FALLING, I FIND WINGS

FALLING,
I FIND WINGS

A novel by

BETTY MORRIS

Betty Morris

MAYFLOWER PRESS

DEDICATION

Having dedicated my book of poetry,
Waiting for Climbers,
to my first four grandchildren,
I dedicate this book to
the darling latest,

Stephanie

ACKNOWLEDGMENTS

I wish to thank Mary Beaudoin, Shirley Cochrane, Brendan
Cullen, Bill Henry, Jeff Hotz, Mae Gaines Kent, Dr. Stephen
Lyrene, Norman Morris, Robert Rovinsky, Jordan Siegel,
Barbara Spring, and my daughter, Carolyn Elizabeth Stevens.
Special thanks to Josephine Nicholls Hughes and Elizabeth
Wood, loyal readers through revisions, and to Glenn Arkin,
who pursued the text, sensitively augmenting many passages.
Above all, special gratitude to my son, Douglas Robert Stevens,
for his generous editing, critiques and substantial involvement
from beginning to end.

Contents

1	MARTHA—*Take a Deep Breath*	1
2	ELINOR, BILLIE, URSULA, SANDY	12
3	MARTHA—*Stardust?*	20
4	MARTHA—*Listening with More Than Two Ears*	34
5	ELINOR—*Small Doses of Anger*	61
6	BILLIE—*I'll Beat You Again Tomorrow*	69
7	URSULA—*What Prescription?*	80
8	SANDY—*Smoking Is Bad for the Baby*	90
9	MARTHA—*Peregrinating*	101
10	ELINOR—*You Got Back Just in Time*	111
11	RALPH—*Nature Abhors a Vacuum on Sundays*	140
12	BILLIE—*I Got Rid of Him*	145
13	MICHAEL—*Who Needs It?*	168
14	URSULA—*The East Wall Beats on the West Wall*	170
15	SANDY—*Is That What Your Shrink Worked Out?*	185
16	DAVID—*Too Sweet for Your Own Good*	201
17	ELINOR—*Let Your Moderation Be Known*	208
18	MARTHA—*Perfect for Chilling Champagne*	216
19	SANDY—*I Know What I Have to Do*	225
20	DAVID—*I Know What We Have to Do*	251
21	MARTHA—*Gumption?*	260
22	BILLIE—*A Phone Call*	268
23	URSULA—*What Were Those Pills?*	284
24	MARTHA—*I'll Buy a New Dress and Enjoy It*	295
25	MARTHA—*A Benchmark*	305
26	SANDY—*American Gothic*	319
27	ELINOR—*A Suitable Gift*	329
28	ELINOR—*Smarty Smarty, No One's at Your Party*	336
29	MARTHA—*Did They Have Good Reasons?*	338
30	MARTHA—*They May Not See from Where They Sit*	345
31	MARTHA—*Four on Wednesday*	350
32	MARTHA—*What Does Billie Want?*	371
33	BILLIE—*Consciousness-Raising Is Free*	382

34   MARTHA—*Blind Spots*   398
35   MARTHA—*A Career Opportunity*   418
36   MARTHA—*The Old Order Changeth*   435
37   MARTHA—*Ten Feet Tall*   442
38   MARTHA—*She Likes What I Like*   460

"The history of love is inseparable from the history of the freedom of women."

Octavio Paz, *The Double Flame*

Take a Deep Breath

Martha stood at the open upstairs window of her townhouse, watching people saunter past toward Greenwich Village. Her thoughts were not in line with the beauty of the evening.

How can I make it alone through the years ahead? It's Saturday night but I don't feel off-duty. All this warm air and soft April moonlight is a come-on, a sweet promise to earth's creatures that they can bask and multiply forever. But Norman's dead, and I've been robbed of spring at forty-nine. Life is a bare, ruined choir where no birds sing.

Two young women on the sidewalk below called cheerfully to two young men who slowed in their car to talk. Soon the car screeched off and the women walked on, their high heels clicking. It wasn't a pick-up—they were chatting in Spanish about their professor.

Norman and I used to stroll into the Village on Saturday nights to the little Tick-Tock Bar and enjoy glasses of kummel, watching men in evening clothes escort women in high heels and long gowns into the glittering night club next door. We'd have a light supper somewhere and wander about arm-in-arm, enjoying the fashions and arts in the small shop windows and the outlandishly dressed young couples mimicking the poses of models. If Barry was playing his clarinet with the high school band we'd attend, but most Saturday nights we'd see an Off-Broadway or Off-Off-Broadway play. Afterward we'd talk about it over frozen custard, then walk home, shower together, and make love in our own bed. These joys had dwindled during Norman's last year, when his heart condition worsened, although the end of love-making was a minor loss in light of the tenderness I felt in taking care of him, and his gratitude. He always wanted me to be happy, so I feel a bit guilty that I can't find a way to have fun. He'd want me to go to the theater, but I'm too busy with my practice to get tickets.

A noisy fire engine paused in front of her brownstone as if preferring it to the other houses on the block. It sat flashing its lights and clanging its bells like a beast wooing a mate. When it moved on, she closed the heavy linen drapes over the living room windows and went forlornly down the hall. Seeing her mother-in-law's bedroom door open, she walked past her own room to say goodnight.

Sarah said, "The fire engine was probably headed for some restaurant in the Village brerling hamboigers."

Martha laughed, enjoying the imitation of Brooklynese, which blended oddly with Sarah's life-long Austrian accent. "Years ago," Sarah went on in her normal voice, "when Norman first brought you from Brooklyn to meet me, I thought you'd talk like that, but you talked lovely, and you always looked lovely, too."

"Thanks. Sleep well, Sarah," Martha said gently, as if she'd never heard the story before. In her own room she resumed packing a suitcase.

Look at this mélange.

She picked up a grey silk blouse and tossed it aside.

None of my clothes are right for reading my paper at Berson's symposium. Something a bit dressy would be okay, but what? I can't go shopping, I'm booked right up to the minute the conference starts. Oh, why did I postpone my appointments for all day Thursday and half of Friday? I should have planned to duck out right after reading my paper.

She pulled the paper out of her suitcase and settled on the bed to read it. A dotted navy and white dress fell to the floor, and she glanced down at its Lord & Taylor label which looked scrawled but was so damn correct.

My paper may be the same: correct and determined

to seem light-hearted. Well, it does have a few good laughs.

She undressed, lay in bed trying to sleep, and reached for Norman's pillow.

I can't bear this sleeping alone, but it goes on and on. It's a trap, and this house is a big cage. I see patients all day, dine on whatever Sarah cooks, and walk straight back to my office to study my notes on patients and read the latest journals. A little TV with Sarah, and then to bed. All bearable because it's routine, but my spring longings could upset everything. Oh, God, help me to help myself!

She sat up in bed in the dark room.

Am I praying? I haven't prayed for years, since Sunday School at the Congregational Church. Where has it gone, the sweet confident Christian faith I had as a girl? I ought to take more time to meditate. Myself my own analyst. I guess my sense of humor is intact—if not, I wouldn't miss having fun. My brain is clear and my figure stays slim, but nothing adds up. I'm a workaholic, have no man in my life, no time for social life. Haven't seen my friend Lucy Woodward for months. Unhealthy.

She threw herself into the middle of the bed, holding Norman's pillow over her face. Finally she relaxed and slept.

The next morning down in the kitchen she watered the hanging plants which fringed the room in lacy green. Sarah was at the table, serenely working on the *New York Times* crossword puzzle, as she and Barry had customarily done with Norman, while Martha kibitzed and spelled words. Barry had recently said, "The Sunday puzzle's been my ritual each week of the year for two decades." Martha refrained from reminding him that two decades ago he'd been only six years old. She felt sorry for her son—he'd suffered two shocks, the death of his father and the unexpected end of his short marriage to Marie. He had lived alone in their apartment until the lease was up, and then arranged with his mother to move back into his old bedroom on the third floor. It was directly over Sarah's.

Martha asked her now, "Is Barry home?"

Sarah nodded, intent on lettering in a word. Then she said, "I cleaned his room yesterday after he went out. Were his clothes ungelegt and ungepechget!"

"I hope that means *not picked up*, rather than *not packed up*. He's not leaving, so far as I know."

"No. He just lives life in a hurry. I left his door open yesterday and it was closed this morning. So he's sleeping."

Martha sighed, knowing Barry's embarrassment at living at home again. To save his pride, she let him pay rent. She loved him deeply, admired his academic record and enjoyed the way he could make her laugh. Above all, she valued the respectful friendship between them with its moments of joyous mutual approval and occasional sharp jabs of criticism, usually taken in a good spirit.

I'd be happy to visit him and cook, if he lived close by. I have no doubt he'll marry again, probably another charming and brainy shiksa. Oh, why do I use that derisive Yiddish word, so condescending to non-Jewish females? That's Sarah's word.

Sarah came from an aristocratic Jewish family in Austria whose language was not Yiddish but high German. Yet on the big occasion when Norman brought Martha home to meet her, she had muttered, "Shiksa!" This didn't stem from a personal feeling, but from ancient loyalty: marriage within a family's faith was preferred. As soon it had become clear that Norman and Martha were happy together, Sarah had warmed to Martha. Norman himself had usually enjoyed his mother's occasional Yiddish, knowing that for her it was a personal slang, a little fling.

Sarah had said, "Shiksa!" on another occasion, as a quick label for Angela, a non-Jewish girl whom Barry had brought home to dinner twice while they were in college. But Norman had made a fatherly point of praising the girl, sensitive to any slur his mother might imply which could refer to his Martha. Who was, after all, a shiksa.

Martha's own thoughts remained loving.

Sarah had a right to feel disappointed when her son presented her with a daughter-in-law who wasn't of their faith. I didn't blame her and was grateful for Norman's idealism and unselfish love of all of us. Now she and I, both widows, have become great friends, and live together pretty comfortably. I feel obliged as a therapist to keep things peaceful, and Barry, like his Dad, keeps us cheerful with his teasing. We can be glad our boy's doing well in his job and is starting to take time for social life. It doesn't hurt that Sarah and I each spoil him a little. If he were my patient and not my son, I could plant the idea of his making a move on his own. I'm sure he'll do it eventually and I don't want to reject him.

A short involuntary groan escaped her, and Sarah looked up, but Martha smiled resolutely. She washed her own breakfast dishes and stared out the back window at her tiny patch of garden. It held a few white snowdrops and lavender crocuses, now losing their petals.

Sarah asked, "How do you spell *ecumenical*?"

Martha spelled it and asked "Does it fit?"

"Of course," said Sarah, "Am I ever wrong?"

Martha laughed, ruefully. "Am I ever wrong?" had been one of Norman's expressions, spoken with a smile after he had taken a chance. A lot of the special language of the family had been Norman's, and without him life's pleasure was diminished.

"I may not go to the conference," she announced. "I don't expect to enjoy it."

"You must *enjoy*?"

"Yes, I must *enjoy*. I have no suitable clothes."

Sarah looked at her steadily. "Maggie," she said, her strong old face working in sympathy, "you always dress very well. You are *Dr. Kaufman* and your paper is important."

"Oh, Berson has plenty of papers without mine. He

5

has my abstract and it will be printed in the conference report."

"When you mailed it you said it left out your stories about the old people's courage. So read the whole paper."

"I need to do something more fun. The only thing going well for me now is my work. And I have to weed my flower bed." She took a jacket from a closet by the back door.

"It's raining."

"It's just a drizzle." She went out and began pulling weeds.

I'm grateful for Sarah's high opinion of my professional standing. Dear Sarah! She has few ego satisfactions herself, and now, after years of homesickness for her sister and nieces back home in Vienna, she's determined to stay with us as long as Barry and I need her. And we do. One of the supportive Jewish customs I've come to love is family helpfulness in the first year after a death, and I'm lucky she likes to cook for Barry and me while I'm trying to get on an even keel with my practice.

The kitchen door opened and Sarah announced, "I'm ready to make a waffle for Barry as soon as he comes down. Maggie, will there be men at this hotel?"

"Of course."

"This Berson. Is he married?"

"Recently widowed. But not my type. Too strict a Freudian."

Under her breath as she went inside, Sarah said, "If you fall for some man you'll have to give up your Barry-baby!"

As she closed the door she almost collided with Barry.

Grinning, he teased, "Was I supposed to hear that?" He gave her a hug, and then sat down in his usual place at the table. "*Was* I?"

Sarah poured his coffee and said, "I'm thinking she should be married again."

"We all should. You too."

Sarah made a face at him. "Your waffle's coming."

"Make it hot and golden brown." He pulled her half-finished puzzle toward him, and studied it. When Sarah presented his waffle he looked up and smiled. "Thank you, Bubbi. Tell me, did you learn to make waffles in old Vienna?"

"Not me. In old Vienna I was strictly a student of languages. We always had two maids at home and one of them taught me to bake. I liked it and it's easy here, with the *Joy of Cooking*."

"How about the joy of cleaning, like my room?"

Sarah laughed. "Somebody has to help the cleaning lady in this big house, so I do your room, dollink boy that you are. You have interesting books and I sit and read."

"Be my guest. And thanks for babying me. So what are you and Mom up to today?"

"She says she may not go to the conference."

"Why not?"

"No clothes. But the conference would surely be good for her work. She might get more patients. Make more money."

"She's too busy now," he said. "And gets paid about max."

"She might get more top-drawer patients like the ones she has on Wednesday afternoons. She always feels peppy at dinner on Wednesday." She rumpled Barry's hair. "*Gib zich a shockl* and tell her to go to the conference. And that means 'really try.'"

When Martha came in from the yard, he watched as she lifted a foot out of a muddy shoe. "Long slender toes, wherever she goes," he teased.

Martha grinned and kicked the muddy shoe toward him.

Sarah nodded toward the waffle iron. "Martha, this is your waffle. Hot and golden brown." She pointed a finger at Barry to show she could speak his language, then demanded, "Who was the Greek goddess of love?"

Martha answered. "Aphrodite."

"How do you spell it?" Sarah asked.

Barry spelled it, "A-f-r-o-d-i-t-e."

"We used to have a school yell," Martha said. "'Aphrodite in your nightie, make our team the winner mighty.'"

"That's poetry," said Barry with an intentionally silly grin.

"Oh, oh," Sarah complained. "It's too short."

"Not Aphrodite's nightie," said Barry.

Martha glanced at the puzzle. "Spell it with p-h, not f."

"That fits," said Sarah. "So, Mr. A-f-r-o, tell your mother to go to her conference."

"Go to your conference, Mother."

"No, my clothes are wrong and I'm just too tired to think."

Barry opened the *Times* and declaimed, "As an advertising executive in the fashion center of the world, I advise you to look at the ads in today's paper."

"It's raining."

"Come on, *gib zich a shockl*, as Bubbi says. You can look like a million if you try."

"She's reading a scholarly paper," Sarah put in, "at the biggest hotel in New York City."

"So dress up for that, Mom."

"It's just a report on my volunteer work with the elderly. I'm reading it in an evening symposium. Nothing spectacular."

"If it's evening, you can dress like you're going to go to an illustrious club afterward. I dated a chick last night—"

"A *shiksa chicksa?*" Sarah asked, grinning.

"Yeah. Hot and golden brown." He waited for a reaction of shock to this but the women accepted it. "Actually, she was white. And I swear to God, she looked so great I had to take her somewhere special."

"To an illustrious club?" Sarah asked, with the accent on *lust*. "What was she wearing?"

"Something like this." He pointed to an ad showing a black dress with a well-fitted top and a full skirt. "With black stockings that sparkled."

Martha laughed. "Very suitable for reading a scholarly paper!"

8

"Why not? Her shoes were only high heels with straps. A shawl instead of a coat. Nothing fancy by itself, and all black."

Sarah joined in. "Didn't your grandmother tell you to use your brains but show your ankles?"

"Yeah," agreed Barry. "Do as your grandmother tells you. I always do." He winked at Sarah, who flashed him a doubting look.

He pushed the front section of the paper into Martha's hand and turned to Sarah. "So where are we with the puzzle?"

Martha went up to her room, sat on her bed and looked into the paper. "It might be a good idea to go shopping," she said aloud.

On Wednesday morning she decisively finished her packing, enjoying the color of her new pink nightgown with its matching negligee and scuffs. Before packing the scuffs, she tickled her nose with their fluffy marabou.

I couldn't have bought these dollops of pink fuzz if I were depressed, even if everything else I bought is black, thanks to Barry's shiksa.

She carried her bag down to the kitchen and told Sarah, "If I eat dinner with you, I'll be late to the conference."

"I'll pack you a supper so you can picnic in your room. My professional daughter-in-law shouldn't arrive late."

"Please, just put a little fruit in a bag."

Martha left her suitcase and walked down the hallway to pick up the morning newspaper. Outside the door she took the opportunity to get a whiff of fresh air, glancing up at the facade of her hundred-year-old house, inherited from an uncle. Not many brownstones had survived in this area, and this handsome one meant security to her, aesthetically and personally. It was tall and each of the two main stories had a row of three high front windows. The steps from the sidewalk were graceful, and led up to the front porch, still called, as in the Dutch days, the stoop.

On the inside she and Norman had not altered the house's dignified personality beyond remodeling the kitchen and her spacious office suite in bright modern style

She took the morning paper to Sarah in the kitchen and carried her suitcase to the coat closet of her waiting room. In her office she noticed that the fern on a bench was drooping. She brought water to it from the sink in the half-bath, a room she had designed with two doors so it could be reached from either the waiting room or her office. On pulling open the heavy green velvet drapes over the windows, she saw that her professional shingle outside was swaying in a slight breeze.

The shingle consisted of two identical boards suspended by a chain from a pole near the stoop. Each board was of dark cherrywood, with letters engraved in gold. The top board read: "M. KAUFMAN, M.D." The lower board reading "PSYCHOTHERAPIST" had hung for years outside the office of her mentor, Dr. Jennette Thornbeck, known to her admirers as "Thorny." Upon retirement she had presented the board to Martha, who cherished it as a tangible proof of a professional's faith in her, and valued it equally with her diplomas.

When I seemed to hear her trenchant voice say, "Take a deep breath!" I decided to go to the conference. So I bought new clothes. Okay, Thorny, I'm going. But first, there's today.

She glanced at the names of patients booked for the morning, and sighed. The first was a man who owned a news agency and gambled away his profits. Then she would see a mother whose teenage children were lured into shoplifting and drugs. Because the mother herself was depressed, Martha found the case so similar to her former work in a low-income clinic that it was tiring.

Also tiring had been her several weeks of volunteer work this past winter, undertaken to keep herself from giving way to grief after Norman's death. Berson, a well-known psychiatric scholar, had arranged for her to design and conduct a research project in a senior center near Prospect Park. Her paper for his symposium this evening would be a report on it. Although she had liked working with the elderly and had woven in anecdotes of their fortitude, Berson bored her. She was glad her work with him would soon be over.

She scanned her appointments for the afternoon—what a lift! Two o'clock, Elinor. Three o'clock, Billie. Four o'clock, Ursula. Every Wednesday they came into the City from various suburbs on Long Island. It was her most bracing half-day, as they were all bright, headstrong and determined to achieve control over their lives. Though their problems were genuine, they sought help in a light spirit which she found refreshing.

I'm lucky to have these patients just now. Maybe my life is dull, but the lives of Elinor, Billie and Ursula are entangled with lively people—teenagers and bosses and husbands and lovers, not to mention ex-husbands.

As soon as Ursula leaves, I'll dash to my hairdresser's and then take the subway uptown. Since rain is predicted, I'll wear my rose-colored raincoat. How Norman smiled from his hospital bed when I first wore it last August! "My pink hiker!" he said. Maybe I'll tie Sarah's fruit into a bandanna and hoist it over my shoulder!

Her doorbell rang and her day's work began.

2

Elinor, Billie, Ursula and Sandy

Elinor wasn't, for once, looking decorative, but letting her auburn hair bounce loosely. Her jogging shoes splashed through rain puddles. She was wearing her silvery-green jumpsuit, matching the color of the lush borders of daffodil leaves in the gardens she passed.

I'll toss these shoes and everything else into the washing machine on the gentle cycle. Gentleness is nice—I should jump in myself. Here I am, passing one big estate after another without seeing any neighbors. Not that I would recognize most of them, as the only one I ever talk with is Adele next door to us. She knows I'm just a sleepy rag doll running to rouse my brain, which would have gone to sleep forever last Christmas day if the old Cadillac had been in the garage with the door shut. I can't bear to think of what I tried to do and how it would have damaged the kids' lives. Well, thanks to Doctor Martha, I don't feel so down now.

In front of her large stone house she stopped to check the mailbox which stood on a stone pillar.

Empty. No bills. Rejoice!

She took a minute to polish the box with the cloth she kept in it, enjoying the hand-painted spray of wheat on its curved top, but not the name of her ex-husband, Howard Bates.

He ordered this design of fantasy wheat, pretending that owning a house was the same as owning a ranch. Fantasy farmer Howard, who couldn't survive the suburbs and moved to Manhattan! I'm probably safer with a man's name out here, but I've really gained safety by his moving out. Safety for my self esteem, anyhow, without his nagging and accusations.

She sprinted up the circular drive to her front door, but instead of going in, ran out to the road again to repeat her route.

Doctor Martha would approve. I thought a woman psychiatrist would chat about a lot of things but she sticks to my emotions. Still, she does breathe energy into me. I'm running right now because she asked me about exercise. How does she get exercise in Manhattan? Maybe I'll ask her on Wednesday. Here, if I don't run I have a big garden to work in, and the beach ten minutes away. Sports always mattered to me in school, thanks to Daddy and his two rules: Number one, girls must be pretty, and number two, girls should play sports. And drive trucks and climb trees— or buildings, like a steeplejack! Ha. But there wasn't any rule that girls should have brains. If I'd finished college twenty years ago, I'd have a job and do better at raising two teenagers on my own without enough money. Oh God, keep the kids willing to eat a lot of oatmeal. And keep me going.

Run, baby, run.

Billie drained her coffee mug, lit a cigarette and opened the *New York Times*.

What stodginess will you put forth today?

She scanned the editorial page, then reached into her briefcase and pulled out a copy of the Socialist Workers Party newsletter.

Thank God nobody else uses the teachers' lounge this period. Dear Colleague Ed keeps track of what I read and would kid me loud and long if he caught me here with what he'd call *agitprop*. Damn, I picked up the wrong copy at home—I've read this one. I should be planning reading assignments, but the kids have no textbooks, since Smartie Artie messed up the book order again. Last Wednesday ol' Socko-the-Shrink Kaufman hinted I could write my own materials, but teaching four classes a day is too much without having to write the damn textbooks, too! Please, no last full measures of devotion for me.

For two classes today she had showed a documentary film, but then the equipment had broken down and the senior kid who maintained it couldn't fix it.

So what would Kaufman suggest for my next two classes? Well, actually I can show those political cartoons I've been saving. Hope the overhead projector is working. *Merde*, I can't just sit here.

She left her coffee mug on the table and marched down the hall. Near the front of the building a man's voice behind her called flirtatiously, "Honey, I'll bet you know the way to the office."

This will be the smart-ass father of some smart-ass kid.

She turned, frowning.

Yes, he took me for a student, when I'm thirty-nine and the mother of a ninth grader in this school, God help me.

"First door on the right," she said with authority, watching his grin fade. To be taken for a teenager didn't amuse her. She checked her faculty mail box to see if Christopher had phoned about tennis tonight, for which she'd reserved a court at the local bubble.

Yes, here's the message. He's coming. Good.

Also in her box was a slip from a school office reporting that her son Mike had cut English again.

Why can't they deal with me like they do with the rich bitch mothers in town and send a notice in the mail? I don't like little handwritten notices stuck into my faculty box. The next kid who stuffs notices into boxes can easily read a slip like this, and spread around, "Mike got caught cutting." I've got enough grief seeing a shrink because Mikey deserves a belt in the arms or legs once a month without his problems becoming public. But I've got to stay polite, do what I can to get him to go to class, and keep my anger a secret.

She strode into the storeroom, pulled out the overhead projector and wheeled it noisily down the hall.

Ursula, wakened by the screeching of air brakes, jumped out of bed and stood looking out the window of her upstairs bedroom, feeling shaky. She'd had a bad night, not unusual for someone seventy. At bedtime she hadn't been able to find the copy of the latest poetry journal with her article. She peered out the window with her failing eyes and discerned the shape of a big garbage truck two doors down, its huge jaw open as it waited for the men on foot to feed it bags of trash. Making out two bags sitting in front of her house, she suddenly guessed that her husband could have thrown out her journal.

I've got to reach those bags before that monster gets there. It chews everything up.

Groping inside her closet she found her robe, worked her stiff arms into it and her feet into slippers. Jerkily, she plunged down the stairs and out to the street. The first bag was heavy with wet garbage, so the other had to be the one. She gave it a fierce tug, splitting the bag so the contents poured out. She got down on her knees and scraped up loose papers from the walk, bending forward so her eyes were just inches above them.

Where is my journal? Only August would reduce me to this. Oh, here it is. He did throw it away, the only thing that makes my life worth living.

She managed to stand and, clutching her journal, marched over the scattered papers and reached her front door just as the trash man took away the bag of wet garbage. Once in her kitchen she dusted off her journal, gritting her teeth.

August will be angry about the mess of papers I left. Well, it was his fault. What meanness! No one would believe my husband could hate my writing so much! When my nice poetry professor asked us to write up imaginary interviews with dead poets, I didn't dream mine would be published! Much less that I'd have to drop the class and not be able to share it. August says my health is bad but I know I'd be fine if I could see. My eyes used to be my best friends, and now they betray me. At least I can show my article to my psychiatrist on Wednesday. She asked to read it. Nice Dr. Martha Kaufman—she's twenty years my junior but tries to talk my language. Too bad her taste in poetry is so old-fashioned. She's read some Shakespeare and the Bible and Robert Frost—as taught in school—but nothing since.

With difficulty she climbed the straight stairs she had descended so recklessly. The door to August's room was closed. Safe in her room, she tried to read, but only the table of contents of the journal was printed in large enough letters. She was listed among the authors as Ursula Friedrich. She had always liked her first name. When she was in the sixth grade, she had told a girl friend that her Daddy called her "Little Bear" for Ursa Minor, the stars known as the Little Dipper. Her friend had laughed and called her "Ursa the Bear" but she didn't mind. As for her last name, her mother had thought when she married August that there was something upright in the name "Mrs. Friedrich."

Well, I don't like that name now. Why did I ever marry that man sleeping in there? A mistake. How can I escape a big fiftieth wedding anniversary party? A Golden Wedding is supposed to celebrate fifty good years but to me it would mark a long misery.

Maybe I can persuade Dr. Kaufman to help me get what I really need—a divorce.

Sandy stood at the breakfast table looking proudly down at the golden popovers she had just baked. Her face was flushed, her eyes full of love, and her small body flowing with happy energy. David gave her a big smile, cheerful as always. "We need a bigger bed," he said, buttering his third popover. "Or twin beds. Yours is twin-sized and mine is too. They'd make one big bed."

She sat down and looked at him, wide-eyed. This was David's practical side. She'd seen it before, but now it was a contrast to his passionate abandon in bed this morning. In the past he had gone home to his own apartment to sleep after they made love, but last night they had drifted off to sleep together as naturally as breathing. Their morning lovemaking had brought a new recognition of dependency, along with the outlandish pleasure. Now here sat David at breakfast, eating popovers and suggesting moving in.

She ventured, "Do you want to bring it over?"

"There wouldn't be room for it."

"I could move my press out to Mom's."

"Wouldn't that interfere with your work?"

"I haven't been printing much. I can use it there when I need it."

"Good. Let's drive it out to Great Neck tonight and coming home we can pick up my bed. We can probably get the mattress inside the car and tie the springs on top. We can set up the bed here tonight and I'll schlepp the rest of my stuff over later. My apartment lease isn't up for a week."

As he hugged her goodbye, she was surprised at how possessively she clung to him.

"It will be great being together all the time," he said huskily, his lips against the curly bright red hair above her ear.

Sandy smiled up at him, the sweetness of her face alight with devotion. "Oh, *yes.*"

She washed the dishes, thinking that only a week ago she wouldn't have believed that she and David were ready to live together. For the past year there had been no attraction to anyone else, but a separateness, partly because she was reluctant to merge money matters, determined to pay her own way. He called her "my slender artist of slender means."

He was fond of art, but his own career was fund-raising for a charity. His dignity, integrity and dependability were making him the father figure in her life, a role her real father had never filled. Even before he left her mother and her, it had been her mother's father she had depended on, not only for his solid virtues but for his sense of fun, expressed in singing show tunes, which Sandy learned. He died when she was in her teens and since then there'd been nobody to join her in their old duet, in which she sang "The Sidewalks of New York" simultaneously with his singing "In the Good Old Summertime." Then they did a little tap dance like old-time vaudevillians. Her thought patterns were still sprinkled with old tunes which provided comfort.

David will never be funny like Grandfather, but he likes my songs and I couldn't imagine a future without him. So he'll be here tonight and I hope he never leaves.

She went into the bedroom, singing with gusto,

> "Frankie and Johnny were lovers,
> Oh, Lordy, how they did love!
> They swore to be true to each other,
> As true as the stars above . . ."

She bounced on the bed which had vibrated beneath them a little while ago and then sat up to think.

It wasn't like us to skip using my diaphragm, but our bodies surrendered to our feelings, and our feelings to something beyond us that made us decide to live together. I even offered to move my press.

She stood to clean the press and found an old print of a sketch she had done of Danielle, her beautiful roommate from the Rhode Island School of Design.

The printing is good but the drawing doesn't do justice to my Blue Danielle. It catches her dreamy look, like Rossetti's "Blessed Damozel," but it isn't easy to catch her modern frankness. The tones of the print are good, though. Odilon Redon, eat your heart out!

She'd signed it "Sandra Lieberman." Now she tore off "Lieberman" and said aloud, "My name will be just *Sandra* and I'll never have to change it."

Then it struck her that to make room she'd have to re-

18

move not only the press but also the noble battered oak table it sat on. Ten years ago she'd been seeing Dr. Kaufman, a therapist who encouraged her to ask her parents for lithograph equipment. She had done so with stubborn independence, still her most outstanding quality, so it was a shock to think of living without her press and its table. They had been her security, a promise to succeed she'd made herself during the difficult days of her mother's divorce. And now they were essentials in her struggle to support herself in the chancy New York City free-lance art world.

With my printing press right here I know who I am. But these days I'm not satisfied with what I'm drawing, so I never print anything. I'm not the person I want to be.

God, what am I facing—a future of great popovers instead of great lithographs?

3

Stardust?

Martha, smiling, heard lengthy applause for her paper.

Is this due to my stories about the old dears in the center, or to the sparkle on my stockings? Anyhow, I've showed my brains *and* my ankles.

Another paper followed, a report on the problem of psychiatrists' making home visits.

Afterward, Martha was aware that Berson, the gray of his suit matching the gray of his hair, was beaming at her. She felt he expected a repeat of last night when, after the general session, he had invited her to supper. At that time she'd been glad not to be dining on Sarah's fruit, and had hoped they'd go into the hotel's famous grill, but he had steered her into the hotel's café instead, saying, "My late wife recommended omelettes at this hour."

Tonight he came to shake her hand and said, "Supper again, to celebrate? I feel at home here in the Hilton."

She responded, "Yes, the home feeling is nice, but my late husband and I liked to dine out in this glittering area. Its threats to safety are more bark than bite. We could go 'Dutch.'"

Berson was silent, leading the way down the hall. As they reached the elevator, a friendly-faced, dark-haired man walked up briskly. She'd seen him come in late and listen attentively to the last half of her paper. Now he held out his hand and clasped hers. "I'm Irving Seymour," he said, and then, still holding her hand, greeted Berson, "Hi, Izzy!"

Berson frowned but shook the man's hand, saying, "Irv, this is Dr. Martha Kaufman, the star of our show tonight."

"A star among stars," declared Irv, "in a good session."

As they stepped into the elevator, Martha said, "We're seeking supper."

Irv, looking at Berson, asked, "May I join you?" Berson nodded and Irv asked Martha, "How about the Plaza? The dinner music is said to be good for dancing."

"Perfect," she said, thinking Sarah would enjoy hearing about her dining with peers.

As she and Irv walked shoulder to shoulder through the lobby, he said, "It's chilly tonight. Better get a coat." He pressed a warm, lingering little push on her back.

"I'll have to go up to my room for my shawl."

"We'll wait here," Irv said. Berson looked solemn.

In her room she found herself humming "Some Enchanted Evening." She dropped her paper onto the desk and looked out the window. Golden lights stretched downtown into the distance.

A star among stars. I never dreamed I could feel attracted to a man so quickly, but ever since high school I've been a pushover for brainy Jewish men with glowing eyes. I married one and we were happy. Creases on the forehead of this Irv make him look less easy-going than Norman, but his smile is dazzling. Dinner tonight will be fun. Afterward he might come up to see the view.

She arranged a pile of bananas and grapes on a bedside table, turned on the bedlamps and touched her ears with the perfume she had bought at the hairdressers.

When Irv alone greeted her in the lobby he said casually, "Berson asks you to excuse him. He's reading his paper in the morning and doesn't want to stay up late."

Martha said, "I'm going to hear his paper. Have you known him long?"

"Only since he kindly critiqued my book."

"You must tell me about your book."

"I will. But here's the waiting line for taxis."

"The Plaza is so near, we could walk," she said, and then remembered her high heels.

"Do you really want to?"

"Well, not really," she said lamely. "I usually walk, for exercise."

"We'll dance for exercise," Irv said, opening a taxi door.

In the Edwardian Room they were shown to a table overlooking Central Park. Outside, the city streetlights shed an eerie yellow glow on the trees, their leaves lacy in April greenery. Beyond, the black stretches of the large park made it seem like a deep woods. Irv took Martha's shawl and tucked it carefully over his own chair. She was a little surprised but not displeased that he didn't want her to escape. A waiter slowly approached with large red-tasseled menus. She nodded when Irv asked if he might order for them both. They started with melon.

"This is the best melon I've ever had," said Irv.

She nodded. "I'm fond of melon, but a couple of years ago my late husband tried to grow some in Vermont. It wasn't a success, though we had good sun."

"Martha Kaufman," Irv said as if seriously studying the name for its importance. His eyes were on her face and now they lit up, as he said, teasing, "I might call you 'Stardust.' "

"Stardust?"

"Because of your stockings."

"Don't be fresh," she said in mock admonition, smiling. "Tell me about your book."

"It grew out of my doctoral dissertation," he said, "and stretched right through my divorce. Thank God they're both over."

"What was your subject?"

"Oh, uh, learning styles," he said absently. He was nodding to the music and watching the dancers. "Tonight I don't want to dwell on it. Shall we dance?"

He danced well and she found it easy to follow. After the set, they sat down to what the menu called "Chateaubriand for Two." After one taste Martha said, "This is fabulous!" and hungrily kept eating. To her relief, Irv was also eating with gusto. Soon, she resolutely resumed their conversation. "I feel envious when my colleagues publish books. I can't seem to find time to write, although ideas come to me."

"I liked your paper for its tight research design and the human touches about the old people. You should publish it."

"Thank you. What else interested you at the meetings?"

"Well, I enjoyed a report on logical problem-solving. It dealt with hypothesis-scanning versus recognition of constraints. I'll use it with students."

"Where do you teach?"

"Stony Brook. Where, I modestly might add, my full professorship came through yesterday."

"Wonderful! This calls for champagne."

When champagne had been poured, Martha raised her glass. "To Professor Seymour. Mazeltov!"

"This is so nice," he said sincerely. "Are you always nice?"

"Always!" She liked this flirting plus exchanging ideas.

"What has interested you so far at the meetings?" he asked.

"One helpful paper was about a particular illusion of some elderly people that persons close to them are impostors, even their chief care-givers. It's called the 'Capgras Syndrome.'"

"A form of paranoia?" he asked, and added, "I've seen a lot of paranoia in young people, too."

"Young people may have delusions of persecution of a deeper sort. But with an elder person's history of survival, this syndrome is treated specifically. Just give them attention."

"No complications?"

"No, and it doesn't take weeks of observation."

"Thank you, Dr. Kaufman," said Irv. "But now, we're celebrating. No more shop talk. But first, what kind of doctor are you? I missed Berson's introduction."

"No more shop talk," she declared, and lifted her champagne glass.

After the waiter removed their empty plates, she excused herself and went to the ladies' room. In the well-lit mirror she noted that her face was flushed but her hair was fine. She dropped her bag onto the counter and used her perfume. When she picked up her bag, she noticed by the sink a lipstick that wasn't hers, attached to a gold tag, lettered "Maggie." She had heard no one else come in.

Some woman left it behind. I'll turn it in to the maître d'.

She put it into her bag, checked the smoothness of her black stockings with their sparkles, and suddenly couldn't wait to get back to dance with Irv.

He rose to greet her and without speaking led her onto the dance floor. She didn't need to think or ask questions, it was enough simply to be. With his touch guiding her she rested her arm on his shoulder and knew that if she let her forehead touch his cheek, he would kiss her. She was following his dance steps smoothly to the old songs the trio was playing, and the warmth of his hand melted her as they moved slowly to "Gonna Take a Sentimental Journey." She brought her cheek up to his, they floated together, and exchanged a kiss, gentle and demanding.

When they walked back to their table through the room she had a feeling of relaxed time, that there would always be time for beautiful things.

"Coffee now?" Irv asked. "They're sure to have thick cream here—it has a way of turning coffee into the real thing."

"Stardust drinks hers black," she said. "Oh, by the way, my real nickname is Maggie."

"I like Maggie."

"May I have my shawl?"

His face fell. "You want to leave?"

"No, I just felt a little draft."

As he wrapped the shawl around her, he squeezed her shoulders. She shivered and leaned back toward him. "I don't really want coffee," she whispered up to him.

He sat down, facing her, his hands clasped. "We can skip the coffee. But I don't want to end the evening. I'd like it to last."

"Me too. But I'll need to get back to my hotel room at the Hilton. My room is up near the top."

"What floor?"

"The forty-fourth. Where there really is stardust."

"You must have a gorgeous view. When I take you home, may I have a look?"

She nodded, matter-of-factly.

His face brightened. "Wonderful." He beckoned the waiter, and eventually got the check.

She opened her evening bag. "I'd like to pay for the champagne. I suggested it."

"Oh, no. My pleasure," he said, counting out a pile of bills which he laid on the table. They danced briefly while crossing the floor and went out into the night, which was clear and not too cold. Holding hands, they strolled across Fifth Avenue and admired the exquisite shapes of Steuben glass and Tiffany's delicate tiny sculptures made of real jewels.

"What do you teach at Stony Brook?" Martha asked.

"Psychology. I work with the young and you work with the elderly."

"Only as a volunteer last winter. I'm a psychiatrist in private practice."

"No kidding? If I'd known that earlier I'd have missed a wonderful evening."

"Are we psychiatrists so terrifying?"

"Don't you hold people up to an impossible ideal?"

"If we don't, who will? But there's one local therapist who's a true believer, to the point that she's joined her own group!"

"Do you think the idea will catch on?"

"It may show the trend."

He sighed. "I'm tired. Let's cross the street again and take a taxi."

As they rode the short distance, he pulled her against him companionably and crooned a bit from "A Sentimental Journey." Yawning, he remarked, "My day started at five this morning, more than twenty hours ago."

On the forty-fourth floor they walked apart, but as Martha was unlocking the door of her room, a tall, craggy-faced man looked out from his room directly across the hall. "Good evening," he said, jovially, whether out of recognition of them or just good feeling, she couldn't tell. Irv replied cheerfully, "Yes. Good weather."

Inside her room, she opened the drapes. "Come and see how high up we are."

"Just a sec. I'm going to loosen my tie. This hotel heat is too much." He hung his suit coat on the back of a chair, and came and stood behind her, hugging her from behind. As he nuzzled the back of her neck her shawl slipped to the floor unheeded. "This is a high nest even for New York. You know how an eagle feels."

"I'm usually more rabbit than eagle," she said.

"Me too." He pushed the curtain completely out of the way and pointed east. "We'd have to be in a room around the corner to see Queens, where my mother lives."

"Do you live with her?"

"Lord, no, I have my own apartment near the campus, an hour's drive out the Long Island Expressway. Where do you live?"

"Not far from N.Y.U."

"Alone?"

"No, my son and mother-in-law live with me. My security and my burden."

"I know that feeling. Divorce freed me, but sometimes I miss the old burden."

"Having interesting work is the only compensation."

"But we need fun sometimes." He gave her a squeeze

and asked in a playful tone, "When you're in a high place, do you ever feel like jumping off?"

"Never. I look and don't leap. That's my most deep-seated characteristic."

"You're nice," Irv said, pressing her closer and stroking her breasts. They turned toward each other and kissed ardently. Then Irv turned back toward the window and opened it. "It's too hot in here for sleeping," he said chattily. "That is, if you'll let me spend the night?"

She was surprised, but nodded, with a smile.

"Do you have some toothpaste?"

"Yes, in the bathroom. But no extra tooth brush."

"I can just rinse." He closed the bathroom door.

She turned down both sides of the bed, marveling that this improbable situation seemed totally normal.

She took off her pearls, tucked them into her suitcase and stood looking out the window. When Irv came out, wearing only his shorts, he put his clothes neatly on a chair and his shoes underneath and quickly got into bed. After bouncing a bit, he reported, "The Plaza was fine for dining, but it couldn't beat this mattress. This is a good bed."

Looking back at him as she stood at the bathroom door, she quipped, "Tune in tomorrow for more consumer notes."

Irv laughed as he reached up and turned off the pink-shaded light on his side of the bed. He lay down, and she noted his face, handsome in the soft glow of the other lamp. Smiling, he said, "I'm apt to be asleep if you take more than five minutes."

Inside the bathroom she saw his tie lying on the floor. She undressed, slipped into the pink silk nightgown and negligee and slipped her feet into the pink maribou slippers, wondering why she was slowing down with each action. Then she sat on the padded lid and sat dangling a slipper from one foot, suddenly wondering what lay ahead. Instead of an answer, she got a question.

How in the world did I land here on the forty-fourth floor of the Hilton Hotel with a man I don't know?

She closed her eyes and recalled his face, which had looked pink and whole.

He's kind-looking. I like the firm way he ordered dinner, and his dancing. There's a lot of life in him. And the minute I get in bed beside him, a new future will start.

She panicked at the thought and sat motionless for a few seconds. Then she heard a distinct snore from the bedroom. She stared at herself in the mirror for several seconds before the humor of the situation hit her.

He's fallen asleep, and I'm hiding. After Chateaubriand for Two, we've both collapsed. My disenchanted evening!

She heard another snore, quite loud, and no longer felt like laughing.

Very soon he'll revive. If I was ever miscast, it's now. Call this act "He Wasn't Ready and Neither Was I . . ." Whatever, it's a flop and I'm not getting into that bed. It's a hundred miles away. I've been suspended above reality all evening, but I'm anchored deep down, like this building. One hastily arranged elegant evening with a charming escort isn't enough foundation. A recently divorced man— what stage of recovery is he in? In the clinic we worked out graphs of behaviors of divorced people, and there's a timetable. It's unfair to judge a good man by a statistic. I know I led him on, unfairly. Above all, I misjudged myself. I too am on a timetable of grieving.

She planted her feet in the scuffs on the floor.

Of course, Irv is considerate—I can either lead or follow. I enjoyed following when we danced. Above all, there's sincerity in this man, which tells me that if we made love he might expect to marry me. And once into an affair, I'd soon become very conventional and want to be married. That would upset Barry and Sarah. It's too soon to start a new phase of life, even dating, no matter how our lonely needs may match.

She gazed at Irv's tie on the floor.

I chose a profession which demands self-knowledge, so I'm supposed to be an oracle dispensing wisdom, not an

Ariel moving to whims. Maybe a similar caution made Irv draw back. His mood changed after we left the Plaza, when he said he was tired. I can't recall what I'd said just before that.

She stood, put her clothes back on, including her stockings and shoes, and hung his tie carefully over a towel rod.

It's green and gold, like one I once bought for Norman. What if Norman could see me now? That's not relevant—he'd want me to be happy. But he'd say, "Intimacy now will lead to new demands on you. Are you ready? For you it would be irreversible." And he'd be right. It's hard, but I have to wake Irv and ask him to leave, or I won't get any sleep tonight. He's at least had a nap.

She opened the bathroom door and he stirred, sleepily.

"Couldn't you please just come to bed?"

"I want to, but I'm not coming."

He raised himself on one arm and said, still sleepily, "Is there someone else?"

"No."

"There's no one else for me, either. I was faithful to one wife for years."

"And I to one husband. So it isn't that. It's just that I can't take on a new relationship at this time. I have prior obligations. And I need to build on a solid basis of friendship, not just glamour."

"I like glamour."

"But it's important to be friends, first."

"I'm always friendly." He gave a little snort and sat up and looked at her with a quizzical grin. "I'm waiting for you."

She didn't smile.

His grin faded. "You're quite a tease."

"I was. It isn't your fault."

"No, it isn't, unless you want to make it so."

She recognized this statement to be true. "You seem very angry at me."

"Don't psychoanalyze me!" he barked, swinging his feet

out from under the covers. "Lucky me. Free bed, free analysis. Happy sunrise at the Hilton Hotel."

He carried his clothes into the bathroom and soon came out, dressed but barefoot. As he sat and put on his socks and shoes he seemed so vulnerable and—yes—lovable, that she wanted to reach out and hug him, but she redirected the impulse. "Wouldn't you like some coffee? We could have it sent up."

"No, thanks. Aren't you afraid that would be the start of a relationship?" His sarcasm didn't conceal that he was hurt. Then he added, "I'll have breakfast with my mother. She wants advice about her property. Where's my tie?"

She went into the bathroom and brought it to him.

Fully dressed, he stood looking at her, his eyes clear again. "Can I see you sometime?"

"Not a good idea."

"May I have your phone number?" She shook her head. "Not staying awake in bed wasn't something I planned, Maggie. This is the first time in four years that I've done anything but grind away at my job."

"I believe you. I led you on. But it wouldn't work."

"Why? Any sincere involvement between two people works on some level. For you, what makes it *work*?"

"I don't know. I'm not ready, career-wise or family-wise. Just failure to leap."

"Well, you're not the way you seemed."

"Sorry." She bowed her head. "And thank you. You spent a lot of money."

"Forget it." His tone was dry, not bitter.

"Let me pay for the champagne. I suggested it," she said.

"No way," he said in a husky voice, buttoning his suit jacket. "I celebrated being a full professor."

"Nobody had a better time than we did, dining," she said.

"Or a worse time, sleeping." He opened the door to leave. "Well, I'll be heading across the East River. Nice seeing you."

After closing the door she stood with her hand on the knob, feeling the emptiness of the room without him.

He needed to celebrate his promotion with a colleague. I have to admire his sportiness, setting up his revels in the Edwardian Room. Oh, God, here I am, cool as a calculator, with no one in my arms.

She took off her dress and shoes and flung herself still half-dressed into bed, too tired to cry herself to sleep.

She woke to brightness and quiet, and stretched.

Irv was right, this is a good bed. My legs feel some tightness from dancing in high heels, but it will wear off. The dancing was great. Oh, dear, I forgot to give the maître d' the lipstick tagged *Maggie!* So I'll keep it. To celebrate there's still some magic left, not only hard work. Berson will be glad to see me, as my paper went over okay. His session isn't until after ten so I'll skip the earlier one.

She ordered breakfast from room service, showered quickly, wrapped the negligee around her and soon settled back in bed with a tray before her. Romancing the prospect of a meal alone, she waved her fingers like a magician, breathed "Ta *da!*" and removed the shiny cover from the platter of Eggs Benedict.

Oh, what nice parsley! This is truly a celebration.

She ate with pleasure.

Now I want to think about the symposium last night. The audience really applauded me, and a good question was asked about one of my hypotheses. Berson answered, and he'd probably help me set up another project. I'll show up early to hear his paper. As for Irv, he's with his mother in Queens. I hope he doesn't regret last night, any more than I do—we both needed a fling and although it fizzled, it was fun.

But I suspect I'm rationalizing. There could have been gentle love-making, true intimacy, but I had a failure of nerve. Out of dread of changing things, for myself and Barry and Sarah. What's happening to me? I'm hardly a happy person any more and what's worse, I never take time out or have privacy. I must look into my dark self.

Resolutely, she put the tray in the hall with a tip, locked the door and sat upright in the desk chair.

Do I want to become a lonely matriarch? I'm worse than some of my patients. What if one of them, Billie for instance, balked at sharing as I did last night? I'd see to it that she faced herself. Well, she's adventurous enough and needs therapy for a different reason, to be more supportive of her son. Still, why did I think last night that something might develop that I couldn't handle? Irv is no monster. In fact his conversation is the sort I like best, shop talk that assumes expertise on both sides. But he had a change of attitude when we were walking down Fifth Avenue. What were we talking about?

The answer flew home.

I told him I'm a psychiatrist. Of course he's a psychologist, a Ph.D., so his professionalism is different. He said, "Psychiatrists work toward the ideal," or something like that. And he was angry when he said, "Don't psychoanalyze me," or he wouldn't have confused psychiatry with analysis. Well, I used to want to be an analyst, but for me, psychiatry was certainly right. I made money when I needed it, for Norman. And I like my practice today. It was nice of Irv to say I should publish my paper but I prefer a full appointment book, and have no urge to publish.

My career decision long ago was right for me, and I'll not be plagued by any more doubts. Irv's feelings helped me clear up my own.

Decisively, she put on a frilly white blouse and her new black suit.

Desire may be gone this morning but I can cherish its memory.

She arrived early to hear Berson's paper. To her dismay she saw him talking with the craggy-faced man who had seen her going into her room with Irv. Berson didn't look up.

Is he being told about the goings-on last night on the forty-fourth floor? Quite justifiably, he wanted to review with me the success of his symposium. Anyone would figure I owed him that. But I cut him off when Irv suggested the Plaza, so he felt snubbed and now he's shocked. After he gave me a professional opportunity.

To atone, she kept nodding in agreement as he was reading his paper, and raised her hand once in the discussion, but was ignored.

Unmistakably cold. He won't ask me again to do a research project. Well, I'll survive. He really isn't my type.

As soon as people began to leave, she slipped out, returned to her room, and packed her bag. Then, with a twinge of sadness, she stood a moment saying goodbye to the eagle's view. There was no stardust out there this morning.

She walked to the elevator, which dropped like a stone.

4

Listening with More Than Two Ears

Martha admitted to Sarah and Barry in early July during their usual Sunday breakfast of waffles, "August is only weeks away, and I'm wavering about going to Vermont."

"It must be hard for you to think of going without Dad," Barry said.

"Exactly, but I need a break, and it's so peaceful in our cottage, like being in the sky. Sarah, would you consider going with me?"

Sarah said, gently, "I'd love to, but my sister in Vienna counts on my coming every August."

"I don't want to keep you from her."

Barry, sensitive to his mother's seldom-voiced need for family support, said, "Let's phone her." He placed the call on the kitchen phone, and he and Martha sat drinking coffee while Sarah cheerfully chatted to her sister in German.

When she hung up, she said, "My sister says one of her daughters is coming to stay a while and I should try Vermont."

Martha hugged her. "It's settled, then. The fresh air will be good for you. You can invite your soul there."

Sarah, serving Barry a waffle, said, "All I know about Vermont is maple syrup. What will I do all day in the sky?"

Barry teased, "Sit on the porch and let the mosquitoes bite you."

Martha said quickly, "The view from the porch is wonderful! And I'll cook for you sometimes."

"Just cook me one special meal. Cooking is something for me to do, and I'm addicted to my own dinners."

"I'm addicted to them, too," said Barry, "and they're going off to Vermont for a whole month."

"Don't worry," said Sarah. "Before we leave I'll cook ahead and freeze some of your favorites. You'd better not be naughty and eat them late at night beforehand, or you'll dine out every night we're gone. And, Martha, shouldn't we list what food to take along? I'll get some cartons from the grocery store."

"We can get everything there," Martha assured her.

"Lox you can get up there?" Barry nodded. "And rye bread? How many kinds?"

Barry declared, "There's good bread there, believe me. And the cheese is the best in the world, melts in your mouth like their maple syrup does."

"Can I take just pastrami, pickled herring, and halvah?"

"Okay," said Martha. "For my one meal, could you please get canned water chestnuts and candied ginger? And I'll make you a non-alcoholic mint julep. There'll be plenty of mint from what Norman planted."

"Dad would be glad you're going," said Barry.

Sarah's shopping also included what she called "jeans" for herself, a denim skirt and red and white checked blouses.

Martha packed hiking boots, and, along with professional journals, a tape recorder and tapes of her Wednesday afternoon sessions.

Barry drove them north one long Saturday, and it was already dark when they walked up the wooden steps into the cottage. Although it was only one room, it delighted Sarah, who said the bright stars seen through the picture window made it seem big. In three corners were beds covered with early American quilts, which Martha said were "vintage L. L. Bean," a term Sarah accepted as foreign, one she didn't need to understand. She understood the large pine table near the kitchen corner, and promptly placed on it the sharp cooking knives she had carried carefully all day in her handbag.

Barry stayed overnight and made pancakes from a mix for Sunday breakfast. "Not as good as waffles," he said, "but it's a small kitchen. Bubbi, can you make do here?"

"I don't know. I'm a spoiled American housewife."

She and Martha went down to the road with him to say goodbye. In the daylight Sarah saw the thick evergreens behind the cottage. "Quite a nice little hunting lodge in Austria," she said, "about the size of my father's."

"Look at all that mint, and all the weeds in it!" Martha said with a moan, but her remark was drowned out by Sarah's gasp of astonishment as she looked up at the mountain.

"Barry, it's beautiful. And tremendous!"

Barry put his arm around her and said reverently, "Up there is where I learned to ski. Those long rivers of green grass between the trees are ski runs—long white streaks of powder in the winter. My country."

"Mine too," said Martha, "for hiking!" Barry put his other arm around her.

"I'd like to stay right through until ski season," he said, "but I've got to drive a long way back to the Village. So bye-bye! Have fun!" He kissed them and left.

The two women comfortably settled down to second cups of coffee. "Doesn't this coffee taste strange?" Sarah asked.

"Barry made it—it's probably been here for months. I'll get you some special Vermont coffee."

"Sounds good. I'm going to wash windows so we can gaze at Barry's rivers of grass."

"I'll cut back the mint and throw lots away."

"Better, bring it in and I'll hang bunches out. This clean air will be fine for drying. We'll take it home and have tummy tea all winter."

In the afternoon they walked down the road, carrying a collection of *Smithsonian* magazines Martha had saved for the children of neighbors, the Altmans. By chance, the Altmans were going for a drive the next day, and invited them to go along to Smugglers' Notch, a pass between mountains. The trip was a happy event, and on the way back they stopped at a supermarket and bought lox and coffee. As her treat, Sarah bought a large leg of lamb for the Altmans, and another for herself and Martha.

The weather remained sunny, and Martha spent a few days weeding and harvesting mint and painting the cellar door, while Sarah polished the furniture and floor.

On Sunday Martha said, "There are probably crowds of people hiking on the mountain today, but tomorrow, let's go climbing."

Sarah responded with a rendition of a hiking song, *"Im frutau zu berge wir siehen, fa la ra!"* which she translated as "We're hiking in the morning, fa la ra!" But in the morning she said, "I'm all out of fa la ra. I'll stay home with my knitting."

Martha, looking forward to a day of solitary roaming, packed herself a picnic of bread, cheese and apples. She also took along a book of Wordsworth's poetry left by Norman, who used to read from it to her and Barry.

At the spot where she started to climb there was a family with young children playing in a clearing, but no one was visible on the higher slopes. Reminding herself to keep an easy pace, she wandered up grassy paths, looking up at trees and greeting new views of trees below. In a half hour or so she hit her stride, climbing steadily and feeling more exhilarated and joyful with each new view. She stopped frequently to notice the wild flowers. Soon it seemed the most natural thing in the world to set a pattern and to stop after every hundred steps and sing and yodel at the top of her lungs. Where she finally stopped for lunch on a high promontory, trees were too small to provide shade, so she rubbed cream on her face and arms to prevent sunburn and napped. Then she opened the Wordsworth and found passages which Norman had marked, and alternately gazed dreamily at the woods below her and read aloud:

"There was a time when meadow, grove and stream,
The earth and every common sight

To me did seem
Apparelled in celestial light,
The glory and the freshness of a dream . . .

Nothing can bring back the hour
Of splendour in the grass, of glory in the flower . . ."

She noted one passage in which Norman had changed the word *fountains* to *mountains*.

And O, ye mountains, meadows, hills and groves
Forebode not any severing of our loves!

It was a message from Norman. She felt that he was close and that the wound in her soul caused by his death was healing. It was all she required of a vacation.

After more hiking she started down, and when she stopped midway to rest, found a poem that applied to her present life.

I have learned
To look on nature, not as in the hour
Of thoughtless youth, but hearing oftentimes
The still, sad music of humanity.

The next morning she brought to the table her tapes of Elinor, Billie and Ursula, telling Sarah, "Good therapy requires listening with more than two ears—you need a third ear for patients' underlying *feelings*. And I use tapes as a fourth ear, to check on what I say, and see how to improve my questions."

"Do they agree to being taped?"

"Yes. At the start I wasn't sure about Billie, but she says she tapes herself in the classroom and it doesn't alter her style. I told her that I destroy old tapes on a rigid schedule and probably that helped her accept it."

"Do you play the tapes for them?"

"Not regularly, only bits sometimes so they can check on their progress. Some therapists send tapes home with patients, but their families might listen and therapy sessions are supposed to be confidential. Which reminds me, you'll hear if I play them here."

"I'll just sit back on my bed and knit. I won't listen."

"Wherever you sit, you'll hear everything."

"I could sit on the porch."

"Bless you, Sarah, you are a darling. But remember the mosquitoes. I should have tried to get earphones." They sat without speaking while Martha tried to think of a solution.

Here I have a chance to grow professionally, too good to lose out of fear that Sarah might divulge secrets. And what is there to divulge? Elinor, Billie and Ursula are just three intelligent women sorting out their lives, and Sarah doesn't know anyone they know.

"Sarah," she said seriously, "Can you be discreet and never, ever talk with anyone but me about what you hear?"

"I promise," said Sarah, her eyes wide with commitment.

Martha smiled and said with affection, "Thank you. Confidentiality's a big deal in therapy. But since you promise and I trust you, you may as well sit here at the table."

"I'll get my knitting. Barry needs wool socks."

Martha readied the machine and said, "Elinor comes first, every Wednesday at two o'clock. She's forty-two but with her lovely face and figure she doesn't seem a day over thirty. She has two teenage kids and sometimes chatters like a teenager herself, being charming to cover up her common sense. Underneath, a dull anger burns in her."

"What's she angry about?"

"That's what I'm trying to get her to examine. Her father didn't believe in education for women and she now blames herself for never aiming high enough. When she feels unable to cope, she stops functioning and gets dangerously passive. She first came to me about twelve years ago, after she had made an attention-getting attempt at suicide. She responded well to therapy, and her marriage became tolerable, but it finally broke up about a year ago and she came back to me."

She turned on the tape and they heard Martha's voice first.

"What is your explanation now of your earlier depression?"

"Well, it was partly because of missing the nice life we'd just left behind in London. We had a big flat where we had a nanny to help with the children and a 'char' to do the cleaning, not to mention a man who came by with a ladder to wash the windows, and a man to hang pictures! I was spoiled in every way—used to have friendly chats with other Embassy wives about specialties like Scotch beef from Harrods and Irish eggs at the PX. On my own, I went to silver auctions and outdoor markets and studied antiques. Howard and I entertained a lot and I'd serve American food—the English love chili, but they don't like pineapple with ham. They do serve applesauce with pork, but it's tart, no sugar."

"You missed that life when you moved here?"

"Oh, terribly. Dear Lord, how I hated Manhattan! We had only a two-bedroom apartment, no cozy morning room where I could write out menus, no separate nursery for games, and no walled garden where the kids could play. I did all the housework and Howard worked day and night at his office. I tried to take the kids, their clothes all nicely ironed, to the park every day like the English, but I could never keep them the way our nanny did. I'd spend the morning cooking and ironing, with Susan sitting in her high chair so I could talk and sing with her. That was fun— one song she liked was 'I'm a little teapot, short and stout.' She was three, a darling playmate! Steven was five and was supposed to play in the kids' bedroom with his electric train, but one day he went into my bedroom and got paint on my satin bedspread and I couldn't stop crying. He was hurt because he tried to be good."

"Didn't you ever hire help?"

"Yes, but Howard's salary didn't cover much beyond rent and food, so when I got a sitter I rushed through the stores to find kids' clothes I could afford. The worst was never seeing Howard until nine or ten at night and even then he'd bring work home. At first he didn't have the right job, and then he found a firm which wanted econometrics, his specialty, and worked like a slave. I guess it's tough, being in business, but Howard *is* tough. He could take it, but I couldn't.

"He worked even on Sundays and one awful Sunday I felt like ending it all. Howard was at work and I was going to call a sitter to take the kids to the park so I could be alone and find a way to kill myself, but when I went to the drawer for my housekeeping money, I found Howard had taken it. All of it. So I sat down and cried with the kids in my lap. But later, I secretly figured out how to kill myself."

Sarah broke in, "I'm glad I know she didn't die."

Martha pushed the stop button "Yes, one day she swallowed some pills and then phoned Howard at the office. Her suicide gesture was basically a cry for help, but Howard panicked. From a list of psychiatrists, they selected me."

"They chose well."

"I hope so. Elinor told me she wanted counseling to save her marriage, but Howard refused to see me."

"Which one of them needed help the most?"

"He did. He *does*. But I got Elinor to pressure him by asking for the phone number of the personnel department at his firm, and just asking was enough. He got alarmed and started leaving money for her. She got sitters regularly, and went to art galleries. On one occasion they entertained Howard's boss at dinner, and apparently Elinor was a charming hostess. Everything got better, including their sex life. In time, his company let him take their account with him when he began his own business, which he still runs, doing statistical studies for big corporations. From the start, he expected great prosperity and bought a house on the "Gold Coast," the north shore of Long Island. Elinor talks about it on another tape. Hold on while I find it."

Sarah said, "While you look I'll make coffee."

Martha found the tape and waited, remembering fondly that Elinor's case had started her champagne celebrations. At the time, her office in the big downstairs front room was furnished with only a desk, some chairs and an old sofa which she hoped looked like an analyst's couch, although she didn't use it with patients.

In those days Elinor came in the evenings, and once, after she left, Martha invited Norman into her office for champagne, to celebrate Elinor's recovery from depression. "There's one marriage in town that's happier and a patient who just graduated from therapy with my blessing!"

Norman warmed to her mood and proposed a toast, "To the doctor in the house."

Then Martha proposed, "To the great librarian who's helping me build a practice." They ended their celebration by making love on the sofa.

How happy we were! From then on, we kept popping champagne corks at special moments, mostly in my work, because it was isolating, not to be discussed with anyone. If a psychiatrist "plays God," as Billie asserts, the resemblance to God is the loneliness. Now there's no one who's happy just because I am.

Her reverie was broken by Sarah's bringing mugs of coffee, and announcing, "You're right, this Vermont kind is delicious. So go on with the story of Elinor."

"Howard eventually wanted out of the marriage, and they split up last year. She got custody of the kids and the right to stay on in their big house. However, last Christmas, the first Christmas after the divorce, she tried suicide again, and later called me and confessed she needed to resume therapy but couldn't afford it. She gets very little child support, and stretches it to do everything right for Steven and Susan. They're seventeen and fifteen now and their father doesn't see them and doesn't approve of therapy. Here's a section of tape I marked for study."

Elinor's voice came first.

"My child support check from Howard usually comes late—at least two weeks and sometimes a whole month—and I have to charge food at an expensive little grocery store. Luckily we grow some vegetables and often eat oatmeal for supper because it's cheap."

"I'll expect his check for your therapy on time."

"Knowing him, I warn you it may be late."

"Is his business successful?"

"Oh yes, he has lots of clients."

"There may be a way I can get my check on time."

Martha stopped the tape and summarized. "I persuaded Elinor to get the minister of their church to put pressure on Howard, and he reluctantly instructed his secretary to send me a check the first of every month. But he still makes Elinor wait, and until her check finally comes, she tries to be patient. My plan is to encourage her to get angry and be sure she gets her money on time, for her kids' sake."

"You seem to make long-range plans."

"Yes. The first long-range plan was to build up what is called transference, to get her to think of me as a kind confidant who really cares about her and then ease her into independence. Some therapists call it being an idealized parent, letting the patient grow up and leave home when a certain level of development has been reached. I try to

43

interest Elinor in planning her own future, whether it's marriage or getting a job, but she can't concentrate on this."

She started the tape.

"You know, I really love my house and was so afraid of losing it at the time of the divorce that I settled for too little. My lawyer worked out the best arrangements he could, but I don't trust Howard. He's to educate Steven, and the house will be mine until both kids are twenty-one. Then I can buy it at half of the market value, *or* it will be sold and I'll get half of the profit, after the mortgage is paid off. It won't bring much profit because I can't afford to get repairs done properly. I also lose it if I remarry."

Martha stopped the tape when Sarah interrupted to say, "Divorce I don't know about, but after a husband dies, children should make sure their mother doesn't have to move. It's very bad to make a widow give up her house."

Martha nodded, and started the tape again.

"I get some strength from going to church. My favorite hymn is 'Dear Lord and Father of Mankind.' I think it would help me to sing it right now—would that be all right?"

The tape of Elinor's clear, yet tremulous singing was the last Martha had made of sessions with her. Sarah asked, "Does it help, hearing the tapes?"

"It helps me play back bits to her, to get her to think harder about her need to defend herself."

Sarah said, "She sings nicely. She's a real lady! Do you know that song?" At Martha's nod, she said, "You'll sing it for me at dinner."

In fact, at dinner, she wanted two songs. "First, sing about the teapot."

Martha's sense of fun took over, and she stood up. "Ladies and Gentlemen, I dedicate this song to my son Barry." She sang,

> "I'm a little teapot, short and stout,
> here is my handle and here is my spout
> I can change my handle to my spout—
> just tip me over, pour me out!"

Sarah, not to be upstaged, stood up and announced, "Ladies and Gentlemen, and Honorable Dr. Kaufman, we will now analyze the confused teapot's appeal to the therapist." She circled the room, tipping and frantically changing her arms from the handle to spout positions, singing:

> "I'm a little teapot, inside out,
> can't tell my handle from my snout!
> If someone doesn't help me, I'll never stop . . .
> never stop . . . never stop . . ."

She pretended to stagger, and Martha joined in and danced her to the sink and tipped her, singing:

> "Sober up on coffee or Freud will flop!"

After they stopped laughing at their own silliness and returned to the table, Sarah complained, "You're not an equal-opportunity doctor. My last therapist tipped me over the right way and I poured her a glass of champagne."

This set Martha to laughing again, and she said, "Oh, Sarah, thank you for coming. We'll have to show Barry our routine!"

"Titled 'Spending August Giggling in the Mountains,'" said Sarah. "Now sing the hymn."

"I can't sing it, but the words are by Whittier, an American poet." She recited,

> "Dear Lord and Father of mankind,
> Forgive our feverish ways.

45

Reclothe us in our rightful mind,
In purer lives thy service find,
In deeper reverence praise."

Sarah said solemnly, "That's a pretty serious song for Elinor, isn't it? You know, I like Elinor."

"I like her too," Martha said, wholeheartedly.

"It's too bad, though, all that oatmeal for supper. How tall is Steven?"

"I don't know."

"I see him as a teenager growing tall too fast. He has to wait for the rest of himself to catch up."

"He'll be okay. One way Elinor is strong is in raising healthy children."

"Do you think she'll try suicide again?"

"That's a good question. I want her to *express* her anger. The theory is that unexpressed anger can build in intensity and lead to suicide, not foreseeable to others. Elinor needs to understand her anger, and learn to cope with her limitations. Eventually a safe time will come when she and I agree that she's strong enough on her own or, more likely, marries a man who can give her financial and emotional support."

Before they started Billie's tapes, Martha said, "Billie is a teacher, bright as they come. She's thirty-nine and still a rebel, wanting her own way—not aware of others' feelings. She works hard and her direct gaze and quick wit give her an air of cheerfulness, so she only shows her down side at home."

"I think I met her once in the hall—she was pretty, but frowning."

"She's never cultivated the facial expressions of a pretty woman. Instead of smiling when you talk, she stares as if you'd just told a lie. Her clothes are in style and show off her good figure, and I'm sure they're expensive. When she marches into the office promptly at three, she throws her jacket onto the sofa or the floor. Then she grabs it up at three-fifty and dashes off, maybe to the N.Y.U. library, but she drops no hints. This section of tape's about her teaching." Martha's voice came first.

"In the past you've spoken of being without textbooks for your students. Have you worked something out?"

"Hell, yes. For once, I outsmarted my friggin' chairman, ol' Artie, who never gets books to us on time. He's always waiting to get new titles—some not even published yet—and I knew there were a lot of old textbooks down in the school basement, so I grabbed some kids and we hauled up stacks of ragged volumes on European history. The facts were there, except for the last twenty years, and I assigned kids different sections to bring up to date. It got interesting. The father of one kid is a diplomat at the U.N. and he came and briefed us on the latest in Tanzania. We all learned a lot."

"Was your chairman angry?"

"Naw, Artie's always asking us to bring in outside speakers, so he was pleased as hell. He often visits my classes, but once when he walked in he got a surprise. The old books were falling apart, so I let the kids make paper airplanes of pages they were finished with, and when Artie walks in they aim at him. He stands there grinning and one kid says, 'Oops, I want that page back, it's the Crimean War!' Artie picks it up and says, 'Take this back and say a prayer to Florence Nightingale!' and shoots it back at him. And everybody laughs. I really like the man, except for his stinking administrative habits."

Sarah exclaimed, "Kids don't behave like that in school in Vienna!"

Martha pushed the stop button and said, "Nor here, usually. But Billie's humor gets her by. While she was in

47

graduate school she placed an article on power politics in the *Nation* which was condensed in *Reader's Digest*, with the radical bits cut out. It resulted in her being hired by her present school district, which pays teachers well. Their students get into good colleges. Politically, though, the district is conservative, so Billie tones down her beliefs in order to play safe."

"That must be hard for her."

"Yes, she hates it. She's also angry because she's been her son Mike's sole support since he was in the 'terrible twos' stage. Now he's a rebellious teenager and demanding a standard of living beyond her means. When she's under stress, she lets her anger out and hits the boy for any little mistake. He went to elementary school in the district where she teaches, and once the school psychologist discovered big welts on his legs. That's how the kid got some help. The psychologist knew Billie and liked her, as men seem to do. He didn't make a scandal but persuaded her to get counseling. She didn't want to risk her reputation by going to a local therapist, and came into Manhattan to the clinic for people of low income where I used to work. 'I just hope,' she told me, 'that God doesn't blab here.' She came to see me regularly for a few years, and her violence diminished a lot. If she came at Mike with a ruler, he turned up his bottom and sometimes this tickled her funny bone and she didn't hit so hard. Mike even seemed to keep the marks concealed. Possibly he has more understanding of her than she has fondness for him. I was just opening my private evening practice when she started coming to me, because her salary became too high for the clinic. I give her a reduced rate as I like the way she manages. She's earned a graduate degree and paid off her student loan. Now she plans to send Mike to college. She's a doer, and sees herself as able to cope with the big world."

Sarah asked, "Is she violent to the boy now?"

To answer, Martha started the tape:

48

"How's Mike doing in school?"

"He likes auto mechanics, but that's about it. I get mad at him for not being a top student, like the ones in my classes. He's got a few semi-literate friends whose parents buy them cars and they play around together, calling themselves the 'BB's'—that means Blood Brothers. Thank God, they're not into guns, just cars and music and what the sociologists call 'playful terrorism.' They think of things like spraying street lamps with black paint. Call it 'ceremonial deviance'—efforts to ruffle the surface of the social order. I hope it's not more than that, but some of their tricks are chancy. Like one kid will hitch a ride, claiming he lives in a nearby town, and a few miles down the road put on an act of having an epileptic fit, and then snap out of it and say something like, 'This is where Jesus said I should go,' so the driver lets him out. Of course, the BB's, with Mike along, have been following, and they all have a helluva laugh about it."

"I gather Mike tells you about these adventures."

"He does, and sometimes I can't help laughing."

"I hear from the way you laugh at the same things that you and Mike are really fond of one another."

"It keeps me from getting too angry. Luckily he gets bored quickly by each trick, but I warn him I'll knock his brains out if he gets into trouble."

"Are you hitting him less often?"

"Once I was tempted to brain him with a pan because of some deviant thing he was boasting about, and then I decided to make fun of him instead. To damage his self-esteem—I'm pretty good at that. I tell him his brain is the 'erroneous zone,' or that he needs 'psychotropic medication.' One of my taunts was that he's a 'paradigm shift,' which he thought was pejorative. 'Go to college, I tell him, and learn some important words.' "

"You haven't hit him recently?"

49

"Not often, although I'm ready. He's actually getting a little better, and doesn't sulk so long. He used to act the martyr for a week."

Martha stopped the tape.

"I keep hoping to probe beneath her anger to the affection which could bring him the confidence to do better in school and get himself some friends who aren't clowns. As a therapist, I try to prepare for such changes."

"Where do they live?"

"In an apartment building on the edge of their suburb, near a gas station. She's always provided him with food and clothing, including sports equipment, a room of his own and spending money. But never enough to suit him, and nothing beyond material things."

Sarah nodded. "She loves him. But she can't show it."

"A lot of what therapy's all about is changing how people deal with loved ones. I firmly believe Billie loves Mike. But she's complicated. She not only wants to dominate, she wants a worthy person to compete with, in life as in tennis, so she can respect herself if she wins. Of course, Mike can't compete, so she scorns him. Fortunately, she acquired a new lover last spring, Christopher. He's her favorite tennis partner, a few years younger, who supports himself painting houses and is saving money in hopes of studying architecture. I hope that hitting a tennis ball with Christopher works off some of her aggressiveness, and that intimacy with him takes the spotlight off Mike. I think the best treatment now is to strengthen the continuity of both motherhood and the affair, while she hurtles along, keeping house for Mike, playing tennis, and reading widely, all on top of a full load of teaching. I think her anger's short fuse is partly due to the heavy load she carries."

"Hasn't the father helped her in any way?"

"Not at all. She used to hope he might help by the time the boy reached his teens, and said if she could find out where he was, she'd ship Mike to him. She did get his address in Florida last winter but she hasn't sent the boy off. Yet." They heard Billie's voice.

"Maybe down there in the land of sun and opportunity he could learn how money is made. I've tried. You know, I bought a secondhand snow-blower so he could sweep the neighbors' driveways. He got paid for sweeping around the service station down the hill. Now he helps the mechanics without pay, crazy about cars. I hope he learns something."

Martha stopped the tape when Sarah asked, "Did you support Billie in helping Mike find work?"
"Oh, yes, fully. A mother's encouragement is important. But I haven't been able to bring her to admit that her own mother must have done something to start her out right, even if she used to strike her. I know Billie used to strike her brother and have asked her if she wasn't also fond of him, but she just pours out swear words. I'm determined to use the sure methods of therapy, not threats, to get this angry, bright young woman to use her motherly influence constructively before it's too late. Mike's violence could appear in an instant, like a switchblade. Even slight abuse might provoke him to strike back and do real damage. He's getting big enough, and you never know the violent influences teenage boys are under these days. Yet if he hurt her, she might claim she'd made a man of him. A paradox."
This word stimulated Martha's guilt feelings about her own in-house paradox, her son Barry. When Sarah got up to get more yarn, she sat reflecting.
I regret the softness in Barry which brought him home after his divorce, but I appreciate that he knows I need him, too, after Norman's death. But this could result in too much dependency, so I can't feel easy with him until he moves away. I should look into my own motives, but it's comfortable to just keep on being hospitable and not pry.

Sarah pries enough. I have faith that our respectful affection for each other will clear everything up somehow.

Sarah didn't return to the table but stood and declared, "Billie's feelings are too complicated. A little quick blow I can understand, so long as she's not starting out with a stick to really beat him. But it's immoral for a mother to try to damage her son's self esteem. When I saw her that day, I thought she'd be a cuddly one."

"Cuddly?"

"Yes. She reminded me of a red-headed boy doll Barry had long ago, named 'Cuddles.' But now I'd call her 'Feisty.' I've heard enough about her."

Martha, suddenly protective of her patient, said, "Well, the scoop on Billie, from my side, is that my unwavering patience is the way to help her. Ursula's tapes are next, anyhow."

"Okay," said Sarah, and sat down. "What's the scoop on Ursula?"

"She's a poet, and a wise woman, nearly seventy."

"That'll be a nice change. What does she look like?"

"She's tall, with the air of a queen. Recently, her sight has worsened and she's less sure of herself, and peers forward as she walks. Her hair isn't gray but faded to apricot color and drawn severely back. I'm sure her face was once beautiful."

"Is she going blind?"

"It's not certain. Legally, she's blind now, not allowed to drive. She's such a brave soul that I was pleased to get some insights at the conference into a problem like hers which causes a patient to become hostile and accuse a family member of being an impostor. This, sadly, is Ursula's problem, blaming her husband for everything, while of course he's her care-giver and very faithful. But his only interests are scientific, and she's a poet, longing for her old world of reading. In fact, it goes deeper, because she needs a life of the spirit and he thinks poetry is too emotional.

52

Oh, that reminds me—the one person in the family who could help is their daughter, Blaine. She helped make arrangements for Ursula to see me and gave me some background. Let me look for my notes."

Sarah put down her knitting and left the table to tend to the mint jelly she was making.

Reviewing Ursula's case reminded Martha of Irv, with whom she had discussed the Capgras Syndrome.

I really enjoyed his conversation, his teasing about the sparkles in my stockings, and saying we were dancing "for exercise." Afterward, more than once, I almost phoned him—I could have gotten his number at the University—but each time I hit the stone wall of my prior obligations. A man to love would be more than welcome, but my career will have to suffice for now.

When she found her old note on August Friedrich, she read it aloud to Sarah. "Daughter lives north of Manhattan. Says she has a sister and two brothers, all of them raising kids out West. Says they had a good childhood. Father is vigorous but has a closed mind. Has been teaching chemistry at the college level, now retired at age seventy-one, doing nothing but housework and taking care of Ursula—a trial to her but indispensable. A good provider, faithful husband and father, loyal to his own."

Sarah asked, "Loyal to his own? What does that mean?"

"I've come to think he's jealous."

"Jealousy hurts. Couldn't the daughter give Ursula a home apart from that man?"

"Maybe, but she doesn't want to impose on her children."

"I feel for her," Sarah said.

"So do I. Once I updated my methods to try to help her. I'd read about psychiatrists making home visits to the elderly, so I accepted her invitation to a New Year's party. Their living room was nicely furnished, all in soft colors of pearl gray and moss green, with a feeling of space and serenity. No ash trays, no cute pillows, no framed mottoes. When I complimented Ursula on it, she said, 'Elegant simplicity penetrates the soul.'"

"Who was at their party?"

"Eight or nine people, neighbors and poets Ursula met in classes at N.Y.U. The talk was literary, except when August took a few guests upstairs to see his photocopier. I joined them, but later I scolded myself, since Ursula considers him an impostor and wants me on her side. At the time I observed that August's room was extremely plain and rigidly neat."

"I wouldn't like him. Was he good at conversation?"

"Not really. He just wanted us to admire his photocopier. I went downstairs again and listened to the poets reading their work. Then a woman who wasn't a poet sat down by me to talk, and we moved to the kitchen. She was a close observer who lived next door, and was full of praise of August. She said, 'When the daughter asked me how her father was doing, I told her I set my clock by when he turns off the lights!'"

Sarah frowned and said, "Let's listen to Ursula."

"I swing wildly in my moods. Usually I hate him but I have to depend on him. Once after I had been difficult, I cried and got him to promise he would take care of me. But he's driving me crazy and I want a divorce."

"I am a family therapist, you know, and I would highly recommend August's coming to see me also."

"Oh, never. He chose your name because it wasn't checked as a family therapist."

"That was an oversight on the list."

"He wouldn't dream of looking into his own feelings. I'm lucky he brings me. If you want, you can phone my daughter Blaine, who's only about forty miles away and keeps tabs on us. She's kind but doesn't realize that I need a retreat. I am Narcissus, and deserve a holy place apart, but Jove hurls thunderbolts. He's driving me crazy. I stay in my room because he doesn't want me stumbling around the house. He brings meals to me, like Blaine used to—when she was only in third grade and her little brother was born, she brought me breakfast in bed. And nowadays in the kitchen I can't see to work, and I start throwing and breaking things. I really need a divorce."

Martha stopped the tape and Sarah asked, "Did you get the daughter's number?"

"Yes, but I haven't called her. I'm considering prescribing an anti-depressant for Ursula, but August stipulated from the start that he's against using such drugs. Still, if her symptoms become unmistakably worse, when I see her next month I'm going to prescribe Doxepin. Doing nothing for her during this long month troubles me."

At dinner, Sarah said, "I may stay awake tonight worrying about Ursula! Wouldn't she be better off divorced, like she wants?"

"Well, not only is she unable to take care of herself and unwilling to be a burden on her kids, she's also set against moving out of her house. Also she still thinks of herself as a helper to the poetry professor at N.Y.U. who published an article she wrote. Poor Ursula bloomed late and then faded."

"She's not sick in her mind, just frustrated," was Sarah's verdict. "You have psycho-everything, why not psycho-poetry?"

"We do have it. Poetry therapy. One of the journals I brought along had a review of a book about it which I'm going to order sent to me at home."

On their last day in the cottage, Martha cooked and served Sarah a lunch in style on the porch. Her menu was a feta cheese dip and crudités, followed by a stir-fry of steak bits with Vermont broccoli, spring onions and water chestnuts. For dessert, she presented a creamy Bavarian pudding decorated with slices of candied ginger. Sarah was obviously relishing each course as she sat in idle splendor enjoying the view. Along the narrow road, the solid walls of pine and spruce were lightly sparked here and there with orange maple leaves. Shadows of clouds over the wooded mountain slopes deepened the dark green that was Vermont's signature. "It's amazing," she said, "The sky hangs way up there."

"You're so hypnotized by the beauty, I know you have to have this," Martha teased, bringing her a mug of coffee. "The Green Mountain Coffee Roasters created this just for you."

"Does it cure mosquito bites?"

"Definitely," said Martha. "And if they're still itching when you get home in a couple of days, you can rub on a little Manhattan grime."

They sat in silence until Sarah said, "Your Wednesday patients are like you."

To herself Martha acknowledged some truth in this. Aloud she said, "They're like everyone else, unique individuals. Maybe suburban women are accustomed to privilege, so they trust the world and have a breezy approach. I call it a coincidence that these three special women all come on Wednesday afternoon."

Sarah nodded. Then she asked, from a full heart, "What goes through your mind when Ursula tells you her troubles?"

"Right now, there's a built-in conflict between her deep fears and her ambitions. Luckily, she's had joy in her life and may find a way to feel it again, with a sense of fulfillment. But I haven't figured out any solution. After she leaves I think over what she's up against, and sometimes it makes me late to dinner."

"I see. But I want you to have your dinners hot."

"You take good care of me, Sarah. And you've done great cooking up here."

Sarah grinned. "Be sure to tell Barry I mastered the kitchen. And so did you."

That night Martha wakened to the sound of thunder. She got out of bed, drew her robe on over her pajamas and, trying not to wake Sarah whose bed was in the far corner, walked quietly in the dark and stood staring out the picture window. She half-believed that Norman stood beside her.

No doubt he'd suggest champagne! The one and only bottle I brought is still in the refrigerator. But for myself, I won't bother.

A crash of thunder brought pelting rain, cooling the warm August night.

Soon Sarah, wrapping a robe around herself, joined her and asked, "Are you okay?"

"Sure. It's just that the thunder woke me from a pleasant dream."

"My dreams have been pleasant, too. It's been a restful month."

"Restful, but sad without Norman."

"So what was your pleasant dream?"

"It was about Elinor. I had a vision of a wedding."

"I'll drink to that, as Norman would say."

"Yes, he always said that." Martha's voice broke, and she shivered with grief, her face screwed up to hold back tears. The two women, their arms around each other's waists, stood side by side watching sheets of rain fling themselves against the pane.

"He's never coming back," Martha said.

"But he isn't gone. His love is around us. He left me you and Barry."

"I need him." Martha dropped her arm and half turned away, her forehead against the cold window, staring into the storm. "I'm not sure I can keep going."

"You're doing very well."

"I'm not. Without you, I couldn't have gotten through August."

"I'm glad I came. I learned about Elinor, Billie and Ursula."

"You know," Martha said, raising her head, "I learned about them too, telling you. I decided to get Elinor to concentrate on getting a job, and to try poetry therapy with Ursula. And I'll try to be stronger with Billie so she'll stop being mean to Mike. So you've helped me." She lightened up. "Even if you did make me sing for my supper."

Sarah laughed. "Now the refrigerator's almost empty again, except for a bottle of champagne. Shall I get it?"

Martha nodded and waited, feeling less sad.

As they lifted glasses, Sarah proposed a toast, "To Elinor! May she find her true path!"

After they drank, she asked, "What was your dream of her wedding?"

"Well, since she's been married before, it's not a white wedding, but all flowery and pink. She's in a pale pink gown and two lovely teenage girls are with her—I wonder why two?—in pale green dresses. I can't see the groom, but I see the tall son in a black suit. The big wedding cake is pink and green. They're in a candle-lit restaurant, all looking rosy and respectable. Then they're off on a honeymoon . . ."

". . . to a hunting lodge in Austria!" said Sarah, happily remembering her father's lodge. They drank again.

"Did you have a vision for 'Feisty'?"

"For Billie? I'm not sure." There was a pause.

"It'll come to you. Skip her for now."

"For Ursula I see a big family reunion for her golden wedding, grandchildren dancing, their parents showing each other cookie caricatures of everyone."

Sarah lifted her glass. "To Ursula! Enjoyment of the imagination she has left, and the security of her marriage."

Martha added, "And wisdom to realize that a creator is more valuable than a critic." They drank.

"And 'Feisty'?"

"Okay. To Billie! More capacity to show the love that

Mike needs. And holiday dinners with him and Christopher." They clinked glasses again.

"Do you think she'll marry Christopher?"

"Maybe yes, maybe no. For now, he's big-hearted—a good model for Mike."

They had almost killed the bottle and were feeling lightheaded when the rain stopped and the moon appeared, not the pollution-drenched dark orange moon of low horizons, but a pale white moon over the mountain, nearly full.

Sarah brought over a chair for herself and Martha sat on the floor by the window, her face unusually animated. "It's a mystery to me, but through my visions—don't mention them to Barry, it sounds kooky—I seem to foretell the future."

"He'd say you were 'spaced out.'"

"Yes." Martha laughed. "There's something mystical about it. Before I've said a word, when I'm really listening, sometimes a patient reads my mind."

"That doesn't happen only to therapists," Sarah said seriously. "I once had a math teacher who only had to be in the room for me to work better than usual. And Norman said that when scholars told him about their research, they'd say what he himself was thinking—reading his mind."

Martha nodded. "I'm interested in this because basically, I'm there to help patients gain insights into themselves, not to prescribe specific solutions. I repeat back what the patient says, nothing more, so it's like they tell themselves their own stories. I hope they can continue this after they leave therapy, and recall the empathy I feel for them."

"You hope they'll keep on talking back to themselves?"

Martha giggled, feeling high as the mountain. "Aplogize for their own emotional histories." Sarah shook her head when she held up the bottle, so she emptied it into her own glass, and slurred her speech, joking, "Remember Freud's famoush shaying, 'Analyshts mush lishen!'"

Sarah didn't smile. "Does that mean they leave the patients to interpret their own emotions?"

Martha became serious. "No, listening doesn't mean being passive. I'm not passive, I'm active when I listen."

Sarah voiced a doubt which had been troubling her. "You have a lot of power, dealing with these women's emotions. But what if you're working toward *your* goals for them, not their goals for themselves?"

Martha repeated, trying to concentrate. "Working toward *my* goals for them, not their goals for themselves? Oh, no. Never!" Resolutely she stood up. "Time for bed, Teapot."

They went to their beds and slept.

5

Small Doses of Anger

Two weeks later when Elinor was due, Martha sat at her desk in preparation. Their first session after the summer break was on tape and she was playing it now because she wanted to let Elinor hear the anger she had blurted out toward her ex-husband, Howard.

Last week I supported her happiness at finding a new lover, and today I want to let her know I support the anger, if I can only locate it before she comes. Where is that healthy outburst?

> "I know I shouldn't feel too joyful, because maybe by falling in love with Ralph I'll be depriving my kids of the love they need. When you've just fallen in love you measure yourself against an ideal and that makes you feel inadequate.
>
> "You know, when my first baby, Steven, was born, I fell in love with him. Not until he reached two and a half did my love become child-sized—not shrinking, but becoming 'tough love.' I had to discipline him, like keeping him from getting run over. Somehow, though, that seemed to bother Howard, and although he became less jealous of the attention I gave the kids, or pretended to, in the end he couldn't really love them. I was a parent without a partner long before our divorce. Now I struggle to maintain a love which doesn't go to such extremes as my suicide attempt last Christmas. I definitely plan to steer clear of any jealousy my kids could have of Ralph. They're my prior obligations, after all. Some day I'll be free, when they leave home, but I dread that, too."

"You need to consider your own goals for the future."

"I sometimes wonder if I'm going to have an empty-nest syndrome when both kids leave."

"Maybe you can add something to your own life, like finding a meaningful job."

"My work record is too ancient. All I'm good at now is running a big house and cooking gourmet meals on a budget. And raising kids. Ralph also has kids, two teen-age girls, and he's a conscientious father. But the problem about sharing love is if there'll be enough to go around."

"Love isn't an apple pie with just so many wedges, you know. It's like the sun shining on everyone. Nobody loses because the next person is also in the sun."

"Oh, that's beautiful! But will I have enough love to give Ralph's daughters? And won't I have to meet his ex-wife and love her in a sort of way for her daughters' sakes?"

"You probably will meet her, but you certainly don't have to love her."

"That's funny! One thing, Ralph won't let Howard run roughshod over me any more."

"Have you heard from Howard?"

"Not really. He doesn't care in the least how we're doing, but now that he smells the fact that I've met someone else, he's sure to turn up."

"Does he come to the house?"

"No, but he sometimes phones Steven. Usually he phones my friend next door, Adele, and quizzes her, but she gives him only the merest bits of news. She tells me later how he tries to check on me. He can't live with the way he himself has changed our lives. I know it isn't Christian, but I hate that! How I hate him!"

Martha played it again: "How I hate him!" and decided that her plan for the day would be to get Elinor to be proud of her anger and to direct it toward Howard.

The light came on indicating that the front doorbell had rung, and she buzzed the front door open. Elinor soon appeared in the doorway, her face pink and glowing.

Martha smiled and said warmly, "Come in."

Returning the smile, Elinor sat gracefully in the chair by the desk. "I had a wonderful weekend."

"Do you want to describe your feelings?"

"Well, you know I stayed overnight with Ralph before, in his apartment in the City, but this time we went to a cottage he has on Fire Island. It's not fancy, just comfortable and private. It's quite a walk along the beach from the shops, and fronts right on the water. Oh, it was so restful. We ate and swam and made love."

Martha waited.

Elinor smiled. "A lot. And each time beautiful."

"How do you feel about that?" They both smiled at this quite ridiculous question, but Martha wanted to determine if Elinor was exaggerating.

"Well, Ralph's more than kind. Maybe he's in love with me. He makes me feel as if I'd never known what it's like to have fun or be tender, or give way to passion."

"You had strong feelings?"

"Oh, yes, I didn't know myself. And yet I knew myself for the first time."

"And you felt comfortable?"

"Oh, yes. Everything seems to be going right between us."

Martha waited longer than usual for her to say more. Eventually, Elinor said, "We had a very nice Sunday morning. At Ralph's you have to walk down the beach to get fresh drinking water, so I braided my hair into pigtails and asked him if he had a robe I could borrow. He found a denim one which barely covered my bikini.

" 'Nobody will see us along the beach this early,' he said. He was wearing a short Happi Coat over his swimming trunks and carrying four empty buckets.

"On the return hike, I felt young and innocent, carrying two full buckets. Well, maybe not innocent, but virginal, like a heroine in a Victorian romance who was learning about life and various ways of making love, each different and wonderful. Once I'd pretended to resist, and he held me so tight I caught fire. Another time I felt a motherly tenderness. Carrying the buckets I told him that if I were home at that moment I'd be in church, so a churchy way to describe our lovemaking could be, *from the rising of the sun until the going down of the same.*

"He said, 'I'm glad to do the Lord's work.' I laughed, then said I was playing the role of a milkmaid walking with the son of the Lord of the Manor who was seducing me. 'You're very kind to be carrying the heavier buckets.

"At the door of the cottage, Ralph put down his buckets and I put mine beside his. We hadn't seen anyone at all along the beach and in the shade near the front door of the house, we were sheltered from view by thick pines. So I took off the robe and spread it over the buckets, and said, 'Master, if I dally here, I'll be scolded for letting the water grow hot.'

"Ralph laughed, and took off his Happi Coat and spread it over the pine needles for us to sit on. 'What if I get hot? Got a doily for me?'

"'Nope,' I said. 'I said *dally*, not *doily.*'

"'How about this?' He flipped the elastic of my bikini.

"'Hey! I'll cool you off if you ask for it.' I reached into a bucket and splashed him. With a mock show of force, he raised my arm so I couldn't splash him again. He pretended to growl, 'Do you dare to splash your lord and master?' He kissed my underarm and pulled me down. I felt a rush of passion as he removed my halter and gathered me to him."

She fell silent, sitting without speaking.

Martha didn't speak, feeling empathy for Elinor's need to integrate new emotions. It could have been the first time her desire was fully satisfied.

As Elinor's silence continued, a past Sunday morning of her own flashed through Martha's mind.

I'd made waffles and was washing the syrupy plates, while Norman sat at the table doing the *Times* puzzle. Barry was at summer camp. The cat was asleep on Sarah's usual chair. It was a snug feeling, being alone with Norman. I was drying my hands when he came behind me and, teasing, pulled my hair. I responded with a hip nudge and he countered with a side bump worthy of the good rumba dancer he was.

"How's your puzzle?" I asked.

He opened his eyes in too-perfect innocence. "I need a word for going back to bed with your wife on Sunday morning."

I leaned back against him, and said, "It's h-a-p-p-y."

We kissed and went up the stairs without speaking, and Norman closed our bedroom door against the cat, who liked to get in bed, too.

Dreamily, Elinor looked up and smiled. "Everything seems right between us. We have fun." Martha nodded approval and Elinor went on, hesitantly. "But something went wrong. When I phoned home, Steven told me that his father had called and said I was immoral and they should pack up their things and move in with him."

"How did Steven react?"

"Well, he has a lot of poise for his age. He knows I have custody, so he just told his father I was visiting a friend for the weekend but would be home when I'd said I would."

"And you returned on time?"

"Yes." She again fell silent. Then she said softly, "There was something else. He told Steven, 'Your mother's shacked up with a stockbroker.'"

Martha wanted to hear anger at this but heard none. She probed. "That made you angry?"

"No, I just didn't think it was in good taste. I *was* shacked up with a stockbroker, I can't deny that. But to Steven it sounded bad, and that's what Howard intended. He has no idea how much I needed that weekend."

"And he criticized you to Steven."

"Yes. Howard is the problem."

This was Martha's cue. "You *are* capable of expressing anger. Listen to this." She pressed the play button. "Oh, how I hate that. How I hate him." She turned off the tape and asked, "How about that feeling?"

Elinor shook her head. "I have to forget that, because getting angry makes me depressed. I always feel I should be prepared, take care of any problems in advance so there won't be any anger, or I'll feel so guilty I'll want to kill myself."

"And so put an end to all feelings altogether?"

"Well . . . "

"Feelings of self-destruction are selfish. They can destroy loving feelings, like toward your children. If something makes you so angry that you want to kill yourself, it may be because you haven't expressed anger at the person who deserves it. Well-placed anger can free you to have warm and joyful feelings."

"I want to have warm and joyful feelings."

"You will. So when someone really does wrong, get angry. As your doctor, I prescribe that you take small doses of anger whenever necessary. Will you do that?"

"I'll try. I planned to tell the kids about Ralph in my own way, but wanted to be sure he was going to matter a lot to me and then have them meet. Otherwise I'd just tell them I'd be easier to live with if I had a vacation now and then. But their father had to butt in, saying he was next door at Adele's but didn't have time to come over. That's typical of his inventive evil ways—Adele told me later that he wasn't there at all, he had only called her on the phone. All she told him was that she knew I'd met a stockbroker, because she didn't want him to think I was eating my heart out. So he enjoyed making the kids feel badly that he was next door, but not interested in seeing them, like a decent father. He only wanted to plant doubts about me."

66

"You seem to resent that more than what he told Steven."

"That's right. Deliberately trying to hurt your own kids' feelings is the worst. I hate that! Oh, I do hate him to pieces!"

There it was again. Martha let it sink in for a long moment. "Your anger is justified. Does expressing it make you feel guilty?"

After a pause, Elinor answered. "Well, I don't feel guilty about being with Ralph or about leaving the kids for the weekend. Susan forgot to go to the dentist—it's quite a walk, actually, and her bike is broken. Otherwise they got along fine. I'll be a better person and a better mother after that wonderful weekend, because someone cares about me. That kind of caring you pass on to other people." Martha nodded. "But of course Ralph and I haven't had time yet to really know each other or foresee any problems."

"You're looking for problems?" Martha's query was sharp.

"Just looking before I leap."

This phrase caused Martha to smile ruefully, recalling Irv.

Elinor continued, mildly indignant. "I'm certainly not *looking* for problems, just want it to be slow and sure. Next Saturday, Ralph's coming to dinner and we'll spend the night either at my place or his. I'm going to phone his office."

"Our time is up," Martha said in a toneless voice.

Elinor stood as if waiting for something more, perhaps a word of congratulation on her happy weekend.

Martha, however, was feeling envy. She had no lover she could call. But a comment was needed, and she asked, in the most pleasant voice she could manage, "Is there a name for the green of your dress?"

"I don't know. It reminded me of daffodil leaves." Martha didn't reply. "Well, same time next week," said Elinor and walked out the door.

At her desk, Martha started to make notes but threw down her pen.

I shop at good stores, why don't I find clothes that color? Elinor isn't the only redhead who looks good in pale green.

I'm angry. Oh, Norman, why did you die?

6

I'll Beat You Again Tomorrow

Billie went shopping late Tuesday afternoon for the dinner she was going to serve the next evening to three men: Mike, her son; Michael, her ex-husband; and Christopher, her lover. Without Christopher she wouldn't want to have a family dinner party. It had to be tomorrow because of her ex's being in town only a day or two longer, and she wanted to confirm that he was taking their son with him to Florida. She had talked up the plan with Mike and kept his clothes clean, ready for a quick take-off.

She dashed along the aisles of the supermarket.

A big roast beef. Sandwich bread. Tomatoes. I have horseradish at home. Instant mashed potatoes. Coleslaw is the easiest salad. Beer. Chocolate ice cream for dessert. Where the hell is Mike? I pounded it into his head that he was to be here by five-thirty. I'm sick of his always being late. He knows I have to get home, so he'd better show up now or he'll be walking.

She didn't like their suburb's lack of transportation for anyone not driving a car. Mike often rode the school bus after school to some friend's home—he had a variety of pals —and phoned his mother to come to pick him up. All suburban mothers were indentured chauffeurs, but unlike most of them, she worked outside the home. If he didn't call ahead, he often interrupted her dinner after she had started eating. The last straw was that he usually didn't know his location and had to take time to relay directions. Houses were scattered on large acreages with no street signs, so meeting her at the store was one solution, since it was at a hub of traffic and he could generally hitch a ride there.

She was in the checkout line when she spotted Mike

behind her. Nonchalantly tossing away an empty banana skin, he strolled forward and dropped a box of chocolate chip cookies into Billie's shopping cart.

"Hurry up, Mom," he said.

She gestured angrily toward the two carts piled high with groceries to be checked out by the woman in front of her.

He took a copy of *Reader's Digest* off the rack and started reading it, and she gazed at him.

My little problem has grown into a six-foot-tall one. His sneakers are dusty, as usual, but at least his shirt and old jeans are clean—I launder them often enough! His features have lengthened but his eyes never lose their watchfulness. He might become handsome like his father but will never have the carefree charm.

When most of her items had been rung up, he dropped the *Reader's Digest* onto the counter to be added to her order, but Billie said, "No, you can read that in the school library."

Silently, he took it back and again became engrossed in it. She paid her bill and to hurry Mike along, snatched the magazine from him. A glance at the cover revealed that the leading article was "Is Your Child Seeking a Cult?" With a shrug dismissing the worth of the magazine, she tossed it back onto the counter, took one bag of groceries, gestured for Mike to pick up the other, and marched briskly toward the car.

Carrying the bag, he followed, and started on his usual demand, "Let me drive."

"Hell, no."

"Hear the fire engines? The police will all be at the fire so they won't stop us. I'm a safer driver than you are. I could pass the test right now."

"There's a law."

"Mom, I need the *practice*." She got into the driver's seat and he grumpily sat beside her. "All my friends drive. Sam has his own car."

"Serendipity Sam is a lot older than you. He got left back in school."

"But how about Gus?"

"Mike, you know where Gorgeous Gus drives—up and down his family's driveway. And I let you drive around our parking lot."

"Their driveway is half a mile long."

"So you weren't born with a silver car key in your fist." He didn't smile and slumped in the car seat. As they waited at an intersection she turned to him, touched his arm, and looked him in the eye. "Mikey, why are you cutting English eighth period? The office sent me a notice."

"The teacher hates my guts."

"Scuracchio?"

"Yeah. All he talks about is birdwatching."

"The school day doesn't end until after the last period, Mike."

"I just go out for some nicotine with the BB's. I'm flunking, anyhow."

"How do you know?"

"I failed a couple of surprise quizzes. Who wants to read a kids' book about funny pigs?"

"It's *Animal Farm*—I know what they teach. It's not a kids' book, it's about the Russian Revolution. Have you ever heard of the Russian Revolution?"

"Mom, I'm a tenth-grader in senior high school. And you know it's a hard school because you're one of the hardest teachers. Are you always going to treat me like a seventh-grader?"

"I'll treat you like a tenth-grader when you act like one. In the meantime, learn to read."

"You bitch!"

Reflexively, she swung out her right arm and belted him in the face with the back of her fist.

He turned sideways, his knees up as close as he could bring them, and leaned his head against the back of the seat, staring at her, silent and unmoving.

Billie drove on in silence, feeling guilty.

Now what have I done?

At her desk the next afternoon Martha was waiting for Billie.

Why did I dream about her? She was playing tennis with someone I couldn't see. She made a fast return and called, "Hey, I'll beat you again tomorrow, okay?" Then a young man walked across the court, his body bent over a potted plant he was carrying. As he shuffled past Billie she hit him hard on the head with her racket, but it didn't seem to faze him. He just stayed bent over and walked straight ahead, off the court. It said "BARRY" on the back of his T-shirt. Why would he be there? Her hitting him points to her ex, Michael. She told me she hit him once with a vase, and he'd had stitches. It left no scar, she claimed. Apparently it left one on me.

Billie arrived, her walk bouncy and her voice cheerful. "Hi! I'm early, right?"

Martha looked up, dragging her tempo, and smiled. "Yes. A little."

"Can we finish early, too?"

"We'll keep it in mind." *Martha did in fact want time to think about Ursula, whose appointment would follow.*

"Well," Billie began, "We have a nice mess now. Michael's come up from Florida and is trying to get Mike to give him the names of the stupid rich people who live around us. He wants to sell some friggin' cactuses to everyone in Middle Cove."

"Cactuses?"

"Yes, he's been growing these fantastic cactuses. He has a van full of them. And he wants us to charm people into buying them, especially the rich mothers of all Mikey's friends. I don't like the idea of Mike making a sales pitch about funky cactuses for his father. Although they *are* amazing—a lot are shaped like penises, some are blue like sea urchins, some are like bunches of flat yellow-green paddles, and some like lacy empty baskets. All prickly and fantastic. I could give you one."

Martha hesitated, wondering what Billie was trying to "buy" with this present. Then she said, "Could I pay for one?"

Billie chuckled. "No, Mikey-baby owes me a few. He's staying in my apartment so I'm saving him hotel bills."

"By 'Mikey-baby' you mean your ex-husband?"

"Yeah. Correction: *Michael*. I used to call him Mikey-baby when we were first married, but later we called the baby that, so he's been Michael ever since."

"What does your son want to be called?"

"'Mike,' but if I say 'Mikey' he'd better answer. I don't know why I called his father Mikey-baby just now. Pretty Freudian, I guess." She grinned at Martha, who looked at her intently until she went on. "He really *is* a baby, arrives on short notice and expects everyone to greet him with open arms. He pulled into town last Thursday at dinnertime in this beat-up van. It's really just an old minibus with all the seats removed, but he calls it a van. He was going to park it on the parking lot of our building and sleep in it, like he did driving up from Florida. That would mean putting a lot of cactuses under the car overnight, but I warned him that people let dogs run around. Young Mike said he could bring his foam mattress into his bedroom, so he did. The second night, I noticed Michael used the bed and Mike slept on the mattress on the floor."

"How did you feel about the switch?"

"Well, the kid has younger bones, and it won't hurt him to put himself out for his dad. Who'll take him to Florida with him, I hope. For several days now, Michael's toothbrush has been on the window sill in the bathroom, sticking out of the top of his thermos jug. Right at home."

"Is he spending time with his son?"

"Well, over the weekend Mike camped out at Montauk as usual, but they talk when they're both around. Mike hasn't seen his father since he was eight. It's his chance for a change, so he should find out what the guy is like. When a kid has the urge to go, you only make him hate you by confining him."

"Is giving a teenage son a stable home *confining* him?"

"I figure he needs a change now. Like a visit to Florida, which is the only way I could afford to send him anywhere. Why not give his father the pleasure of supporting him for a while? He's old enough, or soon will be, to get a license to drive in Florida, and he likes cars, so he might help his dad take care of the sightseeing bus he drives. This cactus business is a sideline, perverse and beautiful as they are."

"I see," said Martha.

"I think it's their prickliness that appeals to Michael. He likes prickly things. He loved me once upon a time."

"You see yourself as prickly?"

"Of course," Billie replied confidently. "Yet this cactus thing is too much. I can't have Mikey panhandling his friends' mothers in the school district—they aren't my friends."

"Some people might be glad to buy an unusual plant."

"Yeah, they do come from all over the world. He can name the deserts where they're native and swears that some have never been seen around here before. But he needs to find a market larger than a few mothers out in the 'burbs. So last weekend I gave him the pages listing florists from my Manhattan phone book. They sell a lot of rare plants."

"You sound angry."

"Yes, because it's no longer my job to establish his manhood. I did that when we were married and it didn't work. And now I'm involved with Christopher."

"How do you mean, establish his manhood?"

"I mean, Big-Mommy him, tell him he's doing great. That's what guys need, the kind I meet, anyhow. But it's a one-way street. They never tell me I'm great."

"Do you find Christopher like Michael in this way?"

Billie sat straighter. "Not really. Chris is different. He

praises me. He may be painting ceilings to save up some money, but he's got a college degree and a big portfolio of art and engineering designs. I've been helping him fill out an application to Cooper's Union for the degree course in architecture. Although he's five years younger than me, he pays his way and he's fatherly, not only to Mike but to me. He says I bring out his creativity and settle him down at the same time."

"No complaints like last week that he lacks passion in bed?"

"Lord, no. Since Michael came on the scene, Chris has been very passionate, like he's trying to get me pregnant."

Martha gave her a startled glance. "Pregnant?"

Billie said airily, "Oh, I see to it that we control the danger. By the rhythm method." Her eyes twinkled as she waited for the effect of this.

Martha picked up the teasing tone and smiled. "And what other method?"

"Everything known to science, except the pill. Just the diaphragm and condoms and common sense."

"Have you thought about having a baby with Christopher?"

"God, no! What kind of garbage is that? I've got a career. But it's fun being the object of desire—you can call that my present from Michael, in a roundabout way." She peered at Martha and relaxed when Martha smiled. "What I want to talk about is Mikey. He's in trouble in school already, and with the term just started the guidance counselor sends me a notice of cutting. The next step is a summons to his office so I can sit with my hands folded while he scolds me."

"What's Mike's problem?"

"Too much like his father. Waiting for the teachers to find out what a great genius he is."

"Does he go to school regularly in the mornings?"

"He gets on the school bus every morning and goes to classes until English, the last period."

"Does he have somewhere to go?"

"He must have, but I honestly don't know where the guys hang out if they cut just one class. Maybe they lie low in some rich kid's car. The girls go to the nurse with cramps, or hide in the bathrooms. But none of my students cut class—they're all vying for good colleges."

"You're lucky."

"As a teacher, yes. As a mother, no. The guidance jerk adds a little comment at the end of the notice: 'He's your son.' Of course he's my son. But he had a father too. I've had enough of this crap—'He's your son.'"

She sat in an indignant posture, postponing confessing that she had hit Mike the day before in the car, and continued angrily, "School is counterproductive for a lot of kids these days. Like Mike's English teacher underestimates them, and teaches Orwell on the level of a kid's book. After dinner last night I sat Mike down and showed him how *Animal Farm* is a satire on the Russian Revolution, and when he got the idea, we laughed and had a beer together. But before that, coming home in the car, he insulted me. I told him to learn to read and he called me a bitch! So I hit him."

"What did he do?"

"He sat like a damned monument, with staring eyes."

"How did you feel afterward?"

"I felt good. It stopped his 'let me drive' refrain."

"How did he feel?"

"That bullet-head? He could be a good student if he'd try. But basically he's a no-good kid. I could kill him!"

Martha looked steadily at her, letting "I could kill him!" linger in the air, then said, "We should discuss this, but it's near the end of our time. Were you serious about leaving early?"

"I'm serious about that but maybe not about . . . about what I said." Billie's voice softened. "He just gets me mixed up."

Martha looked at her watch. "It's two minutes early. Goodbye until next week."

Billie stared at her and rose, angrily. "Goodbye." She stomped out.

Martha was rueful.

I'm glad she wasn't holding a tennis racket—I think she'd have hit me for ending early, when she asked for it. What a love of power she has! And she lets it show. No wonder the school people expect her to manage Mike.

She sat a moment, recalling three occasions when Norman had said to her seriously, "He's your son."

The first was while gazing at the newborn boy in her lap in the hospital bed, and tiny Barry opened his eyes at them. Norman bent over, looking at him closely. "He's your son."

Martha said, "And yours."

"But his eyes are blue."

"All babies have blue eyes. They change in a few months to the color they're going to be. His may turn brown like yours."

"I hope they stay blue like yours," said Norman.

Barry's eyes had, in fact, stayed blue.

The second time was at a teenage track meet where they had watched Barry run a race. He sprinted past them, his arms pumping, his face flushed.

"He's your son," said Norman.

"And yours." Martha squeezed her husband's arm.

"But he doesn't get those long legs from my side."

"Your legs aren't short."

"He may become tall like you and your father."

"I hope he has your disposition," she replied. "My father was athletic but he didn't have your staying power."

The third time was when Barry was a sophomore in college and had brought his friend Angela home. After they had dinner in the dining room the young couple left in the new family car to go to a basketball game. Barry made a ceremony of goodbye, waving with exaggeration, driving half a block and stopping, then backing the car to where his parents stood watching from the stoop and going through a second frenzy of waving. "He's making fun of me for worrying about his driving," Martha said. "But night traffic is scary."

"He'll be all right. He's your son."

"And *yours!*" she said sharply. "We're *both* proud of him."

Norman, unruffled, added, "He has good taste in girls, hasn't he? Wants a girl just like the girl that married dear old Dad."

"But Angela's not like me. I'm not that pretty."

"You're too beautiful to be pretty. It's more her spirit of independence. And she is blonde and long-legged, like you."

"He has lots of time to pick Miss Right. His taste may change."

When they had gone back inside, Sarah looked up from clearing the table and said, "Shiksa!" and Norman scolded her for narrow-mindedness. Martha kept out of it. She told Norman later, "Sarah's not narrow-minded, she was only making end-of-the-party conversation. What may worry her is if he's old enough to drive and have a steady girl, he might soon leave home. We shouldn't worry, just be sure he has time to find out what he wants."

Barry took time, but didn't luck out. After getting an MA in business, he married Marie, another good-looking blonde with an independent spirit. They met in the advertising agency where they both worked. Norman and Martha both liked her, but she was a bit distant and finally became excessively engrossed in managing the art department at a large salary. She had less and less time for marriage, and one day announced she was moving out of their apartment and getting a divorce.

Martha had felt sorry for Barry for having to live alone during his father's final illness, but she'd had faith he could manage. She herself had been spending every possible moment at the hospital and seeing many patients so she could pay the bills. The solution had been Sarah's moving in to keep house, making it natural for Barry to come to dinner regularly. When his lease was up he moved back into his old room.

So now he *is* my son, and I'm worried because he seems to have settled in a bit too comfortably.

7

What Prescription?

Ursula was due, and before four o'clock, Martha set out the delicate china teacup she kept for her and put the kettle on. Today she planned to use with her the poems in the poetry therapy book she had ordered by mail from Vermont.

Thinking of Vermont, she wished she could tell Sarah her thoughts about Ursula, and she fantasized doing so:

The introduction of my book says that writing poetry helps patients define their own ambiguities, but that probably wouldn't help Ursula because she's one of those ultramodern poets who glorify ambiguity for its own sake. She needs help, though. Last week when I first saw her after the summer break, I thought her condition had worsened. Although under my questioning she showed clear memory and good verbal skills, there were warnings, like her intense dislike of August's photocopy machine, which she called a dangerous toy. I saw the copier when I was in their home, a large old-fashioned heavy gray box on a steel trolley, hardly a toy! At first I wondered if she thought that it emitted radiation, but what bothered her was that August wouldn't let her use it. She had given him some poems to copy, her only copies in some cases, and he had lost them, claiming the machine had eaten them. She said he was serious, getting back at her for joking once that her washing machine had eaten one of his socks—it was never found and he had held it against her. In her anger she could no longer recall which poems they were. While telling me about it, she started saying unintelligible words that sounded Japanese.

Also she said that one day while I was away, she'd gotten lost walking a few familiar blocks coming home from the library. She gravely told me about being taken home by the police and having no idea why she had been confused.

That's why I wrote out a prescription for Doxepin and gave it to her last week. I expect her husband has given her three capsules a day—after all, he's the man the neighbors set their clocks by. I hope she's better this week.

Ursula finally arrived with her daughter Blaine, a tall, dignified woman in her forties, a younger, more colorful version of her mother.

Martha asked her, "Would you like to stay for a part of the session?"

"Thank you, but no. I have a long drive in rush hour ahead of me." She kissed her mother goodbye but stood looking at Martha. Sensing that she wanted to say something more, Martha walked her down the hallway, after Ursula sat down.

Blaine explained, "Mother seems to have hit a low point, and has been complaining bitterly about Daddy August." She pronounced the name *Awgoost*. "I believe she may not be really psychotic but just paranoid. I've had her at home with us for a couple of days, and she's been quite normal, especially with our two teenagers."

"She often speaks of them fondly."

"And they love her and her wonderful stories. I'd bring her to live with us, but Daddy wouldn't fit in. Also he's taking care of her and would be lost without the responsibility."

"Yes, it seems to fill a need for him."

"It's hard for her, being unable to read. But what she complains of is Daddy."

"There's a great deal I'd like to discuss with your father," Martha said thoughtfully. "Sometimes the world should adjust, not the patient."

"You're so good for Mother!" Blaine exclaimed.

"Your mother mentioned that she might soon have an eye operation, but wasn't very specific. What is it for?"

"Chronic uveitis. She's getting constant care but if there's a crisis the surgeon will operate. In the meantime, we must wait."

"Does your father take her to the doctor regularly?"

"Oh, yes. I get the Medicare explanations of benefits regularly. But we used up the amount allowed for psychiatry before we came to you."

"I see that my bills are paid by your father, but you reimburse him. Is that right?"

"Yes. I send a monthly check directly to Daddy's bank. My husband and I are better off financially than my parents and we think Mother needs therapy. I'm glad you asked because I'd like you to bill me directly every month from now on." She handed Martha a card. "And be sure to tell me if he tries to cancel an appointment."

After Martha opened the front door for her, Blaine, hesitating, asked, "Do psychiatrists make house calls?"

"Occasionally. Why do you ask?"

"Daddy may not always be able to drive her in."

"It would be time-consuming for me to get to their house and therefore very expensive. Perhaps I could, in a real emergency."

Blaine nodded and left quickly.

When Martha returned, she found Ursula sitting up very straight. She had turned her chair away from the desk.

Martha spoke casually as she poured tea into the china cup. "It's good that your daughter came in with you. You mentioned that I might talk with her sometime and gave me her phone number. Do you remember?"

Ursula nodded.

"She's glad that you're coming in regularly to talk with me. She also mentioned how close you are to her children."

"I'm very fortunate in having my children and grandchildren," said Ursula, more relaxed.

"Yes," said Martha as she carefully placed the teacup and saucer on Ursula's lap. "Here's your tea. I'm afraid it cooled a little."

"Thank you. Am I the only 'schizo' to whom you give tea?"

"Why do you say 'schizo'?"

"I must have a split personality because I am so confused. I have cold feelings and then warm feelings toward my husband. All sorts of crazy feelings at different times toward everyone."

"Labels like schizophrenia and split personality need not concern us. You're right that you have mixed feelings of both love and anger. All these feelings are you and need to be examined."

Ursula said in a threatening tone, "If the threads are tangled, no one will find the way out of the cave." After a moment, she said quite matter-of-factly, "My husband is driving me crazy."

"What does he do?"

"You know what he does. He cooks and cleans. He enjoys looking like a saint, but he's a bully. He tramples my feelings."

"In what way?"

Ursula frowned and shouted, "You don't want to know my feelings. You're just like him. You sit here in your rational room with your shingle outside, and watch your watch. And you don't know anything."

She jumped to her feet, letting the cup and saucer smash onto the floor, and shouted, "You're crazy too!" She stood in the middle of the room, looking defiant.

Martha remained outwardly calm. "It's all right, Ursula."

"I made a mess." She sounded more pleased than sorry.

Martha ignored the shattered cup and saucer and the spreading pool of tea on the floor. "Neither of us is crazy, but the world is confusing, sometimes. Let's look at that together."

"I don't want to look at anything with you. I can't see, anyway."

"You're very angry at me today, aren't you? Well, this is a safe place for you to get angry."

"Nowhere is safe. I'm going under. I'm not myself at home. For fifty years he's been bullying me and I'm not safe." She did a sort of shuffling dance toward the window. "No, no," she muttered. "Shiboo-yee! Wah-bee! Sah-bee!" She was churning her arms, fluttering her long sleeves and fanning herself with an invisible fan.

"Ursula, sit down."

"No, no."

"Yes!" Martha said sharply. The word was a sharp hiss and Ursula turned around with a dazed look and then slumped into the chair and sat, muttering under her breath.

"Ursula, I'm not picturing clearly what's been happening with you."

"Picturing? You have to see if you want to picture things. I'm losing my vision."

"There are visions that don't require sight."

"Please let me sit a while in peace." She sat immobilized.

Martha thought that sitting a while in peace was a good idea, and said in a soothing tone, "Of course. Sit as comfortably as you can, as if you were in your own peaceful living room." Ursula frowned, but settled into silence.

In a moment, the past history of her own living room flashed through Martha's mind. It was the front room on the second floor, directly over the office suite and identical in proportions, so although intended to be the master bedroom it was fine as a living room. It had a working fireplace and was near the bedrooms. The Kaufmans had spent many cozy evenings there.

After our successful renovation of the downstairs room as an office, I thought Norman would enjoy fixing up the living room to his taste. He acquiesced, but his first and only action had been to hang framed duplicates of my diplomas, and to tack up some wedding snapshots which I filed away when they became curly and faded.

84

When Barry was in school, we three spent evenings there, reading and playing games and occasionally watching a TV show. Usually Barry had homework to do, and I had to study when I was in med school. Norman often visited his mother in her apartment a few blocks away.

Now, without him, I don't enjoy the room, with its diplomas, a bookshelf cluttered with plastic sports trophies, and worn-out brown carpeting. There's no color or charm. The old brown leather sofa that was in the house when my uncle left it to us sits there, all lumpy and sagging. It was like that even in the old days when it masqueraded as an analyst's couch in my office.

We didn't entertain upstairs. When Barry brought a college friend home to dinner and Sarah fed us all in the dining room, we lingered at the table, where second helpings of cheese cake were sure to be served. Later the kids would go out, Norman would walk Sarah home and I'd go down to my office.

I'd been keen to give Norman the right to fix up the room as he wanted, but he liked it as it was. I could have made a bright room with inviting furniture. I wonder, did I have a false idea of equality, like a stereotyped feminist? Well, feminist or not, I had a right to be a homemaker, as an extension of my role as wife and mother. All I'm sure of is that if I'd fixed up the living room, we would have entertained more, and Norman would have enjoyed that. Did I secretly not want to share him?

Ursula broke her silence. "You saw my living room at our party."

"Yes, I really enjoyed seeing that room."

"That's the last time I enjoyed it. August didn't want poetry readings at a party and we argued about it beforehand, but I won, for once. I wasn't happy when he took people upstairs to see his copy machine, especially you."

"I soon came down and heard some poetry."

"Yes, and later I enjoyed passing the cookies, the nicest I

ever had. My young friend Robert, the sculptor, claimed he was going to cast a few in plaster, especially one of an elf which he carefully wrapped in a napkin. I told everyone how I get cookies from my daughter-in-law out West, and they laughed when I told about finding old popcorn in the package that was like rubber to chew, so I couldn't offer them any, and they told me it was meant only as packing. They were a friendly crowd, but, truth to tell, I haven't been happy for one day since then because I heard August telling Robert that in a year and nine months we'd celebrate our Golden Wedding. Robert said he'd design a memorial cookie just for that, and August said, 'It will be a big event.' I can't stand the thought of celebrating my long years of misery with that man! I hope one of us is dead before the time comes."

She shuddered and suddenly startled Martha by chanting in a loud whine:

"Shorthand metamorphoses into nothingness.
Barnacles are not noted for being mettlesome."

Martha couldn't make anything of it, but she smiled, glad that Ursula was talking.

"There is high humor in catastrophes.
Annihilation is thrilling."

"Could you explain your poem to me? It is your own poetry, isn't it?"

"Oh, yes," said Ursula, quite sober and conversational. "It's about the whole of life. The first line about shorthand means that all our busy life on land doesn't mean much, and the second means that life under the sea may be calmer. But we're not aware of it. When you're not really living, death—the end of the world—seems thrilling."

"Is it thrilling to you?"

"Oh, yes. As thrilling as birth. Sometimes less painful. I want to be aware of my death when it comes, not miss it."

"Do you think about committing suicide?"

"I think August should commit suicide."

"Tell me more about that feeling."

"Of course, he's the father of my children. I need him."

"Do you think you will be all right through this coming week? The prescription I gave you may take a while to work."

"What prescription?"

"For Doxepin. Didn't your husband have it filled?"

"He didn't mention it. Did you give it to him or to me?"

"I gave it to you to give to him last week. It's medicine you need to take three times a day."

"I didn't take it this week, I know that. I was at Blaine's. Did she say I was taking it?" She shivered. "He's driving me crazy."

Martha quickly wrote the prescription again, put it in an envelope and laid it on her desk, thinking she'd take it out to him when he came for Ursula. "Is there any way you could still study poetry?"

"I can read only what's in large type. And not much *avant garde* poetry is available in large type, only *Reader's Digesty* sorts of things. No haiku. Of course, if there were, it would be a travesty. You don't start with haiku, you work up to it. Americans don't understand its philosophy, they just count syllables."

"Could you get someone to read to you?"

"A couple of friends have tried. I enjoy hearing the poetry. But you can't do real work that way. You need to browse, turn back and forth from poem to poem. You need eyes to do it."

Martha was touched by the simplicity of this, but pressed on. "How about your own writing? Do you need eyes for that?"

"Well, not so much, of course. I can scribble something but it's hard to do any revising unless I can read it. Friends lent us a large magnifying lamp which was a great help but my husband said I'd break it and returned it to them."

Martha hesitated. The teacup still lay in pieces on the floor. "Why do you break things?"

Ursula sat silent. She did not move outwardly but Martha felt her withdrawal, and floated a suggestion. "Do you have a good memory?"

"Oh, yes. It seldom fails me."

"Good. Do you have sight memory—that is, can you recall how things look?"

"Some things. I can close my eyes and see specific flowers and rooms and so on, even from long ago. But not many faces. Faces are hard."

"How much poetry depends on visual images?"

"A lot, especially the Japanese. Each of their three-line haikus contains a clear picture and signifies a season of the year and a philosophy. I write haiku—in English, of course."

"I see. I've read about Japanese flower arrangements, the levels of earth, man and heaven. Is there something corresponding in their poetry?"

"You mean, is Haiku like *ikebana*? Well, like *Ten, Jin and Chi* and *yo and yin* there are connections." She smiled.

Martha sensed it was time for her planned suggestion. "Would it be possible for you to write by concentrating on your visual memories of scenes? Your past must be a vast resource. You wouldn't need to read to do that."

"I . . . I could try." There was dullness in the compliance.

Martha walked to the window and noted that August had double-parked his car and was waiting.

"It must be time to go," Ursula said, rising unsteadily.

"Wait," Martha said. "I have a special book about poetry therapy and here is a line from one of the psalms that I like: 'Thou shalt not be afraid for the terror by night nor for the arrow that flieth by day.'"

Ursula chuckled. "I may know the book," she said. "Was it edited by a professor at N.Y.U.?"

"Let me check. Yes, it was."

"I chose the poems for it. My poetry professor was the editor and he passed the job on to me."

"Oh," said Martha. "You're familiar with that Psalm?"

"Oh, yes. I included many quotes from the Bible and I'm glad that line about the terror by night was kept. A lot of my Gary Snyder quotes were cut."

"It's the idea," said Martha. "One shouldn't be afraid of outward terror, like from a weapon, nor of the darkness of inner terror."

"Easier said than done," Ursula replied. With great dignity, she stood at the door and made a slow gesture, moving her arms wide and then toward her breast, as if folding sorrow into her heart. "Goodbye, Dr. Kaufman." She walked out the door.

Poor Ursula, she has to have power of some sort. I thought the poetry book would help, and maybe it still will. I used to like poetry and know it has real potential for healing. Maybe I should try some myself.

Seeing Blaine, I thought the reason Ursula's well-dressed is Blaine's hand-me-downs. It's sad that she gets to decide so little for herself. She didn't know if her husband got the Doxepin. Oh, the prescription!

She picked it up and ran down the hall and out the front door.

8

Smoking Is Bad for the Baby

Martha's last patient of the day, Sandra, was scheduled to come at five o'clock. Martha had counseled her some ten years before and had reviewed notes she had made at that time:

"Sandra is a cheerful red-headed teenager—wants to be called Sandy. Mother made the appointment, said the girl is very upset, grieving over death of maternal grandfather. Seems to miss grandfather but not depressed. Doing well in school, especially art. Will be art counselor. Friendly and emphatic, often says, 'I swear to God!' but doesn't swear like some New Yorkers, only for emphasis, like Barry."

This note took her back into still-vivid memories of Barry's teens, and she sat remembering.

Once I told him that swearing in the name of other people's sacred figures could offend them. He said, teasing, "Christ, Mom, when you say 'Holy Moses!' it doesn't make Bubbi mad." Later he amused us by inventing his own profanity, like "I swear by Babe Ruth" or "That driver is an unholy goon."

Norman and I took him to visit a popular temple, a synagogue and a couple of mainstream Protestant churches. Maybe, since neither of us was a member of any congregation, Barry ended up neutral about theology, though he shares our convictions about human rights.

When he was about ten, Sarah took him into the Williamsburg section of Brooklyn to the ancient Succoth celebration of Jewish survival. They saw the many different symbolic huts, the elegantly black-suited men, the women drab as brown leaves. What amazed him was apparently the small size of a Ferris wheel he had ridden on with other children. It was parked behind a tow-truck in an intersection and he speculated about other Coney Island amusements which might be towed into Greenwich Village, more convenient for him! He came home with a souvenir of the day, an ornately lettered prayer which Sarah and he hung on the wall in his bedroom. Later he covered it over with a photograph of the earth spinning in space.

She felt an unexpected jab of pain, a side-swipe of grief that Norman wasn't with her to share these memories.

He'd recall how we each, together and separately, talked with Barry seriously when he was approaching thirteen and offered him the opportunity to celebrate a Bar Mitzvah. Norman explained that he would have to convert because Jewish heritage comes through the mother, but that it could be arranged without difficulty. But Barry wanted to spend another summer in his beloved summer camp where he could swim and play his clarinet, and we favored a whole summer of fresh air over one big party for about the same cost. On the day he was thirteen we took Sarah to visit the camp and we all went out to dinner. Sarah gave him his grandfather's *tallis* and he received it gravely, but didn't try it on. One of Sarah's favorite stories later was about a chat she and Barry had that evening about Christianity and Judaism. "Barry says it's pretty simple. Jews believe in divine justice and make good judges because they're for fairness. Christians keep people happy because they're for forgiveness. He says they're both right. My grandson is a moral philosopher!"

One of his high school interests—it pointed to his career—was selling advertising space in the school newspaper to local shops. The summer he was sixteen we took him to Vienna where he met relatives and saw where Freud lived, and to England, where Norman shared with him his own private shrines, the Bodleian Library in Oxford and the British Museum Reading Room in London. From then on it was taken for granted that he had a right to choose his own beliefs.

Now that he's grown, swearing and pretend-swearing are gone, but, thank goodness, his boyish sense of fun has never left him, and he tests me and Sarah at times, acting the ultra-radical or ultra-conservative for the shock effect. We enjoy his teasing.

In the midst of her reverie, the light on her desk blinked. Stepping quickly to the window, she saw a short, pregnant young woman who stood firmly with feet apart, balanced on wedge shoes. Oh, yes, that's Sandy. I was very fond of her.

She pushed the buzzer and when Sandy entered the office said, "Sandra, I'm so glad to see you!"

"Yes, it's me," she responded in a level tone, advancing to the desk to shake hands. There was sensitivity and sweetness in her face as she looked at Martha. "You haven't changed a bit."

"In all these years?" Martha felt motherly. "I've lost a lot of the red in my hair. I see yours is as bright as ever."

"Yes, I'm still Sandy the carrot-top."

"And you still use the name Lieberman?"

"I still am Lieberman. Just five months pregnant, that's all. I'm your unwed mother for today." She walked over to look out of the window. "This part of the City has changed."

"Yes, there's been both renewal and deterioration."

"The story of my life."

There was a pause, until Martha said, "Won't you sit down?"

Sandy sat facing her near the desk, trying to balance a large artist's portfolio in her lap. "I've often dreamed of coming back to talk with you. You helped me in every way. I got along better with my parents, who were getting divorced. You started me deciding on my own what kind of life I wanted."

Martha fleetingly thought, Did I dose both this girl and Barry with self-determination, as one doses a baby with cod-liver oil?

Sandy unzipped the portfolio and brought out a ball of string. She glared at it, and then cupped it on her lap and put the portfolio on the floor.

Martha was puzzled. She didn't generally allow patients to do handiwork during therapy, but more important than saying so now was probing for why Sandy was here.

"What does self-determination mean to you?"

"It means being able to have this baby and live happily with the father, without getting married. I'm an artist and want to make my own way. But my mother's all bent out of shape about it, so I'm coming to you for her sake. And she'll pay after this. I'm paying this week to show I'm serious. She keeps phoning me about what I'm eating and it's driving me bonkers. But nobody could want a baby more than I do." She was tying knots.

"Are you making something for the baby?"

"No, I make macramé baskets to be sold in a shop in the Village, to hold hanging plants. It's funny, after I called you yesterday I started making you one. And sure enough, your plants"—she indicated the bench by the window—"the fern especially, would look better hanging. It needs space."

"Oh," said Martha.

"When I started this yesterday, I remembered how you were like a mentor to me when I was in high school. Gee, string gets so twisted!" She looked up and smiled. "This may seem crummy work for a drawing and lithography graduate of the Rhode Island School of Design, but I don't have space in my apartment for my printing. And I can't seem to settle down to it."

"Does that have anything to do with your pregnancy?"

"Not really. It was like that before I got pregnant. But David's father died—David's the father of my baby and we're in love and have been together for years—and he felt guilty because we didn't get married before his father's death—and that got me mad."

"David felt guilty?"

"Yeah, we knew his father had a heart condition, and David didn't want to do anything that would upset him, so he let on that we were engaged. That was only to his father, the rest of the family knew we were living together with no wedding in mind. Then while we were sitting *shiva* that week—but you're not Jewish, are you?"

"Only by marriage. I know what sitting *shiva* is from when my husband's father died." Martha was struck by a sudden insight.

Do I feel chatty because of Sandy's daughterly attitude both now and years ago? Was she a surrogate daughter to me? A suppressed fantasy?

Sandy said, "You told me long ago you weren't Jewish. It surprised me. My mother thought you were, of course. She pretends not to care about such things, but she does, really."

"And you?"

Sandy shook her head. "David and I are not denying our heritage, which is much the same for each of us, but we're not Orthodox. It was just natural for us to sit with David's mother. A lot of family members and friends came and it was calming. I loved his father, too. All the relatives were wonderful to me, but after three days it was clear they were wondering when we were going to get married, and one of the aunts asked him, 'When exactly?' and David said 'Soon!' I nearly flipped. It was an absolutely rotten double-crossing thing for him to say, because we've agreed all along that marriage is too confining, it's just not for us. Even with the baby coming, we're not going to compromise. At least I'm not."

She jumped up, carried her chair to the window and stood on it, reaching toward the ceiling. "I have to be sure this is long enough to let you water the fern once it's up."

"I see. Be careful." Martha observed her closely and guessed that she was six months pregnant instead of the five she claimed.

Sandy replaced her chair and sat down. "I pictured this

room with its high ceiling and have been tying and tying. It's about finished now. I'll leave it for you."

Martha noted that this was the second time today she wasn't discussing with a patient the reasons for offering a gift. But one thing at a time. Aloud she said, "Thank you. After this, I prefer you not to do handiwork while you're here. We need to concentrate."

Sandy looked at her rather sternly. "If my hands aren't busy I'll smoke a lot and smoking is bad for the baby." She resumed her rapid knot-tying. "David doesn't really like that aunt so he pretended he was just being cool, but he and I had a big argument about it that night at home. You know, in the Jewish tradition a death doesn't interfere with a wedding. Even if a bride's mother dies on the morning of the wedding day, they hold the wedding. David said if we'd been planning to get married the day his father died, we'd probably be married by now and he wished we were."

"It must mean a great deal to him."

"Yes. But not to me. *Que será, será.*"

"You don't want to get married at all?"

"Not ever. It bores me to think of it."

"I seem to hear some anger mixed with your other feelings."

"No, I've had enough of being mad. I'm just sure. My mother's real irritating, though. She thinks I'm mentally disturbed so I told her I'd come for therapy. You helped me before. You taught me to have the courage to follow my own goals as an artist, so I figure you'll help me be independent now."

"You're afraid of losing your independence?"

"Sure I'm afraid of losing it. I won it through a long hard fight, all through my teens and early twenties. I'd be crazy not to protect it, because—whatever people say—it's *not* crazy to have a baby without being married."

"It may lead to other problems."

Sandy nodded but was bubbling over with her next thought. "Of course, a lot of my friends from college think that having a baby at all is crazy, contributing to the population explosion."

"And you don't agree?"

"Oh, no. I love having it. It's the most creative thing I ever did. I'd like to have at least three more."

"With David?"

"Sure, with David. He'll be a terrific father."

"You say that you and he have been together for years. How many?"

"Nearly two years. I guess in five more years we'd be considered married by that common law thing."

"What concerns you about getting married?"

"Well, first of all, the things that happen to women, losing their freedom and getting locked into doing the dirty work. Of course, when I was ten or eleven I dreamed of all the tradition you can think of. A canopy. Prayers. Champagne. Dancing. My grandfather who died used to talk with me about it. And my mother's always wanted to have a big party and dress me up like a bride and get dressed up herself and all that jazz."

"It's not unusual for a little girl to want what her mother wants."

"Sure, but why's everyone assuming I still do? I don't like being pressured. Even when people agree with me that it's not important to be married, dying to show how bighearted they are about the baby, it's another way of pressuring me, to bait the hook. Once I bite on it I'll be pounded with the marriage club like any poor fish.

"Where we live, it'll be good news and bad news on space. My apartment's almost big enough, except I need more space for my art work. When David moved in, we had to move my printing press out to my mother's basement in Great Neck. But we have a big walk-in closet off the bedroom where we'll put the baby's crib. It even has a window in it."

"You sound full of plans."

"Yes, I plan to breast-feed the baby and also keep on

with my art. I can do both, but I have to be on guard that David doesn't think the baby is the only important plan. I'm married now, personally, but not locked into the legal box and not going to be. An affair lets me volunteer to love and lets me go free if I stop loving."

"Like the homeless are free to starve on a park bench?"

Sandy stopped her handiwork and said seriously, "It's years of married life for me that we're talking about. I'm convinced that no woman, once she's married, can fight the vast amount of power over married women that men have built up over centuries, and put into laws. A woman's individuality is wiped right out."

"Which laws bother you?"

"They're all crap." Sandy fell silent but indicated that there were many examples by picking up a handful of colored ribbons from her lap and shaking them toward Martha.

"I can see you're worried about these things."

"It's threatening. Society is so structured."

There was a silence until Martha prompted, "It takes time to change society."

"The only way to change it is for people like me and David not to get into the trap in the first place. I'll give you one example. My aunt died and my uncle married again, a woman I really like. They both have some money and grown children who have left home—except for one mixed-up guy who's divorced and lives with his mother."

Martha felt a pang, thinking of Barry. "And . . . ?"

"So they were really happy to find each other, my uncle and this woman. But when my uncle had a new will drawn up, his lawyer followed a set form that claimed if they were killed simultaneously, it would be ruled that she had died first. Even if they were killed in the same airplane crash! Down on the ground, dead, he would inherit all that she had, and *his* kids would inherit all they both had. How's that for unfair? Why shouldn't her kids get what she had before she remarried?"

"I believe there can be premarital agreements which assure fairness."

"Maybe, but laws favor men so she's got to be the one who insists on an agreement. He's bound to fear he's not trusted. And how's a young bride going to guard against all the expectations? She's expected to spend months and months and years and years of non-intellectual time with the kids—which is only okay if that's the way she sees herself—and every night she's gotta be available for his *enjoyment*. That's a law. Like if she got a little bruised in a car accident, the other driver can be sued, not just for the usual damages but extra because her husband can't *enjoy* her that night. And if his job moves him around the country, she's expected to leave her house and friends and the kids' doctors and all, even her job if she has one. And how often does he leave his job and follow hers?"

"We do know that many married couples have changed these patterns."

"I'll tell you something. I love David very much and I want to have his baby, but I feel that if we were married, my selfish power would be gone."

"Wouldn't his selfish power be gone, too?"

"We'd both lose the voluntary part. That's the trouble. And who'd want duties instead of love? Do you think I'd want to hold David against his will? I'd rather make it alone than force him to stay if he didn't want to. That's what's wrong with marriage—it *forces* people."

"Sometimes. But being forced may be a part of growing up and facing realities, necessary whether you're married or not. Without it there might not be change. I've seen terrible quarrels occur in a marriage that would definitely put an end to an affair, but actually end up strengthening the marriage when both people come to understand the situation. And friends can help."

"I know. I once talked a friend from college into going back to her husband, but it didn't work in the end. David and I decided on this experimental course because we think everyone has just bought a lot of bourgeois values which put women down. Our baby will be loved by both me and David, and it will know we wanted it to be free. And I'll establish my freedom as an artist. Of course, David's career advancement is taken for granted. Men with wives and kids get jobs, and a job becomes a man's selfhood. But where does my selfhood as artist come from except from me? David could help but hasn't caught on. So if I get locked in and come to hate being a prisoner, who am I going to take it out on? The kid? No, thank you. I'd hate myself. We love everything about living together and we love the baby already, but to respect myself, I'll stick to my guns."

"What do you think threatens your freedom as an artist? Is it having a husband or having a baby?"

"It's both. It's biology and custom, everything. But with determination it's possible to live as one freely chooses to live and be happy. I'm old enough, and things seemed so right between me and David. I'd say I'm happy right now if only he and my mother would stop noodging. They make me so mad."

"I hear not only anger but fear."

"My only fear is that my smoking is bad for the baby."

"Do you smoke a lot?"

"About a pack a day. I'd be smoking now if I weren't tying these knots."

"That's something we'd better take up next time. With the baby coming so soon, I suggest that you see me twice a week."

"I can only come once a week. My mom's going to pay and she's a widow and not that wealthy."

"Is that what you want to do, then, come once a week?"

"I guess so."

"All right. Our time is up for today. Can you come at the same time next Wednesday?"

"Why not?" Sandy stood and tried to pull her sweater around her abdomen, but it wouldn't close and she flashed Martha a happy grin.

Martha smiled back and said warmly, "Having a baby really is wonderful!"

"Thank you," Sandy said, preoccupied with getting something out of her purse. "I'll pay as I go." She handed Martha a check. "I made the check out in advance. Is that the right amount?"

"Yes. Each week the appointment is kept open for you alone. If you don't come, you still pay, unless you give two days' notice. That would mean you'd call me on Monday. I'd make an exception in case you went into labor, of course."

Sandy was matter-of-fact. "Okay. That check is for the entire amount of money I made last week. Mom starts paying next week. If I have to cancel a Wednesday I'll call you Monday. Or get Mom to pay anyhow."

Martha said firmly, "I'll see you on Wednesday at five." She stood. It felt good to be out of her chair so she walked with Sandy down the hall to the front door. "It's still light out but soon it will be dark when you leave. Will you be walking toward the subway?"

"Usually David will be waiting in the car. Besides, I can flip any mugger by judo, and I'm a fast runner."

"Oh?" Martha put a slight doubt into the word.

Sandy looked abashed. "I know, now I'm so big . . . but I'll manage. We always knew the Amazon was wet."

"Why do you say that?"

"Well, it's the biggest, widest river in the world and I guess the women were the same. So they took the name *Amazons* and ruled the men."

As the door closed behind her, Martha said to herself, "And now you may learn that ruling the men has its dangers, too."

9

Peregrinating

When Martha returned to her office after seeing Sandy out, she found the plant basket on the chair. Under it was a new hook to screw into the ceiling. She placed the fern in the string basket and held it up to get the effect.

"Okay. Thank you," she said aloud. "What a thoughtful kid, sweet and practical. Barry will hang it for me."

She walked to the window and stood thinking over her afternoon of counseling four complicated women.

I've been listening and only giving hints—to Elinor about sharing love, to Billie about giving her son a stable home, to Ursula about using visual imagination, and to Sandy about not expecting to change society. I'd like to have taped the session with Sandy, but I can't tape at the start. And I couldn't have played it for Sarah, as I did in Vermont. Anyhow, I know what she'd say: "Get yourself invited to that wedding, with the canopy and the prayers and the dancing and the champagne."

She smiled.

It sounds simple, but what I need is Thorny to evaluate my professionalism.

Lights from a passing car hit her shingle and she seemed to hear Thorny's penetrating voice: "I'm retiring but counting on students like you to carry on my work. Please take this old board saying 'Psychotherapist' that hung for years outside my office and hang it under a board with your name. Together they'll be your shingle, announcing your science and wizardry."

Now Thorny is dead, but I hope she'd see that I've gained competence. Mostly, I'd like to tell her the ups and downs I went through before I opened my own practice.

I could tell her in the way Lucy Woodward and I used to

in med school, sending each other letters to Thorny which she never saw. We practiced being therapists and got companionship. But writing takes time, and Sarah's expecting me to dinner.

She went to the kitchen and said, "Sarah, I have some paperwork to do before dinner. Will there be time?"

"Barry phoned to say he'll be a couple of hours late, but not to wait for him. So do your paper work if you're not hungry."

Back in the office, Martha wrote:

A letter to Thorny to be sent to Lucy

Dear Thorny,
You told me to hang my name on a board above "Psychotherapist" and I did get a handsome board lettered. But I wasn't ready. So I put both boards away into a file cabinet until I could remodel the office properly. I kept on working in the clinic, where we saw only low-income patients—that's where I started seeing Billie.

Norman was a dear, never complained about the unused front room, although he stopped saying that he was "raising a rich wife." Through the years he sturdily and willingly traveled uptown by subway to his graduate school library. Luckily, with both our salaries we finally paid off my student loan. To celebrate we bought our Vermont cottage, and the next year, when Barry was sixteen, took him to Europe.

On that trip I got a new perspective on my work, and thought I should leave the clinic and hang my shingle, but I needed a push to actually do it. Norman, with his optimistic faith in me, would agree with whatever I did. His temperament was so rational, he couldn't imagine what strength it took to grapple with psyches imprisoned in painful self-images. Not that I wanted him to be the least bit different from the way he was. Then I got a push, a rude one, when his heart condition became serious. The cardiologists said he could continue working, but for fewer hours, so his salary was reduced, just when Barry wanted us to buy a car for trips to Vermont. To take care of both of my men, I hung the two boards, with another under them saying EVENINGS, and finally was launched into private practice, part-time. Elinor started coming evenings at that time.

Before we could afford a complete remodeling of the office, we put in good oak furniture, a couple of file cabinets and a desk. We had an antique brown leather sofa, and hoped it looked like a psychiatrist's couch, but it was only to fill space! It's now up in the living room. My patients and I sit in sturdy chairs.

We were surprised at how fast my evening practice grew, partly because the clinic referred people to me whose incomes were too high for eligibility there. I felt like a real standard-bearer of the profession.

Amazingly, after a year or so, I had earned enough to remodel the office suite as I wanted it, with an oak breakfront where I keep tea-makings. The most fun was planning to partition the office off from the waiting room, adding a coat closet and a half bath. To gain space we had to remove the fireplace, but we have one upstairs. I get good light in the office from the three front windows, one of which is cleverly fitted with one-way glass. That's a help to me—I can see who's on the stoop ringing the doorbell, and they can't see in. Barry said, "Never stoop to snoop on the stoop!"

However, after a couple of years of working two jobs, I was too tired to enjoy life and couldn't be with Norman enough to keep him from worrying about his health. Luckily his mother, dear Sarah, came most nights to cook dinner. Evenings, while I saw patients and Barry did his homework, Norman walked her home. He'd be home by the time my last patient left.

Sarah saved our morale, but what saved us financially was my promotion to be head of the clinic with an increase in salary, so I gave up the evening practice. My science and wizardry have always told me to save enough energy to enjoy life with the people I love. So the shingle was stored again . . . and might be still if Norman's condition hadn't turned really serious a year and a half ago. He had to quit his job altogether. For once I didn't hesitate. I resigned from the clinic, put out my shingle without the board saying EVENINGS, and went into my present full-time practice. So what you saw as my future has finally come true. You were more than a teacher, more than a doctor. You knew me, really knew me. I'll always be grateful.

Love, Martha Kaufman

Before she sealed the letter, she added a page to Lucy:

Dear Lucy,
Please wrap your good thoughts around this. I seem to miss not only Norman, but my own life, although in a sad way it's reassuring to think of the saintly way he faced death. I wouldn't until then have known the spiritual meaning of falling in love and sharing life with one's true mate.

Love, Maggie

P.S. Without Thorny and you, I'd never have had the smarts to get as far as I am professionally. Love, M.

With the letter addressed to Lucy and sealed, she stopped to speak to Sarah, who was reading the paper and drinking tea. "Sarah, what was the word in the puzzle that meant to go foreign?"

"Peregrinate."

"That's it. So since Barry isn't here, I'm going to peregrinate. Back in fifteen minutes."

She mailed the letter to Lucy and was carrying a bottle of champagne home when she was pleasantly surprised by Barry's stopping his car to offer her a ride. She handed him the champagne, but only pumped her arms and ran in place, to show the joys of exercise. He pretended to take a swig from the bottle and drove off, steering in a wavy path, feigning drunkenness. She walked on, smiling.

I'd love to tell them at dinner how I bought a book to use as therapy with Ursula, only to find she'd written it! But Sarah would then expect to discuss Ursula.

At dinner she said, "I'm never so tired on Wednesdays as on other days."

"Those three on Wednesday are special to you," Sarah said.

"It's four on Wednesday now. I have a new patient, a young woman I saw years ago, now about to be a mother. Barry's age."

"I had nothing to do with it," said Barry, grinning.

Sarah asked, "Is she smart and good-looking like the others?"

Barry quipped, "How do you know so much, Bubbi?"

"What kind of question is that?" Sarah said. "Patients come and go, I come and go. Today I saw Elinor on the stoop."

"Does she look like you expected?" Martha asked.

"Exactly. Very nice. Like Marilyn Monroe. But Martha, I have to tell you. Your sign—the bottom half—is hard to read."

Martha made no reply. She didn't want to change what Thorny had given her.

"So tell more about the new one," Barry said. "I need to get a rounded sense of life."

Martha laughed. "You'd get that from her all right. She's rounded with so much life that she'd better stand under the canopy soon."

"She's pregnant and not married?" Sarah asked.

"Yes, and against marriage on principle. Red-headed and stubborn."

"Look who's talking about red-headed and stubborn!" Barry said.

"My hair was never that stubborn a red," said Martha.

"Come on, Mom. *Schmooze a bissel.* Spill it. If Elinor looks like Marilyn Monroe, I want to hear."

"Oh, Barry, let's don't start using names." Martha became wary. "Mother, have you been making a soap opera out of my practice?"

"No, she hasn't," Barry emphasized, seeing the hurt look on his Bubbi's face. "You asked her what she thought about Elinor."

"So. Elinor?" Sarah looked expectant, stirring her glass of tea.

"Well, this *is* about Elinor, not about her feelings, but a remark that was funny. Her ex-husband criticized her for seeing a new man and speculated to her son that she was 'shacked up with a stockbroker'."

"What does it mean, 'shacked up'?" Sarah asked.

"Having an affair," Barry said, "but 'shacked up' gives it irony. Wait, we've got authority right here. Let's see, which dictionary do we require for this? Oh, yes, here's the Oxford." He took the squat volume from the shelf Norman had installed near the table long ago, assumed with a grin the pose of his father, and placed his finger on the word. "Shack. Noun. A roughly built cabin, of logs, mud, etc."

"Is it logical to be in a *shack* with a *stockbroker*?" Sarah asked. "A stockbroker is wealthy, no?" Martha nodded, and Sarah saw the joke. "An affair. That's good." She laughed and stood to clear the table. "Howard said that about Elinor? To Steven?"

Martha winced, but she had gotten herself into this. "Yes."

"He's a *mazik*, that husband. *Der wilder chazer! Er kricht arein beiner fon nachtigal.*"

"Translate, please," said Martha.

"'The wild pig—he . . .'" She turned to Barry. "How do you say 'comes into the bones like a worm'?"

" 'Worms his way'?"

" 'The wild pig worms his way into the bones of the nightingale.' "

Martha laughed. "Yes, that's Elinor's situation!"

"Who's the pregnant redhead shacked up with?" Barry asked.

"With a man she loves. But she's resisting the shotgun wedding her family wants."

Barry, with exaggerated courtesy, pointed to Sarah. "She doesn't understand 'shotgun wedding.' Unknown in old Vienna."

Sarah's smile lightened her weighty face. "Show me a country where they don't have shotgun weddings!"

Martha didn't wait for cheesecake but left with a quick excuse and went upstairs to take stock of the living room. As she left the kitchen she heard Barry say, "Bubbi, you knew what 'shacked up' means. You were just trying to get Mom to talk."

Martha felt guilty for having blabbed about patients.

She found the living room looking even worse than she had pictured. Her first impulse was to get a big carton and sweep everything away, all the old comic books and games in the book case and the plastic sports trophies. But for now she perched on a chair and looked through a pile of *New York Times Magazines*.

Damn, look at all these furniture ads and not one exploiting leg styles. I want pedigreed pieces where the styles match each other, not like this room where the only style I like is the ball and claw feet on the old sofa. I need to visit a furniture store. Maybe I could find one in the Village, if I look.

In her bedroom she brushed her hair and tied her pink silk bandanna into a turban around her head. On her way out she called to Sarah, "I'm peregrinating again. Back soon!" and said to Barry, "No more second helpings of cheesecake! Bad for your figure, boychik!"

On 8th Street she spotted a new furniture store and

went in, only to discover it was full of air-filled pieces in bright covers. It looked like a fun fair. She sat in one low balloon-like chair and bounced. A thin-faced clerk, maybe sixty years of age, nodded that he would be over to help her. The next chair she tried was foam rubber and so low that she sat sprawled, her handbag trailing on the floor. The clerk grinned down at her, extended a hand and helped her to her feet, saying, "That one turns into a single bed. Here's a bigger model, but I wonder what it's like with two people turning over in these bouncy things. I sleep alone, myself."

Martha, thinking that bed salesmen must read minds, asked, "What about waterbeds?"

"Waterbeds are out," he said. "They leak."

"That's a shame." She tried to speak with dignified detachment but it was a bit late to explain to the nice salesman that she was looking for high quality furniture with ball and claw feet, so she thanked him and departed.

In the nearby big bookstore she bought a large illustrated book on interior decorating, and on her way home stopped on an impulse in the Tick-Tock Bar to look at her new prize. As she slipped onto a stool at the counter she recognized the bartender, a rotund man with a black mustache, who smiled. He wore a bright yellow shirt with a name tag embroidered in red calligraphy, "Alfie Remembers!"

"The usual?" he asked. "For the lady doctor?"

"Yes, please," said Martha. It was at least two years since she had been in and she was curious to see if he remembered what she drank.

He placed a glass before her. "Here's your kummel. How's Norman?"

"I'm sorry to tell you bad news," she said, "but he died."

"That *is* bad news." He sounded truly sorry. "What happened?"

"A heart condition that took over quickly at the end."

Alfie wiped the counter longer than was needed to get it

clean. "I did wonder where Norm was. He was a helluva nice fella. Used to come in regular, twice a day."

"Oh?"

"Yeah, he came in right after work and again later in the evening with his mother. She used to say, 'Norman, you're supposed to be walking me home.' They always had kummel." He moved away to answer the phone.

It's hard to believe Norman was imposing on his leaky heart. I thought the extent of his drinking was the weekly bottle of kummel at home.

Alfie returned and said, "They had crossword puzzles going, and used to ask me for Italian words. They weren't just doing puzzles, they were making them up. One of theirs had only words for grandchildren. Nicknames too. In all languages."

She managed a little laugh. "This is the first time I've been in since he died. I was shopping along the street." She sipped from her glass.

Alfie commiserated. "I'm sorry for your loss."

A smartly coiffed middle-aged woman had come in and was waiting on the stool next to Martha. "I'm still here, Alfie. Don't forget me."

"I forget nothing," Alfie said. "It hits you when you lose an old customer."

He brought a beer to the woman, who noticed the picture on the cover of Martha's book and said, "That's pretty."

Martha was delighted to chat. "Yes, I've got to do something about my living room."

"I just had a decorator do my place. It's all white, from wall to wall and ceiling to floor."

"I've thought of white. But I also like linen color with touches of salmon pink and pale green."

"Nice," the woman nodded. "But my decorator wanted all white, even the carpeting. I had planned on getting Persian rugs from Iran—my brother used to work over there—but I admit all white makes the place look bigger."

"Where did your decorator buy the furniture?"

"Well, they act very hush-hush, only *they* can get the stuff from special dealers, but I saw the same things at Bloomingdales. You can get sofas and chairs that match and everything turns into beds. You can start the evening on a sofa and lie down later in the same place."

"For a nice rest," said Alfie with a cheery leer.

"At Christmas we have grandchildren sleeping all over. They love it. Well, I've got to run."

Martha finished her drink and paid Alfie who promptly put another in front of her. "On the house," he said sympathetically. Her eyes filled with tears. People do care. She savored the drink, thinking of how many people had loved her husband who had wanted grandchildren

Alfie, who had been busy with customers, stepped closer. "Norman had a heart condition?"

"Yes, but he had the best care and we thought it was under control."

"Some types can look very healthy and then surprise you. He was in here a lot."

Martha thanked him and left. She walked home, firmly clasping her handbag to her chest, marching to look tall and strong.

I actually left the house twice in one day . . . Twice a day. Had Norman gone into a bar twice a day?

10

You Got Back Just in Time

Elinor walked serenely out onto the stoop after telling Martha about falling in love with Ralph. On her way here she had chatted with the doorman of a fancy apartment building, and he had agreed to send a taxi for her at three. Now she stood waiting for it to arrive.

There is no crack or flaw in the great dome of my happiness. Telling Dr. Martha about Ralph has made me feel more at home with him in my heart. I'm even obeying him, since he said I should take a taxi *to* the subway, nothing about *from* the subway, and I had to walk here to arrange for a taxi. *A contrite heart will be forgiven.* Ralph might offer me money but I couldn't take it directly from him. He'd drive me himself, but he's busy all week in his office on Wall Street, bless him.

She smiled at a little boy who was walking along, and he smiled back.

I hope no street scavenger comes by, like the ragged old man I saw last week rifling through the gutter. It's funny how a young man might look clean-cut and yet pull a knife on me.

Her gaze rested on Martha's double-board shingle: "M. KAUFMAN, M.D., PSYCHOTHERAPIST."

The gold lettering on the second board is faded, and the wood is peeling. Maybe I could stay late next week in the waiting room and touch it up, after the young woman—I think of her as Short Bob—goes in. But the smell of paint might disturb them. Being in love makes me want to make everyone happy!

Just then Short Bob came along, in a tight brown leather skirt, and boots of worn but polished leather. At the top of the stairs she pushed the doorbell, turned in a neat circle without touching Elinor and sent a cigarette into the gutter with a deft flip. Elinor smiled, hoping for a smile in return, but got none.

She must be Irish, and would be pretty if she didn't look so stern. Even her red hair looks stiff. Well, a friend of Dr. Martha's is a friend of mine, though Short Bob might feel jealous about me. Dr. Martha says there's love enough for all, like sunlight.

The buzzer sounded and Short Bob went in.

Yes, Dr. Martha was pleased about my weekend with Ralph. Even if this happiness doesn't last, it's marvelous. *O come, let us sing unto the Lord. Let us heartily rejoice.*

She made way for a heavy-set elderly woman who trudged up the steps carrying a shopping bag overflowing with celery tops, and opened the door with a key.

She must do Dr. Martha's grocery shopping. *In His hand are all the corners of the earth. The beauty of holiness.*

Her taxi appeared. As they drove north she closed her eyes and thought of her former sorrows.

How much of what I've been through could I tell Ralph? No lift of heart, even at Christmas. There I was, waiting to die in my car with its beautiful end sticking out of the garage, and nothing happened. I couldn't shut the garage door because of that heavy lawn roller in the back. That turned out to be lucky for me. Now I have to keep what I wanted to do a secret from Ralph.

The kids knew they wouldn't get much for Christmas, and worse, they couldn't buy gifts for others. Steven hadn't even wanted to get out of bed. Oh, I miss the bright-eyed imp of Christmas Past who had always swept Susan along with him to a tree rich with lights and sure-to-be-found treasures, like electric trains, bicycles, dollhouses, dragon games, guitars and chess sets. This year I gave them a few necessary clothing items in bright wrappings. Pleasing enough. They watched as I opened my one present, a hand-decorated card with a note, "Your present is that I will polish the silver every two weeks all year. Merry

Christmas. Love, Susan." It was heart-breaking because both kids felt so awful.

And Christmas dinner was a little duck that melted away in its fat. We did the dishes, the kids went to their rooms like on an ordinary day, and I felt everything was my fault for cutting them off from their father's affluence. He hadn't gotten them anything—well, he never did at Christmas, usually grumbled about giving me money. I was mortified trying to sound like a jolly Santa, forcing a *Ho! Ho! Ho!* when I felt like walking right out of the world. I can't explain it, except that I acted on my true feelings, and dashed out to the car, closed the windows and started the motor. I prayed, "Please God, let there be enough gas." I knew people die from carbon monoxide gas when they're shut up in old cars, like if they're stalled in deep snow and run the motor to keep warm. They don't smell anything, just drift off to sleep. But try as I would, I couldn't feel sleepy.

After about an hour Susan came to the car window, and assumed—thank God—that I'd been on an errand. She said, "You got back just in time. I'm serving a snack by the fire." How pretty she looked, with her angel smile and soft brown hair, naturally curly. Her manners are naturally right, too, whatever the occasion. I felt a rush of gratitude for such a darling daughter, and as we walked arm in arm to the house together, the day turned into Christmas.

She seated me in a chair facing the fireplace and then went to the kitchen. Steven sat reading in a chair opposite, poking the fire from time to time. I was thinking how large his face and head are, but that he'll be handsome one of these days when he fleshes out to match his latest six-inch growth. Right now his coordination is poor, like trying to steer a truck with a toy-car wheel. And does he get sarcastic when he's hungry!

Susan bustled in with what she called "perfect cocoa and cake" and presented me with a surprise, a round teapot, bright red. "I couldn't give it from the tree," she explained, "because it came from a thrift shop. Nothing's wrong with it."

I told her, "It's just what I wanted and just the right size, a lovely present." I cuddled the teapot to my cheek, and told it, "You fat, cute thing, you've absolutely made my Christmas."

At this Steven made a vulgar noise, but he was smiling and Susan told us about plans she had for a kid's birthday party next Saturday. She often makes a little spending money by baking and decorating cakes, and she wanted us to try out her idea of doing music as well for this party. She gave each of us a couple of spoons and went to the piano and played "Jingle Bells" with one finger while we banged the spoons. Steven made us laugh by hitting his spoons on his head and reaching between his legs from behind to hit his toes. I went over and banged his nose and he pulled me down on his lap and banged me on my elbows, until I rolled off and Susan said we weren't in rhythm. We had fun.

The following Sunday in church I used the sermon time to think hard about what I had attempted and later called Dr. Martha. She said, "It's right to come to me. Two people are emotionally dependent on you and it's responsible of you to seek help. We'll work something out about paying my bills."

No, I could never tell any of this to Ralph. He knows I have to economize but doesn't know how close we are to being really hungry. I need him to love me in the ordinary way, not out of pity because I need money for food. Right here in this taxi I have to think how to do something about everyday expenses, or temptations of suicide will creep in again. Maybe I ought to marry Ralph.

The taxi pulled up at Pennsylvania Station, where her train wasn't going to leave for twenty minutes. She called Ralph. After saying hello, he asked cheerfully, "Am I going to see you before Saturday?"

"I'd like that, but I won't be in town again. Too busy raking leaves."

"I'll help do that on Sunday."

"If we're there long enough."

"I don't get it."

"Ralph, listen. I've seen your two places and want you to see my place and meet Steven and Susan. But please, let's not put your being in my bedroom right in front of them until they get to know you. It would be nice if they weren't home, but they always are."

"Well, if they're home, please come to the City with me."

"I will. And remember, you're definitely coming to dinner Saturday night. Brook trout paté first, then home-grown chives on baked potatoes, and . . . the meat's a secret. I'll leave the wine up to you. Any color, so long as it's white."

"You're making me hungry. It's a hundred years till then."

"Call me tomorrow night."

When her train was announced, she found a seat, feeling happy that he was to call her the next night.

What a lifesaving event it had been, falling in love with him after all that Christmas moping over her divorce! They had met when her neighbor, Adele, who, having tried without success to get her to go to singles bars, had bought tickets and persuaded her to go to a large private barbecue in the Hamptons. It was a fundraiser for a charity and the two women had been walking on the lawn when Ralph joined them. From the first, it wasn't just his good figure and smiling eyes that Elinor liked, but his natural good humor. They had strolled down the sloping lawn to the dock where the host's sailboat was coming and going with guests. After deciding the waiting line was too long, they walked up the slope and sat in old Adirondack chairs on the grass, gazing at the guests down at the dock.

"Isn't people-watching fun!" exclaimed Elinor.

"I like it best at the beach, and in swimming," said Ralph. "I prefer bars," said Adele, "where you can talk." Elinor said, "My favorite people-watching is at church."

Ralph smiled and said quietly, "I haven't been to church in months." Elinor wondered what church he meant.

It turned out he was Episcopalian too. Their first weekend together, she had made that discovery in his apartment in the City. Alone in his bedroom—not that she'd been alone in that bedroom long—she had found a well-thumbed *Book of Common Prayer*. Inside, a child's hand had written "R. Conklin."

The second time she had been in his apartment, things hadn't gone smoothly. She had driven into the City and after picking him up at his office asked him to drive. He dropped her in front of his building, gave her a key to get in and drove off to park. She enjoyed being in his apartment alone to sense more about him. He had good solid office-type furniture; the bathroom was clean and fairly neat, with thick orange rugs and towels. A man's place. She got drinks ready, dusted a little, remade the bed carefully—somehow she knew he had been sleeping alone since the other time she was here—and settled down with a slice of cheese, feeling at home, until the phone rang. She didn't answer, and it rang and rang. After it stopped she sat a long time before Ralph finally arrived.

"Was it that hard to find a parking place?"

"No," he said with a grin. "I tried to phone you about your car. You do know that I have a Cadillac, too?"

"You do?"

"Yes, and it's the same year and model as yours."

"It is?"

"Yes, and I used the dipstick and found your transmission fluid was so low you'd have sunk that big boat if you'd driven it home."

She was silent, then asked, "You mean it needs transmission fluid?"

"It *did*. I stopped by my favorite garage and personally put some in."

"Thank you." There was another silence, during which she felt defensive. "You know, I didn't want that big car.

But after the divorce, Howard didn't want it in the City and I have to have a car in Middle Cove. There's no public transportation." After they had their drinks they became more cheerful.

Now, after Fire Island, she felt an exciting hope, that she could keep Ralph in her life. He and she were opposites in ways that complemented each other. She was artistic, he practical. She remembered things about people, he facts and numbers. Both had great poise. She recalled with a little thrill the effortless way they had packed up their belongings, closed the cottage and strolled to the ferry in good time. How nice, having a schedule for everything, even lovemaking, without feeling rushed!

As her train racketed into Middle Cove she was happy about the dependable side of him.

In the station parking lot she slipped behind the wheel of her car and started for the local supermarket, whose food specials were the heart of her cuisine.

Little does Ralph know of my planned miracle, to produce a perfect dinner for two, served in a beautifully appointed home. It sounds like *Better Homes and Gardens* and it'll look like it too, if I can finish a million chores. Today's Wednesday, and if the front door is to get two coats and be dry by Saturday, the first coat has to go on this afternoon. If it's sunny tomorrow I'll give it a second coat and deepen my sun tan at the same time. On Saturday Steven will cut the grass, and Susan will help me hang the living room drapes that came back from the cleaner's last year.

She found a parking place and pushed a cart into the store.

How to be free to have Ralph in my bedroom Saturday night without the kids' being home—that's the puzzle of the week, more challenging than how to conjure up a dinner both cheap and elegant, my old trick. At Fire Island we both liked simple things—forgot food altogether before going to bed!—and in the middle of the night feasted on BLT sandwiches. Not exactly a clue to what he likes for dinner. Well, since I don't know what he doesn't like, either, I'll give him my gourmet menu from Julia Child—a whole roasted chicken with umpteen cloves of garlic. Here's a beautiful bird, good and firm. The kids and I will eat the giblets tonight with tomatoes from the garden. And here's a big box of oatmeal for next week. And here are Idahoes for baking, like I promised Ralph. And garlic galore. And I'll splurge on something green to put beside the paté, six of these lovely snow peas.

Luckily I don't have to buy salad greens. Cabbage rolls will qualify as a gourmet dish since we grew the cabbage ourselves. *O Lord, I beseech thee favorably to hear my prayers.* Let Howard's check come on time so I can feed the children. Why can't he just instruct his secretary to mail it, like Dr. Martha's check? No, he gets a charge out of writing it himself and letting it run late.

Here's a day-old cake, very cheap, but I have a better idea for dessert. Susan's doing a birthday party this weekend so she'll be baking some sheet cakes and I can have enough crumbs to make a trifle. A great English invention, and a great name. There's still a tad of sherry in the captain's decanter to flavor it.

At the checkout she chatted with Mrs. Upton from church, who was pushing her granddaughter in a shopping cart. Driving home, she romanticized. Candlelight. Perfume. Wine that Ralph will bring. I hope he likes my transparent negligee with its soft flower blossoms that splash me with orange shadows.

At home she hastened to start painting the front door.

It's lucky I have the right enamel paint left from over a year ago. And it's lucky I feel so at home in this house—which was supposed to rescue our marriage, and not be as lonely as the City. But I used to be lonely here too, with both kids at school all day, and Howard home only to sleep a few hours. It isn't easy to make friends, since each house is like a feudal estate set apart. But there are woods and open slopes which in the spring are covered with daffodils—that's the best time. I think of the poem about daffodils "fluttering and dancing in the breeze," but they're really too stiff to flutter. Glittering and dancing, yes.

This four-bedroom house isn't very big by local standards, but the garden in back and the circular drive in front give it a spacious air. We didn't have proper furniture at first, only the dining table and chairs we brought from England. The living room and library were both empty for months. It was funny when Mrs. Miller raced the vacuum cleaner over the rug that spanned the two rooms, dramatically declaring in an imitated cowboy drawl, "What I like about this house is the wi-i-ide open spaces!" Rude.

Still, I liked Mrs. Miller. She was cheerful. And more respectful after we bought sofas and chairs in old rose, and drapes in grey satin, to go with the rug, which the real estate people had said was an Aubusson. The owners claimed that it was only an *Aubusson type* but worth $30,000. I thought if Howard bought it we'd be broke forever, no college for kids, nothing for our old age. But the sellers had no place big enough for it, and he bargained and got it for $5,000, on time payments.

He was always a hard bargainer. Hard in bed, too. I like a man to be ambitious, but able to relax. He never wanted me to pat him lovingly, touched me only when he wanted sex. I always responded, until the year he had a new secretary and didn't come home some nights. I was getting used to it when suddenly he tried to return to my bed. I surprised him—and myself—by rejecting him. For that he took furious revenge on me and the children, and was difficult all the time, in the kitchen, in the car, at the table. He shorted our weekly allowances, including mine for the household.

He criticized everything, my clothes, my discipline of the kids, my friends, my grammar. It was more like a nightmare than a marriage toward the end. I'm so glad it's over.

As she painted, she listened for the school bus that brought home kids who stayed late for after-school activities.

It's been good having a year in the house alone with Steven and Susan, even with my depression at Christmas. Now it's good to have Ralph coming. It's fun to fix up the house for someone I love. My old uncle said, "Elinor looks like a filly but pulls like a work horse." Do I throw myself into physical work because my mind isn't trained? Maybe.

She heard the bus come to a stop and soon heard Susan calling to her cat, which came to meet her in the driveway. Elinor held up the paint brush with a blocking gesture. "Wet paint! Wet paint!"

Susan nuzzled the cat's head and scrutinized the door. "Why don't you paint it pink or purple or beet color?"

"Because a white door is so right at Christmas, with a big green wreath with a red bow."

"You need a sign. Here." She took a sheet of paper and a magic marker from her book bag and lettered WET PAINT U DUMMY. "Put that where Steven can see it!" She was off into the house.

Her mother called after her. "Remember, you're cooking tonight."

"I know. But I have French homework to do, so don't start getting hungry."

Elinor rubbed paint from her cheek. She was amused by Susan's "Don't start getting hungry." The tone was like her own. What else will she copy from me? Not my too-impulsive nature, I hope.

Suddenly, rock music blasted from Steven's room. He'd gotten off the bus a block away and slipped in the back door.

She was cleaning paint brushes when Susan came and asked, "Did you get sour salt in the City? You said you'd get it so I could make borscht."

Elinor tensed and said, "Oh, honey, I'm sorry, I forgot. Just use salt and lemon juice." Susan returned to the kitchen, disappointed.

Oh, why didn't I think of the sour salt before I phoned Ralph? If I'm going to keep him from coming between me and the children, I'll have to work at it.

For dinner they gathered around a broad pine table in the bright breakfast nook.

Steven was silent but Susan was talkative and announced, "This borscht is terrible."

"It's very *good*," Elinor reassured her.

"Next time you're in the City, if you forget sour salt, I'll—I'll rub salt in your wounds. And lemon juice."

"Lots of lemon juice," added Steven, with a mock threatening tone.

"Do you like my borscht, Steven?" Susan asked.

"Bo-o-o-ring."

"Oh, Steven, it's not! I'm going to use beets a lot. Mrs. Holmestrand, my cooking teacher, says the beet is a neglected vegetable."

"So you'll *mother* it, huh?" He spoke in derision.

"Steven, try to keep a pleasant tone," Elinor said.

"So sorry," he said curtly.

"Mom, you know I'm doing a birthday party this Sunday and I'm doing more than a cake this time, because I said for ten dollars more I'd do a puppet show with the same figures I'm using in the frosting. It's a boy's party and the family has a catamaran, so I'm putting fishing into it, like Huck and Jim on the raft. I'll make a fish puppet and name it after the birthday boy and they'll call out and make jokes."

"Bo-o-o-ring," Steven said.

"Won't it be hard to make puppets before Sunday?" asked Elinor.

"They're just going to be painted and cut out, not stuffed or anything. Judy will help me with them if I can stay overnight at her house Saturday night. May I?"

"Will you girls be alone in the house?"

"Her parents will be away, but their maid Cathy will be there. You know her."

"It sounds okay."

Susan jumped up and hugged her mother. "Thanks, Mom."

"Am I forgiven for forgetting the sour salt?"

"It's okay. I like new recipes. Judy and I are going to make a neat drink in the blender. You take cooked beets and whip them up with apple juice and bananas and yogurt."

"There's a recipe for *that*?" Steven demanded.

"Well, nearly. They say strawberries, but beets are sweet enough."

"Yech! Just to picture the color of it makes me puke."

"What are your plans for the weekend, Steven?" Elinor ventured.

"Oh, he'll be with his fir-rends!" mocked Susan. "If he has any."

Steven blushed and Elinor felt sorry for him. It was a grief to her that her gangly seventeen year old son was such a loner. Susan, two years younger, usually went with a group to school games and parties, but there was no sign of interest from Steven. "Susan," Elinor admonished, "please be nicer to your brother. You know he's smart and interested in lots of things."

Steven was calm. "Mr. Scuracchio, my English teacher, belongs to the Audubon Society and is showing a few kids around the bird sanctuary Sunday morning. I'm going to sleep out there overnight so I can be up early enough to sight birds."

"How early Sunday morning?" demanded his sister. "You get up about noon."

"Oh, shut up. It's *very* early Sunday morning."

Elinor's heart leaped in hope, but she asked only, "What if it rains?"

"My sleeping bag is waterproof. But I need to take food."

"I can pack cucumbers and peanut butter and jelly sandwiches for your supper, and some doughnuts for breakfast."

"Yech!" said Susan. "His diet is so unhealthy, I could puke."

"He'll be okay," said Elinor. "Steven, could you bring in one of your best cabbages for me Saturday morning? I've invited a friend to dinner."

"So *that's* why all the fix-up!" Steven sounded knowing. "Who's coming?"

Elinor knew her ex-husband's remarks about her had worried Steven. "Ralph is coming to dinner, the man I went out with last weekend."

"The stockbroker you were shacked up with?"

"He's a stockbroker, yes. He has an apartment in Manhattan and a nice cottage on Fire Island, hardly a shack. He made me a good dinner last Saturday, so I'm giving him one this Saturday, and I'd like one of your cabbages."

Susan said generously, "Steven's garden is really great. I think your cabbage really *made* the borscht, Steven. It's so fresh and sweet."

"Okay," said Steven, including both of the women in his benign response, "if you're still on those boring beets next spring, I can try growing some."

"Great!" Susan beamed at her brother. "Mom, they gave me money for the stuff I need for the party, so can you drive me to the store after school on Friday? I'll bake three sheet cakes that night so I can help you with the drapes on Saturday morning."

"All right. And may I please have a piece of cake to make a trifle?"

"Sure, I'll bake a little cake for you. With a plain pink frosting, okay?"

"No frosting, thanks. I'm using some of my raspberry jam."

"I have to take the cakes to Judy's Saturday afternoon so we can decorate them. Can you drive me over?"

"Sure. Ralph is coming about five and he can go with us. Will you still be here then, Steven? I'd like him to meet you too."

"Not a chance. I'm going to start hiking east about two. I have to get out there and study the *Checklist of American Birds*. Familiarize myself."

"Can you carry all your gear?"

"Sure. All I have is a sleeping bag and binoculars."

"And your dinner," Elinor reminded him. "And breakfast."

Susan said, teasing, "Honestly, Steven, you're going to look like the original old woodsman, with binoculars hanging off one side and a sack of food off the other and a sleeping bag on your back. You'll look *see-nile*."

Hardly listening, Elinor sat lost in anticipation.

"Hey," Susan said, "you've got paint on both cheeks. Do you want to be the clown in my puppet show?"

Elinor smiled. "No thanks. Whose turn is it to do dishes?"

"Mom, it's my turn, but I made dinner. I have tons of history to study for a test," said Susan.

"I have tons of differential equations," Steven inserted defensively.

"I'll do the dishes," said Elinor. "It'll get the paint off my hands. But Saturday morning you've both got your chores, remember!"

As he started upstairs, Steven kept at his sister. "What do you mean, a plain pink frosting?"

She assumed innocence. "Just a plain pink frosting."

"And what will give it the color pink, stupid?"

"I won't tell you," she said, teasing.

"It 'beets' me," he muttered, and she laughed.

When Ralph phoned the next evening his voice had a hard tone, over-alert in a city way, and he seemed to have a line prepared. "You going to be a mother hen or a spring chicken this weekend?"

Elinor was taken aback, but made her voice express a relaxed warmth. "I thought we'd try spring in September.

124

Both my kids will be away Saturday night so I'm hoping you'll come with your toothbrush."

"And keep you from being lonely?"

"And keep *you* from being lonely." Her voice was husky. "Is five-ish okay?"

"Sure-ish. I'll be driving." She gave him directions. He seemed reluctant to hang up. "Did you get home okay yesterday?"

"Yes, but I forgot the spice Susan wants, so I'm in the doghouse."

"What spice does she want?"

"That special salt for borscht."

"Sour salt?"

"Yes. How did you know?"

"Dear girl, Julia Child's my aunt."

Elinor chuckled. "And the Frugal Gourmet's my uncle."

Ralph's laughter led her to think he was relaxing a little. "I'm bringing the white wines."

"I hope you like to feast on the bounty of the earth?"

"I love to feast on the bounty of the earth."

"Are you with your daughter?" she asked.

"Not yet. I'm waiting for her. Then off to the movies."

On Saturday afternoon she was grateful to her children for helping as she had asked. About three Steven set off for the woods, his gear hanging around him much as Susan had predicted, and his spirit serene. Elinor waved him goodbye from the now dry front door. Susan was busy sketching her puppets and Elinor left her to it and went upstairs for a little rest, sorry she had to rumple her freshly made bed but needing a heating pad at her back. Her fingers and toes were cold. She guessed and then she knew. Yes, her period had started.

Bad, bad luck. Silly to think of it as devastating, but I'm disappointed and Ralph may be mad. I really don't know him well. Maybe, if he knew, he'd feel there was no point in coming. Maybe we can just have a visit without the sacred part. Or would he want to go ahead and have sex?

Somehow, it's not right for me now, though my desire is never stronger than just before my period. When Howard forced me I hated it. If Ralph loves me he won't ask me to. It may be a good test. If there isn't enough between us so that we enjoy being together, talking and eating and sitting by the fire, everything's doomed anyhow. So by tomorrow the whole Ralph affair may have dwindled into nothing but a good excuse to get the drapes hung.

She took an aspirin and fell asleep.

When her alarm went off she felt fine, but too languid to get up. At four, Susan came in to say she had everything packed to go to Judy's and needed to go to the store again.

Feeling heavy, Elinor got up. She no longer felt glamorous, just dedicated to impeccable cleanliness.

I'll have to think of various light-sounding excuses to keep slipping upstairs to the bathroom to freshen up. How far away the white sand and browning sun of last weekend seem! I was seventeen last Saturday and feel like fifty today. Luckily the only thing I've got to wear makes me look about thirty-five.

She put on her waltz-length brown and gold brocade skirt, a clinging ivory-colored top and delicate gold chains. Instead of letting her hair fall loosely around her face, she wound it into a braided crown around her head.

This is one way a redhead like me can achieve what I need. Dignity.

At nearly five Susan was impatient to go, and Elinor was backing the car out of the garage when Ralph arrived. Susan let out a mock gasp. "Migod, he has a Cadillac too! Co-o-zy!"

"Don't start talking like Steven," Elinor snapped. "Mr. Conklin has more right to a Cadillac than we do." She rolled the window down and greeted Ralph with a smile as he walked up to her side of the car. They kissed quickly and warmly. Elinor, alert to what Susan's reaction to this would be, noted only impatience, not disapproval.

"We're taking Susan and cake to Judy's house. Susan, meet Ralph."

He touched his fingers lightly to the hair above his ear, an automatic gesture of manners. "Hi, Susan." To Elinor he said gently, "I'm early. Glad I caught you."

"I left a note on the front door that I'd be right back. You didn't get lost?"

"Well, nearly. I lost the directions you gave me on the phone and had to steer by the map you drew on the sand. I think two seagulls are following me here."

Elinor laughed. "Would you like to come with us? It's not far."

"Sure. I'll just hop in the back."

Susan turned around in the front seat to watch him. "Be careful of my cakes," she warned. Three flat pans covered most of the back seat. "Just lift the first pan up and hold it level on your lap."

Ralph did so with great care, carefully protecting his brown tweed sport jacket and tan pants.

Elinor, glancing behind her, was amused, thinking Ralph was slated for more than one endurance test this weekend.

He seemed undaunted. "This is really a beautiful area."

"Don't forget I have to stop at the store for frosting stuff," put in Susan.

"You're taking all these cakes to your friend?" Ralph inquired.

"Well, not really. I bake cakes for birthday parties, and Judy and I are going to frost these and make puppets at her house. Oh, Mom, I forgot my Elmer's."

"I love cakes frosted with Elmer's," said Ralph.

Susan giggled. Elinor, hoping she wouldn't have to turn back for glue, said, "Maybe Judy will have some?"

"But what if she doesn't?"

"Allow me to buy you some at the store," Ralph suggested.

"Okay. Thanks. And Mom, don't start shopping for groceries like always."

"On Saturday afternoon? You're safe. I'll stay in the car while you two shop."

"I'll go straight in and stand in line," Ralph said.

Waiting for them, Elinor once more had the feeling of acceptance Dr. Martha had given her. And now Susan was included and nobody felt jealous. In minutes Ralph and Susan came out of the store in a comic mood of conspiracy.

"Secret mission here. Lie low until we return," he warned, "then pull silently into traffic."

"Gotcha, chief," Elinor replied, pretending to chew gum like a gangster's moll. She watched Susan guide him two stores down to the fancy local hardware store. They soon emerged, Ralph carrying a brown paper bag.

On the way to Judy's, Elinor pointed out the high school, and its many athletic fields. "Impressive," said Ralph. "One good reason for high taxes, no doubt. Susan, what's your favorite sport?"

"Art."

He laughed. "What's your non-favorite sport?"

"My non-favorite sport—" Susan paused dramatically— "is volleyball."

"I was good at volleyball," Elinor said. "My team won the championship in junior high school."

"Did they play volleyball back then?" Susan asked.

"Yes, believe it or not, in the dark ages, volleyball was already known."

Ralph helped carry the cakes into Judy's house.

"Have a great party," Elinor called. "Save the puppets to show me."

Returning to the car, Ralph took the seat beside Elinor. "Susan's a nice kid," he said. "Is she going out with boys yet?"

"Not really. She's only fifteen. There's a group of school friends, boys and girls, who come by for her. Some handy parent drives them to the school games, and to the pizza parlor afterward. I dread the day when the boys have their own cars."

"You're lucky she's not dating. My older daughter, the one who's nineteen, started at thirteen, and it's been hell."

"That's Helen?"

"Yes. Live in hell with Helen." He wasn't smiling.

"And the other one is Michele?"

"Yes, Michele is fifteen, like Susan. She's the one I was with Thursday."

"She lives with her mother?"

"Yes, at the moment. She wants to live with me. Which isn't feasible, but I'd like to get her away from her mother."

"Where does Helen live?"

"On her own. She may be nineteen but she's a woman of twenty-nine in some ways." There was a silence before Ralph said, "I've never seen a more beautiful suburb."

Elinor nodded. "Thank you." She was finding the car seat restful. "Would you like to see some of my favorite places?"

"Yes, please. Didn't you say there's a beach?"

"I'll show you."

She drove him around the coastline of Long Island Sound, beyond which they could dimly see the coast of Connecticut. In the near waters were dozens of sailboats showing pink sails in the warm late September afternoon. When they stopped at the beach she pointed to the east, saying, "Sagamore Hill is over there a few miles, where Theodore Roosevelt lived. And just over the inlet to the west is Great Neck, the setting of Fitzgerald's novel *The Great Gatsby*." Ralph nodded and gave her a light kiss.

Headed home to Elinor's, as they went down a hill she remarked, "That's our little Episcopal church. Simple but lovely inside."

"Are you an active member?"

"Not any more. When the kids were smaller I used to help in the church school. Now I just go when I can, to worship. It straightens my thoughts out. But I'm allergic to being on committees."

"So am I, though I was brought up Episcopalian too."

"I saw an old prayer book in your bedroom."

"Well, don't be misled. I also have a Bible somewhere, but the only text I can remember is, 'The Lord maketh me lusty as an eagle!'" She laughed and after a short pause he continued, "So you checked me out on that, did you?" He rested his hand on her knee.

Elinor drove calmly a few moments without speaking, and then said quietly, "Isn't it important to check people out?"

Ralph removed his hand from her knee and said seriously, "Yes. I think my daughters' lives would have been better if we'd lived here instead of in the City. Do you find the atmosphere good here for raising children?"

"Yes," Elinor said promptly. "The setting is wholesome, the kids swim and sail and have good competitive games at school."

"Do they have good social activities—with nice kids?"

"Susan does. She doesn't give me any worries. But Steven is a loner."

"He's sixteen?"

"Seventeen. He's young socially, though. After school it's mostly the teachers he talks with. He's off tonight camping in the woods, planning to meet a teacher for bird-watching in the morning."

"What birds are they hoping to see? I'd enjoy talking about birds with him."

"You probably won't meet him because they may be gone all day tomorrow."

"Don't count on that. They'll be early birds with the birds, and he'll think it's lunchtime at ten A.M."

She wondered what time Ralph would leave the next day, as she didn't want Steven to know he spent the night. But it would be rude to ask.

He moved closer to her as she turned the curve up her driveway and braked to a stop. They sat a moment, quietly private. Ralph reached out and turned off the ignition key and warmly cupped her left breast in his hand as he

130

brought his mouth to hers. She felt herself melting, but reached her hand to his hair and patted it, her touch more soothing than passionate.

Sensitive to her coolness, he tapped the wheel. "The old steering wheel is the same deterrent it always was." She laughed. "But I am to stay overnight?"

She became serious. "I hope you'll stay. But you may not find what you expected. I started my period, just this afternoon."

"And you wouldn't . . . ?"

"No. Please, no. In five days, yes."

She was glad he hadn't been angry, but he hadn't taken the news lightly, either.

"Don't you keep a calendar?"

Taken aback but trying not to show it, she said, "I'm slightly irregular." Again silence.

"How were you feeling before you knew?"

"Oh Ralph, so passionate—so longing for you."

"That's good enough for me."

He reached across her and pushed the car door open, nudging her to get out. "Let's see what kind of friends we're going to be."

This is what she had longed to hear. Out of the car, she turned to look at him. "I hope you like my dinner."

"For sure." But instead of getting out, he slid under the steering wheel. "Your gas gauge says nearly empty. I'm taking this bonny boat back to the village to get gas."

She was surprised. "Well, okay."

"You can get some glasses ready for the wine."

"Will do." Inside, she stopped for a second and turned on the oven in which the Idahoes were ready for baking, and went straight upstairs.

When he returned, coming casually through the back door into the kitchen, he dropped her car keys and the brown bag from the hardware store onto the counter. "Is my car okay where it is? Do you want your neighbors to see a strange car here overnight?"

"We could put it into the garage except the lawn roller is in there and it's too heavy for me to move."

"Come on, we'll move it. Show me where you want it."

They got the lawn roller out onto the gravel beside the garage and he turned toward his car. "I'll put my baby inside and get my suitcase. The wine's in it. It won't need chilling."

She hurried in and put out crackers and the trout paté which Adele, her neighbor, had given her. Ralph was a long time coming, and as she stood waiting, her expectancy turned to a feeling of abandonment. What was he doing? Finally she looked in the garage. His car was there.

Just as she returned to the kitchen, the front doorbell rang. Cheered, she hurried to open it, hoping her sparkling white front door looked welcoming. And there he stood, suitcase in hand. Her heart did a thump of pleasure. This was the way she had pictured the evening starting.

"Oh, there you are!"

"Yup, here I are." They kissed. "I took a look around your nice yard."

"My zinnias have lost their color."

"They're fine." He swung his case onto a step of the central staircase and took out a small bottle of sour salt. "For Susan." Elinor wanted to hug him but he bent down and brought out two wine bottles. "The Montrachet is for now, the Chateau Haut-Brion goes with dinner. Corkscrew?"

"I put it out on the kitchen counter."

He followed her, talking. "Elinor, your car inspection has expired, did you know that? The sticker on your windshield says it expired last month."

To Elinor's own surprise, she snapped, "Will you butt out of what's wrong with my car?"

"Okay." He put his arms around her and she reacted by pounding her fists against his chest.

"I'm so sick of being practical—the car, the yard, the house, the kids. I have to think about them all week.

I don't want to think of them on a date." She started to cry.

He held her supportively until she looked up and blinked her tears back. Then, with his arms still around her, he held the bottle behind her and managed to connect the corkscrew with the cork, and with exaggerated twisting of his body, prolonged the task of opening the bottle. "What you need is some wine. Hey, don't wiggle."

She cocked her head. "I'll wiggle if I want to!" She twisted free.

"Now be good! Drink first, dance later."

She did a little dance step as she put out glasses.

As he poured the Montrachet, he asked, "Do you have a tango record?"

"I'm sure we have an old one upstairs. Our collection's in Susan's room."

He pushed the bag from the hardware store along the counter toward her. "Open your present."

She pulled out four plastic bags, each containing a dozen daffodil bulbs. Their labels read King Alfred, Pink Supreme, General Patton, and Mount Hood. "Oh, Ralph, what a wonderful present!"

"Promises of spring."

"And so many! The garden will be gorgeous!" She kissed him the way a child kisses in gratitude for a birthday present, and said, "I'm flabbergasted!"

He grinned with pleasure but said drily, "We aim to flabbergast. Now, lady fair, are you going to invite me into your parlor?"

As they walked through the dining room into the living room, he said, "Elinor, this house is beautiful!"

He lit the fire and sitting side by side they lifted their glasses. Ralph praised the brook trout paté and she snuggled against him. He rested his cheek against her hair and she said in a little girl voice, "Sorry about the scene."

"What scene?"

"When I got mad."

"Were you mad, or tired?"

"Tired, I guess. It feels good to sit here."

As they sat staring at the fire he said, "This is the first time I've rested all week."

"It's good for you. My dinner will make you healthy—lots of vitamin C in the cabbage we grew ourselves. You Manhattanites need that."

"Okay, Mom."

She accepted the term, feeling one of the pleasures of being in love is trying on various roles. When she figured the potatoes were baked through, she led the way to the polished dining table, at one end of which she had arranged white linen placemats and settings of her best silver. She lit the candles in the candelabra and went into the kitchen, to return and dramatically present a platter on which baked potatoes and homemade Chinese cabbage rolls circled the whole roasted chicken.

"Wow!" said Ralph. "The eagle has landed! That calls for the Haut-Brion!" He corked the first bottle of wine, and poured from the second.

During dinner, she asked, "What's your favorite Sunday morning?"

"What we did on Fire Island. What's yours?"

"The same!" she said. "But like the old joke about honeymooners, we have to eat, too. I like breakfast in bed."

"I'm a great cook of breakfast in bed. Ask Aunt Julia. What is your menu, Lady Elinor?"

"For the first breakfast, French coffee, croissants and strawberry jam. Then love. Then for the second breakfast, Canadian bacon and eggs, fried tomatoes, toast and marmalade."

"With the *Times* crossword puzzle?"

"No, the news and editorials first. To sober me up after two breakfasts." Aware that he was frowning, she asked, "Is my menu too European for your taste?"

"Yes. Except the love part. We can have any food we want in the City any Sunday. My idea for tomorrow is to go jogging at five A.M. in your beautiful 'burb."

"You're kidding! It isn't even light by five."

"But there's nothing to do in bed."

"Oh, Ralph, stop teasing. By six o'clock it'll be light."

"Yes, we'll need light. I want to have a look at houses here."

"We have a measured jogging route along some of the prettiest roads."

"How far is it?"

"About five miles. We don't have to run the whole course. I have my own special two-mile and four-mile sections."

"Good. I'm out of shape—a deprived city kid."

"Your swimming didn't look that way last weekend."

When they were leaving the dining room to drink their coffee in front of the living room fire, Ralph saw a college bulletin on the sideboard and took it with him. He looked at it as they sat together on the sofa. "Is this yours?"

Elinor nodded. "It's from our local college."

"Along with your other talents, are you a student?"

"Not me. Not that I wouldn't like to be."

"What field?"

"Art history, I guess. But I never got into it, only had one year of college before secretarial school. I'd love to finish now, but the tuition is too high."

"Were you a secretary?"

"Yes, I was a secretary at the American Embassy in London." He whistled. "It was quite a struggle to get that job. First I went to work illegally at low-paying jobs to get my typing speed up. I was homesick. And there was Howard, an attaché at the Embassy, also American, also homesick. I don't think Howard and I would have gotten together if we'd met in the U. S. of A."

"What's his profession?"

"He's in econometrics. Very smart. We enjoyed London, went to the theater and opera and ballet a lot. We had a nanny to help look after our two babies, so it wasn't hard to entertain. I had a reputation for dinners with international menus."

"Why'd you come back to the States?"

"They phased out some of the jobs there, and Howard wanted to work in the private sector anyway. He has his own business now."

"Howard—Howard Bates." Ralph mused. "I've heard of him. Does he have a business consulting service?"

"Yes, econometrics makes money. But he got overconfident and bought this house and then he did nothing but work. He's never done anything but work, actually. And he spent money before he had it. Like the Cadillac. After our divorce last year, he moved into the City, and I guess now he just rents a car when he needs one."

"He doesn't like maintaining a car, I take it?"

"No. He's supposed to support the children and pay the bills on the house and car, but he hates car repair bills. So it's neglected."

"I see. I'll just check a few things on it tomorrow after breakfast, if that's okay. I brought a few tools."

"Super! Say, are you really a stockbroker or are you . . . ?"

"A grease monkey? Yup, that's me." He tightened his arm around her.

Elinor patted his hand. "What's a typical business day like for you?"

"Well, I get into the office about eight thirty or nine, or earlier if something's up, and there's mail and the market to watch, and I have to study a lot of people's portfolios and give them the right advice—and buy and sell for them. If I have a lull I read the forecasts carefully and call my contacts."

"Sometime will you teach me about the Dow Jones and all that? If I ever go back to work—and I really ought to because the kids will soon be in college—I've thought of trying for a secretarial job on Wall Street."

"I'll explain what I can to you, with pleasure. But the art

history and the international cuisine would lead to an easier life. My secretary, Alicia, has really lost her health having to commute—that's a grind—and support herself and her mother. She wears a wig and does something weird to her eyebrows—sad. A smart girl's better off getting into the centerfold of *Playboy*."

"Ralph, that's the first male chauvinist thing I've heard you say! I protest!"

"Well, about time! I was beginning to think you weren't as much of a feminist as I am. Aren't secretaries stuck in a stereotyped sex role?"

"To me, Women's Lib is still a luxury. I enjoyed being a secretary at the Embassy and I want both my kids to go to college. The divorce lawyer fixed it so Howard will put Steven through, but I want Susan to have a chance, too."

Ralph opened the college bulletin. "Is there a course here you want to take?"

"Yes, I saw one—here it is: 'Art of the Century. Introduction to Modern and Contemporary Art—Cubism, Fauvism, Dadaism, Surrealism.'"

"Sounds good. How much?"

"A hundred and sixty. It doesn't count toward a degree. Anyhow, I probably couldn't learn the *isms* in the right order." She sighed.

"I'd like to invest in something like that for you, pay the expenses."

"But why should you pay the expenses?"

"I could just give it to you sealed in an envelope with a check to the college. A gift. But you'd have to do the studying."

"It's not something I've seriously thought about."

"Well, think about it." His next question was cheerfully disarming. "If you have a guest room, could I sleep there tonight? Sleeping with you would tempt me."

"We have a guest room, but it's partly a store room now. You can help me move stuff off the bed."

"With pleasure. But first, find the tango record."

While upstairs she freshened up in her bathroom, smiling to herself.

He's like a member of the family. And there's so much energy in a man."

In the living room they danced and Ralph said, "We're good enough for my favorite Spanish restaurant. Will you have dinner with me this week?" He counted to five on his fingers. "How about Thursday?"

She answered by holding her fingers open behind her head and doing a stomping Spanish dance around him, with flirtatious glances sideways until he spanked her lightly and said, "I don't know about you, but I'm going jogging at five o'clock."

"*Six* o'clock."

"Well, six o'clock. So I'm going to bed. You'll have to wake me."

Together they made the guestroom bed.

She was calling good night from her bedroom door when he said, "Come here." A bit apprehensively, she approached, and he drew her into the room and to the window. "Harvest moon." He kissed her in a quiet new way, then with a brotherly arm around her, walked her back to her door. As she was going in, he put his hand on her arm. "In the office today Alicia's calculator stuck and everything she totaled came to nine cents. It got to be funny. Rent for the office came out nine cents. One millionaire's account came out nine cents. Alicia kept banging it and sputtering, until I sent our clerk out to buy her a new calculator."

She giggled. "Hardly the sums I picture you dealing with." She moved through her doorway, then turned back. "Ralph, thank you for bringing Susan the sour salt. There's a lot of fatherliness in you."

"Too much for my daughters." He waggled his fingers in goodbye and went to his room.

As Elinor undressed she felt glad he would fix her car. It

was comforting to picture the two Cadillacs down there, his black, hers white. As she drifted off to sleep, Ralph flashed before her eyes, looking benevolent, and she heard his voice from the afternoon. "Let's see what kind of friends we'll be." She smiled against the pillow.

She told Martha all about it the following Wednesday, even the details of her ideal first breakfast which she had served Ralph. "Luckily he left very courteously right after eating. I hated to ask him to go, since he'd been so nice about postponing sex and wanting to talk with Steven about bird-watching. I told him later about the white-throated nuthatch and redbreasted sparrow—or was it the other way around?"

"What was Ralph planning to do the rest of the day?"

"I have no idea, but he understood that I'd worry if Steven came home and found him there. He might tell Howard about it."

Martha grew solemn and gave her some womanly advice. "You should be measured for a new diaphragm. Would you welcome a surprise pregnancy when you're not married yet?"

Elinor heard chiefly the "yet."

After she left, Martha smiled at the contrast of this week's abstinence with last week's joyful romp on the beach.

Elinor is essentially wifely. And Ralph seems right. I hear wedding bells, like my dream in Vermont.

11

Nature Abhors a Vacuum on Sundays

Ralph backed his black Cadillac out of Elinor's garage and easily found the Expressway back to the City.

I feel invigorated. Great, in fact. How could this be, when I didn't get laid? Well, I brought pretty good wine, not deadening to the brain. Then, too, that was a good bed. Firm. Didn't feel castrated by Elinor's prudery, knew she'd be there admiring me this morning, giving me breakfast. Takes leadership from me very well, that woman. I'd be proud of her looks if I took her to a dinner meeting. If anyone asks me how we met, we can truthfully say at a fundraiser in the Hamptons. Socially acceptable.

I like what she said at breakfast about how good the schools are in the towns around here. People spend a lot on houses but see to it that the schools are so good that their kids get into Ivy League colleges.

Beautiful area we jogged through, great place for a home. I may be living here myself before long. Her divorce is final but I'm not sure of the details of the agreement. When I see it, I'll send it to my world-class lawyer, for chapter and verse on how to deal with it. Elinor told me that the house is in her name, with provisions, and her ex makes the mortgage payments until the kids are both twenty-one. After that if she can't make the payments she can sell her share. I didn't ask her what would happen if she married again—no use putting that in her head just yet. But I would enjoy living in this area, and she's a hot item. Refined, too. It could work out okay if our kids get along.

Out here, for the first time in my life, I'd have good weekends. We'd keep both cars or buy new ones the same, with me the grease monkey—and that boy of hers, Steven, watching what I do, impressed, and anxious to learn. Father and son. We could keep my apartment in town so I wouldn't have to take the train out here if I work late, and Elinor loves to come in for the restaurants and theater. I haven't done enough so far to get theater tickets. Maybe I can take everyone to Radio City at Christmas.

I wish my chubby little Michele could have a home like that. Her mother isn't raising her right. Out here in the 'burbs she could have me and the influence of a real lady, Elinor, and that cute kid, Susan. I didn't get to meet Steven, but he sounds bright, can probably get a good college scholarship. Howard's going to pay the rest, though I'd be proud to educate a son. I love my two girls and would take pleasure in educating them, but the thought that I might not get to raise a son always gives me a sharp pain in the gut.

You can bet your ass that smart Howard knew where to buy, to help his image in the City. It would help mine, too, and save me the outrageous private school fees I'm paying now for Michele. I paid plenty for Helen, and then she didn't make it to college, got herself into a mess by leaving home and getting married. Then within months I had to help her get divorced. Kids can fall through the cracks when parents break up. Well, there's still time to save Michele, and out here she'd be away from her mother and have a real home and good schooling. Think what people with several kids save by living out here!

I wonder if Elinor might want to have a kid? Lots of women in their forties do have them, and I want a son. Michele and Susan are both fifteen, a nice age, but I wish Steven was about six or eight, like Belinda's boys, young enough to need a real father, like me.

Okay, God, I'm fussy. I guess it's enough to be in love with the beautiful Elinor. Hope she lets me plant those bulbs.

The Expressway sure moves on Sunday morning, not like what they call it, the longest parking lot in the world.

She gets uptight about some things. Doesn't want her son to know I spent the night, asked me to leave before he came home from birdwatching. My own damn fault, I put it into her head that when a kid's out camping, he thinks it's lunchtime about ten A.M. True, though. I remember. Yet it focused on my leaving early, when there'd be no harm in the kid finding me at the house that I can see.

She's on the rag, I get a single bed, and she asks me to leave early. And yet I had a pretty good time. So, what now? I sympathize with the guy who wrote that nature abhors a vacuum on Sundays.

What we should have planned was for me to put the guest room back as it was and drive around until the kid got home and then show up for brunch like I was just arriving. Could've spent the day reading the paper and working on her car.

Guess I'd better go back to the office, although there's not really anything that can't wait until tomorrow. I hate Sundays alone in the City.

She's the right age, about two years younger than me. Luckily I'm over that herpes for over a year now. The last revenge of my *ex*. Who'd believe I'd sleep with her again, divorced long before? Well, she wanted it. I must have been out of my mind—it didn't take a genius to figure out she'd been sleeping around.

If I marry Elinor, my daughters will have to get used to the idea of a woman on the scene all the time. Introduce them to it slowly.

I could have helped rake leaves. Of course, she has this church thing. Good for my girls, though. If they'd go. Probably would, Michele anyway. Chance to dress up. I'd stay home and read the *Times*. They'd get the Good News and I'd get the Bad.

He chuckled.

Could it be true that she reads the editorials first? Could that be true of any woman? What about the magazine ads and the food section? I like those first. I get ideas so I know what's *in* when I go to restaurants. Elinor isn't a bad cook, but she's the kind who keeps everything tidied up behind her. My creativeness would probably annoy her.

That's something, her wanting to read the editorials first. I should've said, "I read them first on weekdays but I take Sunday off."

He laughed aloud.

What would a family be like if the wife was smarter than the husband? An academic question, as I have to settle the matter of Belinda first. She's blocking any action right now.

Boy, is she! I only slept with her once and that was before I met Elinor. And last week she phones and says she's pregnant! Helen says—and she ought to know, since she goes to Belinda's to babysit all the time—that it's a shame there's no man around. Well, if I did it, I hope Helen doesn't find out. Better get her in fast for a D and C, a good old dusting and a cleaning, as they say. That's better than a lawsuit and sending her a check for eighteen years. Belinda can't object to it, since she has three kids already, and is divorced. God, what if it's my son I'm flushing? Could be—she has boys. That would be ironic, after the times I tried in vain to plant a son, and then to do it by accident—by a sheer coincidence, in fact.

It was only because I tried to help Helen that I got into the picture. She'd been okay as the regular babysitter but she got mixed up on the date and didn't show, and Belinda called me to see if I knew where she was. I didn't know, but thought if Helen was finally doing something useful with her time, I should be a Boy Scout and protect her job, so I said I'd substitute for her and headed for Brooklyn! The little boys wanted to play cars and I finally got them to bed okay. They were really smart and sweet kids. When Belinda came home, she turned out to be a joyful, pleasant person and very fond of Helen. She gave me money in an envelope for her, and then made cocoa and somehow I found myself taking the woman into my arms. Ye gods, lonely women in the 'burbs are a temptation!

That was just a month or so before I met Elinor and I haven't seen Belinda since. She said it definitely had to be me, which I did believe, don't know why, but I did. She said she wouldn't blame me or tell anyone about it, was just trying to figure out how to pay for an abortion. That was pretty straight-dealing.

She's happy-go-lucky, but her life can't be easy. Luckily, her parents take the kids some weekends. Wonder if she's free this weekend? I'll call her right now to see if the pregnancy thing is still for real. A good use for my car phone.

The exit for the Brooklyn Queens Expressway was coming up, so he lowered the cruise control to fifty-five.

Belinda answered the phone. "Oh, Ralph, is that you? I was thinking about you, because the kids are playing with their toy cars and quoting you about dipsticks and transmission fluid! You made a big impression."

Ralph chuckled. "I've been thinking about them, too. What's on their calendar for today?"

"A trip to our garden allotment to collect our squashes and then lunch at McDonald's. Want to join us?"

"Sure. I'll do lunch."

"Okay, but remember, any other restaurant would be wasted on my gang. Give me a rain check just for myself if you have ambiance in mind."

"Okay, wait for me. I'm practically on the way."

It's a funny thing about Belinda—her voice is so vibrant, so near to laughter, doesn't show worry. Obviously, she isn't free of the boys, but that's okay, they're fun to be with, and bright as a medal of honor. Somebody will have to endow scholarships for them, too.

He glided the Cadillac off the ramp toward the Kosciusko Bridge and Brooklyn.

12

I Got Rid of Him

Billie cursed to herself as she left Martha's office after confessing that she'd hit Mike again.

Shitkowsky, Shitteresky, Shittaminsky! So am I cured yet, for Christ's sake?

She glared at the shingle.

Oh, I know you, M. Kaufman, M.D. But your second board is a mess. What's the use of spending an hour with you when it makes me miss the guts of the committee meeting? It doesn't help me with Mikey either—he and I are already a lot farther into the war zone than you know, Shrinky!

Dodging a bus as she neared the New York University campus, she said aloud, "This is the struggle, right here. Cross-fire of imperialists."

She entered a tall building and took the elevator up. On entering a classroom, she found only Dolores and Fern still there.

Fern greeted her. "Billie, it was a short meeting. You should have been here!"

"Bert's given you a special job," said Dolores. "When you're absent, they give you a harder assignment. Especially if you're a woman, Billie dear."

Billie said, "Thanks, Dolores," thinking 'you wrinkled Southern siren, you born address-labeler.' Aloud, she said, "Explain, please."

Fern obliged. "Research reveals that the suffering our party underwent from the Federal Bureau of Investigation needs to be written up as history, and Bert wants you to do it. Here's a list summarizing the data, with the facts that are verified."

Billie studied the paper and said, "The facts are easy. We filed a suit against the FBI for breaking the law and spying on us. They'd spent more than twenty-five million investigating us. We sued for our right to exist as a party."

"I heard that a high school girl in New Jersey was accused of being a Communist because she asked about our party for a school report."

"All they could rightfully call us was 'mildly Marxist'— not traitors who loved Russia. Russian Communism was never true Marxism. What the FBI had against us was that we're for workers."

"It's unbelievable!" wailed Fern.

"Fern, baby, learn," said Dolores. "Reporters like you in the Black press can write it up. Be totally rad."

"Totally rad is out," said Billie. "Still, blame should be placed for the attacks on our members. Bert's papers here say that before we sued, the FBI burglarized our party offices and members' homes on over one hundred seventy occasions. They also secretly set another labor group to attack us. Several of our members were hospitalized. We sued for forty million and won, but got only two hundred sixty three thousand five hundred. Not enough, after thirteen hundred spooks failed to find any evidence of illegal, subversive or violent activity."

Fern proposed, "Billie, you're a social studies teacher. Why don't you assign a report on our party to every kid in your classes? For revenge. Why don't you, Billie?"

"I can't stretch every mini-course to cover political parties. Right now I'm teaching 'Developing Nations' and next month 'Holocaust History.'"

Dolores smiled invitingly. "Bert said today that a snoop who got into our Denver office was named Timothy—a kind of grass, the wrong kind."

Billie grinned. "Uh oh, you gals need recess."

Fern said, "Here are more papers Bert left for you, about others who sought justice." She handed Billie a large legal envelope bulging with papers.

Billie became engrossed in them. "Oh, look at this story —twenty-seven Quakers got arrested for standing in a silent vigil. They figured the law protecting free speech should protect silence, too, so they sued and got one hundred each!"

"Not enough, but they got something," said Dolores.

Billie's voice rose. "This Halperin story is famous. He sued the FBI for three million for wire-tapping, and got four."

"Four million?" asked Fern.

"Dollars," said Billie.

"Sweetie," Dolorous drawled, "he's lucky it wasn't only three ninety-five."

Billie laughed but Fern protested. "It's an insult to give only four dollars in damages to someone who's been proved right."

"Witness for the plaintiff wants to reopen the case," commented Billie, with a glance both mocking and admiring at Fern.

Dolores took a thin cigarette from her handbag and crossed her long legs, once famous in her modeling days but now bony. "Time to share the right kind of grass."

Billie smiled shyly, still studying the papers. Fern teetered across the room in her boots to shut the hall door. They arranged their chairs near an open window and took turns on the cigarette, looking out at the Washington Square arch which gleamed in the late afternoon sunshine.

"What would the professor think if he knew we used his room to spark an economic revolution?" Dolores asked.

"He knows," said Billie. "It's 'Share the Wealth' time now in academia. Hey, here's a list of courses which is a real collectors' item! And look! It features Luke Coursetaker and it's in color!" She held it up for the others to see. "Listen up, Class. Students are offered these exciting new classes by the Division of Student Affairs. Be ready to make your choices. By the way, if the man comes in here to clean, we're just giggly students, not at a meeting."

Fern sighed happily and drew on the cigarette. "I do get giggly with this stuff."

"Giggling is the most sexist thing you can do," said Billie in mock scolding. "Only reactionary women do it. So pay attention to these cool new courses, and may the force be with you."

"It looks like comics," said Fern.

"Oh no," asserted Billie. "This is serious stuff. This is what the division dreamed up to make students happy." She assumed a hearty voice. "Hey, come enroll in 'Open Space'—it's free."

"Free courses at N.Y.U.?" Fern was incredulous.

"Well," said Billie, "It was free if you had a Bursar's receipt to show you paid tuition for regular courses, even if you borrowed the money. Have a look."

"'Basics of Bartending,'" read Fern. "Is this for real? Don't kids come here right out of high school?"

"This 'Clowning Workshop' is for me," said Dolores. "I've always wanted to be a clown."

"I am a clown," said Billie.

"Here's a course called 'Crazy Quilting Patchwork,'" said Fern. "I thought going to N.Y.U. was all studying."

"Well, that was life for the undergraduate," sighed Billie. "Kids had to take courses like 'Economic and Political Disruptions Leading to the Fall of Rome'—I took that somewhere—to get a free course in bartending. So they could earn a living."

They giggled.

Billie returned to the clippings. "Here's another old story—how feminists failed to make the brides giggle at the Garden."

"Oh, yes," said Dolores. "Like Eve in her day, we were expelled from the Garden."

"What garden?" asked Fern. "Why make brides giggle?"

Dolores smiled. "Girlie, Grandma will tell. It was one of our first feminist protests that got attention. We tried to mess up a big Bride's Show in Madison Square Garden, to prove that when men manipulate women for business reasons, they get what they pay for—stupid women. How wrong we were!"

"So what happened?" asked Fern.

Dolores opened her eyes wide. "One hundred mice sure bombed. I've never been in a bigger flop."

"How did you get into it?" Billie asked.

"I was a college delegate, and voted for it at a planning meeting and found out from my biology prof how to get them cheap. In the end I didn't make it to the Garden, but I heard the mice went over like a lead balloon!"

"I still don't get it," Fern said. Now weighty with cannabis, she had taken to staring blankly at equations on a side blackboard. "Did the mice hold the balloon?"

"No, dearie, the garment industry put on a big bridal bash on Valentine's Day. They collected a bunch of local society mothers and fluffy brides-to-be, real ones, and took photographs to show off the latest bridal gowns. It was all schmaltzed up with organ music and a priest—a real priest." She crossed herself in mock piety. "We protesters planned to mess it up by setting loose a hundred mice, expecting the bridies to run around shrieking and holding up their long white satin trains. Our favorite feminist, Robin Morgan, organized it—she was married and pregnant at that time—to show that business was blatantly exploiting marriage vows to sell products. Marriage is sacred."

"Gross!" said Fern. "I hate mice. I'd have panicked."

Billie was reading. "This reporter says nobody panicked."

"No," said Dolores, "the mice were more scared than scary. Only a couple of mothers got excited, the brides just got busy picking up the wee beasties. They loved them. My best friend was there and said our plan bombed as a scare tactic, but we sure interrupted things real good."

"Served the women's wear industry right," said Billie.

Dolores went on, "I did go to the big event in Atlantic City where we demonstrated against the Miss America contest, to show up its false standards for women. We planned to burn our bras as a symbol of getting rid of restrictions, but we couldn't because there'd been a real fire on the boardwalk just before, and the police wouldn't give us a permit. So we hung up a gigantic doll labeled 'Miss America,' all tied up in heavy chains, and underneath we put a lot of empty trash cans, marked 'Freedom.' We'd brought stuff from home in shopping bags—bras and girdles and high-heeled shoes, everything that prevents women from moving freely, and filled a lot of the trash cans. We threw in clothes that were sexy, rather than healthy, like tight jeans and bikinis trimmed in sequins, and permanent wave kits. That was the beginning of that Emily Dickinson style, straight hair hanging down over pale faces with no makeup."

"Like skulls," said Billie. "A couple of my teachers went for it. I never tried it, my hair's too bouncy."

"Your hair's beautiful," said Fern, patting Billie's head. "I love red hair."

Dolores was earnest. "Our real cause is that women are beautiful and sexy when we're just ourselves. We can play outdoors, and work indoors or out, and have husbands and babies and not fuss with hair lacquer and face lifts or any commercial stuff to change us. We love men and are their companions, and all we have to do is be clean and natural. When men try to bind us and decorate us they're trying to dominate. Or sell us."

"I've always lived by those principles," said Billie. "I wouldn't have had much to throw into a Freedom can."

Dolores said, "My hair wasn't gray then, but black and long, and I cheerfully chopped it off and threw it in a can. Everyone clapped. Later I sneaked back for it."

"Oh, no!" Fern exclaimed. "Did you find it?"

"I found the can, but there were pop bottles and half-eaten hot dogs on top, so I just stood there under the Miss America doll and gazed at the ocean. I felt in my heart for the first time that I'd really joined the movement—the human race, in fact. I decided to plan my own life, be what I had the power to be, my natural self, without falsifying. So now I cut my hair short, and don't wear makeup. I eat right, and feel right."

"And you wear low heels. That's healthy," said Billie. She showed off her stubby boots, resting them up on a chair and glancing at Fern to see if she got the hint. Seeing that she didn't, she said, "Fern, you'll crash some day, wearing your high-heeled excuses for boots." Fern tossed her head.

"Not everything bombed that winter," Dolores recalled. "We got a lot of notoriety from the street witches and Bitch Manifestoes. But what still makes me mad about both the Garden and Atlantic City is that the media reported nothing, but nothing, about our real purpose, which was to show that making women into decorated sex objects trivializes them. We're too important for that."

Billie agreed. "The media usually play up what's sensational and only in retrospect can historians pinpoint clues to where things were headed. In our present decade our ideas about economic equality and saving the planet are stifled, but they may win out. Some attention is going to human rights, but not much that's serious is in the papers, and it's ominous how easily media owners can hire reporters who sacrifice their right to tell it like it is."

Fern said, "I'm a reporter and I haven't sold out."

"Hang in there, Fern, and watch the Black Caucus in Congress. They generally get it right. Now listen up—I'm about to give you the scoop of all scoops, more news you didn't read about in the papers, Dolores. By far the most important part of the women's movement is very much alive—consciousness-raising. Women organize groups in order to help one another. There are no paid leaders—everybody's a leader. My colleague, Sally, is in a group, and I'm determined to run one someday. They promote using non-violent means like boycotts and lawsuits to break through the glass ceiling, not by showing off or smashing, but legally."

"Maybe those who smash will win," said Fern, troubled.

"No, they won't," Billie said. "It takes a long time to make a real difference. You can't make a change overnight in men's ideas about women, or in women's ideas of themselves. It's a deep thing. But we'll win."

"Yes," agreed Dolores. "We can do it if we're determined."

Billie stood up. "And now I've got to go home and cook for three men who are exploiting me."

They laughed, ruefully, and Billie added as she left, "I have a thirty minute subway ride and then a long drive."

On the subway she eventually got a seat, and sat thinking about her dinner and whether to try to confirm details of Michael's taking Mikey to Florida, or just take it for granted. She'd learned that if she expected a trip to take place it generally did, and had kept all Mikey's clothes clean up to the minute and given him several large black plastic bags to pack in.

How long have I known that being a single parent is too much for me? Twelve years, anyhow. With no family around to provide money or even to babysit, it's not easy to support a kid and center my life around his emotional needs. Should I tell Kaufman about my escape when I left him alone in the apartment, just mentioning to a neighbor that I was going away overnight? He didn't seem any the worse when I got him from the Children's Shelter, but I suffered over it. I never wanted to give him up, but I can't do a good job with him. The compromise, doing the best I can, is what Kaufman's holding me to, so bourgeois. I'm dead-tired of responsibilities twenty-four hours a day. When I say he's a no-good kid I really mean I'm no good for him. Why can't Kaufman see that it's wrong to think mothers are eternally right? Aloud she muttered, "It's infernally wrong!"

The girl sitting next to her, a gum-chewing teenager with a Rastafarian hairstyle, nodded without looking up.

Only in the past few months has Michael sent money—

ten dollars, two or three times. He hasn't remarried. If he makes money selling his cactuses he might spare some cash for me.

It's no big hardship to let him stay. But what if he stays a long time? He'll have to get a job. Well, he and Mikey could have my apartment and I could move in with Chris. I could keep an eye on Mikey at school, if he stayed in school. But I can imagine the apartment—unwashed dishes, cockroaches . . . and I come to clean up? She said aloud, "Like hell I will!"

A neat black man standing in the aisle next to her seat drew his shoulders together inside his well-tailored jacket and looked coldly down at her. She returned the look.

Christopher really has been loving and not jealous since Mr. Cactus showed up. Some men think only sex goes on when a man and woman sleep under the same roof, but Chris is different. And right to trust me. I could manage nicely, living in Queens with him—it isn't too far from school for me and would be closer for him when he starts his architecture classes at Cooper Union. He's asked me to come stay at his place to save him time driving, but he knows I can't because of Mikey. He could resent the kid, but he doesn't—is darn good with him, in fact. The scary part would be how fast the "BB's" would swarm in if I left Mike alone.

Someday, maybe we can live together and pay only one rent. And take turns buying some of the stuff I buy now, like toilet paper!

She chuckled aloud. The Rastafarian girl had been replaced by a young mother with a baby girl who cooed with delight at Billie. Billie smiled at her.

The solution for everybody would be for Mikey to go to Florida and live with his father for a year. Kaufman thinks I should keep things as they are until he gets through his teenage rebellion and we can settle down like other families, celebrate holidays together until death, but that all seems far off. If I hold Mikey down now, he'll continue to hate me. The right question for Kaufman to ask is, "Is his father the right person to share values with him?" but hell, a father is what he is. A boy gets positive and negative values from both parents. I've talked against his father to him, so now let him find out the good things.

Kaufman is always on the side of old-fashioned virtue. She's a pursuer of continuities. That's the truth—Kaufman pursues continuities. Stability, ninety percent. Striking out on your own, five percent. The rest, no opinion. When you come right down to it, the solution right now for Mikey is Florida. His college chances will be okay if he's back here next year and settles down to work. Michael seems to enjoy what he sees of the boy and can give him a realistic idea of the world. Not, I hope, the attitudes he had when we were first married. How about the time he got himself hired to fix a couple's plumbing and the young wife arrived home to find he'd fallen asleep on their living room sofa, listening to their Mozart records? When she woke him, he just explained Mozart to her. He told me about it and boasted that he didn't apologize.

At first I found his sauciness charming and his love of music an excuse for everything, but my tolerance dried up early. He desperately wanted people to consider him reliable, so why didn't he listen to our Mozart records at home?

When he went on unemployment after Mikey was born, and I had to go back to work right away, I blew up. "No job, no family!" I told him, and scared him across the continent for years. And then he returned and got a job as a handyman on an estate where he had an apartment in a two-story garage. Mikey-baby was eight, proud to be a Cub Scout, and showed his father the binoculars the Scout leader lent him. The boys were taking turns making careful observations. So big Michael borrows the binoculars and spends hours observing his employer, watching the bedroom windows of the main house. Mikey-baby tells me about it and about what his father sees. I laugh all the way to the dresser where I get a big hairbrush and threaten to wallop him if he tells the Scout leader. Poor kid, having to be conventional was no fun.

I recall that Kaufman thought I was right that time.

As for being conventional, I'm in bad shape myself. Well, my shape is all right. It's just that my strict old left brain is boring, getting a lot of linear messages into a nice logical chain. I guess old Rightie isn't dead, though, or I'd never have set up this preposterous plan for tonight, having a dinner party for my lover, my ex and my son, all together. You'll have to wait it out, Leftie.

When she walked into her living room her first view was of Michael putting a record on her hi-fi, "Hi!" he said cheerfully. "I had some label work to do, so I borrowed Mike's key this morning."

She replied, "Oh, hi!" in a dull voice. Neither took even a small step toward the other. He was adjusting the controls and she studied him briefly as she took off her coat.

He's growing a bit stooped, doesn't look his height. His curls are thinning on top, too. Well, he still has his air of handsomeness, and his detached way of doing the unexpected. At least he isn't asleep on the couch.

"Sit down and listen to this Bach," he said.

"I can't, I have to get dinner," she replied, glad that he was apparently going to be on his best behavior. She went to her room and changed from her leather skirt and boots into blue jeans and sandals, but kept on her orange blouse and the black and white checked scarf she wore in sympathy with the Palestinians.

When she returned to the living room, Michael said, "I managed to find some ripe avocadoes in a grocery store. They're in the sink. Shall I make guacamole?"

"No, thanks," Billie said firmly, not wanting him to be working cozily in the kitchen when Chris arrived. "I'll make it in a jiffy. Most everything else is ready. Did you see your son off to school this morning?"

"No, I left before he woke up. Had to get uptown to the florist who bought the cactuses."

"Oh, you sold them?"

"Sure, a piece of cake, not to mention easy as pie. I got a good price."

"Congratulations!" She was setting places at the table.

"I haven't turned them over yet because he wants botanical names and the area each cactus comes from, so I did research in the library and came here and typed labels. I carried your typewriter into Mike's room—let me know if you need it."

"I will." She brought in the roast beef she had baked the night before and started slicing it. "God, it makes me mad when Mike doesn't come home to dinner on time."

"He wasn't too crazy about the idea of all of us being together—dropped a few four-letter words."

"Yech, he can't cut the mustard." She waved the knife with which she was slicing the beef. "He's friends with each of us separately, and I thought roast beef sandwiches would cure his shyness."

"He won't show until after dinner," predicted Michael.

"But I worry not knowing where he is. When it's warm like today, he forgets it's no longer summer. Last week he was late every night so I read him the riot act that he was to be here by six o'clock this week or he wouldn't get his allowance." Michael turned away as if to evade personally any threat of punishment.

Billie noticed and pursued her point. "He has all the freedom in the world in the summer, practically lives fifty miles out near the end of the island at Hither Hills beach. He and his friends hitch out there with their sleeping bags. In fact, he leaves his bag out there. I hope he didn't skip school and go there today."

"Why don't you drive him to school?"

"I have to go early and he's never up when I leave. He takes the school bus, and after school takes another bus home with any one of several friends. Last night I told him to meet me at the supermarket and he did. He even let me help him with his homework after dinner. I haven't seen him today."

"He was still in bed when I left this morning. I said I'd see him here at dinner, and he said eating with all of us was a cockamamie idea. And a few other things."

Billie was about to broach the subject of their plans for Florida, but Christopher arrived and she postponed it. The two men had met on the weekend when Christopher had come in briefly after tennis. As they shook hands she noticed that her lover was the shorter of the two, a surprise because his straight back and confident stance made him seem taller to her. She felt a wave of tenderness for him, a sweet surging feeling.

They sat down at the table where Billie had put out beers and pretzels. "Try the guacamole," said Michael.

Billie knew he wanted her to say he'd brought the avocadoes, but she kept silent. Had he mentioned she'd provided everything else?

"Billie, I got my class schedule for my first term," Christopher announced. "It looks okay."

Billie raised her glass, her eyes on Christopher. "Here's to our future architect!" Amused to hear Michael out of his depth in discussing architecure, she returned to the kitchen.

Soon they concentrated on making sandwiches of beef, lettuce, tomatoes and horseradish. "Great beef," said Christopher. There was silence until he launched a topic. "I clipped this classified ad from today's *Times*. It's for stuffed sharks."

"How much do they cost?" Michael asked.

"Here's what it says. 'Nurse shark eight feet long and dusky shark seven and a half feet long. Bargains.'"

"I love bargains," said Billie. "I'll take one to my shrink. She can hang it up for her professional shingle." Christoper laughed and gave her the victory sign for her quick response.

157

Michael promptly announced, "I'll take the other to my landlord's wife, mark it 'To My Valentine' and sign his name."

"By the way, Michael, I promised my shrink a cactus. You said you'd leave me a half dozen."

Michael flinched but was game. "It's a deal. Big or little?"

"Oh, just three little ones, one for her, one for my classroom and one for this room. Give me labels too."

"Where is Mike?" Christopher asked.

"He'll be home after dinner," Michael said jovially. "How about it, Chris, he's a pretty good kid, isn't he? He doesn't give you any lip, does he?"

"He's fine with me," Christopher assured him. "He's smart."

"As everybody knows except his teachers," said Billie drily. "He doesn't bother to let them discover it."

"Ah, school!" said Michael. "Is it as bad as it always was?"

"No," said Christopher, "kids today don't have to sit still for all the memorizing and grammar that we had."

"God, were they strict at St. Mary's on grammar," said Michael.

"At St. Thomas it was all the Baltimore Catechism," Christopher said. "Nothing about who holds power in politics and economics. I'm learning from Billie."

"What are your beliefs now, Billie?" Michael asked.

"I'll tell you after I pour coffee."

"I'll pour it," Christopher said. "Sit still for once."

Stirring sugar into his cup, Michael persisted. "So are you still the Number One Secret Radical in Middle Cove?"

"You'd better believe it," Billie asserted. "Most people around here don't know the difference between sensible socialism and red communism, but we in the Socialist Workers' Party try to get some of our ideas across. I don't advertise it—Mikey has to eat. So I'm just a liberal, which comes across as radical here."

"You can stay away from Florida. We don't like liberals, even sneaky ones." Michael grinned at Christopher. "And as for Castro-Convertibles, we feed 'em to the alligators."

The music had stopped and Billie turned off the hi-fi. "My party is the Socialist Workers Party, the SWP. We're not the violent Progressive Laborites and not the Socialist Laborites. We're the Workers. For forty years we've been the party for a more responsible economic system than runaway capitalism."

"But who ever heard of it?" asked Michael. "Wouldn't you be better off joining the liberal Democrats?"

"Voters have a right to see a socialist party on the ballot. The rest of the world knows about several kinds of socialism, but Americans are so afraid of the word that we don't even learn the big differences among them. And that's dangerous—it's too easy to spout slogans. We should be an accepted political party."

"How much of this can you work into your teaching without getting into trouble?" Michael asked.

"Not much. My teaching crusade is to get students to state and test their hypotheses, verify their data, and practice seeing both sides of issues. My debate team is learning." Christopher made a stretching movement and she moved behind him and rubbed his shoulder. "Don't let ceiling painting hurt your tennis."

He smiled and pursued the conversation. "Public schools do a better job of preparing kids to run the world."

"We wish!" said Billie. "All educators are racing against the clock."

"But what can we do about it?" asked Christopher.

"What I can do," Billie said, "is teach. I can prepare kids to change things, to use the revolution in information to promote democracy, undo the nuclear dangers, and help the underdeveloped world generate its own industry."

"It's a big order," said Christopher.

Michael was getting restless. "Can kids really come to understand all this? They're pretty spoiled today. I read in the paper about a Bar Mitzvah party where the uncle of the kid zoomed into the Temple riding his gift—a big motorcycle. To celebrate the kid's being a man at age thirteen."

"Ouch!" said Chris. "He was only twelve, one day before!"

Michael said, "Jews mess up their kids more than we do."

"I can think of one way they do a better job," Billie said, as she collected the beer glasses and started toward the kitchen. Her face turned hard. "Child support!" She ran the water noisily to drown out his reply but apparently there wasn't one, as she soon heard his voice from the hall where he had carried the phone. She returned to sit beside Christopher. They kissed once, warmly, before Michael returned and was greeted by Billie.

"Michael, I'm glad you sold your cactuses and hope you're facing what's involved in taking Mike back to Florida with you. You'll get to know your son, and give him a father's leadership. I put some big plastic bags on the bed for him to pack in, and I've been keeping his clothes clean up to the minute."

"I don't have much of a place."

"But it'll be broadening for him and more like real life than Middle Cove. He might perk up in a new school, and next year when he's back in school here I'll help him bone up for the college entrance exams."

"I'm not sure the schools are good where I am."

"That's one way he's getting spoiled. He should have a chance to see how the other half lives. It was a good deal in this country when kids were apprenticed at fourteen and lived with their bosses' families. Mikey needs a change."

Michael did not reply but in a moment said, "I was just on the phone to my aunt and she told me her youngest son, Dennis, was in the Irish Republican Army and was killed in Belfast."

"God," said Billie. "I know they've been protesting against business there for not hiring Catholics. One big ship-builder hired only one token Catholic for years—a night watchman, paid very little. How did Dennis get killed?"

"It was an accident. He was in the lead, ahead of his buddies trying to plant a bomb in a factory and it blew up and killed him. He was twenty."

"God, a regular Roddy McCorley!" Billie said. "But didn't your aunt raise her kids in Brooklyn, not Ireland?"

"Yes. It seems Dennis was visiting relatives. I knew his older brothers, but not him."

"That's a sad story," Christopher said.

"Did it just happen?" asked Billie.

"No, I guess it was a couple of years ago. But I didn't know about it and my aunt was crying, telling me. I'm going to invite her down to visit me in Florida."

"Maybe Mikey can meet her."

"Religious wars are the worst," said Christopher, "like Israel and Lebanon."

"It's the economics of overpopulation. And deep-seated long-lasting hatreds."

"As an architect," said Christopher, "I'm shocked that cities have become battlegrounds. Guerilla warfare belongs in the jungle, not inside a beautiful hotel."

"You'll have to design hotels for fighting," Michael said. "You'll need rooms for artillery, spy equipment, the whole army base. Room service with Spam." The others didn't laugh, and he jumped up and moved to sit on the piano bench. "How's the old Steinway doing?" He started to play an Irish reel, then broke off. "We may be lapsed Catholics but who's a lapsed Irishman? Do you still have that old songbook?"

"Yes. In the bench you're sitting on." Michael took the book out and with an effort managed to get it to stand up on the rack.

"It's pretty ragged," said Billie. "It survived the orphanage but not Mikey's childhood."

"The orphanage?" Christopher sounded shocked.

"Yeah, that book was the only thing I had from my mother when she died. That book made me into a revolutionary and a historian."

Michael began to play "The Rambler from Clare," saying jovially, "Remember this, Chris?"

Christopher joined him at the piano. "I can't even remember 'Molly Malone.'"

Billie went to the bookcase and got a book which she put in front of Michael. "This is a secondhand gem I found in the Village. It's all rebel songs."

"Are there any other kinds?" asked Michael, and swung into "Shan Van Vogt." As they sang, everyone, including Billie, vied to be chief tenor. Next they sang a prison song, "The Old Triangle."

Billie turned the page and said, "Here's the one about Roddy McCorley." They sang:

"Never a one of all your dead
more bravely fell in fray
Than he who marches to his fate
on the Bridge of Toome today.
True to the last he led!
True to the last he led!
He treads the upward way.
Young Roddy McCorley goes to die
On the Bridge of Toome today."

Billie wiped tears from her eyes.

"We need some love songs," declared Christopher. "How about 'Peggy Gordan'?"

They sang, "Oh, Peggy Gordan, you are my da-arlin'," and Christopher requested "Kathleen Mavourneen."

Michael played all requests but at nine o'clock said, "I still have some labels to type. Can I keep your typewriter for twenty minutes?"

"Yes, just that long," said Billie. "I have to type a test."

"I'm nearly finished and gotta hit the hay. My sale will be wrapped up tomorrow and I have to get uptown early." He went into Mike's bedroom.

Christopher offered to do the dishes and Billie gratefully accepted. She took her briefcase to the kitchen table and said, "I have to make up long exams for four classes."

They worked for a while in compatible silence, broken only when young Mike appeared.

"And where have you been?" Billie asked him.

"Out on the Island," he replied. "I'm hungry."

Christopher said, "Here's some roast beef, all sliced, and a lot of good makings if you want to put together a sandwich."

The sandwich Mike made was substantial, loaded with a half-dozen slices of beef, tomatoes and pickles. He carried it off to eat in front of the TV.

Christopher finished the dishes and gave Billie a brief shoulder rub. "It surprises me how hard you teachers work to give exams. I always thought taking them was the hard part."

"The hard part is *marking* them, especially essay questions, so I try to make them only half of a test and the rest one-word answers, which have to be explained in one sentence. This deters cheating because even if they copy the word from someone else's paper, they generally give away their ignorance in their explanation."

"Good luck." He rose to leave. "No musical beds tonight," he said playfully as he kissed her.

"Believe me, the music's over," she replied, "literally and figuratively."

He kissed her again and let himself out. She reclaimed her typewriter and typed out master copies of four exams. Later, from her bedroom she heard Michael and Mike talking in low voices, although she couldn't catch words. She felt left out, but knew she couldn't be of much help, as they were no doubt planning their new life together in

Florida. She set the alarm for six in order to get to school in time to use the copy machine.

The next evening she arrived home carrying stacks of the exams her students had written. In the kitchen she found three cactuses on the table and a typed note on the refrigerator door with a twenty dollar bill clipped to it: "Mission accomplished. Dropping south. Thanx for 6 pack." Underneath he had added: "Socialists own all means of production. Capitalists provoking revolution." It was signed with a crude sketch of a shark, followed by his phone number.

She checked the refrigerator.

Yes, the beer's gone—let them have it.

The thermos jug with his toothbrush was gone from the bathroom. The real news was that young Mike's pajamas, which always hung in the bathroom unused, were gone and his toothbrush, too. She checked his bedroom. His clothes were gone, and also his boom box, a large and heavy radio of which he was proud. One of the four plastic bags she had put out for him was still on the bed but the others were gone.

So his dad has actually taken some responsibility for him!

She felt mostly relief along with hurt that her son had not said goodbye.

It's no surprise, as he'd be scared I'd start up about school down there, and I would have. Michael might not even enroll him. Well, if he misses a few months it won't be the end of the world. If I don't hear by Christmas I'll go down and bring him back. In the meantime, I'll have a vacation.

She poured herself a cup of coffee, sharpened three red pencils, lit a cigarette and settled down to spend half the night correcting exams.

She let her feelings take over the next afternoon in Martha's office.

"I got rid of him," she said, raising her chin and lightly drumming her fingers on the arms of the chair.

Martha let this arrogant remark hang in the air for a moment and then commented, "You sound satisfied."

After a pause, Billie said, wearily, "Wouldn't you be, after all these years of trying to get some help from his father? I deserve a chance to be alone with Christopher and concentrate on my work. In fact, it would serve Mikey right if I went to live with Christopher, so when he comes home he won't find me."

"You want to move in with Christopher?"

"No, not really. But the kid could've said goodbye. It would serve him right to come back and not find me home."

"But you are the parent." Martha sat stiffly upright. "You provide the stability of a home." There was no response. "Are you going to write him?"

"No way. Negative. I've been buying clothes and food and sports equipment for that thankless brat long enough. I've held his head while he threw up because of wanting money, and I'm glad to get rid of him. He can't go too far away for me. Give me a break!"

Martha heard the genuine plea of a parent separating from a child, a mixture of pain and relief. Her tone became softer. "Are you angry at me, too?"

"You preach about motherhood, that's why. You always moralize and tell me what to do—make a home, write to him . . ."

"I recognize that you've done a faithful job."

"Nobody recognizes what it's like to raise a kid alone."

"You've told me how hard it was to take care of him when he was younger."

"Yeah, I made all kinds of arrangements—nursery school, sitters at my house, at their house, you name it. The time spent making arrangements was wasted and I hated every minute of it."

"Yet you persisted and that's a big plus."

"I didn't want to give him up."

"So how long will it be before you miss him?"

"Well, maybe Christmas. That's one day I'm nice to him."

Softly, Martha said, "Is that like your own mother?"

"Hah, you should have seen her, if you think I'm tough. She never gave gifts, except at Christmas. And then she gave my older sister the most, more than me and my brother put together. When she died, my sister ran away, and my brother and I were separated and put in orphanages. After he was killed on his bicycle, my aunt sent me to a Catholic boarding school. The nuns made a scholar out of me and I was on my own. No family. And I never cried."

"Maybe you should, now."

Billie's eyes became bright with tears. "Yes, I should, after the week I've had!" She wiped her face with a savage gesture and shot Martha a hostile look, then rose from her chair, grabbed her jacket and at the door blurted out, "See what you've made me do!" The noise of the door's slamming was followed by the pounding of her boots in the hall.

Martha sighed deeply. "See what you've made me do!" rang in the room.

Well, I have ten minutes before Ursula arrives so I'll do some yoga.

She spread her mat on the floor and started exercising, but her thoughts didn't switch to Ursula.

Poor Billie! This isn't the first time I've failed to get her to explore her feelings about her mother. Brimming with anger and excitement, she dramatizes daily events to cover up her persistent sense of rejection. She can't let herself feel vulnerable. Her need for recognition has been only partially met by shining in the classroom. When she manages to suppress her violence she still doesn't explore her own feelings. Bright as she is, she'll probably never understand the negative view she has of me, transferred from her mother. But it's progress that she can admit gratitude to the nuns. She also found a peaceful way of getting a vacation from the responsibility of Mike.

And the tears are good.

13

Who Needs It?

Michael swept the cactus needles out of his van before he left Billie's parking lot. He felt lonely. His rare plants had taken nurturing, some of them for years, and he had grown fond of them. He was pleased with his financial gain, but it didn't make up for everything.

I'd figured on making sales to Billie's friends and neighbors, but it paid off to go to the florists in the City. Lucky I thought of that. The guy I found was a pro and appreciated my babies—a good gay goy guy. Billie would like that phrase! Glad I was able to leave her twenty dollars for the hospitality.

He roared his engine out onto the street.

I'll check the gas and oil and water and everything after I get out of this area and should be south of Richmond before midnight. I'll park and sleep at the same spot I did on the way north. I'm running late because it took a helluva long time to get back to Billie's from the City. If I'd planned it right this morning, I could've skipped returning to Long Island, but until I was paid I couldn't give Billie a cash token of gratitude. And also the three babies I'd promised her. She got some real beauties, not exactly Saguaros but I'm fond of little ones. Luckily I remembered I'd promised them just when I was unloading the van after I was paid. Nobody could say I'm not entitled to keep out three small ones as my tip, with all that extra work I did on labels. Now I've got a long weekend of driving ahead, to be back at work on Tuesday. No sweat, I feel rested. To my surprise, I enjoyed the visit, especially seeing young Mike.

Fatherhood was never my bag but I gotta admit it's good to see the kid growing up. He got some damn fine genes from me—good health, intelligence, not bad looks, good sense of humor. Of course Billie's genes are okay too, but she's uptight on efficiency and all that college preparatory stuff. She's in high gear on twelve cylinders. So how come she manages to be so sexy? She has that young Christopher in tow. Okay, he likes it. I'm five years older than her, she must be five years older than him. What the hell, it's their life. I wouldn't want to work that hard myself.

New York's too energized, everyone running around and saying everything twice. It could kill you. They don't seem to get any more across to each other than down South where people drawl and yet you hear them. My old girlfriend Henrietta didn't talk much. She was just as quiet and soft and fat as ever.

Last Friday night with her will hold me for a while. Anyhow, who needs it?

He pulled the sixpack of beer closer on the front seat, popped the tab on a can, and took a big gulp.

Nice and cold. Mike-baby was asleep when I left this morning, and he isn't home yet. His mother will get after him, it's after six o'clock. He was interesting last night, talking technical stuff about computers. He's apparently showing the shop teacher all about them, and reading up on their languages, and his mother doesn't even know. He says he likes math, too. He wasn't interested in going with me to Florida. I had to say goodbye to him before I got paid, and luckily I still had exactly twenty bucks left to give him. I'm glad I promised to send him a hundred if he ever needs it, if he writes me how to get it to him without her finding out. I told him I'd leave my phone number with her, and I didn't forget. Stuck it on her refrigerator.

He took the exit for the Verrazano Bridge.

14

The East Wall Beats on the West Wall

Ursula waited on the stoop for August to arrive to drive her home. Having just told Dr. Kaufman that she wished August would commit suicide, she was trying to think of something pleasant, and recalled that Robert in her poetry class had said she had "bone beauty, lit from within." A west wind was blowing, and she touched the barrette at the top of her head which kept her heavy long hair severely pulled up all around.

All my life my curly red hair made me look like a tomboy and now, even if it's getting gray, I'll wear it as I like. This "crested grebe" look shows my ears but never mind, my beauty is within.

A poetry class had been her refuge for the past several years. After a lifetime of writing, she'd finally seen something of hers published, not a poem but a study of another poet, in a journal brought out by the class. It had been mailed to her at home.

If only I had someone to share it with! My eyes are so bad now that I can't go to class, and anyhow we can't afford the tuition. Blaine's a good daughter and she and her husband used to pay it, but they're paying now for my therapy, to adjust me to my eye trouble. How I miss the poetry class! Where *is* August? I hate waiting.

She strained to read Dr. Kaufman's shingle.

All I can see is P-S-Y-C-H at the beginning and A-P-I-S-T at the end. My eyes are getting worse. Dr. Kaufman wants me to keep on writing poetry and rely on visual memories for inspiration. But writing is a much vaster undertaking than that. Destroyer and Preserver, hear, oh hear!

She strained in scrutiny of a short young woman, obviously pregnant, who had walked up the steps and was ringing the doorbell. Ursula guessed she was Dr. Kaufman's next patient. They smiled at one another but the buzzer immediately unlocked the door and she went in without speaking. August, stiff with age, mounted the steps, peering into her face, his brow creased in its usual frown under his parted hair. To Ursula it looked like mildewed straw. She took his arm, saying, "Where were you? I had to wait."

"I was held up in traffic," he said coldly. He guided her safely into the passenger seat and was starting the motor when there was a tap on the window. Dr. Kaufman was waving a small paper at him. He rolled the window down and listened impatiently.

"I'm giving you another copy of the prescription since your wife says she hasn't been getting this medication." She reached in and held the prescription in front of his eyes.

"It'll be taken care of," he said, putting it in his pocket.

"Any pharmacy can fill it. It's important that she start taking it soon and regularly." He was silent.

Ursula said, "Okay!" but he quickly rolled the window closed. He drove off, both of them looking straight ahead and not speaking. Anger hung between them as it had since Sunday when Ursula had accidentally broken his favorite shaving mug, a birthday gift to him long ago from Blaine when she was little. The mug was ceramic with a green frog at the bottom, tiny but real-looking. He'd not responded when Ursula apologized. She tried to put the pieces together but failed and after weeping, muttered to herself, "Stupid ugly mug. That's what he is too." Now in the car, she had the same thought.

Auqust was irked that his wife had told the doctor she'd had no medicine. As he drove toward home through the Midtown Tunnel he pressed the accelerator in jerky spurts.

Always criticizing. Comes from psychotherapy. I don't hold with these mind doctors, treating the body with chemicals. Women become addicts. The mind can cure itself.

Arthritis pain in his heel raised the pitch of his voice. "Why did that busybody doctor march out with this prescription?"

"Because you didn't get the first one filled."

"I did get it filled," he said, rationalizing to himself that aspirin would do the trick. "I'll give you a pill tonight."

"Good." Ursula closed her eyes. When they got home she went upstairs without a word. She no longer helped in the kitchen because he preferred her safe in her room, not stumbling about.

August, after a long career of teaching chemistry, was a somewhat begrudging care-giver but did his best to cook. For dinner that evening he fried pork chops and boiled potatoes and fixed a tray for Ursula. He took it upstairs and after stopping in his own room to add an aspirin, carried it across the hall to her where she lay on her bed, silent. Back downstairs he ate his own meal while watching the news. On his way to his bedroom later he found the tray outside her door, the aspirin gone but the food untouched. He took it down to the refrigerator.

I'll eat it in the morning. Pioneers swore by meat and potatoes for breakfast. Apple pie would be nice, too, but Ursula doesn't bake these days.

Upstairs again, he washed his face and carefully hung the towel over a spare rod which was a reminder of his younger son, Benny, the only one of their children who hadn't married and left home by the time they had bought the house.

Smart young Benny got a scholarship to Stanford and stayed back West. He's married now and has a good job. It's his wife who sends us the Christmas cookies Ursula raves about—Benny says their neighbor's kids call her the "Cookie Lady." He admits that he misses the East, so if he wants he can buy the others' share of this house when Ursula and I are gone. Blaine would be happy to have him close, she was a big sister to him. The odd thing is she's homesick now for the West! I'm going to leave her boy Timmie my chemistry books and the lesson plans I'm revising. They might be published, like my dissertation, but he can have the originals. Blaine and her husband will see that he gets them. We can't complain. Ursula is hard to live with because of her eyes, but there's a chance they'll improve with surgery, safer for her than any mind drug.

He sat on his bed and squeezed and relaxed his toes, hoping the arthritis pain wouldn't keep him awake.

My new copy of *Scientific American* came today, and tomorrow I'll put good morning energy into reading it.

Suddenly he recalled not having cleaned out the frying pan, and went downstairs and washed it.

It pins a person down, being chauffeur, housekeeper and nurse, but I have to do it. My Social Security and pension from teaching will take care of Ursula if need be. She never knew the strain I was under when I stuck to teaching college chemistry in New York City. I didn't feel old when I retired in Seattle, but I aged here in these last ten years of rivalry and prejudice. New York City administrators are hard on part-time colleagues with a German background. I was always assigned the most out-of-date labs to teach in, and still the kids got down to hard work in chemistry, and scored high.

He lay down, jerked the covers up and said his childhood prayer, *Ich bin klein, mein herz ist rein,/ so shau auf mich, du liebes Jesu lein.*

Ursula, on her way from the bathroom, noted that there was no strip of light showing under his door.

He's being a small child again, talking about his pure heart and asking dear Jesus to sleep beside him. Better Jesus than me. *Amen.*

In the morning August brought her a bowl of oatmeal which she hungrily ate.

How come I told Dr. Kaufman I'll survive alone better than he would? Well, since he's boring me out of my mind, he *should* commit suicide. Like the Japanese, to save face, since our marriage is so miserable and I want a divorce.

Feeling guilty for these thoughts, she groped her way downstairs to say something nice to him. She found him in the dining room, holding a book. "What book is that?"

"It's our old botany field manual. I saw it in your book-case."

"Oh, I need to study it and our flower collection be-cause Dr. Kaufman says visual memories might inspire me. But verbal clues work better, don't you think? When I was able to read, a line of my own sometimes came to me." He was silent. "Read me a story," she wheedled.

"It's not stories, it's scientific descriptions."

"I know that. But stories are hidden in it. Find the part with scary plant names. We marked it when we were in high school."

He found it and began to read. " 'Bull thistle. Dogbane. Skeleton weed. Nodding beggarticks.' "

She interrupted. "Nodding beggarticks! Isn't that great! They grew near our house in Pullman, remember?"

He read on. " 'Madwort. Bindweed. Puncture vine. Nightshade.' "

"Don't skip. It's *'Enchanters'* Nightshade.' "

Impatient at being corrected when he knew he'd read it properly, he demanded, "Shall I go on?"

"Never mind. The plants are all poison, of course."

This thought amused him, and brought one of his rare smiles, prompting her to venture, "I'd like to invite Louise, my friend from the poetry class, to tea tomorrow. Will you place a call for me?"

"Yes," he said in a moderate tone.

She wondered why she'd thought something was wrong.

The next day she sat on the sofa before a low table near Louise, who was reading Ursula's journal article. Impatient to start conversing, Ursula sat nibbling a graham cracker, thinking that her friend, perched at her own insistence on a straight chair, resembled a bluejay.

Finally Louise looked up from the article, admiration on her face. "Ursula, this critique is excellent! When we were assigned to write an imaginary interview with a famous dead poet, I chose Keats and got ideas from Cliff Notes."

"I couldn't look anything up so I just used a small magnifier and studied the poems."

"So all on your own, you got published! How come you chose HD? You write that Hilda Doolittle was always called HD."

"Yes. I thought of doing a woman, and HD appealed to me because she became famous very young. I pretended I'd interviewed her in her teens, trying to make her aware of her strong points. If someone had done that when she was still in Pennsylvania she might be more famous today."

"You say she found fellow poets in England?"

"Yes. She was, briefly, the best known of the Imagists, but later her images lost their radiance."

"A young poet is lucky to get good criticism."

"Any poet is! Yet some poets hold up their own standards—Emily Dickinson comes to mind. Oh, that reminds me—there's a Dickinson poem about a vivid sight I'd look for if I could read."

"Could I find it for you? What was the first line?"

"I can't recall, but the poem is a wish that she'd locked up a beautiful moving cloud in her head to remember."

"A cloud?"

"Yes, a glorious cloud that disappeared."

"I'll look for it."

"Oh, thank you. How I would love to look for it myself!" A tremor went through her as she tried to refill Louise's cup, and the lid of the teapot fell to the floor and broke. "Oh, dear," she wailed, "My eyes have caused a shipwreck, again." She called out in panic, "August!"

He immediately appeared and wiped off the table, then pointedly collected the broken pieces. "Now you've broken the lid of your favorite teapot and made a mess."

Ursula didn't argue. "Louise, this is my husband, August." Her voice nearly failed her, but she went on, "Louise might become an interviewer for the poetry journal."

August didn't reply. Louise said placatingly, "I could never be as good as Ursula."

August remained silent. Ursula became more upset. "I've never been as good as I could have been. I mostly raised the children and saved money. And now I'm going blind." She stopped, then shrieked, "Ikebana, help me!"

August turned to Louise. "Go, please."

Louise stood like a bulwark against his rudeness and asked, "Ursula, how can I get a copy of your article?"

Ursula stood twisting her clasped hands, unable to answer.

August snatched the journal and said, "I'll make a copy for you." He stalked off.

Louise touched Ursula's arm gently and Ursula suddenly felt happy. "He's making a copy for you."

"Does he have a copy machine for his work?"

"No, it's just a toy."

When August came back he thrust a bundle of pages at Louise. "Here." His manner said, "Now you can go."

"Thank you. Goodbye, Ursula. I hope to see you soon," Louise said, hastening out.

August picked up the tea tray angrily. "Now we don't have a decent teapot left. And don't ever ask me again to make copies for your friends."

Ursula said, mildly, "Thank you for copying my article."

"We'll take the cost of the paper out of the food allowance."

Ursula started twisting her clasped hands again. "If *you* want to buy something, we can always afford it. But if *I* break something you scream that it takes food money."

August walked silently to the kitchen.

Ursula crawled up the stairs to her room, tried to get to the toilet, but lost control a second too soon. Disregarding her damp undergarments, she went into her room and threw herself down on her knees before a low bookcase in her bedroom. She pounced on books and hurled them to the floor. When she had emptied one shelf, she started on the second, but stopped short, and spoke aloud, "Where is the wildflower collection? It was right here with the field manual." After a few more seconds of frenzied search, she shrieked, "August!"

He came at once, not showing surprise at the scattered books. Now that Louise was gone he had an attentive air. "Yes?"

"I want the wildflower collection. It's not here!"

"I burned it. The flowers had lost their color and were dry and crumbling to bits."

Ursula's whole body jerked involuntarily. "How can we live without the wildflower collection? We made it so long ago—it was like our first child."

"But how old would that child be now? Over fifty." She threw herself down and hid her face in a pillow, silent. "And now I've got another mess to clean up. You'd better take a bath."

She bathed and went to bed in a sort of automatic trance.

In her restless efforts to sleep she relived the overnight field trip their high school science classes took when they were seniors. A world of memory opened up.

In the bus going east she sat beside her friend Margaret, barely aware they were leaning against each other the whole night. But when she woke it wasn't Margaret she was leaning on but August, the senior boy she had long eyed from afar! Blushing, she sat up and looked back. Margaret had moved to sit beside Fred.

August climbed over me to sit by the window!

"I didn't know where I was," she said shyly. "But I know you, you're August."

He smiled. More confident, she flashed him a quick look and combed and braided her hair. He didn't watch openly but she saw how aware he was, leaning away when she crooked her elbow to wind her braid. She felt awkward, having to wear unladylike knickers, but they were required on this trip because of rattlesnakes. August pulled his knee out of the way when she tied her boots.

"Where are we?" she asked.

"Along the Snake River." He showed her a map. "See how the river twists and turns? That's why it's the Snake."

"I thought it was named for rattlesnakes."

"It wasn't, but if Windows says rattlesnakes, watch out for rattlesnakes! He says he grew up around here."

Their teacher had been given the nickname "Windows" because he'd given them a pop quiz on the very first day of class, asking questions about how many windows there were in the school building and what they looked like. Later he lectured on the need for good powers of observation in science. August had gotten the best score, missing only one ornamental window in the tower, the one Ursula recalled most vividly and had sketched from memory on her answer sheet.

She asked, "Did Windows say what town he came from?"

"He said Starbuck. It's not far from here."

She found it. "Starbuck's a funny name, but at least it's English. Here's a town named Wawawei."

"They have some pretty good Indian names all over," he said. "I like Pataha."

"But we have better ones, don't we? Snohomish and Skykomish and Snoqualmie. I guess Puyallup's the best."

"How about Walla Walla?" She smiled, and he explained. "Thousands of years before Europeans arrived, the Indians migrated across the Bering Strait and named everything. When the whites came they kept a lot of names they learned from their Indian guides."

Sincerely and without flirtatiousness, she said, "You're the smartest boy in our class."

Embarrassed, he squeezed his eyes tight shut for a second and then said evenly, "Lewis and Clark explored through here. We'll soon be going down to the river to Clarkston, Washington. Right across the river is Lewiston, Idaho."

"It's romantic, isn't it? Towns with those great names right across the river from each other. Better than Walla and Walla!" He laughed.

The view from the top of the Lewiston Grade was so spectacular that Ursula whispered, "Windows said it's one of the seven wonders of the West."

As the bus descended, their eyes remained glued to the curves of the road. August stretched back so she could lean past him to see out the window. She found his taut body steadying.

"It's a holy land," she murmured and his body grew more taut still. When the steepest part of the descent was over she moved back from the window, until he spotted a golden eagle in flight and reached his arm around her shoulders to pull her forward to look. She saw it and looked up at him, eyes full of wonder. He closed his eyes and lowered his head so his cheek briefly touched hers. When she leaned back in her seat, his arm was still around her. She sat rigid, her heart taking funny leaps.

In the years that followed, she believed the flight of that eagle had determined her destiny.

The bus driver gave them a rest stop, and the students climbed back on the bus to eat the breakfasts they had brought from home. Margaret returned to get her food from the overhead rack and sat down by Ursula again. As Ursula stood and took down her sandwiches, she saw August sitting back beside Fred and knew hunger alone wasn't responsible for her sudden feeling of incompleteness.

Finally they disembarked into dazzling sunshine and stood at the top of a long hillside sloping gradually down to the enormous river. They stared at its wide, quiet flow southward into the distance. A majestic sight. Trees and flowers grew abundantly along draws, making notches in the banks where spring streams had flowed riverward.

Ursula was glad to be on her feet, and when Windows announced, "Watch for rattlesnakes!" she felt better about wearing knickers. As if on cue, August turned up at her side.

The trip's purpose varied according to topics chosen by the students. August, Ursula, Margaret and Fred were looking for wild flowers, many unknown to them. August, carrying his father's old German camera, said he was stalking the *phlox longifolia*. "Would you like to accompany me?" he asked Ursula.

"Yes, I would," she replied, and followed him, carrying the field manual in which they checked sego lilies, yellow bells, wild hyacinths, canyon heather, bitterroot, Indian paint brush, wild larkspur and more. With mouths dry and faces burning, they photographed and carefully pressed flowers, leaves and seedpods. They worked closely side by side and agreed to collaborate on their collection.

Finally, they rested under an alder tree until Margaret and Fred, who had been out of sight for some time, caught up with them. The other two had not collected nearly as many specimens, and Ursula shared some with them, an act which later earned her a scolding from her collaborator.

Back at school, they spent the next three weeks mounting their dried flowers. August carefully spelled out their Latin names and Ursula inscribed them in calligraphy and decorated the pages with sketches of the habitat, based on his photographs. One sketch, copied from a published picture of the dreaded rattlesnake, she labelled "that narrow fellow in the grass we didn't see." She showed it to her English teacher who complimented her on knowing Emily Dickinson's poetry.

The golden eagle she and August had watched remained their secret.

The collection brought them school fame, as well as teasing for the time they spent together on it, and Windows praised it at their graduation (without mentioning

Ursula) when he presented August with the medal for excellence in science.

August finished two years of college. Ursula spent time typing his term papers, and preparing a hope chest of household linens. Joking friends added baby diapers. They became engaged.

On the strength of his being hired to teach in a nearby elementary school they planned a wedding in the community church, for which she made herself a long white wedding dress of dimity. A snapshot showed her in it, looking radiant and poised, cutting the wedding cake and smiling up at August, who wore his first black suit. When the preacher described her as "the perfect helpmate" she felt a stab of envy—August was being regarded as a young professional with a future and she wasn't.

The wedding gift she liked best was a booklet of her own poems, bound in yarn and titled *Poems by Ursula*, written as compositions for her favorite English teacher, who had copied them and printed inside the front cover, "KEEP IT UP!"

This booklet, with the wedding snapshot inside, had been kept beside a group of thin notebooks of poems to which she had steadily added for nearly fifty years. She grew to believe she should have a book of some of them printed, but in the poetry class there was agreement that published poetry was mainly at the expense of the author. August, of course, would spend money on a Golden Wedding, which she dreaded.

August's first job had been as teacher-principal of a two-room school. From the start he worked toward a college degree, setting a life pattern of combining teaching and academic advancement.

Ursula too was ambitious. She bore four healthy children and joyfully raised them to develop their imaginations as well as their intellects. There wasn't much money for rent, so they lived in unimproved houses where she pumped water from wells, washed diapers by hand, and cooked on wood stoves. She also studied wild flowers, birds, dragonflies, clouds and chrysalises, and made them her entry into poetry.

Always a strict man, August was respected by his students and devoted to his family, unfailingly earning enough to support them. Though singularly unable to bring Ursula anything frivolous like a box of chocolates or a Valentine, and unmindful of her hunger for learning, he tried to be a good husband. Often he helped her cope with their Spartan life style. Instead of toys, he brought the children gifts like good wool blankets or knapsacks for carrying books and lunches. By stages he moved up to teaching in large consolidated high schools in country settings, until they moved to Seattle where he taught science in a large high school and also became a candidate for a Ph.D. at the university.

Ursula became the superintendent of a large apartment building, where they lived rent-free in a spacious basement apartment. The children helped by cleaning the hallways and keeping the yard. Ursula, busy making the girls' dresses, often left her sewing machine to inspect their work. August spent evenings, weekends and summers on his doctoral studies, while she ran things smoothly, monitoring each child's schoolwork and studying their books on her own to learn languages and history. Confidently, after teaching teenage Blaine to cook, she turned over the kitchen to her and took a job at the university library, where she spent her lunch hours studying the newest poets.

A tenant who was moving to Alaska gave them an old car in which during vacations she drove her brood to climb Mt. Rainier or camp on the shore of Whidby Island. While they were away August took over the care of the building, not an onerous task as tenants stayed a long time.

The first break in the family, sad but natural, came when Blaine finished college and married Harry Watson, who had come to Seattle for summer school. He liked the West and would have stayed if it weren't for a family manufacturing business in New York which assured his income.

August received his degree and became Dr. Friedrich, but remained a high school teacher in order to achieve the pension he was soon due. Retirement brought new opportunities, and a desire to live in the East where Blaine was. With their youngest child, Benny, they moved to Long Island and, for the first time, bought a house. August's Ph.D. dissertation, which dealt with science education, qualified him to teach college chemistry. Although in a low rank in New York City University's hierarchy, he taught for a decade before reaching the age of mandatory retirement. Then he acquired a new career, taking care of Ursula.

Today, lying in her bed, she felt superior to him.

He knows the formulas for things and keeps his nose in them, but as a human being he's growing stale. To him, the universe has precise truths. As a poet, I know that human truths are often both panoramic and precise. Ocean and land masses are vast, but life starts small and private. The two cells from which Blaine came were minuscule, but how huge she seemed, being born! The pain. The exhilaration! Each birth had been the same. Two daughters, two sons, mysteriously created.

The gigantic and small each has its place, sometimes reversed in importance. Living in a family—repeatedly cooking and eating and taking baths and celebrating birthdays—makes human smallness a part of nature's greatness. The poet Gary Snyder said, "The east wall beats on the west wall."

By keeping a balance I learned to win when August assumed I was losing. Now I'll let the loss of the old wildflower book blossom into a new way of seeing. I don't need those pages with crumbling dried flowers, I will see again with the power of my spirit. I can take a new direction, like I did that day on the Snake. The sun-drenched slopes, the great river flowing below . . . And this time I won't need a partner, I'll be free.

The following Wednesday she entered Dr. Kaufman's office carrying a book of Gary Snyder's poetry.

"I persuaded August to get this book at the library because I want to thank you. I tried your idea of remembering visually, and it brought me ideas that 'dizzy the arithmetic of memory,' as Hamlet might say. Will you read some poems to me?"

This was something new to Martha, who said, "I'll try to read a poem or two. But first, tell me, are you taking the medication?"

"Oh, yes, August counts out the pills and I take them." She handed the book to Martha. "You'll see that Snyder knows about disorientation, and also about divine order amidst nature's chaos."

Gamely, Martha stumbled through a poem about a family bathing. Ursula said, "He knows that moist life can emerge even in dusty canyons."

Martha managed to say, "I've never been West."

"I'd like 'Cold Mountain,' please," said Ursula.

Martha read,

> "Cold Mountain is a house
> Without beams or walls.
> The six doors left and right are open,
> The hall is blue sky,
> The rooms all vacant and vague.
> The east wall beats on the west wall—
> At the center nothing."

Ursula asked to hear it again and Martha found it easier the second time, but was puzzled when Ursula clapped in enjoyment and exclaimed, "I am the West Wall!"

15

Is That What Your Shrink Worked Out?

Sandy walked out of Dr. Kaufman's office feeling happy she'd said she wasn't going to be married, and why.

I'm not sure just where she stands on that, but she liked the macramé basket I made for her plant.

Outside on the stoop the sunlight was warm. She pulled off her sweater and forced it into her portfolio, unintentionally pulling out a piece of orange ribbon. She smiled and reached over and tied a jaunty bow around the chain that held up the shingle. Seeing David standing waiting by his Toyota she waved, and singing "Skip to My Lou" walked carefully down the stairs and over to him. His brown eyes were solicitous as he said, "Hi, Princess. I hope that shrink talked you into marrying me."

"Oh, David, lay off, will you?" She didn't get into the car. "Let's park here a while. Your Princess wants to go to the bookstore—if she can waddle that far."

They strolled arm in arm to the bookstore, where they drifted apart, browsing among the books. She stood checking out books on various crafts until she found one on printmaking and studied it carefully.

Great techniques. I need to own this book. But after that check to Dr. Kaufman, I'm broke. God, I need my own money—that's the secret of being independent. I can let David pay for rent and food, but I have to buy my own art stuff. It's my business. It's me. I'm going to list the worst that could happen if we don't get married, not keep arguing about legalities.

David walked up and looked at her with the radiant smile she evoked in him. He was holding a large book of photographs of the tomb of King Tutankhamen. "Look at this— what an amazing thing, finding it practically undisturbed."

Turning pages, he stopped at a picture of a gold statue depicting the young queen rubbing ointment on the young king.

Sandy moved companionably close to him, "They're a lot like us," she whispered. "Does it say if they had kids? They look so young."

"Being Pharaohs, they could get away with anything. End of story."

Sandy kept him from closing the heavy volume. "The amazing thing about this book, David, is the way it's printed. Look at the marvelous way gold is caught on paper. Printing is a higher art than people realize."

"Yeah. I see that from the prices. Hey, I'm hungry, aren't you? Is there a good quiet restaurant around here?"

"It would save money if we went home."

"I have plenty of money with me."

"Okay. That Greek place with the garden is nice." She showed him the printmaking book. "Please, may I borrow thirty dollars so I can buy this?"

"Sure." He gave her three ten dollar bills and tried to press more into her hand but she refused.

"I'm paying the tax," she said, defiantly. She opened her purse, dumped out her loose change, and counted the nickels and dimes. He waited until she confessed, lamely, "I'll have to borrow two dollars more." David, grinning, gave her five.

During dinner, a song played whose lyric was about the pleasures of dancing at a wedding. David pointedly hummed along.

"Sentimental brute, you're hopeless," she said fondly, lighting a cigarette.

"You shouldn't smoke. Think of the baby."

"I think of it all the time. But I didn't smoke in the shrink's office, so I'm just catching up." She puffed away with bravado.

He scowled. "I'll bet you forgot your vitamin pills, too."

"I didn't forget. They're safe on the kitchen table."

"I'll buy some on the way home. You're supposed to take them with food."

"How did I know we'd eat out? An hour or so won't make a difference."

She often enjoyed his solicitude, but had to guard against the widening of his domain over her. As they walked back to the car, her wedge shoes seemed to chop away at the sidewalk.

On the way home, David persisted, "So what did Dr. Kaufman advise?"

"She believes in marriage. Says it isn't perfect, but the person you marry is probably right for you. But I can't discuss it." Her tone was final.

David sighed and asked no more.

That night in bed she worried that there was a lack of spontaneity in him. After lovemaking, which she desired often during pregnancy, she said, "I'm very happy, aren't you?"

"I would be if we were married."

"Oh, David, try to get over that." She patted him as if he were a child with a nightmare. As he put one arm tenderly over her belly, she felt he was too anxious about the baby.

Alone the next morning she sat down and wrote:

The Worst That Could Happen
If We Don't Get Married

1) If both of us got sick and couldn't work, it would be embarrassing if we had to move in with one of our mothers.

2) If the baby had a terrible health problem we'd have big doctor and hospital bills. But doesn't every couple with a baby have this problem, married or not?

3) People might pity me for not being married. (It might make me a better artist. Or a bitter one.)

4) The worst would be if David turned sour, or our families started to fight. I don't intend to let that happen.

She sat a minute and then wrote "The End" on the paper.

The real story is that if I get my way, the love I'll have for David will bubble in me inexhaustibly. I'll cook for him and take care of his laundry and we'll have fun joking and arguing.

We'll succeed because I'll praise his achievements, and he'll praise mine, and we'll share money and social life. What could change that? And if it changes, why grieve about losing it? In any case, I'll love our baby, breast-feed it, and watch it learn to love me. I'll teach it to laugh and talk and be creative. Plenty of love will just *be* there and for David, too. I'll sing to both of them, "I love you, I love you, and you love me, too."

That evening she confronted David. They went over her arguments and around and around the same points. She smoked, feeling that was a better sign of defiance than throwing a tantrum and screaming. Eleven o'clock came and they skipped the news and continued talking. Sandy declared, "I plan to defend the baby—first from the frustration I would feel if I had to give up my art, and second, from society's hypocrisy."

He slapped the table. "Sandy, I'll tell you what's wrong with you. If you don't give the baby a father, you won't be womanly."

She snorted. "Give the baby a father? Don't be silly. It's up to *you* to give it a father. Whether we're married or not."

"But a *legal* father."

"Legal is what I don't want. Of all our friends is there a single legal father who's any good? Show me one."

"Is that relevant?" David was irritated.

"The best father we know is Jon whose own wife won't agree to a divorce, and he lives with Fran and *her* kids, whose father died. Jon is a wonderful father to them. Legality has nothing to do with it."

"But it's not *womanly* the way you want to do it."

"Isn't that precisely the point? To be womanly is to give in. It's *manly* of you to offer to marry me, though."

This made David angry, as was intended. He marched to the sink and started washing the dishes, his lips compressed in hurt fury.

"What did you hope for, David?" she asked, her voice probing. "I think you hoped I'd trap you, and let you get used to being married without ever *deciding* to do it. That was the *most* noble of your thoughts. In the beginning, you didn't want to consider marriage at all."

"Yeah, I was trapped," he said sarcastically.

"You wanted to be comfortable and then if things went wrong you could claim it was a trap." He didn't answer and she pushed on. "You can't use the excuse of being trapped if we don't get married. That's what really bugs you."

"Is that what your shrink worked out?"

"No! This is my thinking."

"Shrinking."

"No, she's for marriage like all the rest of you cowards."

David changed his tack. "Sandy, our wedding can be fun if we do it now. The baby's showing like crazy, but our parents are glad with us and will share our joy." Sandy melted inside at the word *joy*, but remained quiet. She put the large cooking pots, which David never washed, into the sink, drew water into them and turned off the lights.

They lay separately in bed, hurt and bewildered.

"Lawd, Lawd, gonna cause de death of me," she whispered into her pillow.

The next morning David was his cheerful self. It was so easy to love him; he never sulked. Sandy waited on him at breakfast, singing her mother's old theme song, "That's the story of, that's the glory of *love*." As he started down the building stairs, she grabbed a coat and buttoned it tightly over her short nightgown, walked with him to the subway and kissed him goodbye. It was sunny outside on this fall morning, and as she walked home she sang a song she had learned from her English friend, Danielle, "The Teddy Bear's Picnic," and then "Haida Haida." Once in her building, she hurried up the five flights of stairs and did the breakfast dishes.

Settled down to her new book, one picture sequence made her feel amused at first, then competitive. A lithograph of a fish, head to tail, had been printed from an aluminum plate on which a fish had, in fact, been baked, so its exact shape was clear. The oil had held the ink. Once she had nearly tried this technique herself after baking gingerbread men that left a design in butter on the cookie sheet. It would have been a nice design for kitchen wallpaper, but at the time she had thought she was going bonkers, being domesticated.

I'll bet Blue Danielle will love this book. She's crazy about innovation. Maybe I've been too classical and should innovate more freely from now on, but new techniques aren't enough. I'll use them only to get my ideas across.

I know the next print I'll make. I'll start with a reclining man in the lower left, ready for love—like Michelangelo's David, but lovable, like my David. A lineup of women stretches diagonally down from the upper right, approaching him, one in front of the other, each figure larger than the one before as they near him. The opposite of perspective, more a coming into selfhood. The frontal nudes will be delicate, not shocking, showing woman spirits becoming more real, less shadowy as they come to love. The symbolism is that it's all one woman's different moods, each free, wild, graceful and alluring. The man is always ready for her, generous, welcoming, never changing.

Does it mean that all women are essentially the same? Or that a man will be engulfed *ad infinitum* by the different moods of one woman? Or just that both sexes are trustworthy and strong? The picture will express it, maybe say all of the above. Vigorously. Lovingly.

She got down to work and continued the next day. By Friday afternoon she had finished a sketch that satisfied her.

Celebrating by smoking a cigarette, she said aloud, "So I did it!" and then put the sketch carefully away.

Mom is expecting us to drive out tonight to spend the weekend. The break will be welcome. An advantage of being pregnant is that now she expects us to sleep together. Another plus could be squeezing in a visit to Danielle's. I'll call her, and David and I can drive to her place out on the island. I'll take the book to show her.

That evening, after dinner at her mother's, she slipped downstairs and sat a while looking at her press, secretly anticipating printing her new design.

When she returned to the living room she found her mother and David well into a bottle of Chablis. Judy had on a jumpsuit printed with large fuchsia-pink flowers and gaudy orangey red balloons, and raised a glass in the air, jangling her bracelets. Her hair matched the balloons. "I'm going to put up a bold front, too!"—she made a generous rounded gesture with her arm over her body—"to prove that the mother of the pregnant bride is happy about the baby. I'll wear a hat draped in pink and blue tulle, pink for a girl, blue for a boy—frilly and flouncy. Something to shock 'em, stop all the gossip!"

David laughed heartily. "Right on!"

"What's all this about?" Sandy demanded.

"Wedding rehearsal!" Judy winked mischievously at David.

"Shut up, Mom," said Sandy, cold with anger. She marched out of the room, and called Danielle on the upstairs phone. "Danny, we've got to get out of here. Mom's impossible."

"Come out to a barbecue here on Sunday," Danny said. "I have some new designs to show you. About five o'clock, okay?"

Feeling more cheerful, Sandy returned to the living room where she found a subdued pair. They made plans to go to Temple in the morning and to walk later to the library to see a show by local artists. Nothing more was said about a wedding.

On the way to Danielle's in Sea Cliff, Sandy briefed

David. "If Danny's boss Sol is there, it won't be dull. He's bright and funny and very artistic. They run an interior decorating firm, very *avant garde*, out in Huntington. He's gay and does the cooking."

"Oh, no!" David groaned. "We'll get nothing but salad!"

"I can't believe your stereotypical thinking."

Danielle lived in a two-story frame house trimmed in white gingerbread woodwork. It stood on a hill overlooking a road. The front door was open and Sandy was relieved to catch a good strong odor of barbecue sauce. Two little girls, dressed in identical long Kate Greenaway dresses, tripped down the stairs and laughingly led the way through the hall to the back porch and pointed to their mother and a man at a barbecue grill on the lawn. Danielle waved and walked toward them across the grass. She wore flowing blue cotton slacks which showed off her tall model's figure and Sandy watched David's face light up at seeing her. She hugged Sandy, then David. Sandy observed her leisurely way of catching her breath and widening her eyes when she looked at David.

I'm not jealous, she thought, just aware of Danny's beauty. Her large eyes and hollow cheeks really do remind me of the Blessed Damozel in Dante Gabriel Rossetti's painting, with its mixture of expressions. I didn't catch it in my ethereal sketch of her.

"Come meet Sol at the grill," Danielle said. "He's dizzier than usual, trying to get the charcoal right."

Sol, a large, bearded man of about thirty-five, didn't look up from tending his grill. They stood and watched as he moved chunks of charcoal together and blew on them. Danielle moved to him and caught her fingers in his long hair, turning his head to face them. Finally he nodded, taking Sandy's hand and giving his left hand to David. "I'm Sol Blakowsky," he said, gazing down at them.

Sandy managed to say, "I'm Sandy Lieberman and this is David Steinberg." She knew David was embarrassed about her pregnancy and felt helpless while Sol continued to hold their hands. Then as if it were a mystic rite, he brought their hands together in front of him, laid David's over Sandy's and enclosed them sandwich-fashion between his own. He had an inscrutable expression, mask-like, his eyes veiled. Danielle stood still behind him.

Sandy thought, Do they think they're performing a marriage ceremony?

When Danielle gave Sol a push he dropped their hands and turned back to his grill. Danielle, with a shrug, said, "Sol's more involved in Being than Knowing." Sandy concluded that Sol could be taken as a sort of guru.

A round-faced young woman dressed simply in a pink blouse and black skirt came across the lawn carrying a tray, followed by the little girls.

Danielle said, "Sandy and David, this is Sonia, my helper, with my little angels, Trilby and Christina." The little girls' curtsies were very brief, as their mother took a bottle from the tray and waved it, announcing, "This is the wine Sol brought us. Let's sit down and enjoy it!"

They sat in lawn chairs, Danielle poured wine, and Sonia, standing quietly, watched as the little girls walked around serving hot canapés. "Anchovy binger fiscuits and puffed Roquefort" the girls sang in unison, obviously coached.

Sonia corrected them. "Finger biscuits."

"I like binger fiscuits," said Sol.

Sonia said, "Trilby and Christina helped bake these!"

"How clever you are," Sandy said kindly to the twins.

"Ice cream time!" Sonia said to them, and led them to sit at a table near the back door.

Sandy asked, "Is she a maid or a nanny?"

"Both. She's my helper. I can have a career because of Sonia." She glanced at Sol, her eyes twinkling. "Also help with Sol's new film."

"You're making a film?" said David. "What's it about?"

"I'll call it *'Taking a Chance on Change,'*" was the prompt reply.

Danielle laughed and said softly, "A new title."

"I figured you'd like it better than *My Hypnotist Was a Ventriloquist's Dummy*," Sol replied, with a teasing glance at Danielle.

She's so beautiful, Sandy thought. What a pity if she loves someone on whom her sexy warmth is lost.

But Danielle didn't seem to want Sol's attention in that way. "That hypnotist thing was witty, but too far out," she told him, and then said to David, "Sol is making a video about the development of personality from womb to tomb, trying to catch life-defining moments."

Sol picked it up, "Like just before you're born, or about to be hypnotized, or fall in love—crucial moments of life."

"And I," said Danielle, "have been his guinea pig."

"You've been my co-producer," asserted Sol.

Sandy was trying to think of what to say and was glad when David asked, "So you're making a film about pregnancy, among other things?"

"Yes. Unfortunately, I didn't know Danny when she was pregnant." He and Danielle shared an ironic smile.

"Can I audition for a part?" asked Sandy with a laugh. "I could be a mother about to go on welfare."

David tried to smile but frowned, and asked, "How do you determine a life-defining moment?"

"Well, obviously being born is one," Sol replied. "You can't film the baby's point of view, but you can lead up to it, showing its willingness to be conceived nine months earlier, and the way it sends the mother into labor, particularly if it's a boy. My film's most compelling moment will show the parameter of this concept, the baby's indecision about coming out, or when to present. There are many parameters."

Sandy, put off by his assumptions about birth, asked, "Have you made films before about the thoughts of interior organs?"

There was a pause, until David tactfully said, "You think the baby *decides* to be born?"

"Yes. The way a snail decides to have a spiral design on its shell."

"But *does* the snail decide that?" David asked.

"We film makers will never know. It lives with the decision. It ingests, locomotes and respirates with that mark on it."

"Living things have to live with what they've inherited," David offered. "To state the obvious."

Sol went into a new realm. "I've decided to leave out first communions and Bar Mitzvahs because they're parents' decisions. But deciding something on one's own—which may come at a very early age, long before religious participation—is important. I've been watching the twins." They all glanced over at the table where the girls were sitting quietly with Sonia. "Trilby wants whatever her mother wants, but Christina's my subject. She takes a chance on change a dozen time a day. I want to work with her long enough to *see* her making a decision, deciding to decide something, and show by the music that it's one of life's sacred moments. It should be a decision that affects her life later and maybe her twin's life. Certainly her mother's."

"Do little girls make such big decisions?" David asked.

"Oh, yes. Christina makes them every day. Sometimes hatefully."

"She usually compromises," said Danielle.

"With Sonia, yes. With you, no. We'll know more about her psychic changes when I get them on film. But right now I have to season our steaks." He busied himself at the grill.

Danielle rose gracefully and picked up the wine bottle, at the same moment reaching with her other hand and decisively taking Sandy's matches out of her hand, preventing her from lighting another cigarette. Calmly she poured wine all around, then touched David's shoulder with a brief but firm grip, and said, "I forget what line of work you're in, David."

"I work in a social agency which helps people with muscular disorders."

"Are you a doctor?" asked Sol, one craftsman to another.

"No, I'm in fundraising."

Proud of David, Sandy said, "When they have their annual big promotion on television, he's vice president of everything."

"I bet in your work you've seen people decide to decide about their future lives," Danielle said.

"Yes," David replied. "If that's what Sol's driving at. Kids with muscular disorders have to decide if living is worth it, and decide again and again even when it gets harder. Seeing that, you feel more alive yourself."

Sol was turning steaks, and Sandy, to make sure he was listening, cried out, "That's a wonderful way to put it! I like that, David." David looked pleased. Sandy turned to Sol. "You mentioned hypnotism. Are you into that too?"

"A bit. A gimmicky bit. I have a sequence where I keep the camera focused on a light and twirl the light to produce a hypnotic effect. It's not guaranteed to have a far-reaching effect in real life. I used to have a shrink who was seriously using hypnosis and after I observed what he did, I figured the main thing was getting people to concentrate on what they really want. I could stop your smoking, Sandy," he asserted, "without knowing any more than I do right now."

"If you could stop her from smoking . . . " David began.

But Sol turned abruptly back to his grill and cut in, "Time to get your steaks!"

"Oh, good!" Using both arms, Sandy pulled herself from the chair and moved to the picnic table. She had nearly lost her temper at Danielle's snatching her matches, but now was glad she hadn't lit a cigarette.

After their meal they moved inside to the living room for coffee and for what Sol called a friendly peace pipe. He lit a hand-rolled cigarette, drew on it deeply and offered it to David, who shook his head. Sandy said, "No thank you, I prefer my usual." Danielle drew on it and passed it back to Sol who took a long toke and turned on his video tape. It dealt with an old man in a hospital in a way that Sandy found electrifying and beautiful, not painful.

"He decided to die," Danielle murmured. "Sol really caught that on film."

David had had enough about film. "Where's the bathroom?"

"Top of the stairs," said Danielle.

He left. Sandy waited a minute and then went out to the hall, intercepting him as he returned. "David, couldn't you find a patient for Sol to use in his film?"

"Maybe," David said. Looking very serious, he caught her by both forearms, staring into her eyes. "Would you let him try to cure you of smoking?" Sandy grimaced, but nodded. She forced a grin when David led her back to Sol saying, "Here's a smoker who wants to quit."

Sol went into action and positioned a lamp which he could turn on and off in regular sequence. He told Sandy to concentrate on watching the light while listening closely to him. He was beginning to speak in a hushed voice when little Christina ran in and grabbed Danielle around the hips. Danielle bent over her daughter with a look of apology at Sol, who sat down to sulk, annoyed at the interruption. Sandy felt ridiculous. Fortunately, Sonia appeared and soothingly removed the child. Sandy took advantage of the pause to glance at David searchingly. She felt she was being sacrificed, and that he should be involved. He nodded encouragement.

Sol stood. "Now, Sandra, this is quite simple. As the lamp flickers I want you to picture standing between two lush rows of green leaves growing. Many, many, very, very green leaves. Picture one green leaf coming toward your face, larger and larger until your whole field of vision is green."

Sandy nodded.

"Now you see that leaf turning yellow. Now brown. It

shrivels and starts to burn. It's a tobacco leaf. As it burns, its evil smell gets into your lungs, your eyes. Your teeth are dirty. Your eyes sting. Your lungs are yellow and brown. They become shriveled. Your breath smells foul. You cough and the baby inside you wants to cough. Now I, Sol, and also David and Danielle, want you to be clean again, all through. Clean. Red blood, white teeth, a clean body for a clean baby."

Sandy drowsily heard him repeat over and over, "A clean body for a clean baby." To her it could have been two or twenty minutes later when he finally paused. "When you wake up you won't want to smoke," he said, in a final tone. He turned off the lamp. "Okay, you can think about something else now." He turned to Danielle and said quite amiably, "I have to go. I'll take your car and leave you the van so you can show Sandy your sculptures."

Oh, God, Sandy thought. I wish David cared about *my* work like that. After the back door banged behind Sol, she said softly, "I don't know if he's cured me of smoking, but I feel close to you all."

"I want you to be healthy and clean," said Danielle, leaving for the kitchen.

"So do I," said David.

"Okay, I'll really try if you'll do something for me, David. Stop thinking about getting married."

"I'll try."

To protect her time with her friend, Sandy followed her into the kitchen. "Danny, I want to see your new sculptures."

"Sure. Let's just clean up a bit here first—I don't want to impose on Sonia. Did you bring the book on printmaking?"

"Yes," said Sandy, "David, will you please get my book from the car? And my vitamins?"

David brought them and the Sunday *Times*, which he took out to a lawn chair. After they cleared the kitchen, the women looked at Sandy's book and then walked together out to Sol's van.

"Our firm got the contract to furnish a house in the Hamptons, and I designed two murals for the living room, each three feet square, framed the same and with the same motif. One's done in sandcasting in a spiral like a snail's shell, and the other is like the spiral of the galactic nebulae, done in quilting."

"You're really into spirals!" exclaimed Sandy, laughing.

"They're very religious," said Danielle, seriously. "A basic pattern in our universe." She opened the van and the setting sun brought out the highlights and shadows of the sculptures. "They need to be in the same room for the effect," Danny said.

Sandy studied them soberly and exclaimed, "They're powerful! I like their being the same size and color, one in hard surface and the other in soft. They complement each other."

Danielle nodded, not smiling. "I'm getting paid tomorrow when I deliver them and I've already bought an old car in expectation." She closed the van and they joined David. "Since you'll soon be parents, you'll understand that it's bedtime story time. You can stay if you want."

"We have to leave anyhow," said David.

As they drove home, Sandy said seriously, "I want to be like Danny, a good mother and at the same time succeed in my art."

David seemed not to hear. "Tomorrow's the day Sharon and I are driving to Atlantic City. We have to arrange a lot of details, evening entertainments, facilities for workshops. It's a resort and yet I should look businesslike."

"Well, it's fall foliage time now, a lot of browns and greens. I suggest your tan gabardine pants, brown sports jacket and that burnt orange tie."

The next morning when he was dressed, he said, "I'm a tree, with foliage. Guess my season." He wiggled his fingers in the air as if dropping leaves.

"Don't expect me to *fall* for that," Sandy said promptly, "and it's too early in the morning to harvest your corn."

They laughed. He kissed her goodbye appreciatively and left, feeling clever and ready for the day's adventure.

After finishing her coffee, she realized that she hadn't lit a cigarette since Sol hypnotized her, and knew she'd never want to smoke again. She rubbed her hand lovingly over her abdomen, thinking of the sacred life growing sweetly in her clean body.

On Tuesday she still hadn't smoked. While she was having coffee after lunch, she recalled how David had thought her not wanting to get married was supported by Dr. Kaufman, and asked if it was something her shrink worked out.

Actually, she seemed to favor marriage, and in any case, didn't work anything out. She wouldn't let me do macramé, which would mean I'd smoke. Doesn't she care if I smoke? My friends care. They care about me and the baby.

She went to the phone and dialed Dr. Kaufman. When the answering machine came on, she spoke clearly. "This is Sandra. I'm not able to come on Wednesday. I know I'm giving only one day's notice and you require two, so if you can't make an exception this time, bill my mother at the address I gave you. I'm discontinuing therapy."

She worked all day on her sketch, looking forward to showing it to Danielle as soon as she could print it.

16

Too Sweet for Your Own Good

David took the subway Monday morning to meet Sharon for the trip to Atlantic City. After a brisk walk from the Riverdale stop, he found the building, buzzed her apartment, and waited in the spacious lobby.

He felt reassured about his clothing choice when she emerged from the elevator wearing a tan suit livened by a scarlet scarf. Just five feet tall, she was lively and friendly.

They descended to her Mercedes in the building's basement garage. She patted her briefcase. "David, I have some paper work to do, my bank balance and some office stuff. Will you drive first? I'll drive the last half." She sat in the passenger seat.

"My pleasure." He took the wheel, following her directions to the main road. She got to work, sorting checks on top of her briefcase. David felt pleased to be in charge.

It's good that I studied the map. Driving a Mercedes *is* a pleasure. A world class horseless carriage if there ever was one. I wonder if she bought it herself? She's five years older than I am and makes only a few thousand more—not much for someone as good as she is. She'd make a lot more in business. Of course, having no dependents helps, but seeing where she lives, I bet her family helps pay her bills. Well, today I'm the silent chauffeur and she trusts me.

He drove for about an hour before he asked, "Are we about halfway?"

"Yes. Take the next exit and after we find some coffee, I'll drive." She tossed her briefcase into the back seat. "David, you seem sort of quiet. What's the matter?"

Grateful for her interest, he was frank. "Sandy and I are quarreling. She doesn't want to get married and I do."

"That's a nice switch."

"Yeah. Viva Women's Lib!"

"Why doesn't she want to get married?"

"Thinks it'll change me, make me a traditional husband."

"Does she think it'll change her too?"

"I guess so. She's afraid of type-casting."

"I agree! Marriage isn't working too well as an institution these days, First marriages anyhow. I'd be afraid of marriage, even if I really loved the right guy."

"Why?"

"Because of restraints that women can't throw off. It's partly our fault, but nobody helps us. In college I took a course in Women's Issues and we studied the workings of power, how women have to band together to make social change. It's awful, the way women are exploited all over the world. In this country, we bump our heads against the glass ceiling, not allowed to rise to top positions. I feel handicapped, too, because even if I kept on working after marriage, I'd not only have an office job but housekeeping. My husband would help some but I'd be basically responsible, and I'd want things at home my way. I see why a lot of working women choose not to really share housework—they don't trust men's slovenliness. So they spread themselves so thin the kids run loose and get into trouble."

"Sandy's an artist and can do her work at home. Artists are introverts."

"M-m-m? At our Christmas party, she seemed very sociable. Don't artists have to have contacts or risk being overlooked? The poetry of the Bedouin men in the desert is often recorded when they come to market. But nobody knows about the equally good Bedouin women's poetry, as the women stay in their tents."

"Well, I won't keep her in the tent."

"Radical feminists have trouble with marriage. Take sex—a woman is supposed to be always ready, and if she isn't, she may have to pretend to enjoy it."

David's thought was *You don't know Sandy!* But he didn't voice it.

Sharon continued, "A lot of wives live under restraints, like they have to feed his relatives on Sundays. If a woman has a job and her husband's company relocates him, she's expected to leave her job and go with him. There's a pretty long list of restraints, more when there are children."

David didn't respond to this.

I might have known she'd side with Sandy. Probably that shrink did, too.

He changed lanes and soon spoke in a calm tone. "Sandy and I have settled a few things, and we're working out some others."

"The point is, they take working out, right? It takes time."

"If you have the time. Sandy's five months pregnant."

"She is?" said Sharon. This was followed by, "David, you might start by saying, *'We're* five months pregnant.'"

"Okay. I can say that. I'm glad about it. It's wonderful. *We're* five months pregnant." Actually, he didn't like the words, and said, "It would sound better to say that in four months we're going to have a kid."

"So?"

"So we get married."

"If Sandy doesn't want to? Does she love you?"

"Yes. She insists on that, and I know she does. And I love her. And we both want the baby. We thought of an abortion in the early weeks but it was a horrible idea to each of us. We think we'll have a really great kid together and be great parents."

"So?"

"So we get married."

"Why?"

"I don't want my baby born a bastard, that's why."

"That's another one of the restraints."

David was miffed. "You're the only person other than Sandy who's said that."

"You just admitted that working out new roles takes time. What if you took time, say a couple of years, without marrying? Then when you did, maybe they'd be worked out. You could put a wedding ring onto Sandy's finger without her wanting to run."

"If she wants to run, how can she be the girl for me?"

"If you want to rush her, how can you be the boy for her?" She added as an afterthought, "Shouldn't we change those terms to woman and man?"

"Okay. But why would my ring be a threat? I love Sandy. I want her to have freedom. I'm easy to live with."

"So if you waited a couple of years from now, would that hurt? Fifty years from now, looking back—who would even remember?"

"Sounds great, but you've got to make your bargains with life as you go along, whether you're ready or not. At my Bar Mitzvah I was the usual age, thirteen, and not ready to say, 'I am a man,' but the calendar said I should say it, and I did. It's like taking a hurdle. If Sandy has the stuff, she'll take this marriage hurdle. Now."

He thought, Why can't I speak this eloquently to Sandy? Explain, not argue.

"David, it could be she needs more time. Time to achieve on her own."

"She *is* achieving—making designs all the time for her prints."

"Prints? What does she do?"

"She's been working on a lithograph with women's figures dancing. She can't do much printing right now because we don't have room for the press in our apartment."

"So that makes it tough for her."

"Yeah. But she wanted to move it out so I could move in. She's drawing designs every day, and can print them at her mother's if she wants. When she isn't drawing she's tying macramé baskets for plants and selling them in Greenwich Village. She ties in a lot of colored ribbons and things like cinnamon sticks and real whole nutmegs for a kitchen. They smell good."

"Great! Tell her I'd like one will you? I have a collection of shells that could be used in a seaside motif."

"I'll ask her to call you about what you want. She's always getting orders."

"I'll bet she likes that better than knitting booties for the baby. Isn't that what our grandmothers did, knit booties?" They laughed. "How did you two meet?"

"We double-dated with a nurse friend of hers whose boyfriend I knew. We fell for each other on our first date, and on most dates afterward went to museums. After the guys she met in art school, I guess she liked my having a job and a car. She kids around about educating me, but I keep her from getting nervous. And I like art."

After they left the highway briefly for coffee, Sharon took the wheel. "David, one way you might get Sandy moving would be to pretend interest in another woman."

"I'd never be convincing."

"Not even if it would help your cause in the long run?"

"I don't like tricks. If something doesn't work out in a straightforward way, I'd rather not be bothered."

Sharon sighed. "Well, friend, I've known you for three years now, and you're a sweet guy, too sweet for your own good. But I have never found you to be weak. You have brains and aggressiveness galore behind that pleasant face."

"Thank you." David was embarrassed, but Sharon was his boss, and he had often agreed with her opinions of people. This added to his satisfaction, as her praise soaked in.

Of course I'm not weak or overly anxious about my career. I just don't see how Sandy and I can let the poor kid be born to unmarried parents. It feels like letting my manhood crumble away.

I don't like the way Sharon drives, either. Or maybe I always blame women's driving on the fact that they're women, and take a man's driving as an aspect of his individual personality. Sharon just hinted I might go for another woman. Was she bidding for me to make a pass at her? What if we have to inspect bedrooms today? Will she try to corner me in one? I've heard a man sometimes has to screw a woman boss to keep his job.

He looked over at Sharon, who was concentrating on pulling past a large truck and doing just fine. He felt carsick.

Sandy's my love, my true love. I'll definitely get out of the situation tactfully if Sharon tries to seduce me. Then I'll call home and tell Sandy she has more time.

Aloud he said, "Sandy and I love each other. It's our baby she's carrying. We'll work it out."

One of the songs Sandy sang from her days at summer camp popped into his head and he hummed it, thinking the words to himself:

> If you fall from a boat
> try staying afloat
> with an old New York bagel like me.

That evening he arrived home after a day spent on matter-of-fact business. As soon as they got into bed he told Sandy thoughtfully, "I've reached a decision about our relationship. I've decided that you have as much time as you need to make up your mind to marry me."

She spoke doubtfully. "Even if it takes a year or two after the baby comes?"

He spoke to the ceiling. "Sure. But this is hard for me, Sandy. Don't make fun about it, try to see my point of view. Maybe you should see a different therapist."

"Oh, there's no need for a different one. She's on the side of marriage, probably even more than you are. But I don't want therapy. It kills my creativity to think about adjusting all the time. Can't I just be me for a while longer, David?"

"Of course," he turned toward her and whispered against the pillow case, biting the curls around her ear and kissing the back of her neck with pure tenderness. "You have more time. That's what I'm telling you."

Her response was passionate.

17

Let Your Moderation Be Known

Elinor was perched on the edge of Steven's bed, sewing down a belt loop on his best pair of jeans. "You can wear these tonight if you want."

"What's tonight?"

"The annual thingy—Music and Art Festival at school."

"That thingy is the same thingy every year," Steven said. "Bo-o-o-ring."

"Susan is singing in the chorus and she says a bird sketch you did in art class is on exhibit. You're supposed to take it home at the end of the evening."

"Yeah, I sketched a woodpecker. Okay, I'll go, but I won't wear my black suit. It's too small."

"No problem. Everyone wears jeans and this pair is fine."

Ralph, who had been coming regularly on Saturdays, called up the stairs, "Lunch is ready in the galley! Hurry if you want your steak rare!"

Steven bounded downstairs. Elinor smiled at her son's exuberance, but felt sorry that it showed up only in a spirit of male bonding when Ralph was in the house, while to her his silent frown said, "Shacked up."

She met Susan at the top of the stairs and they linked arms going down.

Ralph's daughter Michele was seated at the table in the breakfast room, where they all took seats. Ralph, standing with an egg in one hand and a bowl of greens, said in a warning tone, "Now this is a man's salad and you girls had better be up to it."

"What's in it?" asked Steven.

"That's romaine in the bowl," Susan said. "My cooking teacher's all for it."

"And this is an egg," said Ralph. "I'm sure you know Caesar was Roman, and romaine was named after him. When he roamed into Egypt and saw Cleopatra he felt romantic—that's Roman too—and inner voices told him, 'Seize her, Seize her!' and they calmed him down with this salad. Please remain seated for today's show."

Steven sat sideways on his chair, fearful of being conned into trying something he wouldn't like.

Ralph cracked the egg and splashed its contents over the romaine.

"Yech," said Steven. "Aren't you going to cook that?"

"No, but I can make it go away," said Ralph, tossing the greens thoroughly. "I'm making the mayonnaise right in this bowl where I already have the magic ingredients—vinegar and mustard and olive oil."

"How do you make mayonnaise, Mrs. Bates?" Michele asked.

"A raw egg," said Elinor, "with vinegar, mustard and olive oil."

"Also lemon juice," added Ralph. He sliced a lemon in half. "Here, Steven, squeeze this half to get all the juice into the bowl."

Steven closed his large hand around the lemon and squeezed it limp, lifting his chin and rolling his eyes at Susan in a look meaning, "Is this guy for real?"

"I generally use a lot of lemon juice and very little oil," Elinor said.

"I'm glad you never cook stuff that's fattening, Mom," Susan said. "I like wearing your size nine clothes and I couldn't bear to be any bigger."

"You could be a model, Susan," Ralph put in, "but I hope you won't get only B's, like Michele."

The girls exchanged smiles, accustomed to his teasing, and said in unison, "We both get all A's!"

"Now we give our salad a soul with these croutons," said Ralph. "There's lots of garlic in them and we add them last so they'll be crisp. Aunt Julia says that Cleopatra found it wise to have this salad ready whenever Caesar came to see her."

"Or to seize her," put in Michele. Ralph gave her an approving grin.

Elinor had the first taste. "I call this a *woman's* salad," she pronounced. "It's that good."

In the end, Susan discovered she liked medium rare steak, and Steven ate three helpings of salad.

Ralph went upstairs and when he came down he stopped by the sink to tell Elinor, "I brought along these old blue jeans to work in. I'll leave them for you to put in the wash."

"Fine," said Elinor. She glowed at the thought of doing Ralph's wash. Saturdays were a joy with him around, although she hadn't liked the two weekends in a row he had stayed away, and still wondered why. On the Saturday morning of the first weekend, he had said briefly on the phone he had to drive a friend to a medical center. On the second Saturday he phoned to say his friend was "doing okay at home." Since then, he had regularly spent Saturdays puttering around Elinor's car, providing lunch and getting to know the kids. He didn't stay overnight but took Elinor back to the City for dinner and dancing and sleeping in his apartment.

When Elinor finished in the kitchen, she too changed into old jeans and went to work cutting off dead peony stems and iris leaves. Ralph was working nearby, lying on a pad under Elinor's Cadillac, singing to himself. She had filled a bag with trimmings and was sitting on the lawnroller resting when Susan arrived with mugs of coffee. Ralph rolled over on one arm, said "Thank you, Snookums!" and drank, watching Susan walk back to the house. He seemed utterly at peace, looked fondly at Elinor, and the words came out, "It would save me a bundle if you and I got married real soon. We could file a joint return for this year and those two long-legged, good lookin' exemptions of yours would come in handy."

"I'm not sure what that means."

"It means if we got married within a month, we'd be ahead financially with the Internal Revenue Service. Dem bums."

Elinor had imagined many romantic ways Ralph might propose marriage, but a money-driven statement wasn't one of them. Shocked, she took a deep breath but didn't have time to respond because to her relief Michele was bringing a plate of cookies. Elinor said, "How nice of you to bring these out! Thanks, Michele." She took only half a cookie, hoping Michele would see how to reject rich food without being rude. Then she moved away to throw away her bag of clippings.

Ralph, grabbing three cookies, crawled back under the car, humming, "Daisy, Daisy, give me your answer true."

Nothing more was said that weekend on the subject of marriage, but Elinor knew it would come up again soon, maybe at Thanksgiving. Ralph was to bring both of his daughters for Thanksgiving dinner, uniting everyone around Elinor's dining room table. It would be Elinor's first real chance to get to know Helen.

She was already fond of Michele, who regularly came with Ralph on Saturdays and was chummy with Susan. Although the girls faithfully did homework, they found time to cook and make up songs, with Michele at the piano. One Saturday after lunch they invited Elinor and Ralph to preview a puppet show they had created for a child's birthday party. It delighted their audience—even Steven had watched and laughed, a real tribute.

Elinor hoped this happy spirit would prevail on Thanksgiving. On Monday she gave Dr. Kaufman two days' notice that she'd be too busy to keep her next appointment.

Early Tuesday morning she was in the supermarket, feeling so thrilled to be shopping that it verged on a religious mission, and, in fact, her thoughts were punctuated with phrases from the *Prayer Book*. Ralph had dropped a hundred dollar bill on the kitchen counter which he said was all for food, as he would bring wine and flowers!

Rejoice in the Lord always!

She waltzed along, pushing a large shopping cart which was soon heavy with a fresh twenty-two pound turkey. She felt sorry for people who had to buy frozen ones, never as good as fresh.

She added chestnuts for stuffing, her specialty. Celery. Olives. No other salad needed. Not meant to be a balanced meal, just wonderful to have food. Thank you, God. And you, Ralph.

At the ice cream freezer she paused.

Shall I get a lot? It's sure to be eaten. And Michele too fat already. *Let your moderation be known to all men.* I'll buy only a half gallon of the best vanilla, enough to garnish my pies of home-grown pumpkins. I'll skip the pineapple sherbet, my usual preference for dessert after a heavy dinner. What about regular meals during the week? Ah! Eggs and eggs and eggs, of all sizes.

It will be a pleasure to use the exact size of egg needed —small eggs for deviling, large eggs for soufflés, medium size for cakes. The Chinese eat birds' eggs—wonder if Ralph could make mayonnaise out of them?

She drove home with many full bags, one of which held a long supermarket receipt like a jolly serpentine, showing a final figure of ninety dollars. She'd kept ten dollars for gas.

On Wednesday morning she tried balancing her checkbook.

It's always a juggling act, deciding which bills can be put off. Heat, light and telephone have to be paid first. My child allowance check is pledged already, so if Howard delays it for a month I'll be in real trouble. If I remind him to speed up his checks, it just delays them a month more. Dr. Martha has seen worse. She says that a common dodge is for men to get out of paying alimony altogether. They quit their jobs, move out of state, or become drunken bums and never pay. Howard in a gutter on the Bowery? He's so super-scrubbed, it seems ridiculous, but maybe that's the kind that topples. Self-destructive, rather die than yield. Steven once talked about an animal on a TV show which let itself be shaken to death because it refused to loosen its teeth and escape. That's Howard, a bad example. It isn't only that he keeps the money from us, he's hurting himself by not getting on with his life.

I'd like to have a career, but I don't really fancy an office job. Dr. Martha occasionally suggests it, but I could never earn enough to support us in this house. Howard most likely wouldn't send any money at all if I earned even a little. It isn't fair, because I gave him a lot of encouragement in his climb to prosperity. I've always economized, yet managed to provide little treats so we wouldn't feel broke. I remember a book I read as a kid, *A Tree Grows in Brooklyn*, in which the mother says they have to have coffee so they won't feel poor. I'm glad Ralph sees me as a student of art but I don't think he'd really want me to have a career, with all the time and energy that takes out of a wife. The problem is that the divorce settlement says I don't get to keep the house if I remarry. Of course, Ralph would buy another house. But what if we don't get along— I'd lose everything. I hope combining the families around the Thanksgiving table demonstrates that things will work out. I'll know, somehow. Maybe. Steven is the puzzle— doesn't seem to be comfortable, acting too jolly with Ralph. I know he's troubled. It's too bad he doesn't want to learn about the Cadillac's insides. Or learn other things from Ralph, like good manners.

I have a strong feeling that even though Ralph mentioned getting married, he won't move until we accept his family and they accept us. Michele likes us and could pretty easily fit into school here in Middle Cove. Susan likes her, but doesn't know Helen and might not be thrilled about sharing me with two sisters.

Oh, Susan, don't change. I know you won't. You and I

will always be close, even while being independent. And Michele's so likable, she'll fit in. She may be heavy in pounds but she has a delicate nature. A lovely girl.

Of course, the real unknown quantity is Helen. That time we met by chance at Fire Island she was friendly, but only on the surface, I thought. She's not as pretty as Michele could be, but sexier. Both of them claim to be crazy about their father, although he says he can't stand Helen. She defies him and knows too much for nineteen. Lives alone. No job. Hard to figure what she does with her time. If she were my daughter, she'd live at home, but she got the apartment by telling her parents she was getting married.

Michele and Helen both dress well, look properly casual. You have to have money to buy that "smart carelessness." Susan needs clothes, and I do too, keeping up a dating life with Ralph. I spent a big share of my clothes money for that gorgeous silk dressing gown for him, but there's been no occasion for it. I'll give it as my wedding gift to him.

She sighed and put away her checkbook.

I can't do it all. When Ralph and I are married—oh, why do I think of that again in connection with money? Oh, Ralph, you seem so far away! We hardly seem to talk intimately any more, just say things like "You're good for my car!" and "You're good for Michele!" Our lovemaking has never again reached the height of that weekend at Fire Island. He seemed to change after that night when he slept in the guest room. I couldn't help that. I *couldn't*. He does understand, I'm sure. It's just that he has so much life. He's a dear, generous person. He's fond of me, but where did the magic go?

See then that ye walk circumspectly, not as fools, but as wise, redeeming the time, because the days are evil.

How much should I budget as absolutely essential for food until Christmas? I'll shop when the reduced fruit is put out, usually Monday around noon. We must be the only family in Middle Cove that knows the good taste of really ripe fruit. Luckily, I eat well in town on the weekends, lots of protein at Ralph's restaurants. My share at home goes to the kids. It's keeping them healthy. And so is using their bikes which Ralph fixed, to save me gas money. And his car repairs save me even more.

"I, Elinor, take thee, Ralph, for better or worse, for richer . . ."

Martha's reaction to hearing about Ralph's proposal was a strange dream. She was in Elinor's white Cadillac, and Ralph pulled up alongside in his black Caddy and shouted, "Didn't Elinor like my suggestion about getting married before New Year's?" She had closed her car window without replying, not knowing what to say to the poor guy.

18

Perfect for Chilling Champagne

"I'd like to invite someone to Thanksgiving dinner," Barry announced at the breakfast table the Sunday before the holiday.

Martha, concentrating on removing a waffle from the iron, managed to say, "Okay, who?"

"A friend I'm working on the parade with. I'm sure I've mentioned Robin to you before."

Martha didn't remember but promised him, "We'll eat in the dining room."

"I forgot we had one," teased Barry.

"It just needs your lively presence," his mother said, placing a hot waffle in front of him. "The living room isn't fixed up yet, but we can go up there for drinks before dinner. Barry, something's got to be done with your old pink and yellow plastic sports trophies from junior high. I'm keeping the white Greek runner from college on the mantel, but the plastic ones are in a carton ready to go to your bedroom."

"Aw, they make the living room feel like home. I love them."

"I love them too, but they don't fit with my plans for an elegant living room."

"Robin can help you with that," he said as he hurriedly brushed her cheek on his way out. "Thanks for the waffles, but I have to run. We're still working out our part of the parade."

It's too bad Sarah wasn't here—she'd have quizzed Barry about Robin. Is she a model, or maybe the liaison between his agency and the sponsor, Macys? But our *Times* wasn't delivered this morning, and Sarah's out getting a copy and fresh ginger for her pumpkin pies.

Missing not only Sarah, but Norman and Barry and the old family warmth at holiday time, Martha determined to keep busy. She went into the dining room and took the best white damask tablecloth from the sideboard. It was heavily creased from being folded away.

No doubt Sarah will want to launder it. Her family's maids in Austria didn't tolerate creases. I'm glad Barry wants to bring a girl home, maybe one he really cares about.

She unwrapped some large silver pieces, took them to a kitchen counter, and quickly polished a pair of candlesticks she had inherited. When she began on the wine cooler, which had been a gift from Norman on their twenty-fifth wedding anniversary, her briskness broke down into sad, bittersweet memories.

Every time we used it we admired its graceful shape, part urn, part bucket, perfect for chilling champagne. At first I teased him about his too careful pouring, but after he assigned us our "homework"—his phrase for dining out, which I called our "not at homework"—he could wrap a napkin around a bottle and pour as deftly as any wine steward. We always had fun!

Oh, Norman, why aren't you here? Our divorced Barry is finally bringing a new girl home. I need you.

She hugged the cooler to her breast and rested her head against the cupboard, leaning on the solid house and its illusion of safety. Then she began banging her head against the cupboard, slowly at first and then faster. Again and again she hit the hard surface, welcoming the pain. She finally stopped, still cradling the cool bucket. She knew she'd been trying to lessen her anger at death's taking Norman away, make it dissolve into sorrow.

Sorrow isn't a pleasant emotion, either, but it allows me some credit for trying to cope. Endlessly. And endlessly, life has to go on.

With a heavy heart, she set the shining silver pieces on the dining table and, hearing the front door close, turned on the waffle iron for Sarah's breakfast.

That evening the two women took their supper on trays into the dining room to check it out. They discovered the chandelier in need of lightbulbs, the rust-colored drapes sagging, and the floor in need of waxing. Sarah volunteered to take care of everything and pointed out that the high-backed chairs were more comfortable than she remembered.

Late Tuesday afternoon Martha found the dining room transformed—the chandelier alight, the drapes hanging neatly, and the white tablecloth smooth under the silver candlesticks. Candles were still lacking. She went shopping and came home with rust-colored wax tapers matching the drapes, and, for a centerpiece, a big bowl of chrysanthemums the same color.

I'll keep the flowers in my inner office for patients to enjoy tomorrow morning, but nobody's coming in the afternoon. That's been planned in advance, so it's okay. I'm glad to give my Long Islanders time to get ready for the holiday.

Sitting at her desk Wednesday afternoon, she was startled to see the light go on. Thinking it must be someone soliciting, she looked out the window and saw a short, smartly dressed woman who looked vaguely familiar. When Martha greeted her, she announced, "I'm Judy Lieberman, Sandra's mother. Do you remember me? I was here once before, about ten years ago when I brought Sandy to see you after her grandfather died."

"Of course I remember. Come in."

"I can only stay a minute. For a long time I've been meaning to mail you a check for the appointment Sandy canceled, and today I was in the Village and decided I'd just drop it off."

"We can talk in my office, if you like."

"Yes, thank you. I'm trying to help, and let you know where Sandy's coming from. Oh, what lovely flowers!"

"Thank you. Please sit down. Would you like to take your coat off?"

"I'll just slip it down and take off my hat." She pulled off a black velvet beret and released a mop of bright red hair, not the natural red of Sandy's. "Call me Judy," she said with a smile, and jangled numerous bracelets.

"I will," Martha said, enjoying the warm fire in the woman's brown eyes. "I see a resemblance to your daughter."

"Thank you. I hope I'm not interrupting your work?"

"Not at all. I'm glad you stopped by."

"I'm fascinated by the therapeutic process, but instead of training in that field, I got my B.A. in anthropology."

"That's also fascinating. What branch of the study have you followed?"

"Mostly the women's movement. But being married to a doctor, I never took a paid job, just tried to be a good mother. My goals were that Sandy should develop her own goals, not restricted by tradition but free to explore new territory."

Martha wondered if Judy was approving of her daughter's wish to have a baby without being married, but Judy continued her theorizing. "Women have to accept some limits, like menstruation, confinement with the new-born, and, on the average, smaller stature and less brute strength than men. But we survive on less food. And live longer."

Martha, impressed with her fluency asked, "So it evens out?"

"Well, we don't have the same freedoms as men, but we do have many freedoms and some new ones. In the past, a few independent women were tolerated as exceptions, but now the sheer number of ambitious women is changing things. Men feel threatened."

"So do conventional women," Martha replied. "There are many of them still."

"Yes, to be truly liberated we should bring our sisters along. We women are on our mythic quests. We'll slay the dragons, burst open the strictures of society."

Martha, tempted to point out that Judy's rhetoric was a lot like Sandy's, asked gently, "And if our daughters are dealt a backlash?"

Judy looked stricken. "That's what I'm afraid of for Sandy. I don't want her hurt." She sat quietly, her bracelets silent, then with a little moan began weeping, tears running down her face. She took a tissue from the box on Martha's desk and daubed her eyes. Then she stood, snatched a check from her purse and thumped it down on the desk, saying, "This is for the time Sandy canceled late." Biting her lip and eyeing Martha sadly, she muttered, "Don't you dare tell Sandy I came here. She knows nothing about it. In fact, she's out of town."

Martha remained silent at this request, but thought she would most likely honor it.

"Thanks for everything," said Judy, and left.

Martha felt chagrined for not having said anything soothing.

But I did right not to. I expect the real reason she came was to ask me to keep Sandy from being hurt, but false comfort wouldn't be fair to her. I too am afraid Sandy may be dealt a backlash.

She was near to tears herself, feeling the hurt that can accompany a mother's love.

A mother's love can be the most unselfish and sacred love in her life, and can be, for a daughter, an unfailing surge on which she is borne along. Yet look at all the empty five o'clock slots in my appointment book, while Sandy rejects therapy her mother hopes will keep her from being hurt. I'd like to summon that young woman and persuade her to welcome the love her mother offers and realize its value. Not wait until her mother is dead, like I did.

A wave of regret, the most poignant regret of her life, came unbidden into her heart and as she had done before, she challenged and quelled it. My mother knew I loved her, and I tried to deserve her love by becoming a doctor. I owe it to her not to belittle my efforts. She shared my loyalty to what I was learning, and got satisfaction from seeing me steadfastly working at my studies, even if it meant being away too long from her. Right now, with the homey smell of pumpkin pie drifting in from the kitchen, I'm reminded that Sarah, too, is full of motherly love. She's working alone in there, creating a great dinner for us tomorrow. The least I can do is give her some company and a little harmless news she'd like to hear.

She went down the hall to the kitchen and was pleased to find Sarah in a cheerful mood, having just made a pot of Vermont coffee. They sat down at the kitchen table. "What are you saying thanks for tomorrow?" Sarah asked.

"Well, I must say Thanksgiving is timely for me this year. My work is going well."

"Your visions for the Wednesday women are coming true?"

"As well as could be expected, yes. Elinor and Ralph haven't set a wedding date, but they're planning to attend church together some Sunday soon. And they're combining their families at Elinor's tomorrow for the first of what may be many Thanksgiving dinners."

"When you say 'their families' it means with Steven and Susan, plus . . . ?"

"Ralph's two daughters, Michele and Helen. Ralph gave Elinor a hundred dollars for the food."

"Not a lot to feed six people."

"But Elinor is pleased about it. She had some worries a while back when she didn't see Ralph for a couple of weekends. He said he was taking a friend to a medical center. Then he started coming steadily on Saturdays, bringing his younger daughter, Michele. She's the same age as Susan, and the two girls make up puppet shows for kids' parties.

"Elinor only met the older daughter, Helen, once at Ralph's cottage on Fire Island, when the girl and her father had a quarrel. She had brought along a man to whom she had promised the use of the cottage for the winter. Ralph grew angry and sent the guy packing, and told

Helen he was going to put bars on the windows and change the keys. Impudently Helen suggested land mines to keep people out. But she was nice to Elinor, who stayed out of the argument. Luckily, Elinor is tactful, which will be a help after they're married."

"You plan for them to get married?"

"It seems inevitable at this point."

"How's Feisty?"

"Guess what? Our Billie is happily living with the architecture student, Christopher. Young Mike is away for the year with his father in Florida. She hasn't heard from him, but when I suggested that she phone him on Thanksgiving she said she was already planning to. That's a breakthrough, as before she had declared she wouldn't contact him until Christmas. His being away has given her a new lease on life."

"How's Ursula? Is your vision of a Golden Wedding also coming true?"

"Not yet. But she got through the eye operation and is to return to therapy next week. Today she and her husband are driving upstate to their daughter's for Thanksgiving. So everyone's okay."

"I see," said Sarah. "Thanks for telling me how they are." She paused as if to say more, but the oven timer sounded and she moved quickly to tend to her pies.

Martha had returned to her desk and was just about to leave the office when the phone rang. It was Sandy.

"Oh, Sandra, how are you?"

"Okay, I guess. I'd like to come to see you once a week, if you have an opening?"

"Oh, yes! I'm glad you're coming in. What time is convenient for you?"

"Any time. I'm still free-lancing."

"Shall I book five o'clock for you then, next Wednesday?" There was a pause. "All right?" Another pause.

Then Sandy said,"I guess. I can't talk. I'm on long distance."

"Okay, then. Have a good Thanksgiving."

They hung up.

I wonder what's bringing her in. Has she split up with David? Or married him? I couldn't guess from what Judy said, and obviously Sandy doesn't want to tell me on the phone. I'll give thanks tomorrow that she's returning to therapy.

With verve in her step, she was soon on her way to the liquor store.

What a joy it is to celebrate a holiday on which the whole family agrees! Of course, I've always enjoyed the Jewish holidays, especially the Seder, and Sarah's never objected to my favorite bits of Christmas—the cookies, the tree, the great classical music broadcasts. Of course, Norman loved all the holidays! But Thanksgiving is the most harmonious. Luckily, Sarah approves of turkey, a reminder of game birds her father shot from his hunting lodge. She's roasted a lot of beautiful birds for us, including one during the year of Barry's marriage. I remember I thought it my duty to tell his new bride, Marie, about my mother's Thanksgiving specialty, the red currant jelly Marie was eating. Daddy always praised it as better than cranberry sauce with turkey. But Marie wasn't interested. I suppose that was an omen, a clue that she didn't love Barry. When you really marry a man, you take on his family's recipes.

In the liquor store, she found her neighbors standing in line, joking and ordering lavishly. She knew of no other place where New Yorkers became so chatty in public, except maybe waiting for half-price theater tickets, as she used to do in med school. Today they recommended their favorite drinks for toasts—rum coladas, Lemon Squeegies with gin, or—as one man aggressively insisted—Salty dogs with vodka. The man ahead of Martha in line, wearing a plaid shirt and blue jeans, turned toward her and said, "I certainly prefer champagne."

"Oh, so do I!" Martha said fervently.

She listened when he told the clerk in a clear voice, "A bottle of Dom Perignon."

She also noticed that the price rung up on the cash register was three times what she usually paid for champagne. Her temptation built up as she watched the reverential way the clerk wrapped the bottle, and the equally reverential way the customer took time to pack it in a highly polished leather briefcase.

Shouldn't we celebrate? Isn't my calendar full all week, now that Sandy's coming back? It's the Wednesday Four again. And Barry's bringing a girlfriend home! I'll spend some of the money I'm too busy earning every day, since these days I never spend anything on *fun*.

Within seconds she was saying softly to the clerk, "A bottle of Dom Perignon, please."

19

I Know What I Have to Do

A couple of weeks before Thanksgiving, Sandy felt good. She wore for Sunday a peach-color dress which went well with her hair. The fall weather agreed with her, as did her pregnancy. She hadn't resumed smoking and felt no need to see Dr. Kaufman. Proud that she'd sewed the dress herself, she made up her face in delicate shades, dabbed perfume behind her ears and went to sit close to David on the sofa. Engrossed in *The New York Times Magazine*, he automatically slipped his arm around her.

"There's a new show at the MOMA," she said. "I have one of those cravings. Mama wants MOMA."

Marking his place, he kissed the top of her head. "You'd better watch where you go. It says here, porn cravings satisfied in Museum of Modern Art."

She poked him. "We had a big breakfast, so we won't need a meal soon, and we can get coffee there."

In the museum they walked around slowly, in a comradely way. Just beyond the biggest Picasso, David spotted friends. "Hi! How's my roommate?" About to bring her handbag to her front to conceal her bulk, Sandy stood with her arms at her side beside David while he talked to Tom and Brenda, close friends from college.

"Wow!" exclaimed Brenda. "Davey, you didn't tell us you'd gotten married. Oh, Tom, everybody's getting ahead of your poor little wife. I want to be a mother—now—this year."

"We aren't married," David said gravely, "but soon will be."

"Well," said Tom, after a pause, "the art isn't all that's modern here."

Sandy felt angry at David's prediction of marriage but

tried to be friendly and light. "You came to the right museum."

They all went for coffee, chatting about art, and Sandy and later Brenda went to the ladies room. Sandy was surprised to hear herself blurt out, "Our not being married is my idea, not David's. I worship the ground he walks on, but I can't face the confinement of marriage."

Brenda said nothing, tossing her head with what Sandy took as a snide smile.

That night at home and again in the morning, David was quiet, not like himself. Sandy knew he was feeling stress and working hard at the agency, which had been hit by inflation; a cost of living increase was all he could look forward to. Without being married, he couldn't use his approaching fatherhood to seek a higher salary. To compensate, she tried to show contentment and made sure they ate well. Now she sensed he was going to force the issue. If he did, she would let him stew for a while and go visit her mother.

Monday evening when he came home she had dinner ready. It was complete with popovers like the ones she had baked for their first breakfast together, but David ate only one.

"Sandy," he began, "maybe there's no way to tell you why I don't want my child born out of wedlock, but I don't."

She interrupted. "Wed *what*?" Even to herself her voice sounded harsh. She repeated at a higher pitch. "Wed *what*?"

"Wedlock."

"What's *that*?" She put disgust into the question.

David exploded. "It's what I don't want my child born out of, dammit!" He banged the table so hard their coffee mugs jumped.

Sandy grabbed them, put them in the sink, and turned to face him. Her face was serious, the skin drawn tight over her cheekbones. After a silent stare into his eyes, she walked behind his chair, put her arms around his shoulders and pressed her enlarged, warm breasts against his head, holding him tensely. "It's the lock part, Davey," she said slowly, her voice husky. "It's the *lock*. I have to win this argument about getting married."

He didn't reply.

In bed later they made love tenderly, in desperate truce.

On Wednesday, after two days of David's unusual silence, Sandy imploded. Choosing a soft blue sheet of paper, she sat down and wrote:

> Dear David, try not to feel hurt, but I am fed up with the situation and I'm *going home to mother*. I need a breathing space. Don't worry, I'll eat right and take my vitamins. Be good. Sandy.

Knowing the sketchiness of David's cooking, she added:

> P.S. There's leftover onion soup you can heat up—float toast on top, add parmesan cheese—and some sliced pastrami and carrot sticks. Also stuff in the freezer.

She placed the note on the kitchen table along with the ticket for his suit she'd taken to the cleaners.

It's hard to know what clothes I'll need, as I don't know how long it will be. I can spend a couple of days at Mom's and print my "Images" sketch. Some time at Danielle's wouldn't hurt, as her artistic energy is inspiring, and I can learn about children. A couple of days should bring him around. If he calls me at Mom's after I've left for Danny's, she'll tell him to call me there. Then I'll come back and make him so comfortable that he'll stop nagging about marriage.

She rode by subway, the Long Island Railroad and a taxi in Great Neck to get to her mother's. Wearily dropping her backpack onto the marble slates of the front porch, she rang the bell. Judy opened the door, expressed surprise and delight, and hugged her warmly. Sandy murmured, "I might stay a few days."

"Trouble!" exclaimed Judy, cheerfully enough. "What's wrong?" She drew Sandy to an easy chair and offered her sherry.

"I've stopped drinking. And smoking too."

"Good!" said Judy, and brought her a glass of water. When Sandy was silent, she blurted out, "Well, Sandy, if there's a tempest in a teapot at your place, it's no doubt about getting married, and that of course can only end one way. You kids are deeply in love with each other, so a little crisis may bring some action."

Sandy sipped her water. "Thanks for this. I was thirsty."

"How are you feeling? Morning sickness all gone?"

"Yes, long ago. My back bothers me sometimes, probably because I don't get enough exercise. Swimming is what I need. Is the pool still open?"

"Only the indoor junior high pool, evenings. But it's sure to be full of pee."

"Mo-*therr!*" Sandy used the intonation her mother hated, and they laughed.

After a silence, Judy asked in a neutral tone, "So when ya gettin' married?"

Sandy winced, made a quick excuse, and went to the bathroom.

Why doesn't Mom ask me about my backache? Why doesn't she listen, like Dr. Kaufman? Mom loves me, but she's stubborn, like David. I don't want to start quarreling after the strain of getting here.

She walked into the living room talking. "David's okay. He's full of notions about wedlock, but he's eating and sleeping well."

"You haven't quarreled?"

"Sure, we've quarreled. Why else would I be coming home to mother?"

"I like having you come. Any time." Sandy managed a

tight smile, expressing gratitude, she hoped. Her mother smiled warmly. "What's the trouble?"

"In case you haven't noticed—David says we have to get married."

"Well, you wouldn't be the first bride by a long shot—I could name girls I knew in high school who had to get married."

"Why?"

"Someone insisted. Sometimes the guy did. I learned that you only lose people's respect if you act guilty. At my friend Lillian's wedding her mother was the sour note. She sat around looking ashamed, when she should've been proud of how her daughter looked. Which was beautiful. I've made up my mind that a bold front wins the day."

"So have I," said Sandy. "And so has the baby." They laughed.

Judy stuck out her chest. "Wanna hear my poem? 'I'm the mother of the bride/ who takes pregnancy in stride/ with grandmotherly pride.'"

Sandy laughed. "I hope your snapshots of the baby will be better than your poetry."

"So what are we waiting for? We have to get the restaurant for the banquet well ahead." There was no explosion, so she risked, "I hope you'll wear a white satin bridal gown."

The song in Sandy's head was "If You Don't Know Me by Now," and her voice had a bitter tone new to her mother. "There's no bridal gown because there's no bride. Why do you and David make it so hard for me?"

"It's for your own good."

"But I'm the one who has to have this creature inside me and eat right and have the backaches."

"But basically, you want to marry David. You do love him. We all love him. And everyone in his family loves you."

"I'm beginning to wonder. With all the talk about freedom for women, this simple little freedom is denied me, to love David and our baby without getting married."

"So you couldn't go through a short legal ceremony? It would be a recognition of your relationship."

"Couldn't we do that by just having a party? Forget the legal stuff, nobody will notice. Hire a band, dress up and say all the prayers, spend all the money, but no legal papers. That's fine with me." She looked at her mother steadily.

Judy, her lips trembling as she failed to return the gaze, retreated to the kitchen and stood at the sink struggling with her anger. Sandy followed and put her arm around her. "Don't cry, Mom. You'll always be our baby's proud grandmother."

Judy sobbed wordlessly against her daughter's shoulder.

On Thursday morning Sandy breakfasted alone on some cold cereal and milk and went to the basement where she put a few touches on her sketch. Suddenly it was done and she wrote its title in the lower corner, *Images of Woman*.

Judy drove her to shop for printing supplies and then to their favorite delicatessen for pastrami sandwiches. Afterward she drove around and slowed down when they passed a large restaurant on Northern Boulevard. Judy said, "That's *the* great place for wedding banquets. There's a big staircase where the bride can throw her bouquet to the bridesmaids, and whoever catches it is the first to get married."

Sandy stiffened, but managed to say only, "It's nice. My friend Rachel had her reception there. I caught her bouquet."

Back to her printer, she thoroughly cleaned it, but didn't start printing. She obsessively went over her drawing, line by line, doubting that it was good enough, and finally gave up and went to bed early. Feeling anxiety about it and denying to herself that she was homesick for David, she couldn't sleep. The only thing she couldn't deny was that her childhood bed was a strange place to be.

How long can I stand this? The eleven o'clock news is over. Why doesn't he call now?

On Friday her back felt better, but she still couldn't face the printing job. She was considering a third cup of coffee when Judy suggested a shopping trip to Altman's and she accepted. Judy dropped her at the back door of the big suburban store and headed for a space in the parking lot.

Sandy hummed "Bye-bye Birdie" as she waited.

Well, today Mom will be in a good mood for getting stuff monogrammed. It goes with weddings and it's not just Sandy *now, it's* Sandy and David. *She'll think it's a step forward. I like having both names because I love David, and getting ready for a wedding would be fun, even if it's not fun afterward, when you have to accept a lot of wedding gifts and then rent a bigger apartment to show them off and make jokes about how you're having trouble with your joint tax returns. I don't want David and me to be like that. We'll be happier doing things my way. Mom may think that monogrammed stuff is for the married, so I'll string her along and stay single. When friends visit us, they can play with the baby and see my art.*

Anyhow, I'm proud that she's not ashamed to be seen with me. If we run into one of her stuffy friends who'd think, "Horrors! So pregnant and no wedding ring!" Mom could carry it off without blinking an eye if she wanted to.

When Judy came, Sandy led the way to the counter for ordering monograms, where they agreed on styles of paper napkins, guest towels and an address book, all to be inscribed in capital letters in gold, SANDY AND DAVID.

"Mom, those cotton tee shirts lettered R.I.S.D. were nice. They washed well."

"Why not order more? You choose the lettering."

Sandy lettered on the order form: SANDY AND DAVID DID THIS. "I want that printed right here, over the baby." She patted her abdomen.

"Oh, Sandy, do you really want to wear that?"

However, the clerk stated with confidence, "The letters can go wherever you wish. We can measure how far down from the center of the neckline."

Sandy stood proudly to be measured and said, "I want one pink and one blue, as we'll be happy with either a girl or a boy. And please order two more, a pink and a blue, with this." She lettered "MY UPROARIOUS BABY." As they left the counter she told her mother, "I stole the idea from you, Mom, about pink and blue."

"You're a thug. A tubby mama thug," Judy said, pleased.

They strolled among the clothing racks in the junior department where they had often shopped. Judy commented, "I'm glad you're not wearing a tube top. But I do sort of wish they'd had these rounded-bottom blue jeans when you were in college. You have such a nice round bottom. Real curves."

"My curves did their work and I got my man. So forget it."

"My, aren't we prudish!"

"I've never approved of exploiting sexiness, making it marketable."

Judy was contrite. "I know. Forgive my remark." She paused. "I wouldn't think of you as . . . marketable, if you were married."

Sandy held her tongue, humming to herself, "Mother Earth will make you strong if you give her loving care."

That evening she phoned Danielle who offered to pick her up on Sunday afternoon. Only one more day at home with her press.

On Saturday she woke up singing and full of energy. David hadn't called, but she was rested.

I've been fooling around but I swear to God, today I work.

Cheerfully singing an old Scottish Union song, "If It Wasna for the Printers, What Would Ye Do?" she worked steadily, printing and numbering fifty copies. By Sunday noon she had signed and dated each copy. She knew it was the best print she had ever done and proudly carried copy number one upstairs and gave it to her mother in the kitchen. Judy, busy at the moment chopping mushrooms on the marble top of the work island, stopped to examine it and said, "I love it, Sandy. I'll always remember you did it here, with me." She grilled a filet mignon steak for her daughter, the same dish she would prepare for her guests that evening.

Sandy felt grateful. "Mom, don't be worried—David and I will work out our problem."

"I never let the sun set on a quarrel with your father."

"Yeah, and look what happened to your marriage! You didn't live by your true feelings, just kissed and made up for the look of things. That can lead to divorce like it did for you. David and I know we're quarreling, and that it's about something important."

"I think it's scary. With the baby coming."

"Don't be scared. Hey, this steak is delicious. Sorry I can't stay for your dinner party tonight."

"Danielle always steals you away."

"Because she's a working artist, and can't see me except on weekends. She's gotta be the most romantic person I know, lives in a gingerbread house near Locust Valley and dresses her cute twin girls in Kate Greenaway dresses. Don't you remember meeting her at college? She was my best roommate, looks like the Blessed Damozel. You know, the Rossetti painting."

"Mmm," said Judy, inspecting a mushroom. "How would I know? We can't all afford to go to the Rhode Island School of Design."

Sandy's spirits sank at the disparagement of her mother, who was often jealous of her only child's friends, though not, luckily, of David. As gently as she could, she said, "I'm grateful for the education you gave me, and I'll make you proud of me. I hope to be a really super artist someday."

"Good. Does Danielle's mother live near her?"

"No, unfortunately. Her father came from England to

work here when she was in high school and after R.I.S.D. she married an American guy but it didn't work out. By that time her parents were back in England and not too prosperous. She works for an interior decorator and supports twins and a mother's helper. She has a car and is coming for me at two."

"If she lives near Locust Valley you can drive yourself there in my car. The people coming to dinner live there and when they go home tonight they can drop me at Danielle's to pick it up. Write down her address and directions."

"Sure. Thanks." Sandy recognized her mother's curiosity about how Danny lived and was glad to spare her friend the driving. She left her pile of prints carefully packed in her bedroom, taking only copy two for David and copy three for Danny. She thought David would soon be driving from the City to get her, but she packed her backpack ready for a train ride to Manhattan from Danny's, just in case.

Judy carried the pack to the car and pressed fifty dollars into her daughter's hand as a good luck gift. "Come back soon. You and David come soon."

"Mom, be sure to give him Danny's number when he calls. I left it by the phone. I know he's lonesome for me and might come for me today."

"Drive carefully."

"I always do. Have a wonderful dinner party."

When Sandy got to Danielle's she parked and mounted the steep stairs to the porch. The door was open. "Hey, I'm here!" she called, dropping her pack in the hall. The house was quiet except for the sound of running water upstairs. She went through the house to the kitchen and looked out the open back door. Danny was in the far part of the yard using a shovel.

"Hey there! Can I help?" Sandy called.

"Oh, hi! I'm coming."

Sandy, not finding any railing, descended the steps with care. Danny called, "Mind the bottom step. It's broken."

"Going down is harder then going up. I can't see over me."

Danielle, in tattered blue jeans and a black tee shirt came toward her, an empty plastic bag in her hand which she put into the garbage can, saying, "Just planted this week's veggie peelings, good for compost. Now, let's look at you." She lifted Sandy's right hand over her head and Sandy obligingly twirled like a dancing doll. The purple dress she was wearing had a bias peplum which swung out as she turned.

"Migawd, you're big! How long ago was it you were here?"

"About two months," Sandy said.

"Well, you sure grossed out in two months."

Sandy beamed maternally, proud of being gross. "How's my beautiful Blue Danielle?"

Danny hooked her thumbs into her belt, flapped her arms like a bird that can't fly, and frowned. "Pretty pissed off. But it's nice to see you. Let's go inside."

"Where are the twins?'

"Sleeping. I had to have some time for housekeeping this morning, so I gave them each a little pill."

Sandy gasped. "Isn't that bad for them?"

"Not especially. My grandmother said that during the bombing in London people were under such strain that the only way adults could cope was to knock the kids out at times. Necessary for the survival of all concerned."

As they sat side by side on the living room sofa, Sandy said, "Danny, you're doing great, getting practical." She patted one of her friend's hands, noting that it was red and rough to the touch. "I'm really glad to be here."

Danielle squeezed her hand and withdrew her own, smiling wanly and tucking both hands under her arm pits as they sat. To Sandy she was all the more lovely with the faint bluish tone of tiredness in her face.

She's so vulnerable. We're all so vulnerable. *Nobody knows the trouble I've seen.*

She felt her lips begin to quiver and suddenly tears gushed forth. When Danny put an arm around her, she broke down and wept with deep sobs against her friend's shoulder.

Danny patted her on the back until the sobbing diminished. "What's the matter, Duckie?"

Through sniffles, Sandy got out, "I've left David. He wants us to get married."

"Well, you don't have to marry him if you don't love him."

Sandy raised her head. "But I do love him. For sure I love him. And the baby. I just can't stand the thought of marriage, and he's stubborn."

Danny produced a short hand-rolled cigarette. "Here, let's get into something comfortable." They alternated tokes until Danny rose and threw the roach away. In the light of the window, she stood looking less like a Rossetti and more like a Vermeer. "What are you afraid of? David? Yourself?"

"It's more David plus society. I'm struggling to find and maintain a new me, as an artist. Part of that is loving a man and having a baby. But he's always worrying about what people will think, and pulling down the window shades and emptying ash trays and taking out the garbage."

"But does he take it out—the garbage? For real?"

"Of course," said Sandy. "He'd better! But all he talks about is did I take my vitamins, and how do I want the laundry done and how to save money. He's nothing but a husband!"

"Does it hurt to be practical? Kids cost money."

"Okay, maybe I'm complaining about the wrong things. What really gets me is that he was so unconventional before, and now he's acting the uptight, moral man. It's dull. I've—I've got my creativity to protect."

"I see what you mean and you're right."

"I need more time. To make my way as myself, an artist."

"You need more time." Danielle led the way to the kitchen, a room painted apple green with an old white gas stove and chipped porcelain table. She started laying out plates and cutlery.

Sandy, sitting in a wooden chair which had a leg mended with a tape, said, "Women are more independent than men."

"Sounds great, but hardly true. Some individuals are more independent than others, that's all."

"Yes, I guess it's not a man-woman thing."

"No. I'm very dependent myself. And Sol—you know, my old boss—he's independent."

"Did you change jobs, Danny?"

"No, the job changed. Soon after you guys came to our barbecue, Sol split for Iowa to make films at the University. And my new boss is awful, scolds if I'm ten minutes late, so I'm hardly creative at all on the job. Sonia quit, and I can't keep regular working hours unless I can find people to look after the twins."

"Did Sonia leave without notice?"

"She gave me two weeks' notice but I just couldn't believe she'd go off and live with a dumb beer-guzzler she met at a bar."

"Don't be prejudiced. A guy can drink beer in a bar and be a good man."

"I guess. Are you okay? I felt great when I was at about your stage."

"You must have been big with twins."

"Not much more than with a single. After all, the twins' combined birth weight was under twelve pounds."

"When did you learn you were having twins?"

"Not until the sonagram, when there were definite double heartbeats. Why? You're not having twins, are you?" Sandy shook her head and Danny speculated, "I'd say you look about average for eight months."

"But I'm seven months."

"Nobody knows for sure. You're short and your bones

are average—I'm tall and my bones are small—and—well, I don't know all the factors but I'd say you were eight months if I didn't know otherwise."

Sandy unwrapped the print. "I brought you a present. It's called 'Images of Woman.'"

Danny was delighted with it. "Sandy, you have a real draughtsman's sureness, and get marvelous color into even your black and white. I love it. And the idea of the man and the images of women. God, you're really in love! This will be the jewel of my decor."

She pinned the print reverently to a beige window shade where children's art was also pinned, and then led the way to the dining room where there was a basket of clean clothes on the table. Starting to fold kid's clothes, she confided, "It was a shock to lose Sol and Sonia both. Every morning I have to drive Trilby to nursery school but the school won't take Chrissie, so I drive her to my friend Betsy's in Queens and then drive the other direction to work in Huntington. I pay Betsy a lot and Trilby's school a lot, and nobody will take both girls. Chrissie is the problem—she could stay overnight at Betsy's, but even though she's the bigger twin she isn't housebroken and Betsy is having doubts about keeping her at all."

Sandy was shocked. "But how old are the twins now?"

"Four. But toilet training isn't easy for twins."

"Danny, it can't be because they're twins. Because you're overworked, maybe."

"Whatever. Anyhow, Betsy's in Texas for a week because her grandmother died, and I don't know what to do with my poor kid."

Sandy didn't hesitate. "I'll stay with her tomorrow. Maybe Tuesday, too, unless David calls."

"David could come here for dinner. Ask him any night."

"Could you get someone by Tuesday?"

"I can try. Maybe I'll get an inspiration."

"What's the procedure?"

"Well, I look in the local paper, to see if there are any

new ads, and I call a few friends to see if any of them or their friends will take Christina. And I ask people I meet during the day if they know anyone near my job who babysits in her own home."

Sandy thought this seemed a bit haphazard but said forthrightly, "Here, I'll fold while you start phoning."

"It's too early to phone about Wednesday, since you're staying anyway . . . "

"I said I'd stay *Monday*," Sandy said, folding a small tee shirt. "Try to find a sitter."

Danny moved uncertainly out the door and came back in a minute with a newspaper. "Here's an ad. 'Childcare needed for five-year-old, nine A.M. to noon, four days a week. Steady. Call immediately.' She probably won't get anyone even for those short hours. Here's an offer for a kid to get free tuition in nursery school in exchange for the mother's driving a school bus. I could do that but I have a job. Here's somebody else needing a sitter—in fact three more. There's nobody who wants to keep kids—just people with kids, needing help. I'm lucky to have Betsy in Queens."

"If you pay so much for child care, how do you manage?"

"Well, this house is free—that is, the divorce agreement takes care of the mortgage payments and I skip the repairs for now. I get our clothes in thrift shops and this summer we grew a lot of our food. We're vegetarian mostly, anyway. My big expense is the car. I drive more than sixty miles a day. So far I've been putting the gas on my Master Charge, but that won't be any good soon, if I can't pay."

"But don't you realize the interest you pay on charge cards? David says you should borrow money only from a credit union."

"Oh, Sandy. It must be nice to have a man to rely on. But I'm not going to feel bad. If I have to quit work I'll go on welfare. There are worse things."

"You like to work, though. I loved your sand-castings and quilting. You're really good."

"That's what Lippy used to tell me—remember Lipstein, my design teacher? He sure hyped me on all my talents. But I married wrong and unfortunately had the talent for twins. Speaking of those cuties, it's time to wake them up for a meal."

"Can I get it ready?"

"Okay. There's stuff for salad in the fridge."

Sandy found the fridge bare of anything beyond salad greens, and recalled passing a supermarket only a few blocks way. She went to the bottom of the stairs and called up, "I'm driving to the store while I've got Mom's car. If David calls, tell him I'll call him right back."

When she returned with food the twins hurried to the table where Danny had a salad ready, and Sandy produced bread and cheese, bananas, raisins, and milk, all ready to eat.

She herself couldn't stop eating the salad. "What's this crisp white vegetable?"

"Jicama. Sweet Mexican radish. Spelled j-i-c-a-m-a, but called *heeckama*."

Sitting side by side in their tee shirts and blue jeans, the twins were wolfing down cream cheese and bread, bananas, and glass after glass of milk. Between swallows they giggled and said, "Heeckama, heeckama!" pretending to hiccup.

Sandy smiled broadly at them. "Where do you buy jicama?" she asked.

"Actually, I don't. A friend brings it from the Bronx market where he works."

"Oho, who is this friend?"

"He's nice plain Bill who works for a grocery store, and is the principal reason we haven't quite stopped eating." Danny winked solemnly and made a clown face. The twins laughed and made faces themselves but Sandy felt her own eyes widen and dropped her gaze.

For dessert she had bought oatmeal cookies and marshmallows which started another eating frenzy until Danny told the twins, "No more sweets, or you can't go to the movies when Bill comes for us."

"We're going to the movies!" the twins sang.

"I get to sit by Sandy," Trilby said.

"No, I get to sit by Sandy," said Chrissie.

Sandy smiled warmly and said, "I'd like to sit by both of you, but I'd better stay here and wait for a phone call. And I might get an idea for a sketch."

A honk outside signaled Bill's arrival, and Danielle and the twins disappeared. Before washing the dishes, Sandy opened the door so she'd be able to hear the phone. When she was done she walked into the hall and heard again the sound of running water. She went upstairs and bent the wire holding the float in the toilet and the noise stopped.

It would be satisfying to clean this bathroom properly. And best to have a clean living room where I am to sleep on the sofa, as Mom's sure to come in when she comes.

She cleaned the bathroom and living room.

When Danny's entourage came home, Sandy was watching *Masterpiece Theater* and said only, "David didn't call." Danielle and Bill invited her to join them for a smoke in the kitchen, but the little girls came to join her on the sofa and told her about the movie.

Her mother arrived about eleven o'clock and was so shocked at seeing the twins still up that she could do little more than say hello and goodbye. Sandy whispered, "They slept all afternoon," but her mother snatched the car keys and left. Sandy was too tired to do anything but kick off her shoes and fall asleep on the sofa in her clothes.

The next morning she woke when Danny brought her coffee and only then realized that a blanket had been tucked over her. She thanked Danny and tried to listen to her instructions. "I'm leaving for work and taking Trilby to school, so all you have to think about is yourself and Chrissie. She's in the loo right now. There's homemade yogurt on the table and lashings of vegetables that Bill brought. I cooked enough oatmeal for both of you. I'll be home around six. Have fun."

Before Sandy was fully awake, Chrissie came thumping downstairs. She was big for her age, and was going to have her mother's blondeness and beauty except that her expression was pouting. Sandy soon found her in the kitchen eating cookies. She tried to persuade her to eat the cooked oatmeal instead but Chrissie just stuffed more cookies into her mouth.

They're made of oatmeal anyhow so what the hell. I can't start by laying down minor rules that aren't worth enforcing. I'll eat the oatmeal.

She ate it. Her smile disappeared when the child started eating marshmallows.

What if she eats the whole package?

She quickly removed the bag from Chrissie's hand and counted out four marshmallows, which she laid at intervals along the edge of the table. "See if you can reach them with your tongue." Chrissie grabbed them with her hand. Meanwhile Sandy put the package into a large brown bag and walked it carefully down the stairs to the garbage can.

"I want marshmallows!"

"Marshmallows all gone. Let's play a game." Her voice promised fun but Chrissie dashed down the stairs and almost got to the can before Sandy grabbed her. "No, Chrissie, marshmallows all gone. Dirty." But the child went limp, slid out of her grasp, ran to the bottom of the yard along the wire fence and slipped through a small opening into the neighbor's. Sandy trudged to the spot, and cleared some nettles away but couldn't squeeze through. She patted her belly.

Poor baby, I won't mash you.

She couldn't see anyone in the neighbor's yard although she felt Christina was still near. She waited, rubbing her arm which had been stung by a nettle. She looked closely at a nettle leaf.

I'd like to sting her with one. Little brat. Actually, a nettle leaf would make an interesting lithographic emblem. One Shakespeare line I like is "Out of this nettle, danger, I pluck this flower, safety."

After several minutes she walked back through the house and over onto the neighbor's front porch. A dog inside barked but no one came to the door. She returned to Danny's back yard, wishing she had something to sit on. The whole situation was baffling, on top of David's failure to call. Her back ached.

What did he do all day Sunday? Today he'd be at work, but he never makes personal calls from there

A cat came through the fence and she talked to it, hoping the kind tone of her voice would bring Chrissie back. Then she looked up and saw her at the window of Danny's bedroom upstairs. She walked back to the house and climbed the stairs. On the floor of the hall near the bathroom lay the empty marshmallow bag, a pool of urine beside it. Chrissie was on Danny's bed, muddy shoes dangling.

"So while I was at the neighbor's you got the marshmallows and have been gorging on them the whole time. I hope you're satisfied, you rascal you!"

Chrissie just sat watching as she wiped up the floor, "How did this happen when you're wearing a diaper?"

"Diaper too full," said Chrissie. Sandy approached her with a new diaper but she squirmed to the other side of the bed.

Sorry for the child, Sandy sat across from her on the bed and spoke cheerfully. "Do you want to play with your toys?" She shook her head. "Do you like to sing songs or say nursery rhymes?" Chrissie wriggled off the bed and ran into the bathroom. Following her, Sandy found her fishing in the cosmetic bag she'd left there.

"That's mine, Christina." She retrieved the bag, scowling, but the little girl kept hold of a comb and was trying to pull it through her tangled hair. She looked up engagingly and Sandy again felt compassion, and helplessness.

243

I give up. I cleaned yesterday but I'm sketching a nettle today. She can have the comb.

Downstairs, she put the cosmetic bag into her backpack and stored it on a high empty shelf in the kitchen, and took her sketch pad to the table outside. By using a large maple leaf as protection for her fingers, she picked a nettle leaf and was idly sketching it when Chrissie appeared, sat at the table and fingered the edge of the sketch pad. Sandy smiled. "Would you like to draw a picture?" She tore off a clean page and spread it out on the table for Chrissie, who promptly stood up on the seat of the chair, turned around sat down heavily on the paper. It was quickly printed with grime from her diaper. Sandy looked at her in disgust. "You're a real pest!" Chrissie stuck out her tongue and Sandy stuck out her own, hoping it would appear playful, although she didn't feel it that way. She went on sketching.

When Chrissie ran out again through the hole in the fence Sandy made a decision. The next time the child came near her, she went into action, managing to wrestle her into a clean diaper. Chrissie struggled but didn't cry, seeming to enjoy the physical contest as she gave Sandy a violent bump in the abdomen.

Oh, God, she'll end up hurting the baby.

She sat down and did nothing. David didn't call.

Danielle came home at six, quickly bathed Christina and dressed her to match Trilby, who was shyly proud to show her art work from school.

Sandy ate heartily of salad again and was pleased when Danny said, "Sandy, you've been a real help today. My mind was free at work and I figured out how to change a closet into a half-bath. It solved a remodeling problem."

"Do you know about architecture too?"

"Enough to know that hot and cold water pipes were inside that wall."

The twins were fighting and Danny got them interested in working a puzzle.

"Would you have liked to be an architect, Danny?"

"Oh, yes. Or an engineer. But I didn't have the guts to go for it."

"Weren't we all chicken, though? I wanted to be a sculptor, of big outdoor things. I imagine great structures, like attaching the wings of the TWA building at Kennedy Airport onto the top of the Empire State Building."

"You'd have to move more than hot and cold pipes," said Danny. They laughed.

"Last year," said Sandy, "near some construction, someone fastened a lighted Christmas tree a few hundred feet up in the air. The tall crane which held it was invisible at night so the tree just flew there against the stars of the winter sky. Modern art could be like that. Huge and outlandish and cheerful. That's the kind of art I'd like to do."

"Maybe the engineers of beautiful bridges are the great artists of today. Their work is permanent . . . mostly. And some airplanes are sculpture."

"But *I'm* not designing them, I'm tying macramé baskets."

Danny didn't laugh. "I need a plant basket."

"I'll make you one. Do you have string? It takes lots."

"There's lots in a drawer somewhere. I think it has a nice uneven texture. I'll look for it after I read the girls their bedtime story."

"Okay. While you're doing that I'm going to take an evening stroll. If David calls, tell him I'll call right back."

Sandy walked but didn't feel calmed. David was toughing this out. At a phone booth, she dialed her mother, hoping to hear that she'd just heard from him, but Judy said, "He didn't call. Why don't you call him?"

"I have my pride."

"That may be all you have if you're too independent."

"Oh, Mom, c'mon. I had an awful day taking care of Chrissie. She's the big twin. She's disturbed, I swear. And I'm going to keep her again tomorrow, so *I* must be disturbed."

Tuesday was like Monday except that Sandy took

Chrissie for a walk and bought her an ice cream cone, but afterward the little girl sulked and hid from her.

In the evening, Sandy went to the phone booth and called the apartment, hoping to talk with David, but what she got was, "This is David Steinberg. Leave a message." She hung up without speaking and called her mother, who, after hearing about Chrissie's behavior, said, "She and her mother both need a psychiatrist."

Although this was also Sandy's private opinion about Chrissie, she said only, "Danny has no money for it."

"Therapists help you figure out how to earn the money."

On Wednesday Sandy sat in the backyard tying a plant basket for Danny, while Chrissie went in and out. She did eat her oatmeal that morning and some bread and butter later. They walked to the store and Sandy bought hostess gifts of a big canned ham, and a barbecued chicken. She and Chrissie lunched on hamburgers.

It was hard to abandon Danny, but she had decided to return to Manhattan the next morning. Danny said bravely, "I'll take Chrissie to work with me tomorrow, and persuade Trilby's school to take her for the day on Friday. I'm sure they'll do that in an emergency, as they're fond of Trilby. And Babysitter Betsy will keep Chrissie next week."

On the early commuter train on Thursday, Sandy did some serious thinking.

I'd rather talk with him on the phone, whichever one of us calls first, because I'd know what to expect, not just run into him in the apartment and start quarreling.

From Penn Station she phoned Debbie, an old friend from high school. Debbie, now a capable young nurse, was a generous friend for whom Sandy had both love and admiration. Her modern apartment wasn't far from the hospital where she worked and where her boyfriend, Stan, was an intern. They had introduced Sandy and David to one another in the first place, and had recommended the doctor in their hospital who was to deliver Sandy's baby.

Luckily Debbie was at home, having worked two shifts the day before. She sounded delighted that Sandy was near and insisted that she come for lunch. Sandy took the subway to Chelsea.

Sandy warmed to Debbie's efficient manner and the way her navy slack suit set off the shine of her short blond hair. Hopefulness seemed to surround her as she served lunch in a clean kitchen with orange drapes, a pottery bowl of fresh pears on the polished table, and and a drawing of happy bunnies on the wall.

Practical and experienced, Debbie heard Sandy's news and invited her to stay. She answered questions about what to expect in the hospital and soon had the mother-to-be on a blanket on the living room floor practicing her breathing. Sandy asked, "Will it really be all right for David to be there all during the birth?"

"Your doctor has agreed and that's all that counts. Still, Sandy, if I were you, I'd go ahead and get married before the baby comes. Like tomorrow. You'll have visitors in the hospital, and they'll feel better if its name is Steinberg, not Lieberman."

"Next week is Thanksgiving."

"Well, do it. For the baby's sake."

Sandy knew she'd never make dear, generous Debbie understand how she felt about the threat of marriage to her art. But Debbie did know why she didn't want to call David herself. He might be angry at her and his direct anger would be hurtful to the cause of their making up. Or, if he concealed his feelings in order not to hurt her, she wouldn't learn how he really felt, which he most likely would tell Debbie. Instinctively she knew a mediator was necessary. They decided that Debbie would call him at home that evening.

At nine, Debbie called the apartment but got the answering machine. She held the phone so Sandy could hear. "This is David Steinberg. Leave a message." Sandy signaled her not to answer but to hang up. Debbie tried again at eleven but got the same reply from the machine.

Sandy herself dialed the number at midnight. She could picture their apartment, the sink full of dirty dishes and David's clothes and newspapers scattered about. She got the machine and hung up.

In the morning as Debbie was leaving for work, Sandy gave her David's office number, asking her to call him about ten, tell him where she was and see what he said.

At eleven the phone rang and Sandy picked it up on the first ring, sure that it would be David. But it was Debbie with news. "You'd better be sitting down, Sandy. David's office receptionist said he's in Atlantic City. He drove down with two women from his office, Sharon and Becky. Sounds like a party."

"Oh, I forgot! He had a conference."

"I got his home number, and it wasn't your number but his mother's. She said he's out of town and she expects him back tomorrow evening. She sent you her love if I see you. So call him at his mother's tomorrow night."

"I want to call him today. Listen, if I find out from his office his hotel number in Atlantic City, will you call him there?"

"Sure, when I get home, about five."

Sandy got the phone number and waited. She knew who Becky was, a fake blonde who David said always went to the coffee machine when he did, and made eyes at him from her desk. Before the office Christmas party, David had appealed to Sandy to stick close to him, to show Becky that he had a girlfriend. It turned out, however, that at the party Becky gave all her attention to a man fixing the photocopy machine, so Sandy only glimpsed her.

Debbie called the Atlantic City hotel twice on Friday evening but there was no answer in his room. Sandy felt she was unable to wait until Saturday evening when his mother expected him. She didn't know what to do, or if she was right to be so sure that Debbie should speak to him first. Leaving a number for him to call would spoil the shock value. What if his true feelings never did come out? She felt unsure about everything.

On Saturday one last phone call by Debbie to the hotel brought the news that David Steinberg could be reached at another number. With Sandy sitting next to her, she dialed and David answered.

"David, this is Debbie in New York. Sandy's at my place and wants to know how you are." She listened a moment, gave him her phone number and hung up. "Sandy," she said, "he's in a meeting but will call me right back."

The phone didn't ring at once and Sandy gritted her teeth to keep calm. When it rang, she wanted to try to overhear David's voice on the phone, but when Debbie said, "Sandy was here but she went out, and I don't know when I'll see her," she walked into the bedroom so her friend wouldn't be a liar. Finally Debbie hung up and came to sit facing her.

"What was he saying all that time?"

"He sounded like an executive. He's at a post-conference meeting and not coming back until tomorrow. Then he said stuff like he wanted a meaningful relationship, but you threw it back in his face, and with his upbringing this was a terrible experience for him. He said you're a far-out type who falls for silly notions and he doesn't want to talk with you. I said, 'Yet,' and he repeated it, 'Yet,' so it's not hopeless, I guess."

Debbie went into the kitchen, and Sandy felt an ominous stillness in herself, a cold recognition of trouble.

I know what I have to do. His mother thinks he's coming home tonight, and I can tell her he isn't coming until tomorrow, as if he had called me. I'll tell her I'm back in town after helping out a friend while Davey's been gone and ask her to have him call me when he comes. I know she's on my side.

Right now I'll pay Debbie for all the phone calls and take her out to lunch. Then I'll take a taxi home and leave my backpack and go right out to the grocery store and get food galore, bread and milk and butter and eggs to make popovers, and green groceries and fruit. I'll clean the apartment. I'll have it all fixed up and good food ready when he comes on Sunday.

If he doesn't come, I'll call him at work on Monday and ask him to come home to dinner. He'll come, and I'll tell him we can be married right away. Thanksgiving day's a holiday, and we'll go to dinner with first one mother and then with the other and break the good news about a wedding. My mother can arrange whatever she likes, and both mothers can invite everybody they want.

Going home, she rested in the taxi. It supported her back better than most chairs she'd been in lately. She felt old with ancient wisdom.

I learned what David needs. And I'm the only one who can give it to him. We'll get married, and have a healthy baby.

20

I Know What We Have to Do

David, on the evening after Sandy had left him to go to her mother's, found her note on the kitchen table and scanned it.

She *is* cute when she's mad. And what spirit she's got! So darn spunky. That baby of ours is going to take prizes, exploring everything, full of himself.

His supper menu was crackers and cheese and beer, with raisin bran and milk for dessert. He pondered the note as he ate. She needs breathing space? Hmm. It's good she remembered about my suit because next week I go to the conference. I'll call her at her mother's and tell her about my day.

He picked up the phone but put it down again, recalling the shock on the faces of Brenda and Tom when they heard that he and Sandy weren't married. He did some checking.

Yes, she took the bottle of vitamin pills, also her tooth-brush. She left me the toothpaste.

He wandered into the bedroom, took off his business clothes, put on his old brown bathrobe, and rested on his bed.

Her name is on the lease of this apartment, but I'm not her guest—I pay most of the rent, and this is my bed which we bridged with hers. I could stay with my mother but she'd start asking questions. She'll have to know, if Sandy doesn't come back soon. I could call Sharon, but I'll see her in the office tomorrow and decide then if I want to tell her. A boss can look for your work to deteriorate if there's trouble at home.

Hammering in the apartment above annoyed him.

Damned inconsiderate, hammering when people have just finished dinner and are resting.

He turned on the kitchen radio full blast, opened the window so it could be heard upstairs, and sprawled out on the living room sofa to read some *Times* pages he'd clipped. The first was an editorial titled "Crisis Mediation."

Maybe I should find a go-between for me and Sandy. Marriages used to be arranged by brokers but aren't now, anyhow not by my family in the Bronx nor by Sandy's. Judy Lieberman could be a mediator if she weren't Sandy's mother. There is our friend Debbie who lives in Chelsea. She has a great heart. If Sandy's not back in a couple of days I'll call her.

He watched the news, then changed into his pajamas and took off his shoes and left them neatly pointing forward under the standing suit rack which had belonged to his father.

I know Mom's feeling lonely these days.

The next evening he rode the subway to the Bronx. His mother, a small but vigorous woman, was thrilled to see him, and, to soothe his feelings, acted indignant over Sandy's desertion. After dinner, she showed him a snapshot in her album of his young cousin who resembled Sandy. Warmly, she exulted, "Your baby could look like both families."

David had hoped she'd be more sorry for him. Her parting remark, however, was strategic. "Don't call her. She'll call you."

On his long trip home, every pay telephone he passed sent a pang through him. But he had worked out a formula. "I don't have the right change. Millions for freedom but not one cent for tribute." It didn't make sense, but it sustained him.

On Friday morning he realized the weekend would be too rough for him if he stayed in the apartment alone. Anyway, he had work to do. He packed a suitcase and ate a big breakfast of the onion soup, pastrami and carrot sticks. He drove to work and parked in a garage near the office so he could drive straight to his mother's at the end of the day.

His mother was pleased to see him but opened her eyes wide when she saw the suitcase. After dinner she made a sober remark. "David, you love her. You'd better call. You have to face a quarrel sooner or later, so you might as well get it out in the open."

"I can't. Calling her will mean I'm a crumbling cookie."

"In a marriage there are a lot of cookie crumbs."

He slept overnight on her sofa.

On Saturday he painted her small kitchen, as he had long ago promised to do. He was touched that she still had some of his old clothes on hand to work in. On Sunday he read the *Times* thoroughly, took his mother out to lunch, and washed his car. He called the apartment, hoping Sandy was there, but the answering machine chirped, "This is Sandra, the lithographer, with a message for the Madison Purple Art Gallery. Please let me know the deadline for submitting a print for your next show." He hung up.

She isn't home. She forgets to change the machine after her outgoing greetings are out of date. Well, something outgoing is on now. We've both gone far out.

At home that evening he recorded on the machine, "This is David Steinberg. Leave a message."

Monday and Tuesday were busy office days. The conference was to begin Wednesday evening, so he had to do the regular week's work in half the time. He worked late on Tuesday evening with Becky, the youngest professional on the staff. She was bright and forthright, and made several suggestions which helped them finish sooner.

He walked her to the subway entrance where she reminded him that they would both be riding to Atlantic City the next day with Sharon. He told her he was glad she'd be along, thinking that her presence would spare him any more of Sharon's personal advice. He wouldn't have to hear it coming back either, since Sharon planned to visit friends in New Jersey after the conference. He and Becky would return to Manhattan by bus.

The next afternoon on the drive to Atlantic City, Becky kept things lively with jokes and light talk. Time passed quickly, and once at the hotel, they soon joined the staffs from their agency's offices in other cities who gathered in Sharon's room for wine. The faces of the group of young professionals gleamed like pink moons with the pleasure of looking at the ocean out of Sharon's window. She was the only one with an oceanside room, although David claimed he had a clear view. "Of the beach?" someone asked.

"No, the fire escape," David quipped.

During the laughter, Becky said to David, quietly, "My room is tiny but I have it to myself. It's right next to yours."

All of the guests worked for a charity benefitting victims of muscular disorders, and talk skipped from problems of funding to stories of courage.

David enjoyed the first day of meetings, partly because he had shared in the planning. It was late Thursday night before he felt lonely. The man who was supposed to share his room was no longer expected. He missed Sandy.

I can't expect her to phone me. She knows about the conference, but probably wouldn't remember what hotel it was in, if I even told her. I don't want to call her—I'm sticking to my views. Of course, if she's changed her mind and come back to the apartment, she's missing me and feeling guilty she left before we could kiss and make up. Well, she can have her "breathing space."

As he tried to sleep, he heard the shower running in Becky's room next door and pictured her getting into bed.

By Friday morning his thoughts about Sandy had shifted.

She's been using me. There are lots of warm, dedicated young women who are working to help sick people at sacrifice salaries, like Becky. She lives at home, and pays her parents for room and board. She's cheerful, with a ready laugh and wink, not cute when she's mad but sincere. New York City and fashion go together, so she dresses well.

Sandy, on the other hand, is an artist and does her own thing. Neither her own mother nor mine can understand her. She's letting me be exposed to a lot of women on the make, hot for bachelors, like they are at conferences. Well, I can have the game as well as the name.

At the cocktail hour Friday evening, he and Becky had a couple of drinks together and joined the group at dinner. The entertainment finale included good music. They danced, Becky quiet and dreamy in his arms. There was a floor show with a funny comedian, and during a singer's heartfelt rendition of "September Song," he felt her hand on his knee under the table.

He stood up and beckoned the waiter for more water.

While it was being poured, she soothingly rubbed her hand over his ear and neck, and later followed it with a seductive look through heavy-lidded eyes, which moved him. She was part purring kitten, part siren.

After the entertainment ended, Sharon and a group left to try gambling, and David and Becky were alone in the elevator going up to their floor. She leaned against him, smiling and comfortable. As they walked down the hall to their adjoining rooms she chatted about how they could sleep late in the morning, since there would be only one late morning session before lunch. At the door of her room she gave him a warm hug and a little tug. "David, would you help me open the window in here? It's stuck." He went in and after he opened the window she placed her hand in his. Suddenly he was kissing her and she was kissing him back, holding him close.

He didn't return to his room.

On Saturday morning after breakfast he went to the pay phone in the hotel lobby, and again dialed his home number. The answering machine reported, "This is David Steinberg. Leave a message." He waited for the tone, and said, "Sandy, this is me, calling you from Atlantic City. It's Saturday morning." He was thinking what to say when he saw Becky approaching, and hung up quickly.

The conference was to end after lunch, and as they ate, Becky said, "Tomorrow's Sunday. I hate Sunday at home. Couldn't we move to another hotel and keep on enjoying Atlantic City?"

He didn't answer, and she hung her head, submissively. He thought of his loneliness at his mother's the weekend before, and said, his voice husky, "Okay, I guess."

"I like the looks of that hotel next door," she said. "We won't need a taxi."

In the hubbub of goodbyes after lunch, Sharon reminded David that she wasn't driving back to New York and that he and Becky should save receipts for their bus fares, for reimbursement. He didn't mention they weren't leaving until the next day.

He and Becky checked in at the new hotel about one thirty. She wasn't shy and asked the clerk if there was a honeymooners' rate for a room with an ocean view, and if there was a discount for honeymooners for the evening entertainment. They got the discounts and she said to David, with a wink, "Pay the nice man, dear." When they got to their room she promptly put her share of the money on the table by the phone. David pocketed it, and put in a call to their first hotel asking the desk clerk to give anyone who called his new phone number.

Minutes later, the phone in their new room rang and David answered.

"David, this is Debbie. Sandy's here at my place and wants to know how you are."

He was relieved that it was Debbie and not Sandy herself who called, as he didn't want to explode in anger to Sandy, and didn't want Becky to hear it, either. He decided to make it sound like a business call. "Yes, this is David Steinberg. I'm in a meeting, but give me your number and I'll phone you right back. And you're the only one I need to speak with."

He took the elevator down to the lobby and put through the call on a pay phone. "Let me explain things to you,

Debbie," he said. "You can tell Sandy whatever you want."

"Yes, David," Debbie said mildly.

"I don't want to talk with her because she left me. She's not interested in having a meaningful relationship, only wants to live in sin and feel artistic. I want to act responsibly and she throws it back in my face. With my upbringing, this has been a terrible shock to me, her being such a far-out type who'll throw away solid values for silly notions. It's gotten me confused, and I don't want to see her."

"Yet," said Debbie.

"Yeah. Not yet. I'm too angry. Now I have to go."

At nine-thirty the next morning, David realized what an enormously boring weekend he was having. Following breakfast in the coffee shop he wanted some exercise outside, but Becky was interested only in sex or domesticity. About them she was healthily matter-of-fact, but he couldn't fathom why enjoying something else was such a big hurdle for her.

"Let's walk on the boardwalk for fresh air," he insisted.

"In these high heels?" she asked. "Didja think I'd bring sneakers to Atlantic City?" So they walked across the street to a shop where he bought the *Times* and she bought souvenirs made of clam shells.

"We haven't seen any clams," he said.

She waved her hand toward the ocean and with a flirtatious smile said, "They're out there."

David bought a *New York Times*. Outside the shop, he gazed at the skylines of the many hotels, but she wasn't interested in comparing styles of architecture. In their room she sat doing her fingernails and chatting, and "frankly admitting" she believed in marriage. He tried to concentrate on the editorials and asked her if she wanted to see the paper.

She asked for the sports section but soon started watching TV. David read until it was time to leave to catch the bus.

At the bus station he bought hamburgers which they ate as they stood in line for a bus which was due to arrive in Manhattan at about six. It was so crowded that they couldn't sit together, and David was soon lost in thought.

I was caught off guard when I spoke to Debbie yesterday. What I said isn't really the way I feel. What if Sandy was by the phone listening? My lively Sandy. I've made her unhappy, and she doesn't even know yet that I've been unfaithful. When I tell her—and I've got to tell her right away—she'll leave me for real.

One of her songs popped into his head:

> Frankie and Johnnie were lovers,
> Oh, Lordy, how they did love.
> They swore to be true to each other,
> As true as the stars above.
> He was her man
> And he done her wrong.

I've been stubborn in two ways, one right and one wrong. I'm right to know that marriage is what I need, and wrong to overlook how much it means to Sandy to establish herself as an artist. If I'd paid more attention, she might not be afraid to get married.

I know what we have to do. I have to convince her that I understand she'll be a good lover and a good mother and a good artist, all three, and that I'll be more help with the artist part. And she'll have to forgive me for being unfaithful, and understand how much it hurt that she refuses to marry me. We know our families expect us to do right—not make our whole lives unhappy. We want to have a happy baby. So help me God, we're going to have a happy baby!

At Port Authority, he and Becky found the taxis and David asked the first driver in line, "Can you take this young lady to Brooklyn?"

"What address?" asked the driver.

Becky told him, but he shook his head and let another

couple into his cab. Becky told David, "You have to pay in advance."

Luckily, when David gave Becky's address and thirty dollars to the next driver, he replied cheerfully, "Sure, that's on my way. I'm going home to watch *Masterpiece Theater*."

Becky gave David a grateful hug. However, when he put her bag in beside her he said, clearly, "Goodbye, Becky. I'm sure I'll see you around when we're back to business in the office."

When he closed the door she blew him a kiss.

He started for home.

21

Gumption?

Martha and Sarah sat at the kitchen table with glasses of champagne in front of them. Barry and Robin had not arrived. Martha had opened a bottle of her middle-priced brand hoping to keep Sarah from worrying that her big Thanksgiving dinner, all ready, wouldn't be at its best much longer.

Earlier, in a holiday spirit, Martha had set out in the upstairs living room their real wine of the day, the beautiful bottle of Dom Perignon. She thought of it standing up straight in its silver ice bucket, as if bracing her for whatever was ahead today, in case she was to meet her future daughter-in-law.

Sarah was suppressing anger at her beloved Barry for being late. "She may live far away," she said timidly.

"More likely, their work hit a snag and they couldn't call. I wonder what she does in connection with the parade."

"Maybe she's part of a float," said Sarah.

"Yes. Those giant cartoon-figure balloons that dance by the skyscrapers are only part of the parade. The floats at street level often feature beautiful models wearing the upcoming fashions. Maybe Robin is a model."

"Maybe the one who wore all black and sparkling stockings," said Sarah. "Here's to her!" She took a sip of champagne.

"Here's to her! And I have reasons of my own to celebrate—all my fondest hopes for my Wednesday patients are being fulfilled. Elinor's engagement to Ralph is imminent—they're combining their families at dinner today. Ursula's operation is over and she's taking the antidepressant I prescribed. She may make it to her Golden

Wedding after all. And Billie's phoning Mike in Florida to wish him a happy Thanksgiving." She raised her glass. "Here's to my visions coming true!"

Sarah raised her glass slightly. "From your mouth to God's ear!"

"Thank you, Sarah. And I've another thing to celebrate. Do you recall Sandy, the pregnant feminist who didn't want to get married? She phoned and asked to come back to see me."

"Mazeltov! Did she have her shotgun wedding?"

"I don't know. She just asked for a weekly appointment, like before. I said, 'Okay!' and she hung up. So here's to her happiness."

They heard the front door open, and Sarah moved immediately to the stove. Martha hurried into the hall and then stopped cold. With Barry was a tall man of about thirty-five, blond, with a trim mustache.

"Mom," Barry said, "this is Robin."

Martha was shocked, then mad, then hurt, then scared. In milliseconds her mind went from preparing to meet a future daughter-in-law to wondering if Barry had changed his sexual preference. My God!

Robin took off his coat, saying in a cheerful midwestern accent, "Nothing smells better than roast turkey." He was holding a package wrapped in gift paper.

Barry, hanging coats, said, "Sorry we're a little late, but we've been working like miners and couldn't get away."

Martha nodded. "We'll go upstairs for champagne to celebrate the day."

"Aw, Mom, we're starved. And Robin doesn't like champagne, do you, Rob?"

"I only drink it if I get to kiss the bride." His voice had a tone of perpetual amusement.

Barry strode down the hall, saying, "Just come to the kitchen and meet my grandma!" Robin bounded after him.

Martha stood watching them, stunned. Robin, indeed!

She felt sad at what she knew would be a shock to Sarah. As for herself, she knew she had a problem ahead. Could she cope with this development, if it was one? She was reassured when she heard Sarah's normal tone, shooing the men upstairs. Obviously, serving dinner was uppermost with Sarah just now.

They all went up to the living room, Sarah bringing the open bottle of champagne, forgetting that it was supposed to stay in the kitchen. When they were all seated around the Dom Perignon, Martha exclaimed, "Oh, I forgot something. We need a corkscrew."

Barry said, "Don't open it. This Chandon is fine." He filled glasses for everyone except Sarah, who left them, saying she had a glass in the kitchen and would soon call them to the table.

Robin rather shyly offered Martha the box he'd been holding. "I brought you a couple of bottles of Napa Valley Riesling. We think it's good with turkey, so maybe you can use it if you have any leftovers."

"Thank you. It's nice to have it." Then, noticing he wasn't drinking, "But wouldn't you like some now?"

"Oh, don't bother. I seldom drink."

Barry took the box. "I'm opening a bottle for you," he said and dashed down the stairs.

Left alone with Robin, Martha was glad to sense that he was quite at ease. Observing that he was glancing around the room, she said, "This room is overdue for redecoration, but it takes more . . . whatever . . . than I've got to get started."

"Gumption?" suggested Robin.

Martha laughed. "That was one of my mother's words. Where did you grow up?"

"I was born in Cincinnati, though my parents were English. Now I live in San Francisco but do consulting everywhere."

"Do you often come to New York?"

"In the spring and fall. Barry and I work together on

fashion promotions every Thanksgiving, grabbing the momentum of the parade to work toward spring."

"Oh, yes. Barry said something about fashions." She wished she'd worn something more colorful than navy blue, but had expected to play the role of a serene mother-in-law. San Francisco?

"I started out as an interior decorator, and liked to do a room like this, spacious with great windows."

"Where should I begin?" she asked coolly, wondering if he was fishing for a job.

"You have these good linen drapes for a start. They're fine."

"So far I plan sofas and chairs in linen color, too, with spring green and salmon-colored touches, but I haven't acted."

"Your scheme sounds fine. What about the floor?"

She shrugged. "This old brown wall-to-wall has been here forever."

When Barry came back he found them dusting off their hands. "We've been tearing up the carpet," Robin said. "Your mother didn't know she had classic parquet under here."

"Oh, I used to play that game, a cross between parcheesi and croquet!"

Robin laughed and Barry handed him the bottle of Riesling he had just opened. "Bring it downstairs. Bubbi says to tie our bibs on."

The two men started down briskly and Martha followed, closing the door of the living room with a grimace of regret at the Dom Perignon embedded in its casket of ice.

Poor corpse, your being unopened is only one of the surprises. Robin. An interior decorator. A good hardwood parquet floor. What next?

Martha and Sarah noticed Barry's astonishment when he saw the new elegance of the dining room, but he rose to the occasion and held the chair for Martha to sit. Robin graciously poured Riesling for everyone.

Sarah, at the head of the table carving the turkey, remarked, "My father had a large wine cellar in Vienna."

"European wines have always been the best," said Robin agreeably, "but I'm here to tell you that you should do the wine trip through the Napa Valley. They have some damn fine wineries—the Robert Mondavi is great—and Charles Krug, too."

Barry said, "I know you don't drink sherry, Robin, but how about Christian Brothers? We like their sherry."

Martha wondered who Barry meant by "we." She never bought sherry.

"Yeah, they have some fine sherries," continued Robin. "And there's some very nice Cognac-quality brandy in the Eastern Mendocino, where you don't have to worry about a lot of tourist traps, funicular railways, and such. You know, cable cars. A distraction, when the grapes are remarkable enough."

Explaining *funicular* to us? Martha thought to herself. Is *he* my son's lover?

Before their first bites of Sarah's dinner, Barry proposed a toast to the cook. Soon Robin praised the paprika in the dressing. Sarah said, modestly, "I always use paprika in veal and *Wildgeflügel*." She looked at Robin, then glanced at Barry, and lowered her eyes sadly. Clearly, her heart ached that Barry had not brought a girl home. Martha fleetingly thought that right now Sarah would gladly settle for a shiksa.

What would I settle for?

Dinner progressed from a period of silent, concentrated eating to conversation about the parade. Martha scarcely dared look at Barry for fear he'd guess what she was wondering. He described how his firm worked up seasonal ideas for the fashion industry and how Robin coordinated the work with designers. He claimed that the two of them had been "knee-deep in models and hairdressers and photographers" for years, and he and Robin laughed over some memories.

They had had only a few sips of after-dinner brandy when Robin said apologetically that they should leave. Martha urged them to stay longer but Robin said, "Barry's doing me a favor, driving me to Kennedy to meet my wife. Her plane is due about an hour from now."

"Barry, why didn't you tell us?" Martha said. "We could have waited dinner for her."

Robin said, "It's okay. We're going to my aunt's in Brooklyn. Barry and I will be eating another dinner in a couple of hours."

"Barry, you *can't!*" said Sarah.

"After what you've just eaten!" said Martha.

"You see why I didn't tell you dieters? I knew you'd tsk-tsk about it."

"My wife works with me and is coming on business," Robin said. "She couldn't get here yesterday because she had to keep our San Francisco office open and then drive the kids to Sonoma to have Thanksgiving at their grandmother's."

Sarah flashed a radiant smile at him.

After the men left, Martha went directly upstairs to get the bottle of Dom Perignon and to think. She sat on the ancient sofa which had once masqueraded as a patients' couch. Inescapably the place to think through her fears.

Why did I assume that Barry's guest would be a woman? Of course, he has men friends like he's always had. There were a couple of girls besides Angela whom he dated a few times, but many more boyfriends—reporters on the school newspaper or fellow players in the orchestra. But none especially close that I knew about. There was his marriage to Marie, of course, that didn't work out. Is Robin gay? Is Barry?

Why didn't Barry tell me more about Robin beforehand? I do recall something about a colleague working with him on his firm's account with Macy's, so maybe he took for granted I knew who Robin was. What if I have to face a whole new set of facts? Barry would be frank with me, I know, and I'd become the Mother of a Gay. Is there an association, the MAG's? They'd be dubbed the Nags.

Your time is up, she thought suddenly, and stood up. There's Sarah down in the kitchen doing all the clean-up.

She carried the bottle and bucket of ice downstairs, and remarked to Sarah, "Let's face it, Barry's taking a long time to bring a girl home."

"It's only a year and a half," said Sarah, loyally.

Martha wrapped the bottle in aluminum foil and in spite of Sarah's mild protests about space placed it in the rear of the refrigerator. It would most likely wait for a long time. She felt a little cheated that she hadn't even tasted it, but maybe something joyful would eventually turn up. The evening ahead seemed long.

Sarah was cross, unusual for her, and Martha helped put away the leftovers. They cleared the dining table and started a Scrabble game but it didn't seem as much fun as in the kitchen. Sarah took a long time over her turns, and finally made an impatient movement and scattered her letters. "Barry's new girl was a real catch!" she said sarcastically.

"Yes," said Martha. "Maybe he had sparkling socks on, under his trousers!"

Sarah laughed ruefully. "Well, he was a nice man, and he and Barry seemed to have things to laugh about. It makes them so happy to eat! What worries me is you, not having more friends. And you're deciding too much for your Wednesday Four."

Martha felt angry at this but tried to remain calm.

"It's good for you to be concerned, Mother," she began. Sarah winced. Martha hadn't called her that for years. "But the theories I am working on are well-founded. It gives me genuine pleasure to know that each of the Wednesday women has been growing in self-esteem. I need that."

"I know you need it. But you should have a life of your own, not just get reflections of their lives."

Martha's tact evaporated. "So what else is new? It isn't

266

that long since Norman died. I'm earning a good living. We eat well. Do you know how much that bottle of Dom Perignon cost?"

Sarah stood and took off her apron. "We are both tired."

Martha felt chagrin. "Your dinner was the best," she said quickly. "And you did wonders in this room. I do appreciate it." She found words inadequate. "Hey, we actually had a real dinner with company in a real dining room! We must entertain more—I do have friends." She smiled affectionately. "Besides you."

Sarah grinned. "Time to get my feet up," she said. "My dogs bark. Hope there's something on TV besides football." She went heavily up the stairs.

Martha put away the Scrabble game, then wandered into her office. Not turning on a light, she pulled aside the uneven and faded green velvet drapes and studied the street. It was a dark rainy afternoon and puddles on the pavement glinted red and green from distant traffic lights.

Sarah says my life is a reflection. Plato believed that all our human concepts are reflections of big original ideas, which have actual existence outside our minds. The notion never appealed to me, my truth is inside. The biggest idea I have is to help my Wednesday women grow into full womanhood. Not some sort of Platonic ideal but a truly fulfilling life—maybe that's what Irv called the overly high hope of psychiatry. Still, if therapists don't believe in it, who will?

Certainly, I'll be supportive of Barry. It'll be sad if he tells me he's gay, but I won't ask him outright because surely he isn't and would be shocked if I brought it up. I love my son and whatever he does he'll do with full integrity, I know.

The room was chilly, and the gloom of the City, almost without traffic on the holiday, made her feel lonely. She folded her arms on her desk, rested her head on them and slept. A phone call roused her.

22

A Phone Call

Christopher had moved in with Billie as soon as Michael and Mikey left.

On Thanksgiving morning she enjoyed being lazy and stayed in bed watching him get dressed. "How come you're wearing your suit already? Aren't you going to go to your apartment to clean it up?"

"Yes, but I'll change into old clothes there and change back to my suit for my folks' dinner. Then I'll come back here for your dinner. Are you sure you don't want to come to my folks'?"

"Yes, I'm sure. Right now I'm figuring out when to call Mikey in Florida. A holiday to him means sleeping late, but by noon he won't be mad if I wake him. The turkey's all defrosted, and I'll get it stuffed and start it roasting a couple of hours before we want to eat."

"What time will that be?"

"Sally and Duncan are coming about five and she's bringing wine so we'll eat about five-thirty."

"I'll be here by five."

"Don't forget, you're carving the turkey."

"I am if the knife is sharp."

"I'll see to it, you . . . you *manly stereotype*."

Still in her pajamas, she cooked eggs the way Chris liked them, "over easy." After he left, she planned how she would serve the dinner. She had recently bought tray tables which she now placed so everyone could have eye contact and elbow room. First she'd pass crackers and her own special dip, and Sally would pour her wine. On the long narrow table by the wall, there'd be plates and silverware, with cranberry sauce, olives and celery. She'd bring in the hot food and the big turkey, all brown and fragrant. Chris would stand to carve. He'd arrange pieces on a platter so people could help themselves, buffet style, along with stuffing and vegetables, including sweet potatoes baked with marshmallows. At dessert, if Sally wants to, she'll cut the pumpkin pies I bought, and I'll do coffee.

She removed Christopher's gooseneck lamp and other drafting paraphernalia from the table, as well as piles of her school papers. For a festive air, she spread a white paper tablecloth and placed on it a row of white candles in motley holders.

Memories of her dinner party with Michael and Christopher and their Irish songfest came to her as she polished the piano, her luxury item.

It's only an upright, but it sounds wonderful, and as long as the word "Steinway" is in the room, I can make do with corduroy couch covers and mat rugs. The etchings that Christopher gave me are pretty classy too.

In preparation for a long phone conversation with Mikey, she worked steadily, stuffing the twelve-pound bird with dry bread, chopped onions and sage. By noon it was covered with foil and set inside the cold oven. Michael's phone number was still posted on the refrigerator where he had stuck it before he left with Mikey. She went to the phone and dialed it.

Her ex-husband answered gruffly, sounding sleepy. "Oh, Billie! In New York. Long time no see."

"Hi," Billie said matter-of-factly. "It's about time I caught up with Mikey. May I talk with him, please?"

"Mikey? Why should he be here? He's with you."

"He left here with you in September. Wake him up."

"Excuse me?"

"He hasn't been here since the day you left," she said. "He *must* be there."

"You mean you've thought since September that he was here?"

"Where the hell is he?" she shouted, choked with fear and anger. "It was *obvious* he went with you. His clothes were gone the same day."

"He might have gone to the beach," Michael said dryly.

"Migod!" she cried. "He's drowned!"

"Naw, he's a great swimmer. He probably hitched somewhere. Ask his friends. You see them at school, don't you?"

"I never see them. I just barely know one or two."

"They're around. My guess is that Mike knew you wanted him to come with me, so he grabbed the chance to cut out on his own. Weren't you telling me he was ready to split?"

"Yes, I thought you'd help. Now I have no idea where he is."

"His friends will tell you. Check with them."

"Great!" she shouted. "Maybe I'll call you if I find him!" She slammed down the receiver. "I'd like to cut out your liver for your bad example for my son."

She found the number of Sam, the wealthy boy she'd nicknamed Serendipity. After dialing, she waited, dreading what lay ahead. At length a woman answered and said with finality that Sam was asleep. Billie said sharply, "Will you wake him, please? This is important."

When he came on the line after a considerable wait, she asked, "Sam, this is Mike Halloran's mother. When was the last time you saw him?"

"Couple of months back. I picked him up at your apartment building—he had some plastic bags packed. I took him to school. We left the bags in the car until lunch time and I drove him out to the gas station near the Expressway. He said he was getting a ride to Florida with his father."

"He was, but he didn't get there. Listen, Sam, don't tell anyone he's missing."

"Okay, I won't mention it."

Fat chance, she thought. "Sam, promise!"

"I promise. Anyhow, we're leaving for the day in my

270

dad's plane to fly to my grandmother's on the Eastern Shore. I won't be back until late tonight."

"Sam, you know where my classroom is, don't you? Room one-oh-five. Will you please stop by to see me the first thing tomorrow morning?"

"Okay. I have to hang up now."

The only thing Billie could think to do was to dial Florida again. "Michael, I phoned Sam, the kid he rode to the beach with, and he said he drove Mike out to a gas station on the Expressway to wait for you. Sam believed he'd gone to Florida. I swore him to secrecy about Mikey's being missing, but didn't have a chance to ask questions. He's coming to my classroom tomorrow morning. What time did you leave that day? Did you see Mikey at all?"

"Only asleep on the floor on my mattress. I had to get to the library to do more research on labels, and finally delivered the cactuses to the florist's. Then I drove back to your place and got my mattress. Nobody was home. I pulled out about six o'clock."

"That was a Thursday, the day I work with the debate team until six-thirty."

"Didn't Sam say anything else?"

"No. I may learn more tomorrow. Do you think I should call the police?"

"No, wait until you talk to Sam. It's obvious he's struck out for a little freedom. I'll bet he's gotten a job. He did tell me he wouldn't go to Florida, because some people needed him."

"Needed him?"

"That's what he said."

"God, how shall I start looking for him?"

"Let me know when he turns up," Michael said calmly.

Billie hung up. Sure, St. Michael, I'll let you know, Your Excellency, if I find him. Or the body. Maybe you can sell some of your damned cactuses at the funeral.

In spite of her anger, Michael's attitude helped her to stay matter-of-fact.

A couple of month's ago she'd made a space in Mikey's room for Christopher's clothes by stuffing things Mikey had left into the bottom desk drawer. She now emptied it onto the bed, vaguely hoping to find a note of goodbye or some clue to where he might have gone. However, she found only a cassette tape about computers, a copy of *Animal Farm*, his good shoes, an old sweater, and a broken toy car. The prize was one battered sneaker, full of sand and the smell of Mikey's feet.

"Nothing very revealing here," she said aloud with a forced brusqueness, marching back to the kitchen. As she jammed the sneaker into a garbage bag and put it outside the back door, a picture flashed into her mind of herself holding it out to a pack of bloodhounds and watching the dogs scatter over the empty beach, sniffing at everything until they all reached the water line and stopped dead.

Should I keep the sneaker after all? No, his good shoes will be enough if his scent is needed. Anyhow, that's pure panic. The kid was all set for a move. He can look after himself in many ways. And wherever he is, he's sure to be learning a lot. For one thing, that you have to work for what you eat. I have a strong hunch he's homesick today, and would like to talk with me. Probably hasn't money enough to call home, nor enough nerve to call collect.

I can't cry for him. Whatever love I have for him is too mixed up with pain and trouble. I tried to phone him to tell him I miss him and I get this.

She opened canned cranberry sauce, holding back tears.

I'll have to wait and talk with Sam first. But can I get through this day without doing anything?

She phoned Christopher at his apartment and heard his sharp intake of breath as he heard the news. "So he split, huh? Well, he's old enough to look after himself, Billie. In most ways."

"Yeah, but there are lots of dangers."

"Wherever he is, he's been there for a while so there's no use worrying today."

The common sense of this appealed to Billie. "Thanks," she said.

"I'll come home as early as I can. And Billie, you should call Dr. Kaufman."

"Right. I'm sure he's at her place."

"Don't joke. She can advise you. Shrinks know about runaways."

"I don't feel like calling her—she might be at dinner."

"Do it this evening."

"Sally and Duncan will be here and I don't want them to know."

"I'll take them up to the roof to look at the lights and you can call her then."

The rest of the afternoon Billie alternately tended to her dinner and cleaned Mike's room, giving herself a shot of whiskey to help the process.

When the roasting turkey began to smell, it unnerved her. That smell held memories of the years when Mikey was little and their food budget incredibly small, but she managed to have turkey and cranberry sauce and pumpkin pie on Thanksgiving. The year Mikey was eight he heard from the other Cub Scouts that Thanksgiving had a game of its own—it was the meal of the year for gorging yourself, a challenge. So Mikey overate with zeal and fell asleep like a lump of lead in front of the TV afterward. I undressed him and put him to bed. A baby.

Christopher arrived at four-thirty. He looked concerned and gave Billie a hug of sympathy. He too went through the things from the desk drawer. And then he examined the bed also, and found between the mattress and the springs some cigarette papers and last September's *Reader's Digest*.

Sally and Duncan arrived, bringing wine and a bouquet of chrysanthemums. Billie took the flowers gratefully, burying her nose in them to catch their special smell in a slow way unusual for her. Even through the aroma of roast turkey she sought some new scent, some whiff of the outside world where Mikey was. Fortunately, her friend Sally thought he was in Florida, and didn't mention him.

Sally and Duncan both taught in Middle Cove High School and lived together outside the district. As in the case of Billie and Christopher, the woman was a few years older than the man. Sally, robust in both face and figure, was a master teacher of English. Like Billie, she kept her classes lively and was helpful to her colleagues. Duncan taught art and was what Middle Cove considered artistic—timid and talented. His eyes were a clear violet under dark brows, his skin white above a handlebar mustache. In class he had an odd mixture of qualities, positive about his views but so ill at ease in explaining them to the uninterested that he stammered. Students exploited the lack of discipline in his classes but not openly enough to jeopardize their own privileges. Sally had helped him. They fell in love.

Billie breezily introduced Christopher and Sally poured wine to go with the onion dip and crackers Billie had set out. Soon the women took their drinks to the kitchen, where Sally confided, "I'm glad Duncan is chatting easily, not stammering."

"It's the wine," said Billie absently, balancing the turkey carefully as she took it from the oven.

During dinner, Christopher's skill as a host pleased Billie. He carved the bird correctly and was solicitous about slicing more dark or white meat, as preferred. Billie noticed that his own appetite was good despite his having eaten already.

"So give us the scoop on Cooper Union," Duncan requested. Billie started to answer but stopped abruptly when Duncan turned his face from her and waited for Christopher's reply.

"We have Environmental as well as Architectural Design Science," Christopher said. "It takes five years. We'll end up with Bachelor of Science degrees, then can go on to a graduate program. After that I hope to be apprenticed for a couple of years to an architect before I take the exam."

Sally asked, "Do architects have a certification exam?"

"The New York State exam is so tough it's unreal," replied Christopher.

Sally shook her head in sympathy, looking sideways at Billie and speaking to Christopher. "It's a long program you've started on. How old are you, Chris?"

"I'm thirty-four. One guy in my group is older. I can work on the side to support myself but it's tough for those with families."

"How did you and Billie meet?" Duncan asked. Christopher gave Billie a warm secretive glance, and she smiled at the thought of the natural way they had first shared tennis, then his art, and then passion.

"Did you ask her to your place to see your etchings?" Sally added playfully.

"Sure did," said Christopher, without embarrassment. "I showed her my stuff and she helped get it together into a portfolio with new drawings."

"He's done some beautiful pen and ink things," said Billie. She lifted a framed drawing of the Verrazano Bridge from the wall and showed it to Duncan. "He did this when he was in high school."

"Wow!" said Duncan. "This is good. I wish my students could do this well. Or that I could."

Sally and Billie began discussing Billie's chairman, whose shortcomings had been the occasion of a stormy department meeting, held without him. "Sure, Artie's inefficient," said Billie, "but he has broad views and gives us a free rein in curriculum."

"I thought you organized that meeting to protest."

"Only to protest against his ordering books late."

"I heard you were the first to show up in his office to tell him what happened."

"Because I'm a strike-breaker," Billie joked. Christopher

gave her a questioning glance, and she said seriously to him, "A teacher in our department named Ed is goofing off and Artie's trying to replace him. But Ed's making a stink with the union to keep his job, claiming due process. He fantasized that our indignation meeting was to defend his job. I went in to tell Artie that Ed hadn't scored with us but that we were setting up a committee to order books on time."

"And he agreed," Sally said with a look of admiration.

"Of course," Billie said, grinning.

After dinner Christopher glanced at Billie and, at her nod, invited Sally and Duncan to the roof to view the panorama of coastal lights on Long Island Sound.

As soon as the door closed behind them, Billie called Dr. Kaufman. "I phoned Florida. Mikey didn't go with his father but left the same day for parts unknown." She reported what she knew.

Martha's voice reflected shock and pain, but her words were unhesitating. "It's probably a phase of growing up, running away. Yes, you'll want to see Mike's friends in person, not quiz them on the phone, and make it clear that you're only seeking information, not trying to place blame. Mike himself apparently left them thinking he was going to Florida, so that's a plus."

After Sally and Duncan went home, Billie sat quietly next to Christopher on the couch while he studied.

The next morning before class, Sam came by her classroom. He was a ruddy-faced, heavy-set young man who seemed older than most high school students. In a voice too low to be heard by students arriving for homeroom, he said, "Usually Mike and I didn't go to the beach at all. I have a girl friend in Easthampton, so Mike would ride with me that far and then hitch out farther where he had made friends with a family. I don't know who they are."

"Who would know?"

"I think there's a girl in Mike's homeroom named Eve who has a sister there."

"A girl in his homeroom named Eve?"

"Yes. I don't know her last name, but I'll find her and send her to see you during her lunch period." Waving two fingers to Billie as if dismissing an employee, he merged into the stream of bodies in the hall. He seemed to Billie like a young executive, and for the first time she dared hope he wouldn't blab about Mike being missing.

Lunchtime varied according to each student's program, so Billie didn't leave her classroom from third period on. During her free period at midday she sent a student out to get her a sandwich. Finally, during sixth period while she was teaching, a girl with stringy long hair and a sallow face appeared at the door. Billie stepped out into the hall with her.

"My name is Eve," the girl said, her green eyes on Billie's while she cradled her books on one arm. With her free hand she pushed a lock of discolored hair into place. "Sam sent me."

"You know my son Mike?" Eve pushed back her hair again as if it were a brute truth which had to be suppressed repeatedly, and kept her face blank.

Finally she nodded, but said nothing. Behind them in the classroom the students' talk and laughter were growing louder. Billie feared she might fail to learn anything. Finally Eve found her voice. "I'm supposed to be in gym. Can you give me a pass?" She opened her notebook to a fresh page and held it out to Billie, who duly wrote the date and time and signed her name. Eve solemnly took the notebook back, extracted a pamphlet from it and said, "Mike gave this to me. You can have it." She pushed her hair back one last time and left, not in the direction of the gym but of the cafeteria.

The pamphlet was entitled "Soul Only" and was from a group Billie had never heard of, at an address in Eastwick, Long Island. Billie didn't know the town, but a clue to its location was hinted by a sketch of the Montauk lighthouse, the beacon at the eastern end of the island.

She read the tract carefully. "God's Messenger calls you to Develop your Soul," it headlined, and went on to say, "Parents today are overprotective of their children's bodies and don't promote the development of their souls. Freedom of religion and freedom of speech are your rights. Members of Soul Only support one another wherever they go."

On Saturday morning, Billie and Christopher drove east, speeding along the Expressway. The land and sky opened before them. For some thirty-five miles, clusters of brick-brown oak leaves slipped past, looking rich against the silver trunks of leafless birches. Then, in the last ten miles, where scrub oak and sparse pines were all that had survived the seacoast winds, they got glimpses of the sturdy red and white lighthouse.

Before noon they had located Eastwick and the street named on the pamphlet. After checking the numbers of adjoining houses they parked in front of a good-sized dingy white frame house with a mailbox on a post in the yard. It had no number, but Billie thought that a tattered banner drooping from it read in faint letters "Soul Only." They sat watching for signs of activity in the house. Soon, two pallid teenage girls came down the front steps and walked silently up the street. They wore blue jeans and tee shirts, but something in their way of walking seemed tired and restrained.

A long wait brought no new sign of life.

"Here goes," said Billie. She walked up the steps and knocked. A chunky young woman in her mid-twenties, wearing blue jeans and a man's workshirt, opened the door.

Billie smiled. "I'm Mike Halloran's mother. Is he here?"

"No." Her voice was flat.

"Has he been here?"

"I don't know. I just transferred here."

"Who's in charge?"

"That would be our leader."

"What is his name?"

"He's out of town today."

"May I come in and talk with someone who knows Mike?"

"No, you can't." She looked at Billie with eyes apologetic for her lack of hospitality. After a short pause she said, "Maybe someone else can help you. A girl who's been here a long time will be home soon on break. Wait in your car and I'll ask her to talk with you."

Relieved at not being totally turned away and sensing it was lucky the leader wasn't there, Billie sat with Christopher and they speculated about what was meant by "on break." They decided to concentrate on watching both directions to catch the point of origin of anyone who approached. After a few minutes, Christopher spotted a young woman less than a block away, who must have come around the corner or from the modern brick diner. They tried to watch without staring as she came nearer and went in the front door. Within a couple of minutes she came out again and walked toward them. She was wearing blue jeans and a tee shirt spattered with tomato sauce.

Billie rolled down her window and said, "Hello!"

"Hullo," the girl said dully, and waited. Billie thought she resembled Eve, the girl at school.

"We're looking for Mike Halloran," said Christopher in a friendly voice. "Do you know him?"

"Yeah, I knew him," said the girl, without smiling.

"Is he here?"

"No."

"Is he working nearby?"

"No."

"Are you on break now?" asked Billie.

"Yes. I have to be back for the lunch rush."

It was true, then, that she had come from the diner. Billie said, "I know that's a lot of work."

The girl nodded. "You can say that again." She smiled thinly.

Christopher said, in a jovial tone, "So you know Mike. Where is he?"

"He isn't here any more. He tried to organize us in a protest to get more time off and meals as good as the ones we serve—we get the stale food and aren't allowed to keep tips. So Father Gus was going to transfer him. But I think he left on his own."

"Where to?" asked Billie.

"I don't know. Maybe Maryland or West Virginia. That's where the other homes are. I think."

"Father Gus?" asked Christopher. "Who is that?"

"He's our boss. Spiritual leader. He owns the restaurant. He's gone with the truck to pick up supplies. But if you wait it won't be any good, because he won't talk to you and it may make trouble for us."

"When Mike was here, did you talk with him?"

"Oh, yeah. We worked together. He made me laugh."

"He wasn't too miserable, then?"

"Not at first. Then he got to thinking it was unfair not to have more rights, like keeping our tips. So he began to gripe a lot and everyone stopped being friends with him. We had to. Then he escaped."

"How long ago was that?"

"Oh, after Halloween. He left his boom box here. You can wait and one of the sisters will bring it out. I have to go in and rest—I only get one break."

Christopher waited on the porch and the chunky young woman who had first talked to Billie appeared with the big radio. Taking it from her he asked, "Can we eat at the diner?"

"Anyone can eat there. But you can't talk to the help. We have vows of silence at work. We may get in trouble for talking with you as it is."

"Thank you for all you've told us," Christopher said. "We'll try to keep you kids out of it."

When he got back in the car, Billie drove slowly down the street and pulled into the parking lot in front of the diner's glass and chrome entrance. The building was set in neat gravel beds planted with shrubs. She turned the ignition off, closed her eyes and sat motionless. Relief swept over her, mingled with annoyance. She sat looking dolefully at Christopher. "Shall we go in?" She was fishing for advice, rare with her.

"Billie, this could be risky. Whoever he is, the guy who runs this place has a firm hand on it. The kids in there aren't going to talk. We've probably got all we'll get and darn lucky to get that."

"I'd like to have a few words with that Soul Only guy. It's clear he's using these kids as slave labor to run his business."

"If you go and talk with any of the kids you'll arouse suspicion. Those girls at the house probably won't report it to the boss, but the next kid might."

"Je-sus Kee-rist! How did Mike stand this for even a month?"

Christopher could not suppress a smile, and Billie started to laugh. Her laughter then turned into sobs and she fought for control, pulling herself in when Christopher touched her shoulder in sympathy. Finally she gritted her teeth, raised her chin and took a deep breath. "What bothers me, really, is Mikey's being angry at me so long. When he escaped from here, why didn't he come home? His wild moods are usually open, never this secretive."

"He could be afraid of this leader guy."

"We've got to find that bastard."

"I don't think you should tackle him now, Billie. Wait until we know more."

They decided not to go into the diner, but learned at a gas pump how to get to the police station, where they hoped to talk with someone who could deal with "abstract issues," as Billie put it.

"We don't want to put them on Mike's tail," she said.

At the station, she told the person at the first desk, "We're a team of writers doing a story about cults where kids are exploited."

They waited until they were ushered into the Chief's office where they talked with a young officer who explained that the Chief was out on business. He was pleasant and frank, knew about what he called "the commune with the diner" and said the force was keeping an eye on things.

"The leader's always inside the law and we can't abridge freedom of religion," he said. "It's their right, and all anybody's noticed is some chanting the postman heard from the porch. They moved the mailbox to the yard. We figure they're imitating some bigger cult, but that Filler's mainly running a diner."

"But isn't he overworking the kids?" Billie demanded.

"They work hard, but everything's clean and the food is good. A few of our officers eat there and nobody's seen anything wrong. There's no evidence of drugs. So we've had no reason to confront Mr. Filler."

"Is that his name? Father Gus Filler?" Billie inquired.

"He calls himself Gus, but his real first name is Joshua. He started out as one of those Southern holy rollers or whatever they are. That's about all we know."

"The girl at the house hinted there are other homes in the network, in Maryland and West Virginia. Does he have a hand in them too?"

"Is that what she said? I'll make a note of that. Did you get any other information?"

"No, we didn't press for it," Billie said. "The only girl who was talkative was on lunch break and anxious to get off her feet."

"Are you going to try to interview Mr. Filler?"

"Not today," Christopher said flatly. "The girl said he was due back soon, but would be mad if he learned she'd talked with us. So we're not talking with him until we find out more."

"I bet he's breaking some law," Billie said. The young cop shrugged.

"Please, tell us your name," Christopher asked.

"It wouldn't help you. I'm only a rookie here, just answering the Chief's phone at the moment. He has a lot to look after here in Eastwick, mostly to do with fishing boats and the Coast Guard. If you want information, I suggest you talk with Joshua Filler."

23

What Were Those Pills?

Ursula sat in a wheelchair by the nurses' station, waiting for August to come and take her home from the hospital. The surgery over, she felt sad and abandoned by everyone, even the surgeon. All he could predict was that her eyes would most likely not get any worse soon. The only thing she had to look forward to now was seeing Dr. Kaufman again, after missing two Wednesdays.

The nurse in charge came to speak with her, handing her a glass of water. "You didn't get your morning Doxepin, so you'd better take it now." She shook a capsule into Ursula's hand from a white pharmacy envelope.

Ursula recognized the capsule as like those she'd been given in the hospital, not like her usual pills. "This is a different shape from the Doxepin we have at home."

"Oh?" said the nurse. "Well, medicines can come in more than one shape."

Ursula swallowed the capsule, and asked, "What is Doxepin, exactly? Is it for schizophrenics?"

"It's for anyone, if the doctor gives them a prescription," said the nurse. "We ask patients' families to bring in all their regular medications so we can make sure they're safe with what we administer."

"But my husband would have brought little white pills."

The nurse gave a dry little laugh. "Actually, he didn't bring in any medicine. But when you told us you were supposed to be taking Doxepin with meals, we asked your daughter about it. She got your psychiatrist to call in a prescription to the hospital pharmacy. It's on your hospital bill and these are yours to keep taking." She pressed the envelope into Ursula's hand.

"I'll take them," said Ursula, folding the envelope tightly

closed and snapping it into her handbag. "Thank you, nurse."

After eating dinner at home that evening, she didn't take the usual pill from her tray, and instead swallowed one of her capsules. August was sure to resent the new medicine, so she hid the pharmacy's envelope among her scarves. The white pill she washed down the drain.

In a couple of days of doing the same after every meal, she felt better, more even-tempered and active.

On Friday she was downstairs and answered the phone. It was Blaine who said, "I'm making plans for your visit. Daddy seems so agitated by traffic that I'm driving down to pick you up next Wednesday. You'll sleep here overnight and after Thanksgiving dinner on Thursday, Harry will drive you home. I've cancelled your Wednesday appointment with Dr. Kaufman because I have to come for you about two. Tell Daddy all of this. Are you bringing your usual cranberry-orange relish?"

"Oh, yes. I've already made it. It's better made ahead of time."

"Good, it's my favorite thing with dinner! I'm counting on picking you up early enough on Wednesday to bake my pecan pies that evening, so be sure to be ready by two o'clock."

"We will. Your pecan pies are *my* favorite thing!"

Ursula was upset to learn she would miss another session with Dr. Kaufman. On returning upstairs, she found August by the bookcase in her room. He was taking pages out of a folder, tearing them up and feeding pieces into the vacuum cleaner.

"My poems!" she shrieked, flying at him and knocking the folder out of his hand. Paper spilled out to the floor.

August looked at them indignantly and announced, "All this paper mess clutters up the place."

Distraught, Ursula picked up the folder. "Are these my poems? What does the label say?"

"Chemical formulae."

"That's a folder you threw away. I only use it for notes for poems I might write. Where is the poem folder?" Blinded by anger as well as poor eyesight, she knelt and peered closely into the shelf. "Here it is! You stay away from it, do you hear? You stay away!" She took both folders to her bed and lay down on top of them, her body trembling. After August went out she hid them under the mattress.

They'll be safe only until he changes the sheets on Monday. I have to find a way to get away early and take my poems to Blaine's for safekeeping. Granddaughter Jeanne will store them in her bedroom. She loves me.

A first step toward this end came when August was out on his Friday task of sweeping the front sidewalk. She went to the kitchen and located an empty grocery bag and hid it behind her bookcase. The rest of the day she made plans.

He'll go grocery shopping on Tuesday morning and the minute he leaves, I'll go by taxi to the subway that goes to Penn Station. I went to Blaine's by myself once before and I remember. From Penn Station I'll take a taxi to the Port Authority bus terminal and catch a bus to Hillside-on-Hudson. I'll ask people to help me find my way. I'll leave my suitcase for Blaine to pick up when she comes for August, so I won't be carrying anything but my sack of poems and handbag.

The trouble is, there won't be any money in the handbag. So how will I pay? . . . Oh, I know! Timmie gave me a ten dollar bill when he visited me in the hospital. He said it was in case I wanted candy from the gift shop! That's a teenage boy for you! He grandly pressed the money into my hand, saying, "You always gave me money for my uniform and badges when I was a Cub Scout and now I get paid for my paper route. So I can help." Grandchildren are such a pleasure!

This ten will pay for the taxis and subway at this end, but won't be enough for the bus upstate. August doesn't let me handle money any more. I have saved about a hundred dollars from tutoring the Cooper boy three years ago. If I can get to the bank, the taxi will wait while I get cash. I'll take all of it out, as I'll be staying at Blaine's a long time. I certainly can't stay here.

She planned to copy out some phone numbers to take along and thought of leaving a note for August to find after she left, to let him know she was going to Blaine's.

If only I still had that magnifying lamp!

She decided to appeal to August tactfully, and on Saturday after breakfast calmly said, "It would be helpful to borrow that lamp again from the Coopers. They said we could have it back any time. You know, I did help their boy graduate from high school."

"But what if it gets broken?"

"Well, they aren't using it. And so it's a chance we have to take. I'm better since my operation."

She accepted that August's not objecting was as close to agreement as she'd get, and that afternoon walked down the street to the Coopers'. As recently as two years ago, when she was still able to drive, she had often stopped there and given the children rides. Now she talked with Mrs. Cooper, who sent her younger son, a ten-year-old, to carry the lamp home for her.

With the help of the magnifier she sorted papers and wrapped them neatly in the grocery bag, ready for her move.

Once I get to Blaine's, I'll stay all winter. So how will I get my winter clothes into my small suitcase? My shoes and snow boots alone will just about fill it. Well, I can wear my warmest coat over my heavy red sweater. Underneath, I'll wear my long flannel nightgown. It'll hang down to my ankles, so to cover it I'll wear my long black evening skirt, which I haven't worn since forever. People will think I'm a visiting celebrity. Well, so I am.

In preparation for her getaway, she looked in the phone book for a taxi's number, but found that even with the lamp she couldn't read the small print. Finally, she found an ad with a number printed large, and copied it out carefully.

When Tuesday arrived she walked down to the kitchen and ate her breakfast, wondering how she could make the time pass faster until he went shopping. To her consternation, he looked in the refrigerator and said, "Maybe I don't need to get groceries this week, since we'll be eating two dinners at Blaine's."

"Don't you need anything?" she asked. "Aren't we out of peanut butter?"

Then, to Ursula's relief, he said, "Yes, there are still a few things I need in my revolving inventory." He departed in the car at ten-thirty.

She immediately went to the phone and ordered the taxi. Then she put on her layers of clothes and went with her package of papers to the front porch. When the taxi came she waved to the driver to wait and, moving sedately, left the note to August on the kitchen table. At the bank the taxi waited, and money in hand, she went elatedly through the steps of her getaway.

She wondered if people thought her long skirt odd in the middle of the day, and on the bus to Hillside confided to the woman sitting next to her, "I had to leave a literary hoo-ha in order to catch this bus so I'm wearing my glad rags." Then she feigned sleep to avoid having to chat, smiling to herself.

I did indeed leave a literary hoo-ha if hoo-ha means an exciting escape with my papers. I feel freer than I've felt since my eyes went bad. It's heady stuff, handling my own affairs.

In the bus station at Hillside an obliging young man dialed Blaine's number for her. Granddaughter Jeanne answered, "Mom's out shopping."

"Darling Jeanne," said Ursula, "tell her I'm in Hillside at the bus station and she should come get me. If you go anywhere before she comes back, be sure to leave a note that I'm here waiting."

"No problem."

To Ursula's surprise, about twenty minutes later Jeanne arrived on her bicycle, a blonde thirteen-year-old in a pink- and- white jumpsuit. She looked the part of the nickname "Gretel" her grandfather had given her. "I left a note for Mom like you said." She hugged her grandmother. "Where's Granddaddy?"

"He's coming tomorrow," said Ursula. "How do you like my outfit?"

"It's great. You look like a pioneer."

Ursula laughed. "Well, I guess everyone was a pioneer when I was a girl in Seattle!"

When Blaine arrived she frowned. "Whatever possessed you, Mother? Daddy phoned you were coming on the bus, but didn't say when. It's disconcerting. He could have come, too, so I wouldn't have that long drive tomorrow."

"You could phone him to take the bus. But he might not know how, and he couldn't carry both our suitcases and the cranberry relish."

Not one to do battle with a *fait accompli*, Blaine said, "Well, thank goodness you've arrived safely." She put Jeanne's bicycle into the station wagon and drove home to the four-bedroom brick house.

During dinner, Ursula enjoyed the flattering banter of her son-in-law, Harry Watson, a businessman with good common sense whom she had come to love dearly. He asked sympathetic questions, but she didn't mention that she'd come on her own in order to rescue her poems.

Anyway, they wouldn't believe August would try to destroy them, so why tell them?

As soon as she rose from the table she realized how tired she was, wanting only to fall into bed in the guest room. But first, she went to visit Jeanne in her bedroom and asked her to keep her papers, explaining, "Your grandfather can't stand old papers around the house and I'm afraid he'll throw these out by accident. They're my poems, all I've written my whole life. Don't tell anyone."

Jeanne nodded her head solemnly. "I'll look after them, Grandmother. Don't you worry. If the house catches on fire, I'll save them first, along with my snapshot album." She tucked the package into a shelf in her bookcase, and choosing a stuffed toy dog from her collection, squeezed it into the shelf above. "I'm putting Snoopy here to guard your package." She kissed her grandmother goodnight.

Ursula went to bed with a strong sense of well being. *The ready wisdom of youth on top of kindness is a miracle. Thanks to Jeanne, what I value most in the world is safe. Snoopy's guarding it.*

The next day, alone in a happy house, Ursula didn't feel lonely until Blaine returned with August. When Harry came home from work, he found his wife determined to serve supper and make her pecan pies for the next day as soon as she'd fed everyone. Observing a kitchen already swamped with the makings of tomorrow's big turkey dinner, Harry announced, "Tonight we're eating out." In the restaurant Ursula and August had no need to converse.

Everybody was on his own for breakfast the next morning. No one but August had noticed that his wife hadn't spoken to him since his arrival. So Blaine was surprised later when Ursula asked to have her Thanksgiving dinner brought to her on a tray in the guest room. "Mother, that's a pain in the neck," said Blaine. "The family is together. You've been eating at the table. Can't you sit with us for my big dinner?"

"I can't. I often have dinner on a tray in my room at home." Without saying more, she went upstairs and sat down on her bed. Young Timmy later brought her a large tray of food. "I have a terrible *Weltschmerz*. But thank you, especially for the delicious cranberry-orange relish I made myself."

Back at the table, Timmy said, "Grandmother has something wrong, a 'schmertz' or something."

Harry kept carving the turkey and Blaine didn't answer. But Jeanne, who had suddenly grasped the situation, blurted out, "She won't come because she's not speaking to Granddaddy."

August gave her a quelling look and said, "Gretel, we're saying grace."

"We're gathered together to ask the Lord's blessing," they sang.

After dinner, Blaine felt a stabbing pain of homesickness for the mother she had always known.

Here she is, right in the house, and yet lost, not able to be the engine of efficiency she's always been in the kitchen.

Jeanne helped by clearing the table and stacking the dishwasher and was then dispatched to take pie up to her grandmother. Blaine finished putting food away, boiling turkey bones for broth, and packaging sliced turkey to send home with her parents. At last she joined the men in the living room. "Daddy," she ventured, "I wonder if it's too much for you, taking care of Mother?"

"We do what we're put on earth to do," August said with finality. He then went on talking about his days of teaching chemistry. He was criticizing chemistry textbooks, claiming that he had devised a more sequential curriculum. Feeling guilty that her father had so little real companionship, Blaine settled at one end of the long sofa, listening and relaxing after the success of her dinner. However, she soon dozed off. Harry, in his recliner, also yawned from time to time, while August talked about the chances of publishing his old lesson plans. He had brought along copies made on his photocopier, and sought advice. But Harry said he was out of his depth, and called in Timmie from his bedroom, where he was at that very moment studying for a chemistry test. August was placated when Timmie promised to take the lesson plans to his chemistry teacher for an opinion.

When this was settled, Harry moved and sat on the sofa where Blaine was fast asleep. To wake her, he took her hand and squeezed it. "It's pretty late to start driving our Long Islanders home. What do you think?"

Blaine woke and quickly grasped his meaning. "Daddy, why don't you and Mother stay overnight again? I'll drive you home in the morning."

"That's all right, if it isn't too much trouble."

"It's better than tonight. I'll have to get an early start, because I must be back here by one o'clock. I'm entertaining the executive board of the League of Women Voters. I'm President of our local chapter, you know. We'll have to leave here by twenty minutes past eight. Tell Mother."

By eight the next morning, Harry and the children had left, and Ursula and August were at the table finishing breakfast. Blaine's plans were on schedule. On her way to the living room with a tray of brownies and coffee cups for the board meeting, she sang out, "Private limousine to Long Island leaves in twenty minutes!"

"Count me out," Ursula said promptly. "I'm staying here."

"I love having you, Mother," Blaine said, "but it wouldn't work this weekend. We did have a longer visit since you came early. Maybe at Christmas you can stay all week." She stood behind Ursula's chair.

"I can't go home " Ursula said with panic in her voice. "I'd go crazy."

She began to cry and Blaine patted her shoulders gently, with a look at August which said, "Poor Mother, and you too, poor Daddy."

"I'll get our suitcases," said August. He stumbled as he got up. Walking as if on ice, he went up the stairs. Ursula dropped her chin to her chest, grasping the seat of the chair with both hands so tightly her hands turned white.

Blaine sat down beside her. "Mother, what's the matter? Are you disappointed that your eyes aren't better?"

"It isn't my eyes, it's bad for me to live with your father. He doesn't like the things I like, or me. And he hates my poetry." She looked at her daughter, all defenses down. "I've always been only a flag that he flies—at first I was an obedient young wife and mother, diaper-washer and cook.

Now I'm a burden. He enjoys looking like a saint, but he's a bully. It's time I had my own life."

Blaine was silent. Ursula knew she felt sympathetic, but when she spoke, it was with the voice of reality. "Mother, it's been bad for you, but it can't be that bad. Dr. Kaufman will help you straighten things out. And Daddy needs you, more than just to make him look like a saint. Without a job—and you're his job—he'd age quickly. His being jealous of your poetry means he wants to come first with you. It's a sign of affection."

"A poor sort of affection."

Blaine stood and forcibly pulled her mother's hands away from the chair. "Mother, you have to let me take you home, right now. I have to be back here by one for the meeting." Gently but firmly, she pulled Ursula up, out of the chair. "Get your coat on. I'm starting the car."

August came down with their suitcases and followed her out to the garage. Shakily, Ursula groped her way upstairs to the guest room, intoning "Shiboo-yee, Wah-be, Sah-bee!" She put on her winter coat, wrapped her nightgown into her long black skirt, and draped them over her arm. Making a detour into Jeanne's room, she bent over and gently patted the head of Snoopy, and touched her papers lovingly with one finger. Then she walked downstairs sedately and out to the big station wagon with its motor running. She took her place in the back seat.

The next Tuesday morning, while August was out shopping, she carried the lamp into his room to see if she could operate the photocopy machine. She wanted to copy a thank-you poem she had written to Jeanne.

A black plastic tray labelled "Paper #1" sat on top of the machine, empty. Looking for paper, she opened the top drawer of August's desk, and finding a stack of paper, lifted it out. Underneath she saw two rectangular notes which looked vaguely familiar. Scrutiny under the lamp showed them to be two prescriptions for Doxepin, with the name Martha Kaufman, M.D., at the top.

So he never got them filled! What were those pills?

Checking the drawer again, she found a bottle of white pills and took it to the lamp. It was clearly labeled "Aspirin." Just to be sure, she broke off a bit of a pill and tasted it.

Yes, that's what I was taking. Aspirin. It couldn't do me any harm, but it couldn't help like Doxepin. He didn't want me to get better!

She stood, her eyes squeezed closed, trying her best to find the forgiveness she had forced into her heart for years, the excuses for him that she had summoned time and time again.

I half-believed Blaine's idea that his jealousy shows he cares and wants to come first in my life. That might be true if he was jealous of somebody. But I have a right to my poetry. That side of me doesn't belong to him, any more than his science belongs to me. If he wanted me to get better, how could he stop me from getting medicine? That's not a form of love, it's more like hate. It's a reprehensible act of destruction. Monstrous.

She sat down on his bed in a daze, until a cold fire possessed her, and she rushed at the desk drawers and pulled them out, one by one, dumping their contents on the floor. Then she scooped everything off the desk, shouting "Ricka! Hayka! Showka!" She threw copies of the *Scientific American* out of the bookcase. "Hi-yah! Aspirin! Doxepin!" She pushed the copy machine toward the door and with superhuman strength shoved it over the doorsill. Just as August appeared at the bottom of the stairs she pushed it off the landing. It slammed down the steps and crashed at the bottom.

He jumped back in fear and astonishment shouting, "What's this? What's this?" and glared up at her, shaking his fist. "You've ruined it!"

At the top of the stairs she stood straight, head held high, rotating her fingers in a condescending queenly wave. Then, with a vague smile, she disappeared into her bedroom.

24

I'll Buy a New Dress and Enjoy It

Martha saw all four of her afternoon patients on the Wednesday after Thanksgiving.

"Thanksgiving makes me think about money," Elinor confided. "I can save it, like growing our own pumpkins, and I can spend it, like buying a fresh turkey. But I can't make it." Martha was glad for this opening and listened without comment. "I know you've mentioned that I might get a job, but I'm trained as a government secretary, and for that the offices are miles away. The hours are long, and it's not right to leave teenagers alone after school."

"Might there be a small business where you could work part-time close to home, something to give you new references?"

"We couldn't live on what I'd make, and the minute I earned anything at all, Howard would stop his support. I know him. I'm surprised he sends *your* check on time. Mine always comes a month or two late. And he's so slow in paying the plumbing bills that the plumber doesn't come any more. Also the roof needs repair. He doesn't pay the water bills but we get water because it's added to the tax payments, and he complains about that." She was blinking her eyes to keep from crying.

"Have you thought of legal action?"

"I had a lawyer for the divorce, a married man who made a pass at me when I let him hold my hand before I signed the damned divorce papers because I needed someone just then. I pushed him away but after that he kept phoning me, so I dropped him."

"You could see a different lawyer."

"How would I pay him?"

"You might find an attorney who wouldn't get paid until you did."

"But it would be such a hassle. And so would working. Maybe I should marry Ralph. He said it would be a help on his income tax if we got married before the end of December."

"He said that?"

"Yes, but it wasn't a real proposal. He said my kids would be 'good-lookin' tax exemptions.' I didn't say anything negative, just quietly let him know I couldn't respond to a proposal of marriage that sounded like a business transaction. I figure he was testing my reaction."

"Has he tested your reaction again since?"

"Well, we finally went to Trinity Church last Sunday, to worship like we had talked about. But I think he's mostly testing his daughters' reactions to me."

"How do you feel toward them?"

"Fine toward Michele. Both she and Ralph say she's better off with me than with her mother. But Helen, the nineteen-year-old, is something else. You know, after we finished dinner on Thanksgiving we all sat around the table and the kids were topping each other's stories about breaking school rules. My kids didn't have much to say, but Helen said she'd smoked in a closet at school and cheated on exams." She paused. "Ralph was pleased the kids were laughing together but after a while he saw I was tired, and announced that they were to take complete care of the dinner clean-up. 'All of it, not one turkey bone out of place!' he said. Then he and I drove to the City. Susan and Michele did all the work, they said, and Helen followed Steven to his room to listen to music.

"Later I talked to the girls about the cheating and smoking, and made it clear it wasn't behavior I'd tolerate. They were sweet, and promised they wouldn't start. Michele told us that Helen had been married and divorced."

"And didn't you say she's only nineteen?"

"Yes. It was a shock to hear that someone so close to Susan's age had been divorced."

"It may be a shock," said Martha, "but it's good that she can be free of a marriage quickly if it's bad for her. Some young people try on everything for size. They learn the hard way."

"I hope mine won't, as long as I give them tender loving care. Which they need all the time. That's the main reason I don't want an office job."

After Elinor left, Martha reflected on what she had heard.

If Elinor marries Ralph it will be because an old-fashioned marriage is what she wants. She's good at raising kids, as Ralph knows. People who are needed usually manage to remain right side up.

This comfortable thought got a jolt when Billie arrived, slammed the door closed, and threw herself into the chair. "Goddamn that Michael for not letting me know that Mike wasn't going with him to Florida. Goddamn that cult leader for ripping off kids in Eastwick. Goddamn that police chief for not having the balls to shut down that sweat shop. Soul Only! My ass!" She took a pack of cigarettes from her handbag but, under Martha's sharp scrutiny, put it away, saying, "Don't worry, Doc, I'm not going to self-destruct in front of medical personnel." She bent forward. "Most of all, goddamn that Mikey for falling for that Father Gus crap." Then she leaned back. "Well, let him worry about it. He's made his bed."

"I'm behind on what's been happening. All I've heard is he's not in Florida."

Billie told her about the pamphlet Eve gave her and how she had seen a girl at Soul Only who said Mike had made her laugh. "God only knows where he is and I hope God cares. I don't."

"He'll need a friend," said Martha.

"If he wanted me to be his friend, he'd write to me or call. He could call collect. I'm not going to search for him. Let him have his cruddy cult!"

"Some cults serve a purpose by giving young people a community to belong to. Kids need emotional support sometimes."

"If you had a kid of your own, you'd mollycoddle him to death. Not me. Let him hang himself."

Martha, ignoring Billie's accusation, said in a level tone, "Some parents get in touch with the special branch of the police who search for missing persons."

"The hell with them! He's been missing too long. I'm not looking for him."

"The police might be helpful. It's been some time since Mike left—he may have left a trail. You can tell the police what you know. Did you say you heard the same group might operate in other places?"

"Yes, in Maryland and West Virginia, but no address and maybe not the same cult name."

"Both of those places are in driving distance for you."

Billie was silent.

Martha hoped lack of objection was a positive sign, and ventured, "Have you thought of getting in touch with the girl from Mike's homeroom?"

"Eve? She was a zombie."

"How about the girl who said Mike made her laugh? She may have an idea of where he is."

Billie shrugged. She felt the need for a cigarette, and said, "You're really a pursuer of continuities, aren't you?"

Martha nodded, a smile curling at the edge of her mouth. This patient was unfailingly bright, even when her tone was insulting.

Billie changed the subject to the inefficiency of her chairman at school who failed to keep needed items on hand, like bulbs for the overhead projector. Martha asked questions focusing on how Billie could write up her innovative lesson plans so other teachers could use them. Surprisingly, Billie responded, and described her ideas for new courses. At the end of their session, Martha said, "Keep me posted on your search for Mike."

"Didn't I have enough to do before he split?" Billie retorted, slamming the door shut behind her on her way out.

Martha felt a bit more hopeful.

Knowing Billie, I'll look for progress next week. Her loudest outbursts usually foreshadow change, as if she has to protest one week before she listens the next.

She was making tea for Ursula when the phone rang. It was Blaine, who said that Ursula was with her in Hillside and had a request. "Mother really needs to talk with you. She wanted to come see you, but I couldn't drive her today. Is it possible for you to talk with her on the phone and bill me as usual?"

"Yes, it is, but she should be in a private room."

"She will be. I should explain, my father's in the hospital. He hurt himself lifting his photocopy machine."

"Oh, I'm sorry. Is it serious?"

"We don't know yet." Blaine lowered her voice. "Mother keeps saying made-up words. Maybe you can find out what they signify."

In a moment Ursula's voice, too close to the phone, raspily hailed her. "Shiboo-yee, Dr. Kaufman!"

Martha's impulse was to reply, "And a happy Shiboo-yee to you!" but she refrained.

Ursula had news. "You know, being at home with August was driving me crazy so I took the bus on my own to Blaine's for Thanksgiving. I brought my poems here because August was destroying them."

"He was destroying your poems?"

"Yes. And more. After they made me go home with him, I found two prescriptions from you in his desk drawer that he'd never had filled. There was also a bottle of aspirin there, with pills like he'd been putting on my dinner tray. I found out that Doxepin isn't in pills, but in capsules, because the nurse gave me some. You phoned in the prescription, she said."

"Wait a moment. I'm trying to recall what happened. Yes, Blaine called me and said your husband forgot to take your Doxepin to the hospital and I agreed to call the prescription in to the hospital pharmacy."

"Thank you. Doxepin is different from aspirin. He didn't want me to get better."

"Did you confront him with your discovery?"

Ursula let out a glad cry, a high-pitched chuckle. "I certainly did. I pushed his machine downstairs."

"A machine?"

"Yes, I was in his room and there was that machine. Hayka!" She talked rapidly and shouted. "I wanted to make a copy of a thank-you poem I wrote to my granddaughter, Jeanne, and he wouldn't make copies for me. But the machine was out of paper so I looked in his desk and found the prescriptions. Showka!"

Martha recalled seeing the standing photocopier in August's room. "I don't understand what you did with the machine."

"I ruined it. He came home in time to see it crashing down the stairs. Doxepin!" She fell silent.

"Did it hit him?"

Ursula's reply was unintelligible. "Ricka! Hayka!" Martha could only interpret the sound that followed as a chuckle. But Ursula then said clearly, "It didn't hit him. It was when he tried to lift it off the floor that he twisted his hip. He couldn't get up, but I got help from neighbors and they called Blaine and an ambulance took him to L.I.J.H."

"Long Island Jewish Hospital?"

"Yes. That's where he is now. It's a good hospital."

"I know," said Martha. "Did he break his hip?"

"Oh, yes. But they found there was a crack in it already."

"Is he in pain?"

"If he is, he can take aspirin." Martha had to suppress a chuckle. "I don't have to look after him any more. I'm safe at Blaine's, and Jeanne rides her bike downtown to copy poems for me."

"I see," said Martha.

"Thanks to you, Dr. Kaufman, Doxepin really helps me. Without it I wouldn't have thrown that machine at August. Thank you."

"That wasn't my intention," Martha said, and paused before asking, "How long will your husband be in the hospital?"

"I don't think he'll ever come out."

"Does the doctor say that?"

"I say that. For sure, he's not coming to Blaine's guest room. It's mine now. I have a card table and Blaine bought me my own new magnifying lamp. I'm revising and writing new poems."

"You sound well cared for. I'm glad we had this phone conversation. Now could I please talk with Blaine again?"

Blaine told Martha, "We're on the lookout for a suitable nursing home in our area, depending on what kind of care Daddy needs. I'll know more on Wednesday. I'll drop Ursula off at your office on my way."

"Won't Ursula wish to go with you?"

Blaine lowered her voice. "No, she refuses to see him."

They said goodbye, and Martha sat at her desk feeling drained.

Ursula's made-up words are less worrying than her glee at her husband's condition. I thought August was taking care of his wife, but I was wrong, as those unfilled prescriptions prove. Ursula's right. But no medication can reach the root of her anger—it's my skill that's supposed to do that. What's ahead for Ursula?

She stood at the window in sorrowful thought.

Just at five, Sandy climbed the stairs. She was really large in front, and walked awkwardly, carrying a bulging portfolio. A drawn look about her mouth made her look older, but when Martha inquired how she was feeling, she replied with a satisfied laugh, "Outrageously wonderful! And it's not just my pregnancy that's wonderful, but my love life."

"You and David are happy?"

"Yes, after a bad quarrel. That's why I called you and made the appointment for today."

"You wanted to see me because of a quarrel?"

"Yes. I got fed up with his nagging about marriage, and I went home to mother. That week he went to a conference in Atlantic City that I forgot about. And a horny woman from his office seduced him."

"David was seduced?"

"Yes. For real. He'd told me more than once about how Becky was always pursuing him. He'd made me come to the office Christmas party last year to show her he was taken. But in Atlantic City he was so mad at me, he let it happen. It did just happen—they'd been put in adjoining hotel rooms. I kept trying to phone him at our apartment and finally reached him in Atlantic City, and got the most awful news I ever heard. He said I had sleazy values, was just getting a kick out of living in sin with him, and had silly notions about not getting married. He said his up-bringing was insulted and he didn't want to see me."

"That must have been painful news."

"I knew he didn't mean it, but it hurt. There I was, with a baby almost here, and I had to make peace with getting married. It turned out that we each headed home, where we had a real truth-telling. He told me right away how he happened to sleep with her, and he felt so low that I had to take him in my arms. I forgave him. We talked about how stubborn we'd both been. He said he understood that my desire for a career in art was my real reason for not getting married, and that he'd help me. And I told him I'd found out that making him happy was more important to me than my big ideas about freedom. So we're going to have a wedding in three weeks!"

"He's a lucky man, that you love him so much."

"And I'm lucky that he's honest with me and wants me and the baby to be happy. We both cried when we whispered how much we love each other. It was sort of our private wedding."

"I'm glad you decided together to return to each other. It sounds as if you had, in your own style, a ceremony of forgiveness and commitment."

Sandy's face was radiant. "We did. We truly did."

"You know," Martha said, "true love between a man and woman doesn't interfere with the freedom of either of them, if they keep trying to understand and support one another. Each person can gain real personal strength in a good marriage."

"I think we may be growing into that."

"It's rewarding when you do." Martha paused. "How does your mother react?"

"We told her on Thanksgiving. She was ecstatic, and set the date with the rabbi right away. We'll have the canopy and all. She's reserved a big restaurant for the banquet, hired a band and ordered invitations from the printer. Would you like to come?"

Martha smiled, her eyes filling with tears. "Yes."

"I thought you would. Mom will send you an invitation." She smiled warmly.

A new thought brought again the drawn look. "While I was away from David, I stayed with a dear friend and I'm worried about her. Her name is Danielle. It would be so good for her if she could come and see you, because she has to support two little girls. I babysat one of them and found out how rough it is when you're a mother with no man to rely on."

She talked until the end of their session, telling Martha about Christina and her failure as a babysitter. As she left, she declared, "I'm getting so wifely I brought a check from David to give you." She rustled through her portfolio, taking some papers out in order to locate the check, which she finally produced. At the door she said, "I'm getting new ideas for lithographs I want to do. Next Wednesday, I'd like to talk about how I can manage to do my work after the baby comes."

"Okay!" Martha replied.

After the door closed, Martha heard her own "Okay!" echoing in the room.

It didn't meet the standard I try to maintain in the office. I should have said simply, "Yes, if you wish." But never mind.

She smiled and sat in a reverie, feeling the happiness of the young lovers.

Sandy went straight out to David's car and tossed her portfolio onto the back seat. Clasping both hands under her abdomen to support the weight of the baby, she bounced into the passenger seat. "I hope you're ready for good news," she said with delight in her voice. "Dr. Kaufman's great. She understood the importance of our making up and called it a ceremony of forgiveness and commitment."

"That is nice," David said sincerely. "I guess we're learning to solve problems. Wish it transferred over to my job."

Out of her reverie, Martha sat reviewing the events of a full day.

Just last week I drank a Thanksgiving toast because everything seemed to be turning out roses. And yet at that very time, Sandy and David were almost breaking up. And we're still not doing too well around here. Sarah's upset because Barry hasn't been home all week. And face it, my going to Sandy's wedding is unconventional for a therapist.

Well, to look at the bright side—haven't Elinor and Ralph gotten their families together? And isn't Billie's adamant refusal to look for her son just about to turn into a search for him? And maybe Ursula is safer now, with the Doxepin working. And isn't it best that Sandy accepts marriage now, with the baby almost here? My saying I'll come to her wedding shows that I care. Judy has invited me so I'll buy a new dress and enjoy it.

25

A Benchmark

Martha, finishing lunch the following Wednesday, looked forward to her afternoon. "Elinor, Billie, Ursula, Sandy," she said to herself in anticipation.

Elinor arrived with an announcement. "I'm making a big decision."

"Oh?" Martha said, ready for an invitation to another wedding.

"Ralph's daughter Michele's been staying with us because her mother's away on a trip, and Ralph wants her to move into my house permanently and be treated like one of my kids. She'd have the guest room, and go to our high school. And guess what? He says it will save him money, even though he'll pay me twice as much for Michele alone as Howard pays me for everything!"

"This would be quite a step."

"Yes, I'd have the responsibility for fat Michele. Of course, she won't be fat when she gets a balanced diet and a lot of tender loving care."

"Are you really fond of her?"

"Oh, yes. I love the way she gives me a shy goodnight hug, waiting until Susan has kissed me a big one. She's never pushy, but has such happiness in her eyes when she's included! Steven stopped teasing her after they talked once about European geography and she knew more about it than he did. Of course, she's traveled more than my kids. In fact, one of Ralph's educational schemes is to send us all to a cottage in France next summer, along with Helen and three young boys from the family where she lives. They all have to be good in French before they can go. So our theme song at home these days is 'Alouette.'"

"And the decision about keeping Michele?"

"I want to do it, because I like her and need the money, but not if it will change my relationship with my kids. It's a little late to add another child. Steven is noncommittal, but Susan says she can share me, and thinks Michele is easy to live with. I agree, judging from their weekends together. So we're on a trial run—she goes to school every day with Susan and likes it. Both girls like the piano teacher Ralph has hired for them. I drive them into the City on Fridays after school for their lessons. Steven and I go in too. Ralph takes all of us to dinner and afterward Michele goes home with him to his apartment. He brings her to us again the next morning."

"So Steven is having new experiences, too?"

"Yes, he likes going to the City. His Social Studies teacher, a Ms. Halloran, has gotten him interested in the U.N. and he's becoming friends with a classmate whose father works there. So day after tomorrow I'll drive everybody into the City right after school and while the girls are at their piano lessons, Steven and I will tour the U.N."

"Are there signs of jealousy among the kids, someone feeling cheated of time with you?"

"I don't think so. I guard against it. Susan and I still talk privately, and she doesn't seem to mind that I also talk privately with Michele. When they come home from school we all snack and laugh and joke in the kitchen, or they bring me tea and we talk in my room. Sometimes they prepare dinner by themselves. I love that. Maybe I dread future change more than they do, as they have each other. It does give me more time with Steven."

"What do you think now about what you said in the past, that you expect to have an empty nest syndrome when your children leave home?"

"I remember you said I should find some new interest, and Ralph is that for me."

"Oh? How is he?"

"Fine. He says I have a good influence on Michele. But I'm not sure I can live up to it."

"It strikes me," Martha said earnestly, "that raising children is a talent which you have already, and perhaps you need to think the way a social worker might about keeping Michele. You can find the subtle ways it's possible to be a parental figure to someone without trying to possess her. Leave her free to be close to her father and her own mother and yet give her a feeling of belonging in your family. You might, for instance, help her make plans and find transportation to visit them, and also, when she returns, fill her in on what's been happening in her new home. Make it feel like home, while reassuring your own children that they and their history are yours. It's a tight rope to walk, but in this day of remarrying, many parents are doing it."

"Could you give me something to read about it?"

"Trust your own thoughtfulness. You already have skills you can perfect."

"Do you think Susan will get seriously interested in marriage at an early age, to get away from home?"

"Well, having intimacy at home is the best way to keep kids from marrying to get away. You need to keep Steven close, too."

"Steven's hard to predict. He's already more self-sufficient than us females. In fact, I worry about his not being sociable, and have a wonderful idea for a way to center things at home and let the kids have fun. I'm thinking of our giving a big party on New Years Eve, with adults in the living room and kids down in the rec rooms. I'm going to talk with Ralph tonight and get the invitations out. I think it will further establish his and my belonging together. It feels right."

"I see." It felt right to Martha, too, and left her in a cheerful mood.

When Billie breezed in, she was wearing a new leather suit in dark brown. She flipped a bright orange-colored tie at the neck of her plum-colored blouse and said, "This color clash symbolizes the violence in my nature." She laughed.

"In nature, those colors don't seem violent."

"Right. Actually, I've turned over a new leaf. Turned peaceful. Things are going well between me and Christopher, and I'm not working all the time. I bought some crazy pajamas for him—it says on the chest `Below lies a sleeping giant.' And we made far-out tropical drinks. Once he made me a drink from a Fiji Island recipe called a 'Coconut-tumble' and said it made him feel like a Billie-tumble. So I made him one called 'Jump Up and Kiss Me!'" She laughed. "That's the name of a drink, 'Jump Up and Kiss Me!' And I've been thinking that even when I'm happy, life isn't complete without Mikey. I remember him as a little boy, and want to find him."

"So you've reached a decision?"

"Yes, and it will cost money. I'll have to quit therapy altogether."

"Because of money?"

"Yes, and time. I'm driving to Maryland this weekend and maybe to West Virginia the next, and that means correcting papers evenings all week." She launched into a complaint about Michael, who didn't tell her he'd offered Mike a stay in Florida and been refused.

Martha listened, knowing this talk was a buffer, that when the time came for Billie to leave today she'd do so with an air of saying goodbye for good. Consequently after a time she said, "You mentioned quitting therapy, and that seems rather drastic at this stage. You might think of it as a leave of absence. I believe you will find Mike and that will challenge you to new adjustments. You may need support."

"Yeah, I'm not that peaceful when I'm making adjustments. God, sometimes I'm right back where I started with you, when I used to wallop Mikey with a belt. That's why I'm wearing clashing colors today."

"You wore them as a sign to me?"

"Well, it strikes me there's a lot of violence that escapes being labeled. I'm sure my physical violence didn't hurt Mikey as much as my sense of martyrdom over what I did for him. And he responded with violence toward me by not liking school. I plan to find him, and when he comes home be more frank, show him I'm fond of him. It won't be easy for me. I don't like to show my feelings."

"It strikes me that you show your feelings to most people."

"Only some. There's a lot I don't show you."

"Like what?"

"Like why are you so old-fashioned? There's a whole new world out there—transactional therapy, Jungian therapy, primal therapy, hypnotherapy . . ."

"In my view, primal therapy is psycho-babble—all those patients cooped up in a room together, screaming, hitting walls and pounding pillows."

"Well, for a Freudian, you don't do much with Freudian theory, never ask me about my dreams. Aren't they super-important?"

"Research has shown that we all regularly dream disconnected dreams, and no particular one is especially significant. I base my practice on the work of analysts who have modified many Freudian theories."

"Well, it moves at a damn slow pace."

"It has to. Real change comes slowly."

"I suppose so," said Billie, absently. "I want to pay you what I owe you, up to date for a change." She dropped a check on the desk, and said, "Well, that's that."

Martha ignored the check, looking at Billie and smiling warmly. "I want to hear how your search for Mike progresses. It's wonderful that you're going to show him you care about him, and keep a home for him, even if it won't be easy for you. But if you do it, a lot of other things may become easier. Family members gain confidence from sharing. Stable family life is often a step toward success."

"But it's so bourgeois, steering a middle course! I've had

enough of it, teaching in Middle Cove. It's making Chris and me more discreet about living together, because some of the cults, after capturing kids, hang onto them if their parents are living in sin, as they might consider it. Some of them are strict. So he parks his car a block away now."

"I see," said Martha. "After Mike comes back, we can discuss some aspects of ongoing family life. For instance, with a cooperating husband, there's a triangle which can reduce anxieties compared to a twosome. If there's affection on all sides."

"Maybe. *If* I find him, which isn't guaranteed." She left with her usual speed.

Afterward, Martha shrugged off Billie's labelling her old-fashioned and felt pleased she planned to find Mike.

Actually, I could have accepted some smidgeon of appreciation from that young woman. She's indifferent to my trying to help her. As for her quitting therapy, that's bound to be temporary. She'll be back, to exult over finding Mike or to swear about not succeeding. And, glory be, she wants to make a real home for him! For that I'll take some credit, after the efforts I've made to get her to see that she and he are basically fond of one another. Primal therapy, my foot!

Ursula was overdue, possibly because of the increase in traffic in the holiday season, and Martha watched for the arrival of Blaine who would have to double park. Five minutes late, her car pulled up, and Martha went out and guided Ursula in.

Once seated, Ursula smiled graciously. "How are you, Dr. Kaufman? I missed seeing you last week, but was glad we talked on the phone."

"Thank you. You're looking well." It was true. Ursula's skin, though wrinkled, had a new glow.

"I should be grieving over my husband but I'm not. Blaine will find out today at the hospital what sort of care he'll need if they discharge him. I'm hoping they won't discharge him, ever, and most likely even if they do, he'll have to stay in some sort of nursing home. Shiboo-yee! Showka!"

Martha asked, "Tell me, Ursula, what do those words mean?"

"Shiboo-yee means 'I'm free! I'm free!' The others are swear words. Showka is my best one. I started using Ikebana terms for swear words when August knocked over my flower arrangements. I don't know any other Japanese."

"There's often a connection between swearing and religion. Do you think of these words as religious?"

"Oh, yes!" Ursula replied fervently. "There is so much in Ikebana that expresses my beliefs. We extend one branch in a flower arrangement to show a need for individual freedom—in a sprightly way, not getting uptight about it, realizing it's illusory. Like creating an illusion of space by good manners. Asians may live in small quarters, but they give each other space by not being nosy or bossy. With flowers, the design is balanced but not symmetrical, like a mass of darker colors at one side and one tall flower at the other. Balance without symmetry. We Americans could learn that. Well, I've told you more than you wanted to know about Ikebana."

"I gather you feel the need for space?"

"I try to get it through a sense of order. Of course with cut flowers we can create perfect order, but flowers don't last, and growing plants are disorderly, always dropping seeds and leaves. So the Japanese invented an art based on slowing down growth by constantly clipping bonsai trees to preserve the artistic shape. A symbol of continuity. Flowers are also a symbol of privacy. Japan is a crowded country. People don't have private gardens, so they create order in their homes by having a niche with flowers, often just one flower, before which they meditate. No matter how cluttered the house is, they escape into serenity."

"Have you visited Japan?"

"Regrettably, no. What I know is from reading and my

imagination." She chuckled. "I know my idea of Japan is an ideal. For instance, Tokyo is a noisy big city—that's the real world. But the world of the inner life is real, too. I need it to survive." Martha murmured assent, and Ursula went on. "I've lived fifty years with a man who doesn't respect my right to compose poetry, and it's driving me crazy."

"Crazy? How? Through anger?"

"More through fear that I'll never have respect. It's made me work hard to create a serene, beautiful house."

Martha sat silent. Here was a paradox.

Ursula regularly shows coldness toward her husband. How can a house be serene without love? Am I showing a lack of love by packing up Barry's sports trophies? No. Beauty and love go together.

Aloud she said, "One has to decide which values transcend others. It takes discipline."

Ursula spoke thoughtfully."I wish my husband could remain in the hospital. They wouldn't tell Blaine on the phone what treatment would help, so maybe there is none. And I can't feel sorry. I don't want him to die; but I don't want to see him again, either. The Japanese solve questions of honor by suicide. August could do that and never have to face the end of our marriage, which we should have faced years ago." She bowed her head and murmured, "*Nobo, hara, sogetsu.*"

"What do those words mean?" Martha asked softly.

"I don't recall. I learned a lot of Ikebana terms but I forget what they mean. Right now I *want* them to mean that death can be very handy."

A chill went through Martha.

Someone this much in need of a niche of privacy, who has gone on so sorrowfully long without it, can forget how to love. This must be what she means by the east wall beating on the west wall. There's no buffer at the center.

When Ursula rose to leave she asked, "May I sit and wait for Blaine?"

"Of course," Martha said, and after Ursula settled herself on the sofa in the waiting room asked, "Will you be bored?"

"I'm never bored after my sessions with you. What I've told you comes back to me and seems interesting. Often surprising."

"Another patient will be arriving soon to see me. But when your daughter comes I'll buzz the front door open for her. Goodbye until next week."

Back in her office, Martha stood at the window thinking of Sandy's wish for advice. She soon saw her walking up the street, her petite frame nearly overbalanced by the size of the baby. Still, she walked with her usual springiness on her wedge shoes. She came into the inner office with a look of mock annoyance.

"This here kid's been kicking me," she said, patting her belly proudly. "Like always on the subway, the noise drives it bonkers. And I'm bonkers wondering how I'll be able to work after it comes." She sat.

"Well, first we're safe in assuming that you and the baby will be healthy," replied Martha. "From birth, a baby is learning, mastering biological processes."

"Like what?"

"Breathing air, for one. And swallowing. It takes practice to learn that food goes *down*, not *up*."

Sandy's eyes lit up. "I never thought of that! Is that why babies spit up so much?"

"Partly." Martha laughed, feeling grandmotherly. "So a mother gives a baby time to learn. Communication, like eye contact, is just as essential as feeding at the one end and cleaning up at the other."

"Can David help communicate?"

"Certainly. He can take over with the baby if you have the detachment to use the time for your art. Say you want to finish some lithographs in six months. Little by little you work toward the goal and may even reach it sooner than that, since a baby sleeps so many hours a day."

"I guess it's asleep right now, glad to be out of the subway."

"The safeguard is knowing you can change gears quickly. When you finish nursing and the baby is asleep, don't just sit—move on to the next activity. A change may be as good as a rest. After you eat, start your art work right away. Leave the dishes—they can be done when the baby is crying for exercise."

"Is crying its exercise?"

"Sometimes. Or entertainment, something to pass the time. If it has a pain, you'll hear the difference. If you can't do your art work while it's crying, you can use the vacuum cleaner to drown out the noise."

"How do you know the crying will stop?"

"You learn by experience. After you've fed a baby and burped it and walked with it and changed it and sung to it, it may just want to cry itself to sleep. Unless it has a fever, and that can be checked with a thermometer."

"You make it sound easy," said Sandy, "but how do I get out to arrange for the sale of my work?"

"There I'd advise a different approach. You can schedule a definite time out of the house for yourself when David is home, and get out some on weekends."

"But it has to be business hours if I contact galleries."

"You may have to postpone business for a while. Use the first year to build up a solid pile of finished work, a collection to take to galleries later."

"It makes sense," Sandy agreed. "The idea of a pregnant artist puts people off somehow. Like when I phoned about a job designing book covers the job was open, but when they saw me, it wasn't."

"They may be wrong, but experience has shown that it's hard to work to two schedules, a job's and a baby's."

"I suppose," said Sandy. "Anyhow being pregnant has given me some ideas. One is for a sort of cartoon, with a baby asleep in the womb and a train, a radio, rattles and other noisy things in three dimensions in the frame around it. The baby is frowning."

Martha smiled warmly, and Sandy said a bit shyly, "Your invitation to the wedding's in the mail. In the meantime, mark the date, a week from next Sunday. I won't be seeing you before then, because I have an appointment next Wednesday afternoon."

"An appointment?"

"Yes, with a gallery. But I'll be here the Wednesday after the wedding. I'll no doubt have problems to discuss."

"You're not going on a honeymoon?"

Sandy patted her belly. "No, we'll wait and take the kid down to the islands later. We're going to love being parents."

"Well," Martha said, drily, "that's what you'll be, forever after. You'll never have to give up that job."

At the door, Sandy said, "I'm going to wait until David comes for me. He has to work late tonight. Is that all right?"

"Of course," said Martha. "I'll see you in two weeks."

"Yes, we'll be married by then. But I won't be Mrs. David Steinberg, my professional name will be just *Sandra*."

When Sandy entered the waiting room, she saw Ursula still there on the sofa. She seemed asleep. Sandy sat down quietly at the other end. In a moment Ursula jerked her head up, stared around vaguely and said, "It's a myth."

"Did you speak to me?"

"Who ever heard of getting divorced on a Golden Wedding Anniversary?"

"Oh." Sandy considered the idea on its merits. "It could happen. If I were married and it didn't work out after fifty years, I'd get divorced."

"I plan to," said Ursula. Her head dropped again. Sandy wondered if her own hair would be that same grayed peach color when she was old.

Ursula looked up again. "You're not married?" She edged herself closer to Sandy.

Sandy did not reply but sat proudly erect.

People often move close to me these days, like I'm a warm stove. Maybe the baby is radiating love.

She hummed to herself, "Bumblebees a'buzzin' 'round the honeysuckle vine."

Ursula peered at her abdomen. "Is this your first baby?"

"Yes."

"I had four. Wonderful experiences. But hard work bringing them up. Too hard for me to discover I'm a poet."

"Oh, you're a poet? How do you manage?"

"I don't." The finality of this bothered Sandy, who began to wonder if Ursula had said her final word, but then she said, with bitterness, "I published a critical article but had to stop going to my class at N.Y.U. and couldn't really discuss it with anyone. My husband took no interest, and I didn't have a magnifying lamp to read by. I can't live my life my own way."

"The right equipment is so important, isn't it? Artists need their tools, right? I need my press under the same roof with me; but I gave it up on purpose, temporarily, and so far I don't feel deprived. But I might after the baby comes, as it'll be harder to get to my Mom's to print. David won't be deprived of anything, but I will."

"Being happily married is a myth for many people. Equality in marriage is the wildest dream."

"The funny thing is that David isn't too far from perfect! In fact, he's become more understanding that I can be okay as a mother and also create works of art. At last."

"At last?"

"Yes, now he's encouraging my work, after I left him stewing for a while. I had to show him, train him, and it had to be done before marriage."

"I admire you for having a plan. Somehow my frustrations just grew."

"Once, before I got my idea across to David, I talked with a two young guys in a coffee shop, one a divinity student and one a future rabbi—but they turned out to be real M.C.P.'s."

"M.C.P.'s?"

"Male chauvinist pigs."

Ursula said, "My word!" and chuckled. "A divinity student and a rabbi?"

"One of them said, 'Housework is stabilizing.' Of course I'm the one to be stabilized, not David."

Ursula cleared her throat and spoke carefully. "Sometimes the gentler types of men—men of God and scholars and poets—are bullied by the big money men. So the gentler types end up bullying women."

"Well, David needs me so much that I agreed to get married. My Mom is planning a big affair, and I owe it to her because I'm an only child. But I dread it."

"I dread it for you. Won't your David support you and the child if you don't get married?"

"He would, but he'd be miserable." Sandy realized that meeting Ursula earlier, someone who took calmly the idea of going her own way, might have helped.

When Blaine arrived, Ursula rose to leave, not hurrying. At the door, she stopped and added with dignity, "There are some things you can never buy back if you give them away. Give away your love but not your time."

Sandy, still considering these words when Martha came out of her office, told her, "I had a wonderful talk with your other patient."

"Good."

"Do you think responsibility is stabilizing, Dr. Kaufman? Or is inner freedom more important, even if it means ducking responsibilities?"

Martha, hearing pleading, became judicious. "That's quite a question."

"I need to know."

"Both are important. Are you comfortable where you're sitting?"

"Oh yes. In five minutes I'm going out to meet David."

"We can talk about inner freedom next time."

Back in her office, Martha sat at her desk.

Today was my benchmark. I can't prove why, but I feel

it—Elinor through Sandy, a full Wednesday. Maybe the last one, since Billie's quitting. I took her impertinence well, and softened her gesture of paying me off—didn't beg her to stay and didn't say goodbye. At the end she said, "Maybe," so the way is open for her to come back, especially after Mike is found. She'll need to tell me all about her search.

I'm becoming less directive.

The awareness that she had given copious advice to Sandy flitted across her consciousness, but she was too hungry to think about it. When she went out, the waiting room was empty. She recalled Sandy's saying she'd had a wonderful talk with Ursula.

That's interesting. Those two independent women and their men!

26

American Gothic

Sandy and David were finishing dinner in their kitchen the following Tuesday. "I met Bernie's boss at lunch, and their man in fundraising is leaving," David said. They're going to offer the job to me. It'll be part-time, but pays well and I can keep my present job."

"David, that's super. Do you think you'll like it?"

"It shows there'll be some things to choose from, and it'll be better when we're married and I can ask for more money." He started doing the dishes.

Sandy brought his after-dinner coffee to him at the sink. "You're so smart!" She patted him on the back. "Did I tell you I have an appointment tomorrow with the director of a gallery? It's a good place for a one-woman show."

He raised two soapy fingers in a victory sign.

Sandy went into the living room and lay on the sofa. "David, you should feel Him-or-Her," she called. "It's dancing, I swear."

He sat beside her, resting his hand firmly on her abdomen. "Hey, Him-or-Her, which are you?"

"Not to worry, we'll know soon enough. The wedding will keep us busy. One good thing, boy and girl babies wear the same clothes, and Danny's collected a lot of the twins' hand-me-downs for me. She's bringing the girls to the wedding, but I told her not to bring the clothes, because we'll drive out and get them, okay?"

David grinned. "And show off our kid."

"Of course. The twins will be thrilled. Danny says she has little blue jeans of all sizes, from six months old on."

"You arty roommates have become practical women, haven't you?" She nodded, vigorously. "So how was your day?"

"I get tired, carrying this weight." She put her hand over his, sorry to be complaining. "I have to guide my portfolio into crowded elevators and ask receptionists to see if someone will give me a chance to design a book jacket. Eventually, jobs will come, I know. One nice editor said some illustrators don't read the book and make goofs like giving the heroine the wrong color of hair. She gave me a novel to read so I could submit a sample. If it's trash, I'll go back to macramé."

All fall she'd been attending classes in prenatal care and, inspired by Debbie, had resumed practicing breathing in preparation for labor. She had some anxiety about the pain of delivery, but felt she could rely on her doctor, who laughed at her tee shirt with the word UPROARIOUS above the word BABY. She did get a little tired of his joke about his golf partner, called "Fizz" for Physiotherapist, who disliked pregnant women because they interrupted golf. Yesterday, however, during her routine examination, her obstetrician hadn't joked, but spoke crisply to the nurse, something about centimeters. The nurse nodded and didn't detain her afterward to schedule another office visit.

David brought some work from the office to the kitchen table where Sandy was wrapping up a drawing which she showed him. "This is what I'm peddling to a gallery tomorrow. I hope they like it."

He scrutinized it and asked, "Is this the one you call 'Sea Dreams'?"

"Yes. I told Mom about it and she liked the idea of sleepers with relaxed bodies and closed eyes and tousled hair, all wrapped in blankets of sea kelp."

"Oh, is that what the brown ribbons are?"

"Yes."

"I like the little fishes swimming by."

"I hope it makes people sleepy to see it. I'm sleepy right now." She undressed and went to bed.

She woke later in the dark with a pain she recognized, a menstrual cramp.

So, old buddy, all those years you were preparing me for this!

The pain held her in desperate, silent sweat and then let go. She turned on the light and looked at her watch—three o'clock.

David was sleeping soundly and she decided not to wake him.

"I swear to God," she said softly, "everybody will flip. Here I am having it before the wedding. Well, we'll have it anyway." Dutifully she corrected her thought. "We'll have both, the baby and the wedding." She dozed but an undercurrent of fear kept her alert. In her head she heard, "Turn me over, doctor, turn me over slow."

The second pain came in twenty minutes. This time she controlled her breathing, but was soon aware that a contraction was the opposite of relaxation until it let go.

God, I should have opened my mind when people said I was one month farther along than I figured. But the books say predictions are often wrong, and I felt sure I conceived the night David moved in. Maybe my notion of the date was a myth, but since we don't know for sure, I'll keep to my story. It's romantic, and this experience is all my own. Nobody else owns it.

I'm in for it now. This will be my night of trial.

In the aftermath of the third pain she realized that during a contraction she would be out of action, just enduring and nothing else, so she'd better make practical use of the in-between times. She had in her handbag a long shopping list of items she'd been told she'd need. So far only two of them were ready, a second-hand crib from a Salvation Army store and a gross of disposable diapers. She put the list in her handbag to give her mother.

Right now I'd better think what to take to the hospital for myself.

She had a tote bag with the logo of the Public Broadcasting System always ready for sudden overnight trips to her mother's, but wanted a suitcase big enough to hold a sketch pad.

I'll make a record of the experience. And take along the book the editor gave me so I can think about the cover.

It was nearly a half hour before the next pain, and when it was over she located her bathrobe and slippers and three of David's old white shirts.

One of these over a hospital gown will be my bedjacket.

In the kitchen she tidied up her latest sketches. Lovingly regarding "Sea Dreams," she signed it "Sandra" and put it away. She had meant to show it at the art gallery, but the fact that she wouldn't be keeping that appointment didn't seem to matter. "It's their loss. I have a rendezvous with destiny," she said aloud.

When she returned to the bedroom she put a large towel under her place in the bed and lay down ready for the next pain. David stirred and woke. "I'm having regular labor pains," she said through clenched teeth. "Don't jiggle the bed. It hurts." His hand shot out and clutched hers in panic. "They're still pretty far apart," she said to reassure him.

His hand was so tight on hers that she patted it with her free hand until he relaxed his grip. "Could they be false pains? The baby isn't due for a month."

"There's nothing false about them. Friends have said I'm a month farther along than we thought and I guess they're right."

"God, it's coming before the wedding. Does it hurt a lot?"

"It's bad for a minute or two each time. I hope it doesn't stay this bad."

"Shall we call the doctor?"

"Not yet. We're supposed to wait until they're a lot closer together, then go to the hospital and they'll call him. He asked me to try to be sensible. Go back to sleep."

"I couldn't sleep now," David insisted, but in a few minutes she heard his measured breathing. She got up and paced back and forth through the living room and kitchen, and then brought the kitchen clock-radio back to bed with her.

At five o'clock David rolled out onto his feet, upright and alert. "How is it now?" he asked. He wrapped his robe around him and came to stand by her side of the bed.

"They keep coming but not at regular intervals. It's okay at the moment," she said with a warm smile. "I'm just resting up from the last one."

"So was I."

She grinned up at him, and watched fondly as he ran his hand through his curly hair like a sleepy kid. She reached out and rubbed his knee.

"Can I get you some coffee or anything?"

"No, I shouldn't eat anything. But you can go down to our locker for my suitcase. The blue one."

"Down in the basement of the building?"

"Yeah. Take the locker key."

"Christ, I hope there aren't any rats or muggers around. It's dark down there."

"David, get it . . . No, wait, here's another pain." She gritted her teeth and he dropped down on his knees and held her hand. When she relaxed, he touched her face reverently.

"Are you sure this is normal? I don't want anything to happen to you."

"I don't know what normal is, but this is what the books said. Get the suitcase."

When he came up with it, Sandy took it to the kitchen and sponged off the dust, then opened it and tossed in a bar of fragrant French soap. The next hour was a long one, with pains during her preparations. Having heard that a woman's feet are the main part of her anatomy on display during birth, she decided to go into battle looking brave. Although she usually wore toenail polish only to the beach, she twisted to reach around her enormous abdomen and painted her toenails bright red. Then she wrote out instructions for David to cancel her appointment at the gallery.

After the pains became regular at nine minutes apart, she took a quick shower. She didn't object when David insisted on calling the doctor at his home, and was told she should go to the hospital when the pains were five minutes apart. When suddenly they were coming every six minutes, Sandy, in panic said, "Bring the car to the front door."

"I got a parking place right in front last night. We can take the elevator down together."

"Not yet," she said, changing her mind. "I want to call the doctor myself. After the next pain."

This time the interval was nine minutes, but she called him.

He was friendly, said he was eating a muffin. "Not to worry," he announced. "If you've been clocking them at nine minutes they won't settle down at six for a while, maybe a couple of hours. I'm playing golf early and we'll limit ourselves to nine holes. You can check in at the hospital in an hour or so, but there's no rush. I'll be there before noon, in plenty of time to deliver you."

"You're going to play golf?"

"Yup." He pursued his joke. "Take pity on Fizz and don't rush it. The hospital knows how to reach me at the clubhouse if necessary. And if it comes sooner, another good doctor will be there."

David's ear was pressed against the phone and he spoke firmly into it. "What's the name and number of the clubhouse?"

To their relief, the doctor gave him the number which he wrote down on the back of Sandy's shopping list.

Outrage at doctors who had to play golf on Wednesdays seemed to merge with Sandy's next pain, but when it was over she saw the interval hadn't really been six minutes but closer to nine, and sent David out to buy the day's *Times* and some muffins. While he was gone she made him coffee.

They forced themselves to read the news—they'd keep

this paper, with the date of the baby's birthday—and when the pains were very predictable at six minutes, Sandy surveyed their kitchen with new eyes. It was a plain but serviceable room and she scrubbed the sink and counter and said, "I'm going to brighten up this place. Life will be all different when we come back here. Debbie had cute bunnies all in a row around her counter."

"Bunnies?" David asked. "They're fertility symbols."

They laughed and proceeded in high spirits to the elevator. Going down, the mirror reflected them, each with a hand on the handle of the suitcase, looking proud and fallible and absorbed in their destiny. Her cheeks were pink, her eyes were bright, her long red hair hung in two pigtails over the shoulders of her dark green coat. David, short and solid-looking in a business suit and coat, needed a shave. His eyes were solemn, wet with love.

Their eyes met in the mirror and Sandy grinned. Then she thrust her belly forward, bumping the mirror. "American Gothic," she said.

"Yeah, I feel like a pioneer," said David.

When they arrived at the hospital, David let her out at the front door and went to park. She proceeded to Admitting and was directed to Delivery. Going up in the elevator, she realized she hadn't had a single pain on the trip there, which had taken about twenty minutes. When she was examined she was told, "You're not ready to be here. It will probably be hours. You should go home."

David was mystified when he returned from parking the car and heard she'd been sent home, but took her down in the elevator to the main waiting room. "Wait here," he said and went out again for the car.

Sandy decided to call her mother while she waited and on the advice of the volunteer "pink lady" at the desk, started for the pay phone in the corner. Before she got there the real thing hit, a hard pain raging so suddenly and fiercely that she went down on her knees between a sofa and a heavy standing ashtray. A kind Black woman who had been reading a magazine jumped up and helped her up after the pain began to lessen. She squeezed the woman's hand, remarking, "A bolt of lightning. I'm supposed to call the doctor. Thank you."

She walked to the reception desk and asked the pink lady to let her use the phone, saying, "This is definitely hospital business!" A man at the golf club answered and she left a message for the doctor, "Sandy Lieberman is rushing up to Delivery. Please report to the hospital immediately!"

David hurried in and caught her waiting at the elevator. "The car's right outside," he said.

Impatiently jabbing the elevator button marked "UP," she growled, "I am not going home. Go park again."

To the nurse in Delivery, she said firmly, "I am definitely in labor. Please examine me."

The nurse did not need more than a glance. She quickly called the resident who also was convinced by a quick look. "Time for the delivery room," he said.

The nurse helped her undress and supported her through another pain and then helped her onto a gurney.

David returned in time to find her lying flat on her back. Seeing his look of amazement at her size, she reached to the top of her abdomen and said, "My volcano!" He smiled wanly.

They were sent to a birthing room and during the next two hours, pains came and went and nurses came in and out.

To their relief, the doctor arrived and said to David, "I told you it would start slow but when it happened, it would go fast." David frowned, having no recollection of ever hearing this, but Sandy, looking anxious, shook her head to signal that he shouldn't respond to what the doctor said, right or wrong.

"Modern technology," she said, as she and David watched a monitor being plugged in. Soon the *glub-glub* sound of the baby's heartbeat filled their ears. It slowed with each contraction and disappeared, only to re-emerge as the contraction eased.

The doctor left and came back at noon to check. "You have about an hour more, so hang in there!" he announced and quietly vanished. But at twelve thirty there was no baby and the pain was becoming worse. David tried to interest Sandy in doing exercises, but she had long since given up trying to relax or breathe according to directions.

"I have no more will to cooperate," she announced to David, and then called out, "Don't I have any rights? This baby is still way up here." She circled an area closer to her lungs than her abdomen. "This baby will suffocate. This baby . . ."

David squeezed her hand and her hysteria subsided.

"Don't I have any rights?" she screamed as the doctor came in for another look.

"Let's have this baby," said the doctor.

She felt exposed with her feet in the stirrups but knew she was in the most convenient place in the world for what she was going through. The next five minutes she alternately felt disorientation and pain. The doctor told her when to push, and she pushed. She was sure that one huge pain was the moment of birth, but it exploded into the next one and then suddenly she was only hurting, with no work to do.

"It's a boy!" David whooped.

While the doctor clamped and cut the cord, the baby was laid across Sandy's knees and she was catapulted into a dizzying new world. This sensation was beyond all her imagining. It was life and death and fate, and all hers.

The doctor examined the baby carefully.

"Why is he so blue?" David asked.

"He's pretty red. And listen to him!" There was a baby sound, a cry which Sandy felt she had heard before although she had no idea where or when. "On a scale of ten, we'll give him a ten," the doctor said with satisfaction.

A nurse deftly wrapped the tiny body in a receiving

blanket and put it into a waiting isolette. The doctor supervised the eye-cleaning procedure and waved his hand with a sweeping motion. "On your way," he said to the nurse.

Suddenly the baby was gone and also David, who followed the isolette down the hall.

Sandy felt dazed. The afterbirth came and the doctor stitched her up and she was put into bed in a regular hospital room. She slept.

Waking later, she was humming, "Sleep, Kentucky babe." The rhythms of her body were normal, but she felt excited and at the same time, safe. "I'm a mother!" she said aloud, telling herself the joyful news. "It wasn't so bad."

She pushed the button behind the bed and sat up expectantly until the nurse appeared. "Nurse," she stated in a not-to-be-mistaken tone, "I want to see my baby!"

27

A Suitable Gift

Elinor saw Ralph on Saturday evening in the City as she had told Martha she would. After dinner at an elegant seafood place, she served him coffee at his kitchen table. "Ralph, I'd like us to have a New Year's Party at my house."

"A party?"

"Yes, and I'd like to invite Adele. You remember her—the skinny dark-haired woman I was with the day you and I met in the Hamptons? She's my talkative friend. And I'm sure you have friends you'd like to ask."

"They couldn't find the way there, and they'd get too drunk to drive home."

"Not everybody," Elinor said, trying to remain cheerful. "Those who can't drive can stretch out on the sofas, and I'll serve breakfast with croissants and Eggs Benedict and lots of coffee. Then we can take them jogging."

"Not my friends. They don't like exercise much."

"But the general idea of the party is a good one, right? I'm hoping you'll bring the liquor and I'll make special canapés."

"I feel obligated to give my girls a good time."

"Of course. That's part of the plan. If we get the invitations out right away, we should get a lot of nice people, especially teenagers. One wonderful thing about Susan's friends' parents is that they really look after their kids and want to keep them happy right in their home town. Especially on a night like New Year's when drunk drivers are on the roads. The kids play fascinating games. Michele is getting to know these kids too. Although Helen may not know them, a couple of the girls have older brothers in college who are Helen's age, and they can dance if they want to.

We can arrange one rec room for table games and one for dancing. Maybe Helen would enjoy shopping in the Village for crazy hats and noise-makers. A lot of the parents will come to our grownup party upstairs and your friends will be welcome. I love New Year's parties."

"I don't," Ralph said, sounding cross.

Elinor made no reply but took something out of her suitcase and went into the bathroom. A few seconds later, she emerged, wearing only a bright yellow bird headdress with blue paper streamers which curled down over her breast. "I found this in the rec room closet," she said, "and thought it might put you in a festive mood." She sat down on the bed and Ralph playfully tickled her with the streamers, then knocked the headdress to the floor and drew her to him possessively.

Their lovemaking was a perfect pleasure to her, and she slept soundly until he jounced the bed later. "Are you getting up?" she asked.

"No, I had heartburn. Too much of that hot sauce with the crab at dinner."

With light fingers she rubbed his stomach and back until he relaxed. She was drifting off to sleep again when he stirred and abruptly rolled over on top of her. She was taken aback by his approach which was too forceful to be amorous. Pinning her down he said in a didactic tone, "Elinor, why don't you save yourself some trouble? There's a big New Year's dance at the singles' group on the West Side."

"You're in touch with a singles' group?"

"Off and on. Mostly off."

"And you're saying I ought to go to their party?"

"It would save you a lot of work."

"I never go to singles' groups."

"There's a big one at a church on the upper West Side in Manhattan."

"In *Manhattan?*"

"Yes. On the upper West Side."

"Whatever side it's on," she retorted, sliding away from him and sitting on the edge of the bed. "I don't need any group. I'm with you." He grunted, and she appealed to him with a shared memory of the night he had slept alone in her guest room. "Honey, guess what your West Side story is worth? Nine cents!" He laughed, but rolled back to his side of the bed.

He said no more and was soon asleep. Elinor lay awake for a long time.

On Monday, Martha received a call from Blaine.

"Mother's staying with me and won't be able to come for therapy any more," Blaine said, hesitantly. "You know Daddy's been hospitalized, and now he's been moved to a nursing home near us, and I have to visit him every day. Mother refuses to see him so it all falls on me. I can't drive her down to you any more."

Martha listened, her heart sinking. "Oh, I'm sorry," she said.

"We also have to economize. Am I canceling the required two days in advance?"

"Yes. But not having more therapy will be a shock to Ursula. Have you discussed this with her?"

"Not yet."

"When you do, please give her my regrets. It would be better if I could see her a couple of times more, to prepare her for the adjustment. How is she doing?"

"She's quite rational, and getting along fine, actually. For the long pull, she doesn't want to stay here and talks about going home, but her living alone is out of the question. We'll have to keep her here and find tenants for their house. I know she'll miss seeing you."

"Tell her I hope she'll keep on with her poetry. She should also continue taking Doxepin. Would you like me to mail you another prescription?"

"Yes, please. And I'll mail you a check for your last bills."

"Fine. This is a difficult time for all of you."

"Yes, especially with the limit on how long Daddy's health insurance will cover the nursing home, which can become astronomical. We'll do our best. Anyhow, Mother's happier here than she was at home with Daddy."

"Yes, that's probably true. Oh, and tell her I understand about the West Wall."

"The what?"

"The West Wall—her symbol of self-reliance. From a poem."

After Blaine hung up, Martha felt dazed, and through the day on Tuesday had recurring moments of sadness over Ursula. She also had a hollow feeling about Wednesdays. She had lost Billie and Ursula, and Sandy wouldn't be coming in until the week after her wedding. Only Elinor would be coming as usual.

Wednesday morning was cloudy, with dust blowing in the street. Martha's first patient of the day was late, so she hadn't yet switched the phone to her answering service, and picked it up herself when Elinor called.

"Dr. Kaufman, I need a favor. Instead of coming in today, could I have my session with you on the phone? Michele has a sore throat, and Ralph said to take her to my doctor, but we can't see him until two."

"All right. Call me at four after you get home," said Martha.

"I will."

"I'll be here when you call. Please make sure you call from a place that's private."

Elinor was relieved that she wouldn't miss her session that day. She gave Michele breakfast in bed and learned that this kind of attention was new to the girl, who also confessed that at school the assistant principal had asked her if she lived in the school district. Elinor comforted her as well as she could, assuring her that her father would take care of things. Later Michele didn't want any lunch, and Elinor fixed herself a bite which she took to the table in her breakfast nook off the kitchen, fondly recalling Ralph's good humor while serving them Saturday lunches at this table.

I wonder what he will say to the school people? I know the district is pretty strict about where students live. Howard used to become irate when we heard about outsiders who used fake addresses, hoping for free education in our superior system. Of course, no fake address has been claimed for Michele, as she definitely lives here now. I once might have expected Ralph to decide that we should get married and everybody live here. But since he doesn't want to have a New Years party, and even worse, says I should go to a singles' group, getting married isn't in the cards right now. Telling Dr. Martha about it won't be easy.

Fortunately, Michele's appointment at the doctor's went quickly. On their way home they made a stop at a pharmacy to pick up the antibiotic the doctor had said should help the sore throat. After giving Michele lunch and medicine, and settling her in bed with a magazine, at four o'clock Elinor was on the phone in her bedroom spilling out her hurt feelings to Martha. "I think Ralph's suggestion of a singles' group is utterly preposterous," she said.

Martha didn't seem to take the subject very seriously. "It's not much of a rejection," she pointed out. "Probably he was testing, to be reassured you didn't want to meet someone else. He's entrusted his daughter to you, and is regularly taking you out and making love and discussing things."

"Yes, he's always seemed just as much in love as I am. That's why I was surprised. Of course, he was suffering from an upset stomach."

"And sharing night thoughts with you. Men do think about singles' groups."

"It wasn't only that, it was his not being enthusiastic about our giving a party. Maybe he doesn't want his friends to meet me."

"Could it be that he hasn't kept up his social relationships since his divorce? Or maybe his city friends would be envious of your house?"

"I'd hate to invite people and have them refuse. My grandmother used to say, 'Smarty, smarty, no one's at your party!'"

When she got off the phone with Elinor, Martha felt the emptiness of the afternoon. It was a change, not getting Billie's outbursts immediately after saying goodbye to Elinor. Trying to feel efficient, she opened her appointment book and crossed out Billie's name.

She's anxious about her son, that's why she called me old-fashioned.

Determined to cope, she also crossed off Ursula's name, and made herself tea.

This is like the empty office the afternoon before Thanksgiving, but everybody's been coming since then, including Sandy. In fact, she only cancelled today because she has an appointment. At a gallery! I assumed she'd be having a fitting for her wedding dress, and pictured our short, bouncy Sandy being measured over "the outrageous baby!" I wouldn't be surprised if she asks people at her wedding to feel where it's kicking her! Of course, the dress could still be beautiful white satin and look very . . . well, very feminine. She's so radiant in her pregnancy, she can get away with anything. It's the human story. I recall an old Dutch painting by Rembrandt or Van Eyck or someone, called *The Wedding*, with a serene-looking bride who's obviously about to give birth.

She settled down to read her latest professional journals.

Just before six, as she was about to go to dinner, the phone rang. It was Judy Lieberman, so full of excitement she was nearly shouting. "Sandy had her baby this afternoon, a boy, seven pounds, three ounces. Both mother and son are doing great. The wedding is just postponed a month. I'll send you another invitation."

"Oh, thank you for calling," Martha said, joyfully. "That's wonderful news!"

Judy's voice became less strident. "Oh, *yes*. And Dr. Kaufman, we'll have to cancel Sandy's therapy from now on, under the circumstances."

Speaking loudly herself, Martha said, "Sandra should definitely continue therapy now." She was startled at her own decisiveness.

"The wedding is just postponed a month," Judy chirped and hung up.

Martha sat thinking.

I'm really glad the baby's all right. Not premature, with that weight. I felt all along she'd figured the date wrong.

Winter darkness penetrated the office as she opened her appointment book.

How can it be that all my Wednesday afternoon slots are empty except for Elinor's at two? Well, actually, there's good reason to rejoice over her progress. She was upset by Ralph's remark about the singles' group but not in despair. Not suicidal. She's hardly the helpless woman she was a year ago. She's more aware of herself as being good at raising kids, and is more secure financially, through keeping Michele. A case where everyone wins.

She closed the book, washed her teacup and watered the fern hanging in Sandy's macramé basket.

In my free time next Wednesday, after Elinor leaves, I'll pay Sandy a friendly visit to see her little son, all seven pounds and three ounces of him. I'll take a suitable gift to show I wholeheartedly celebrate his safe arrival. Champagne is called for. The beautiful bottle of Dom Perignon is still in the refrigerator. My Thanksgiving plan for it fizzled but it's just the thing for this special event. Sandy and David can drink it to celebrate the birth of one of the world's lucky babies!

28

Smarty, Smarty, No One's at Your Party

Elinor walked into the office the next Wednesday looking pale and somewhat tousled. She slumped into the chair facing Martha and said, "Bad news like you'll never believe. I can hardly bear to tell you."

"What's happened?"

"It's Howard. He sent me a letter. Here, read it." She handed a letter to Martha, who read:

> To whom it may concern:
> As of this date, I have instructed my staff to send no further checks to Dr. Martha Kaufman for treatment of my my ex-wife, Elinor Bates.
> > Yours truly,
> > Howard Bates

"When did you get this?" Martha asked.

"Yesterday. And along with it came this letter to me." She read aloud. " 'Elinor, You have no right to house someone else's *brat* in my house. I am in receipt of a letter from the school superintendent about the residency of a *brat* named Michele Conklin at the address on which I pay taxes. If you don't get rid of your lover's *brat* I'll stop the mortgage payments. I know that shrink down at N.Y.U. is behind this, and she'll get a letter from me, too. Take care of our children or I will.' " She asked anxiously. "Did you get a letter too?"

"No," said Martha. "It may come today."

"How can he call Michele a brat?" wailed Elinor. "She's a well-brought-up young lady whose father is a respected stock broker."

"This is a shock to you, and I must compliment you on being in control. Now, as to his forcing you to quit therapy, that may be temporary, and a break will not be fatal. I think you'll weather the storm until we see what can be done." Secretly, she wondered if she herself could weather the storm of losing all of her Wednesday afternoon Four. "Have you talked with Ralph about it?" she asked professionally.

"Yes, and in a way, his response was reassuring, but it was scary, too. He told me he himself has absolute confidence in my parenting, and has every confidence in you as a therapist, but probably I should stop seeing you. Because if Howard tries to get custody of my kids, my being in therapy might open me to a charge of incompetence. Do you think it would?"

"My experience has been that in a custody case, the mother usually wins, all things being equal. But in this case, Howard is the one with the means to support kids and hire powerful lawyers."

Elinor kept her composure, but great tears rolled down her cheeks. Martha handed her a tissue from the box on her desk and nodded in sympathy.

"Did Ralph say anything about Howard?" she asked.

"Yes," said Elinor, wiping her eyes. "He said he's surprised he's so obsessed about it, this long after the divorce, so there's no telling. He thinks Howard should remarry and stop going over the past. I gave him my divorce papers so he can ask his good lawyer about it."

"Did he say anything about your keeping Michele?"

"Oh, yes. He says he's going to pay me a lot more for her care, since in the past he's paid a private school thousands of dollars on top of child support to his ex-wife. He says he's getting my care for Michele at a bargain rate, and under my good influence she's becoming more cheerful and well-mannered. And above all, she's begged him to let her stay with us and in our school, and he wouldn't dream of taking her away."

"I'm glad to hear that!" said Martha. "Not everyone could be so successful with a teenage girl!"

29

Did They Have Good Reasons?

Martha felt indignant after Elinor left.

How dare Howard threaten to take Elinor's kids? And say I'm a bad influence? Even Ralph suggests that she stop seeing me. Personally, I'd swear in court that Elinor is no longer suicidal, and I'll so testify if summoned. But Howard could be a tough opponent, playing on the distrust some people have of psychiatrists. And he has money for powerful lawyers.

In a gloomy mood she set off for Sandy's, taking the subway to 72nd Street, and walking through damp streets crowded with Hanukkah shoppers. She was carrying a bottle wrapped in blue paper sprinkled with teddy bears. On reaching Sandy's apartment house, she studied the directory of names.

Am I looking for Sandy's last name, Lieberman? Or— what's David's name? Oh, here it is, "David Steinberg and Sandra," on the fifth floor. And lettered at the bottom of the label, "Baby Jordan." I guess at this moment he has his mother's last name. For sure, though, he's not worried about his label. Bless his heart, he deserves a good one, like this Dom Perignon.

She pushed in the code and the front door opened.

Upstairs, Sandy was waiting in the hall with her apartment door open. "Hello, Dr. Kaufman. Please come in." She was pale and looked like a tired teenager in her loose maternity jeans and a blue tee shirt imprinted "MY UPROARIOUS BABY."

Martha, smiling, crossed the threshold and held out her gift. "I brought you a little bottle of congratulations."

A look of pain crossed Sandy's face as she placed the

bottle on the coffee table, saying, "Thank you. This is nicely wrapped. Blue for a boy."

Martha, a little disappointed that she didn't unwrap it, said resolutely, "Yes. A boy is wonderful."

Sandy, who seemed tense, indicated the sofa. "Please sit down."

Martha sat, not immediately ready with small talk. Fortunately the phone rang and Sandy said, "The phone's in the kitchen. Please excuse me."

Martha glanced around the room with its basic pine furniture, dark red drapes, and blue and yellow pillows. The gray walls were strangely unadorned. She'd expected to see some of Sandy's art work. On the coffee table lay a large book on printmaking, which she assumed was Sandy's, and a page of classified ads from the *Times*, with job openings for executives, which she assumed was David's.

Sandy returned and immediately started showing snapshots, the top one introducing a dreaming baby held by an exuberantly smiling grandmother.

"That's my mother," Sandy said, and Martha recalled red-haired Judy's recent visit to her office, although she didn't mention it, in accordance with Judy's request. "And this is David's mother."

Martha examined the face of another exuberant grandmother. "She's happy."

"Oh, yes!" Sandy said. "One of the best things about Jordy's birth was his coming now, the year her husband died. And here's one of me and David, beaming."

"Oh, yes, I've seen him by his car, out my window." Martha too was beaming like a grandmother, imagining pouring champagne for these happy people.

Sandy put the pictures away into a file cabinet. Stepping around a couple of stacks of folios propped against the wall, she remarked, "Artists always seem to have messy apartments. My drawings are everywhere."

"I'd love to see some of them."

"I'd like to show you. Sometime. I feel too tired today."

"The baby came just a week ago today?"

"Yes. Luckily it was an easy birth and I came home the second day. Last night I had to go out shopping for baby bedding, so today I'm taking it easy."

"You look happy. Motherhood suits you."

"Thank you. Would you like to see him?"

They went into the bedroom where Sandy gently lifted the corner of a blanket and Martha got a quick glimpse of a very pink, solid-faced tiny fellow with dark hair, sound asleep.

They tiptoed out of the room. Martha had hoped for a cup of tea, but from the bedroom came a soft cry.

"I guess I have work to do," Sandy said. "Thanks for coming." She walked over to the door to the outside hall, opened it and waited. "And thank you for the gift."

"You're welcome," Martha said, as the door closed behind her.

Walking along the street, she felt a lack of energy in her feet, which were getting wet from puddles.

In years past only a theater ticket could have unplugged me from the office on a Wednesday. I never feel lonely or exposed in the midst of a companionable audience. Well, from now on I can book seats for myself and Sarah for Wednesday matinees. Hardly a cheering thought today.

As she walked toward the subway, dreading the unpleasant ride ahead, she passed a building which had dentists' offices upstairs and a small restaurant downstairs. It had clean windows, a luxury in New York. She decided to have tea. Inside, she heard Strauss music and saw chocolate éclairs, cream puffs, meringues and Napoleons displayed under soft lighting in a sparkling glass cabinet. An elderly bearded man sat alone at a small round table, reading a book and drinking tea from a glass. Resisting the pastries, she ordered a glass of tea and sat at a table by the window, feeling solitary.

The man was smoking a pipe and now and then slicing a pocket knife through uncut pages of his book, European style. He looks like Freud, she thought, recalling a group photograph on Berson's office wall at the senior center, in which Freud stood with some twenty other dark-suited doctors.

Berson had explained that they had come together to honor the great analyst, and pointed himself out to Martha, saying, "Of course I was very young, and now I am the only one in the picture still alive." It impressed Martha that the great Viennese psychoanalyst had been in this city to which he would have had to travel by ship. Perhaps he had followers in the prosperous Jewish neighborhood she was now in. He himself had been prosperous, the tenant of a now-famous apartment in Vienna. She had seen the building years ago when she and Norman visited a family friend, a woman who had been Freud's neighbor before he went to England to escape Hitler.

This man's pipe even looks like Freud's. How ironic that the founder of the most powerful means known for changing human behavior smoked a pipe so long that he had cancer of the jaw and died. Heal thyself? Is anything more difficult?

Entering a crowded car on the subway, she bleakly wished she had avoided the rush hour, especially when the lights went out. She felt uneasy, standing among the herded people going home, and felt that her life, too, was unlighted and stale. Like the train, she was rattling along in the dark, and any bright spots were reflections of the lives of her Wednesday patients, in false vicariousness. Now all shut off from her.

When the lights flickered on again, she found a seat from which she saw herself reflected in the window, dirt-streaked and distorted. She closed her eyes, a vision of turning wheels greasy in her head, many interlocking gears, enormous and black, revolving against flickering lights. Wheels spun wildly, then jammed and broke loose repeatedly, grinding out deafening noises.

When the lights failed again, she kept her eyes closed,

heavy with fatigue. She was a dentist leaning over Elinor, drilling into a cavity. Elinor looked up and said, "Do something for your own tooth," and pulled away. Martha said to her, "Don't be sorry for me, Elinor. I'm sorry for you." Then Billie was in the dentist's chair and Martha was holding a suction pump in her mouth to keep her from talking. But Billie yanked it out and snarled, "Why the hell don't you look after your own son? You need to learn from me, not me from you," and stomped out in her boots. Martha followed her out the door in bare feet, and found Ursula and Sandy in the waiting room. "The doctor will see you now," she told them, but both women walked out, shaking their heads.

When she woke, she discovered she was three stations beyond her stop, so she forced her way out the door, and caught the next train back. She felt utterly alone.

It wasn't for them I sought solutions, but for myself. I couldn't heal others because I lacked wholeness, so everyone was betrayed. Especially Ursula and August. I wanted a Golden Wedding myself but Norman is dead and I can never have it.

At her stop, she walked down the long black platform on Fourth Street, up the steep stairs, and through the cold, wet streets home.

The Christmas holidays did not rout the gloom from the brownstone house. Barry was skiing in Vermont, Sarah was homesick for her sister in Vienna, and Martha was marking time in place, counseling a heavy load of patients as always on holidays. She spent evenings in the office and was withdrawn at meals, unlike herself. Sarah studied the reviews until she found a Broadway play about three generations of women, and got Martha's agreement to go to a Sunday matinee.

After the show they chatted about it in an ice cream parlor, but Martha soon lapsed into silence, staring at nothing. "This is good frozen custard," Sarah ventured.

"I need it like a hole in the head. I should lose fifteen pounds."

"Ten would do it," said Sarah. "I'm the one who should lose fifteen." Martha did not respond. "You would have dieted to please Norman."

"Yes." Martha said, twisting her wedding ring. "Tomorrow is our twenty-ninth wedding anniversary."

"You had a long time together."

"Not long enough."

"It's a long stretch after your man is gone. I know."

"Happiness is rationed."

"That doesn't sound like a therapist talking," Sarah said.

"This therapist is getting nowhere fast. All the Wednesday Four have quit."

"All four of them?" Martha's reply was a slow nod. "Well, they'll be the losers," was Sarah's comment. "Did they have good reasons?"

"Yes, all contradictory to my visions," Martha said with a shiver. "I tried too hard. The first process a therapist must follow is to establish transference from patients, which means to build up the trust they have in the therapist as solid as the trust they felt in their parents. But transference is supposed to go only one way, from patient to therapist, and I betrayed the trust, and assumed I had a place in their lives and a right to plan their futures. That's countertransference."

"Were you compensating? For losing Norman?"

"Whatever. I'm trained to know better. I didn't help them or myself. I didn't take time to exercise, and my mind got foggy."

"So do it now. Lose weight, in Norman's memory."

Martha smiled at last. "You're a good friend, Sarah. But you'll have to do your part and serve salads and lean meat and vegetables. No cheesecake."

"I'll diet too." Sarah's eyes grew serious with commitment. "Now that your Wednesday afternoons are free you could visit Norman's library. Say hello to the people he worked with. They were always his friends."

That evening Martha sat slumped in her office chair.

Why did I stray so far from professionalism with Sandy? I lost my detachment and regarded her as a daughter, and fantasized that I was a grandmother to her baby. I need to learn more about avoiding countertransference.

And face the hard fact that I will never have a daughter.

30

They May Not See from Where They Sit

The next day was a cold Monday. Martha was tired but managed to see all her patients before she knew she had to have some "spontaneity time." Decisively, she rescheduled her patients for the next two days. Among them were a woman being harassed by a parole officer, and a pair of teenagers from Stuyvesant House referred by the court. Cases of real need.

But it can't be helped. I've been chained to my desk. I'll reschedule them later.

On Tuesday she slept late, baked a pineapple upsidedown cake, and she and Sarah walked into the Village. They each bought a hand-wrought necklace from a Zuni silversmith on the street who said he wasn't feeling the cold.

On Wednesday morning she walked through a light snowfall and took the subway uptown, headed for Norman's library.

I'd like to speed up my way of helping people, without succumbing to the current rage for quick cures. I hear stories about the shenanigans of amateurs, with their contempt for the uniqueness of each psyche, and lack of accountability. Billie says I'm old-fashioned and I plead guilty to not hobnobbing with the new demagogues, though I've healed damage they've done. Patients have brought complaints to me about feeling worse rather than healthier after hours of treatment with people screaming, pulling hair, punching pillows, and acting out in general.

One woman was locked up and told to write all day— about anything she wanted; afterward not a word was shared with anyone. One well-known leader kept roomfuls of clients sitting all day like kids being punished, not allowed to move, even to go to the restroom.

From what I've heard, a patient longing for family life is expected to make a swift transference to the leader as a parental figure to be loved or hated, according to the patient's history. There's no follow-up. No results are verified. This profession has taken a long ride on people's gullibility! Patients want instant cures for their anxieties, but sadly find they've paid chunks of money without gain. They may not see, from where they sit, a way to go on trying.

Still, some solid new techniques are being developed along lines I agree with. To help people, you have to tap the real energy source, the motivation of the patient to change. If the desire is there and there's guidance, patients can come to assess themselves and see how they affect others. Change is possible at any age. These are the lessons of therapy. At the library today I plan some wise self-assessment of my own.

Once inside the familiar high-ceilinged reading room, she shook snow off her pink raincoat and sat at the table where she had often waited for Norman. Usually they'd left carrying new books, and stopped for a quick dinner on their way to a lecture chosen from the many offerings at Columbia.

I studied the new books at home and enjoyed advising him which ones would be useful to teachers and guidance professionals. I never guessed that some day I'd be looking to the same books for help! I'm like Ursula, who edited the book on poetry therapy but needed to learn to apply it to her own life.

She scrutinized the range of titles on the shelves.

Yes, most of these books hold out the promise of emotional health to those who make sincere efforts to change. People do need help in identifying their needs. They can learn wisdom from others, and this collection is a great resource. The present librarian seems to know what she's doing, as the newest titles seem excellent. Someday I'll go into the office and meet her, and maybe take her and Norman's old colleagues to lunch. We were fond of them. But I'm sure they're busy, and today I have work to do.

She took a pile of books to the table, feeling Norman close by.

How safe I felt in his love all those years! He'd be glad my mind is eager to be used.

She turned pages rapidly, her eyes devouring paragraphs. At lunch time she sat in a quiet corner of the big cafeteria and ate quiche and a big rosy apple.

All afternoon she systematically placed markers at dozens of pages she wanted to study. On her way to supper she dropped off books at the library's photocopy service. In the cafeteria, elegantly turbaned Africans joined her in the line, many of them experienced teachers who would take progressive methods back to their countries. They were friendly, but she ate alone. Back at the library table she felt time was getting short and to keep herself alert stood up in the stacks to read.

Becoming engrossed in a new book on group therapy, she sat down again and wrote the publisher's name so she could order it. Then she wrote an appreciative note to the librarian and left it at the desk. At closing time, after collecting her photocopied pages, she went out the massive front door. A chilly wind had blown most of the snow from the wide stone steps. Clutching her copies, she felt she was bearing home new wisdom from a temple. The clean air was the right sort of incense.

She walked a block to reach the uptown stretch of Broadway on Morningside Heights, thinking of its history.

A battle of the Revolutionary War was fought right here on this hill. Now these massive university buildings stand as ramparts in the war against ignorance. For me, the battle is for clear thinking. I went too far in designing my patients' lives. I know that therapists do this all the time, calling it a working alliance, and that I had a personal need, but I knew better. Sarah, who is no therapist, saw that I was being too directive. It's antidote time.

She hailed a taxi with her pink umbrella and, once seated, didn't allow an opening for small talk with the driver.

Today has proven that there are valid new methods, to be added to our old ones. I'm free to experiment, develop ways to help patients find their true directions. Free to try harder with the Wednesday Four. How can I get them back? Could I convene the Wednesday Four into a group? It would cost them less than individual therapy and they'd all like that. And everyone's free on Wednesday afternoons.

When she got home she went into her office and sat in deliberation.

If I invite them to come for group therapy, will they come? And if they do, will they be compatible? Well, Ursula and Sandy quickly got friendly that day in the waiting room, and if the oldest and the youngest can communicate, those in the middle may find a way. They could be a great help to one another! Since the goals I had for them have all gone off target, I would try to stay out of it and let the group structure itself.

Do I have the skill to lead a group? We didn't do much with groups at the clinic, so it will be a learning experience for me. Surely, since I know each woman so well already, I can let them find their own separate destinies. This idea is experimental—they'll be free to choose the lives they want, and I'll stop trying to influence them. I picture them seated in a circle, confiding their stories. But where? There's too little space in my inner office, but we could meet in a small circle in the waiting room.

In the reality of daylight the next day, she still favored the idea.

One promising reassurance is that each of my Wednesday Four has given birth, so important for maturity in a woman, but they still need to learn self-discipline.

She looked up at her diplomas and licenses on the wall. I threw away the copies which Norman put up in the living room, but these originals showing my training are important. What's needed is discipline on my part to make them mean what they're supposed to mean. My exceptional patients, four sensitive, courageous women who've been coming to me for help on Wednesdays—if I put my non-directive utmost effort into helping them, may I not still succeed?

Pursuing her hope, during the rest of January she studied several books on group therapy and countertransference. Near the date of Sandy's wedding, she sent a conventional note of regret. She had paid due homage to the real event, the baby's birth.

The last Sunday in January, Sarah and Barry shared a drink with Martha in her office to celebrate new drapes they'd given her as a Christmas present. The gloomy green velvet was now replaced by golden translucent satin which hung in deep folds, giving the room a sunny glow. Martha poured champagne. Barry, full of fun, repeatedly pulled the cord which opened and closed the drapes, chanting "Cha, cha, cha-cha-cha!" Sarah squeezed behind them, put her head through and sang, *"Im frütau zu berge wir ziehen, fa la ra!"* her mountain-climbing song. Barry quickly learned it, ready to celebrate anything that went with skiing. He sang it for her in English the next Sunday morning, "This morning we're going up the mountain!"

Martha was celebrating more than the new drapes—her plan was ready. That afternoon she opened her appointment book and, shakily sanguine, started making phone calls.

"Elinor, I'm calling to let you know I'm offering my patients a new opportunity. It's group therapy, a chance to work with a few others toward personal development. The cost is considerably less than the individual rate. I think you'll like the others in the group, all women, and am sure they will benefit from working with you."

"I'll try to come," said Elinor. "When will we meet?"

"At four on Wednesday."

31

Four on Wednesday

Elinor took only a day to think it over, even after Martha reluctantly reminded her that being in therapy might endanger her custody of Steven and Susan. "Who needs to know?" Elinor had said. "I'll pay for it out of what I make taking care of Michele." Martha accepted this hopefully.

Ursula accepted next. Blaine would be driving some League members down to N.Y.U. for a Wednesday series of lectures, so Ursula could ride along. She had been sorely missing Dr. Kaufman, and Blaine was glad to help. However, the lecture series would last only a few weeks.

Sandy said she'd try it. "I still get orders for macramé, so I can pay, as group therapy costs less. Mom'll come to babysit and I can visit one or two galleries the same day."

Billie left a message that she wasn't sure she could join. She might have to teach a late afternoon class this semester. Two days later, she called, saying she could just make it to Martha's office by four o'clock.

There were seats for only four people in the waiting room, so Martha brought in a straight chair for herself from the office and left her appointment book on it to show it was meant for her.

Elinor and Ursula were the first to arrive, and Elinor took Ursula's coat to hang up. "I love the smell of cold that comes in on our clothes," she said. "This morning I took a long walk in the new snow."

"You walked in velvet shoes," Ursula intoned.

Elinor knew this was poetry, but didn't reply, thinking poetry was a private matter and they sat in silence. When Martha came to the door, Elinor gushed to her, "Oh, you look great!."

Ursula, peering as close as possible in trying to see, agreed. "Oh, yes, you're very beautiful."

Embarrassed, Martha said a quick "Thank you" and escaped into her office.

Sandy arrived in a rush, bustled to the closet to hang up her coat, and began a private conversation with Ursula as if Elinor were not present.

Just as Martha returned, Billie marched in, rolled her jacket into a ball, threw it on the floor behind the remaining empty chair, and sat down.

Martha introduced them to each other by saying their names around the circle. The women sat, their eyes darting from face to face. Billie was learning faces as if the group were her class. Elinor broke into a delighted laugh. "I've just noticed something—we're all redheads."

Billie's look became brazen, Ursula's curious, Sandy's uninterested.

"Yes," said Martha, "by coincidence, all my Wednesday afternoon patients are redheads."

Elinor turned to Martha. "And so are you."

"I used to be," Martha said.

"Mine's not red anymore," said Ursula, patting her topknot. "I guess I'm a strawberry blonde."

"Could it be," Billie said, "that we're all fantasizing? Creating a symbol of our common . . . our common . . ."

"Denominator?" offered Elinor.

"Sisterhood?" asked Sandy.

"Naw, bitchiness!" Billie declared.

"It doesn't apply to me if redheadedness means having a quick temper," said Ursula.

"Well, if it means being passionate, it applies to me," said Elinor.

"I think it means having a sense of humor," said Sandy.

Billie grinned. "Naw, bitchiness is all it means."

Elinor enjoyed this, but looked to see if it offended

Ursula, who promptly remarked, "Bitch is the term for female dogs. It just means *not male*."

"There are red-headed men, too," said Martha. Everyone was silent and Martha caught the moment. "I'm glad that you can all resume working with me, or more accurately, start working together. We will need some agreed-upon procedures which you as a group may develop. As a start, I'd like to mention two important guidelines. First, whatever is said here is confidential, not to be discussed outside this room with anyone. Second, the same rule will apply as in individual sessions—attendance is expected on a regular basis. The new group fee will be charged unless I'm notified two days in advance, that is, no later than four on Monday. We'll limit ourselves to meeting for an hour and a half, and start promptly at three-forty-five or four and stop at five-thirty—or five forty-five. The group should decide." She waited.

Elinor spoke politely. "Starting at four suits me. I'll be meeting a friend for dinner so I'd want to finish by six."

"That sounds all right to me," said Ursula. "My daughter will pick me up. She'll be driving some ladies to lectures at N.Y.U. and says if they finish before I do, they'll go for coffee and wait for me. Then we'll eat dinner."

"My mother will come to babysit and get dinner ready at home," said Sandy.

Noting that Billie was nodding yes, Martha said, "Starting promptly at four and stopping by five-thirty suits everyone then?"

There was a silence of agreement which Sandy broke saying, "I plan to see an art show each Wednesday."

"Oh, I like art shows," said Elinor. "What's on now?"

"I prefer shows in private galleries where the really new stuff is," Sandy said, "especially drawings and prints. I'm a lithographer."

"I first saw Picasso in a private gallery," said Ursula. "A very stimulating artist."

"We're getting long-winded about art," Billie said. "Let's organize our procedures."

Elinor turned to Martha, her eyes searching for guidance. "What do you suggest?" Martha indicated it was for the group to decide. Elinor asked, "Has anyone been in group therapy before?"

Billie responded. "I hear about it from a colleague at lunch where I teach. She says each group makes its own rules and puts a time limit on each person. Her group has men in it, and one topic the men talk on and on about is ex-wives and sex lives. So you can't let everyone talk without limits."

"I imagine that is so," Ursula said, peering earnestly in Billie's direction, "but as there are no men here, do we need to take time on them?" Billie was silenced.

Sandy spoke up. "I hope this group won't have a lot of rules. I think we should start by going around the room with everybody taking the same amount of time, but after we get acquainted we should have more flexibility. I mean, someone may need to discuss a problem one week and not have much to say the next. Do you agree?" Elinor nodded and Sandy continued. "Let's each talk fifteen minutes today and answer questions right after speaking."

"Is that the wish of the group?" Martha asked. Everyone nodded yes except Billie, who did not frown. "Shall we go around clockwise, then, starting with you, Billie?"

"Okay," said Billie. "I'm on. Since the last time I was here I've been all over looking for Mike." She was gazing steadily at Martha, who gave her a warm smile.

"Who's Mike?" Sandy asked.

"My fifteen-year-old son, who joined a cult and then disappeared. I drove to a couple of the cult's possible locations. But nobody knew him."

"Did you have to go alone?" Ursula asked.

"No. Christopher went with me." She caught Elinor's eye. "My manfriend," she smugly explained. "Finally, I heard from Mike on Christmas Eve. He was in jail in Atlanta. He said the police had arrested him at a demonstration in a park, and kept him locked up. Finally, he was told he could get out, but only into the custody of one of his parents. So he called and wanted to come home."

"Why jail? Were drugs involved?" Sandy asked.

"He says it wasn't drugs, but trouble with some gang he didn't even know."

"I'm glad you found him," Martha said.

Elinor asked, "How long was he away?"

"More than three months, but I thought he was with his father." Billie told the story with her eyes on Martha. "He started out in a sort of commune out near Montauk, a houseful of kids run by a tyrant of a man. There wasn't as much brainwashing as in the big cults and Mike got permission to transfer. He was dropped off at the dormitory of a restaurant outside Baltimore. Luckily, before he went inside, a kid came out who was escaping and they set out for a different commune the kid knew about, in an old mill across the state. They were hitching rides but something happened to the other kid. Mike went to the gas station restroom and thinks the leader snatched his friend back at that time.

"Mike found the old mill, full of kids. They baked honey-bran muffins. Newcomers had to stay in a tent outdoors. I felt better about the whole thing when he said he read books from their library, but it was mostly about Indian religion. After it got too cold to sleep out, he headed south and somehow got to Atlanta and thrown in jail."

"Poor kiddie," said Ursula. "Was jail terribly depressing?"

Billie drew a deep breath. "You'd better believe your poor kiddie was depressed. There was a rape threat that scared the shit out of him, but he managed to protect himself and got put into solitary for nearly a week. In a way, that was the real pits because he kept saying a mantra and came to think that hypnotic crap was helping him. He'll never be the same."

"But he didn't get raped?" Sandy asked.

"No, and he finally called me." She spoke more softly. "It was my Christmas present."

Martha intervened. "Billie, your calling Mike's mantra 'hypnotic crap' may not be fair. He's been on a journey of new understanding. This could be important to his character."

"Well, he's back, anyhow," said Billie.

"I know that means a lot to both of you," Martha said. "He came *home!* Is he back in school?"

"Yes, if he sticks. Our new term just started this week, and he went to school Monday and Tuesday and I hope today. I left home this morning before he did. He doesn't know yet if he can stand school and I'm worried he's planning to get back in touch with that 'Soul Only' group. God!"

Elinor had been listening with rapt attention, shivering at words which she'd normally find offensive. This Billie was indeed the woman of the leather skirt and boots who was not only hard, but foul-mouthed. "Please," she said, holding her fingers in her ears in what was only partly a mock gesture, "I'm embarrassed that—" She turned to Ursula, "What is your name again?"

"Ursula!" Martha and Ursula spoke together.

"I'm embarrassed that Ursula has to listen to such language."

Billie turned to Ursula with a disarming smile. "Do I shock you?"

"Not really," said Ursula. Her tone was open and assured. "I am a poet and very interested in words. There is a time for each word and sometimes nothing will do but the vernacular. My husband used to discipline the children's language, but I didn't. They could use all the bathroom talk they liked. I even encouraged them, told them there was a word, 'flatulence,' but I liked 'fart' better. Of course now they're grownups and use bathroom words only when they apply."

Elinor looked at Ursula admiringly. Billie sat stone-faced, then said, "After what I've been through, I still have nightmares about the police station. I sat across from Mike at a scratched-up table, as if I were visiting a life prisoner. He seemed frozen and hurt. And he still does."

"Could you bring him in to see Dr. Kaufman?" Sandy asked.

"He wouldn't come," Billie said.

Ursula cleared her throat. "In the way we're organizing this group, is there going to be time for questions and discussion? And are you going to participate, Dr. Kaufman? I've always listened to your advice."

"We try not to give advice here," Martha asserted. "But yes, we will have time for discussion, and yes, I will be participating. I have a question now for Billie. How have you gone about debriefing your son?"

"I'm having enough trouble debriefing myself," Billie said. "Christopher talks with him."

"How does he get along with Christopher?" Elinor asked.

"Okay. Better than with my lovers in the past. I figure it's because Chris lets him drive his car."

This gave Elinor a pang. Neither she nor Ralph had tried teaching Steven to drive, and he wasn't interested in what Ralph wanted to show him about repairing Cadillacs.

"Does Mike ask you for money?" Ursula asked. "Like for drugs?"

"Well, I haven't given him any, except a ten-spot on the trip back from Atlanta for cigarettes and stuff. When he got home he went down to the Mobil station and hung around until they let him pump gas. Now he's busy helping the mechanic every chance he gets. He gets a few cash tips, not regular pay."

"Maybe working there would be better for him than going back to school," said Sandy.

"No way!" Billie's fist hit her palm for emphasis. "He has a brain, he's going to college!"

Sandy flashed back, "Then you should get the truant officer after him the first time he skips school."

"Are you asking questions or giving advice?" Billie retorted. "The friggin' truant officers never accomplish a thing. You don't know the situation."

"I meant it as a question," said Sandy.

"I'm sure Billie understands that, so don't feel badly," Elinor interposed.

Billie looked daggers at Elinor who seemed saccharine to her. "The flamin' grammar isn't feel *badly*—it's feel *bad*. And Sandy was telling me what to do."

Sandy gazed at the ceiling, her lips pursed to show she didn't agree.

"It's hard to separate asking questions and giving advice," Ursula said. "Should we make some rules about that?"

"The aim of questions in a group like this," Billie said, "is to keep to how the speaker *feels*. After I talked I was sure someone was going to tell anecdotes about communes instead of keeping to my feelings."

Ursula, who had in fact been ready to tell the story about one of her neighbors, felt threatened. "All of this may be too hard."

"I'm sure we'll learn by doing," said Martha, "so let's continue around the circle."

Ursula wasn't silenced. "I have a problem with only asking questions. What's the point of getting together if we just find out how we feel, and don't give each other the benefit of our advice? So, even if I'm breaking the rules, I want to say to you, Billie, that I think your son probably will go back to his group to show off what a lot of the world he's seen. Parents have to act fast to rescue a kid from a cult. One of my neighbors took a truant officer, a lawyer and a priest to where their daughter was, and they brought her home. They didn't lose any time."

"I agree!" cried Sandy. "There's a lot of trouble now about kidnapping your own kid away from the cults, so act fast."

Martha was impressed by the worldliness of the group,

but looked at her watch. "Can we hear from you next, Sandy?"

Sandy frowned at her new wedding ring, and kept twisting it with her right hand around the fourth finger of her left. "Well, I just got married, so I'm a blushing bride."

"Oh, why should brides blush!" exclaimed Billie, scornfully.

"At my wedding because the baby kept crying while we cut the cake."

Billie's mouth fell open and she didn't reply.

Elinor looked lovingly at Sandy, whose defensive glare softened when she perceived the kindness of Elinor's scrutiny. Ursula stretched out her hand and let it rest on Sandy's wrist. Billie took out a cigarette and held it between her fingers, but put it away again.

Sandy found her voice. "David and I love each other but I didn't want to be trapped in marriage too early. My girlfriend hinted that it would be embarrassing to go through the birth in the hospital as an unmarried mother, but nobody was embarrassed that I saw. My mother was the only problem. She showed up the first afternoon—it was a dark December day—wearing a big spring hat and stood peering through the window of the nursery where all the babies were, staring at Jordy for hours. The hat was a riot, all covered with pink and blue flowers."

"She sounds like a good sport," said Elinor.

"The nurses were laughing about the woman in the hat, but the parents looking at the babies couldn't see around it."

Martha laughed out loud in enjoyment of Judy's enthusiasm for her grandson.

"How much did he weigh?" Ursula asked.

"Seven pounds, three ounces, which is big since both David and I are short. And he had eyelashes and fingernails and everything. Great equipment."

"Ooh, babies are so cute," crooned Elinor. "What's his name?"

"Jordy. For Jordan."

"And you had a regular wedding afterward?"

Sandy shrugged. "Oh yes. My mother saw to that. I won't go into the details now. It was your routine wedding."

"Still, I expect it was nice," Elinor said. "Could you bring pictures next time?" When Sandy only shrugged again, Elinor changed her line of questioning. "Was it hard while you were carrying the baby? Did people know you weren't married?"

"Some knew, but it wasn't that hard."

Ursula said, "You were cheerful when we talked here."

"Well, I felt fine up to the time Jordy was born—hormones or something. Of course, being so big slowed me down, but I did get some work done and that pleased me. But no more. He cries for three solid hours every evening. We can't eat dinner in peace, and the people upstairs knock on the floor to protest. David has to go to the Burger King to do the work he brings home from the office. God! Burger King! He says it's noisy but quieter than home. I'm stuck with this crying machine and when he does finally stop, I'm out of my mind unless I phone a friend or read before I go to bed. By then it's late and as soon as I lie down, I swear the crying starts again. Last night it was one o'clock when I turned off my light and two o'clock when he woke me."

"Did you feed him then?" asked Ursula.

"Oh, yes. Whenever he cries. I breast-feed him and have plenty of milk and he's gaining, but he cries."

"It sounds so familiar," said Elinor. "I remember never getting enough sleep. I used to bake oatmeal cookies at night so being awake would count for something."

"Three of my children were colicky," Ursula said. "There isn't much you can do but wait until they grow out of it."

Billie sawed the air with her hand flattened. "Colicky or not, a baby is boss. Mothers have no life of their own."

"It gets better when the toilet training is over," Ursula insisted.

"When my two could both dress themselves, I felt ten years younger," Elinor said. "Susan was about four then and Steven, who was six, used to tie her shoes. It was cute." Noticing that Sandy was frowning, she quickly said, "Oh, I'm interrupting!" and held two fingers over her mouth.

"Everybody's interrupting," Martha said. "Go ahead, Sandy."

"What bothers me most is when David holds Jordy all evening with no crying. Daddy gets the good times, I get the shit."

"Oh, oh, that's my word!" Billie laughed, drily.

"This is not your *abstract* shit," Sandy said, with a grin. A current of humor ran between her and Billie.

"Continue, Sandy," Martha said.

"I expected to stay on top of things, planning my work for six-week periods, and saving time. Like running the vacuum cleaner during Jordy's routine crying. But I cry too. Just before he was born I rented a post office box, using the last cent of my own money, to keep a business address so I could sell prints. But for six weeks now I haven't even been able to look in the box." Her face contorted and she began to cry, sitting immobile and angry. "It's so awful."

Ursula seemed about to cry, too. Grief linked them as they sat hunched side by side. Elinor's eyes sought Martha's and she asked, timidly, "Is it time for ques—?"

Billie cut her off, speaking to Sandy. "Why can't your husband go by the post office for you?"

Sandy ground out an answer. "Why should he find out about my wanting orders for prints? He'd probably think I'd neglect the baby!" She drew a sobbing breath. "Don't you see, that's why I didn't want to get married. Husbands don't trust you."

"That's true," Ursula said bleakly.

"Couldn't you go by the post office when you take the baby out in his carriage?" asked Elinor.

"What carriage?" Sandy's tears had not taken the snap from her voice.

"We called it a 'pram' in England. I'm sorry it's already been given away," Elinor said.

"You picture a baby carriage cruising along Broadway to 72nd Street? The air's not clean enough."

"Isn't there a park? I used to walk my kids along the edge of a park on Riverside Drive."

"I'd be mugged."

"How did you feel about leaving him today?" Ursula asked.

"Mom couldn't come today, but David came home to babysit because he has to work tonight, give a speech."

"Bring the baby here with you," said Billie.

"No, that wouldn't work," Martha said quickly.

"Why not?" Billie flared. "Nursing mothers are everywhere."

"I'd like to see him," Elinor said. "Couldn't we try it at least once?"

"I think not," Martha said firmly.

Elinor did an about-face and supported Martha. "Sandy, you need to get out on your own to believe you're still you."

"As for clean air," Martha put in, recalling her visit to Norman's library, "there's usually a breeze uptown."

"Those over-the-shoulder baby carriers look handy," said Elinor. "I wish I'd had one when we lived in England. I used to feel stir-crazy, stuck indoors with a baby."

Billie's annoyance with Elinor had been smoldering and now threw off sparks. "Spare us your frustrations, *please*." Pointedly turning her head toward Sandy, she ordered, "Check your post office box tomorrow."

"Okay," said Sandy.

Ursula's voice wavered. "We're not doing so well on not giving advice."

Martha sighed, but maintained a wan smile, not trusting herself to conceal her annoyance if she spoke.

Ursula went on. "I'll try to do better. If you'll time me, I'll speak for ten minutes and leave time for questions."

"Good idea," said Elinor. Billie yawned.

"My husband is trying to drive me crazy," Ursula began. "But I gave him a shock and so he landed in the hospital."

Billie looked up. "No kidding? What did you do?"

Ursula gently raised a hand in restraint of interruptions, lowered it slowly and went on. "I destroyed his favorite toy, his photocopy machine. It served him right because he wouldn't make copies of my poems, even destroyed them. Then I discovered he'd been giving me aspirin instead of the medicine Dr. Kaufman prescribed for me. So I pushed the machine downstairs. It didn't hit him. He hurt himself picking it up."

Elinor made a sympathetic noise in her throat, but Ursula continued without pause, "Since we're talking about feelings, mine are better now because I'm living with my daughter Blaine and her family. I have a room of my own and a table with a magnifying lamp. I am revising my poems and can write new ones. However, the future is distressing. My husband's not getting better, and Blaine and one of the children visit him every day in the nursing home. Blaine is planning to find tenants for my house and this upsets me. My own house, so dear to me, is empty and I want to go home, but they won't let me stay there alone and nobody in my family can stay with me. I feel old and alone, but I wouldn't if they'd let me live in my own house."

Her voice shook and she stopped. The room was silent. Then Ursula's straight spine arched backward and she opened her handbag. "I'm sure I haven't used all my time so I'd like to share my new poem."

Martha felt a chill, dreading another poem about inscrutable barnacles.

Ursula held out a sheet of paper to Elinor. "Would you please read it?"

"Wouldn't it be better for you to read it?" Elinor was

touching the paper but not taking it, courteously making it a link between herself and Ursula.

"I think I know it, but I may need prompting."

Elinor accepted the paper.

Ursula announced, " 'From the West,' " and recited:

"From this rounded hill
stretched lines of poplars,
their shadows dark stripes
on the great carpet
of spring-green winter wheat.
East, apple trees marched far away
to other hills with shade and fog
in their valleys.
North, gullies of gray sand
climbed to the timber culture
with its seagreen light
between columnar trees.
What space we had when we were young!
Now, confined, my mind's eye
sees by memory
the roundness of my hill.
But pain
dashes the images
because my doomed, actual sight
cannot zoom in
through seagreen light
between columnar trees
to see a single trillium."

Sandy clapped. "I like poems that I could illustrate."

"I like the description," said Elinor, "but isn't it sad, a sort of homesick poem?"

Billie turned teacher. "It could be called 'Homesick for Seeing.' " Ursula nodded. Billie went on. "But aren't words like 'doomed' and 'actual' pretty leaden for poetry?"

"Emotions have weight. Lead's okay in poetry." Ursula was smiling, welcoming responses.

"I wonder about 'columnar trees,'" Sandy said earnestly. "Could you say 'groves of trees'?"

"That's less musical. I used *l* and *m* sounds on purpose. and 'columnar' shows the big trees standing like columns in contrast to the tiny trillium below. I use interior rhyme and alliteration, too, like 'doomed' and 'zoom,' and 'seagreen,' and 'see' and 'single.'"

"Could you say it again?" Sandy asked. Ursula repeated the poem and Sandy said softly, "I love the seagreen light."

Martha, feeling she ought to participate, asked, "What's a trillium?"

"A small wild flower, very white and fragile, with three petals," Ursula said. "A member of the lily family."

Martha knew the poem couldn't bring to others the message she got, that Ursula was close to admitting that poor vision was her major problem. She said, "I think Elinor and Billie said it—homesickness for seeing."

"Have you published any poems?" Elinor asked Ursula.

"No, but I wrote a critical study that was published. And now, with Dr. Kaufman's encouragement, I'm writing poetry again. By visual memory. I can't see. I'm legally blind."

"But you do see a lot," Sandy said. "You saw me perfectly well when I was pregnant, and you seem to see now."

"Not well enough for them to let me live alone in my house. And that's all I want. I want to go home." She dropped her chin on her chest and struggled against weeping.

Surprisingly, it was Billie who stretched out a hand and patted Ursula's knee. "Don't cry," she said. "We'll think of something."

After a pause, Ursula raised her head. "I was going to show such a good style and then I had to blow it."

Sandy said soothingly, "We'll start now and ask questions. How do you feel about being a grandmother?"

Ursula's face lit up. "That's what I feel best about. My

granddaughter Jeanne saved my poems in her bookcase. And my grandson is an upright young man, excellent in science."

"Get one of them to take you for walks," said Elinor.

"That's giving advice," Billie said.

"I know, but getting outdoor exercise is so important!"

"That's good advice and should be allowed," Ursula stated. "And I have some advice for women. Don't let your important papers, your old school work or diaries or music or snapshots lie around the house. Don't keep anything in cardboard boxes which could look like trash. Get a regular steel file for them, with a lock, and treat them the way you want others to treat them. I wish I'd done that. A woman has a right to protect her personal work."

"Oh, *true!*" groaned Sandy.

There was silence, broken by Martha. "Thank you, Ursula. Now it's time to hear from Elinor."

Elinor, feeling a threat to her privacy, looked down at her slender black suede shoes, and then up at Martha. "I don't know where to start. It's been hard."

Martha nodded her head slightly and prompted, "At the time we last talked, your ex, Howard, was threatening to cut off the mortgage payments on your house if Michele didn't leave."

"Oh, yes," said Elinor, grateful for a clue. "Ralph, my manfriend, has a daughter, Michele, who's fifteen. She's been living with me and my teenage daughter and son. Ralph contributes to household expenses, more than my ex does. But my ex insists that she has to leave! It's unfair because Ralph and I are trying to combine our families. So far, she's staying. We think Howard was bluffing, as he's still paying the mortgage. Ralph offered once to pay it, but the divorce requires Howard to pay. He did stop paying you for therapy," she said with a troubled look at Martha, "and that wasn't fair."

"No," said Martha, "it wasn't."

Elinor looked downcast but said, "I'm going to squeeze

the money for this group out of the money I get from Ralph. I don't know what I'll do if he and I break up."

"Is there a chance of that?" Martha asked.

"Well, we have a big problem now that I learned about yesterday. Ralph has an older daughter, Helen, who's divorced already at the age of nineteen. She was with us on Thanksgiving and after dinner, Ralph and I left the kids to clean up. Susan and Michele told us later that they did all the work. Helen went with Steven to his room and stayed in there a long time. Now Helen claims she's pregnant and he's the father! It's preposterous! Steven is a complete innocent. He told me that they didn't really have sex, just tried. Poor kid, he was trying not to cry. But Ralph questioned him and says there's a chance that Steven's the father. These things do happen. But why should Steven be blamed? She started things. He couldn't have led her into it, for heaven's sake— he's never even taken a girl out. He told me he doesn't even like her. She made fun of the music he likes. He's an introverted studious type, and now he'll never be normal."

"I wouldn't say that," Sandy said, trying to be soothing.

"Young men grow up through such experiences," Ursula said. Hearing these reactions, Elinor looked happier.

"What trimester is the girl in?" asked Billie. "She must be still at the safe stage for an abortion if she got pregnant on Thanksgiving."

"It's just under two and a half months. She missed her period in December."

"That's when I had my baby instead of my wedding," Sandy said.

"And when she missed another one in January," Elinor continued, "she had a pregnancy test, and it was positive. She told Ralph yesterday and he called me. He sounded worried. I'm seeing him tonight for dinner, and we'll talk more."

"The gals in my school have to get abortions sometimes," Billie said, "and they sail through fine if the timing's right."

Elinor cried out. "Oh, I absolutely don't believe in abortions! But what can you do? Helen's not in any shape to take care of a baby. Ralph told her he'd arrange for an abortion, but she's planning to keep the baby. She plans to go to Western Canada to live on a group farm, and says he can send her money or not."

"She'll need money," said Billie.

"She's probably angry at men. She's got to be if she's divorced at nineteen," said Sandy.

"She's probably jealous of her father and Elinor," said Ursula.

"Also jealous because her younger sister's at Elinor's," Billie said.

Elinor nodded solemnly. "It's all those things, but if she has the baby, it'll break up Ralph and me, and force Steven to live a guilty life. And *she* seduced *him*. It's a real mess."

Martha spoke calmly. "Maybe when you talk with Ralph this evening you'll figure something out. He has influence over his daughter, since she'll need money from him, whatever happens. And the younger daughter, how is she?"

Elinor's gaze focused levelly at Martha. "Before I talk about her, I want to say I was expecting to marry Ralph but I don't want to be in the same family with Helen."

"If things are going well with Michele, couldn't things still be . . ." Martha stopped herself, amazed at her own disappointment at this news from Elinor.

"We hope Michele can stay in our school. She likes it, and she and Susan play clever duets on the piano and make up musical puppet shows—quite funny ones. Ralph hired a piano teacher for them. It's the one bright spot, seeing them so happy, fixing their hair and mine, and doing homework and gossiping about boys. If it weren't for them, I'd go bananas."

"And Steven? Has the problem with Helen interfered with his schoolwork?" asked Martha.

"Well, he's trying hard. Half the time he seems paralyzed over this thing with Helen, and then he'll say something that shows he's holding his own. Michele and Susan have been very sweet to him and have vowed not to say a word about him outside the house. That's helped him. Oh, how could I marry a man whose daughter has hurt us so much?"

"Remember to love," said Ursula. "You can love people right out of their queer notions."

"But who can love Helen out of her hatred of the whole world?" cried Elinor. "It would take a lot of therapy, and that takes money. I could be more help if I had money for a lot of therapy for myself."

"You could ask Ralph for money for therapy," Sandy said.

"Negative!" Billie cried, her eyes blazing. "Never beg for money! How'd you support yourself before you were married?"

Elinor was taken aback but answered with a touch of pride. "I was a private secretary. To the second Secretary of the American Embassy in London."

"So get a job, for God's sake," said Billie.

Elinor's eyes glazed over and she remained silent.

Sandy stood up. "I have to go. I have so much milk it hurts if I'm late."

Martha looked at her watch. "Yes, it's five-thirty and we must stop." She said on her way into her office, "See you all at four on Wednesday."

Sandy and Billie left without saying anything.

Ursula got slowly to her feet. "My daughter's coming for me shortly in a big car," she said to Elinor. "Can we drop you somewhere?"

"Oh, lovely. Just to the subway stop. I'm going to meet Ralph on Wall Street." She and Ursula walked down the hall. Outside, while waiting for Blaine, Ursula asked, "Do you know Frost's poem about old snow?"

"I only know 'Stopping by Woods on a Snowy Evening.'"

Ursula said, "This is different," and recited:

> "It is speckled with grime as if
> Small print overspread it.

The news of a day I've forgotten—
If I ever read it."

Seated at her desk, Martha was possessed by a very good feeling about the group.

It's like making candy. When you think it's nearly done, you test a drop in cold water, and if it coalesces into a ball, it's going to be right. Today was like that, the women coalesced into a group. It's wonderful, after weeks of wondering if I could make it happen!

She went into the waiting room and looked around, recalling the openness, the humor, the dearness of the women.

I hardly talked at all, only facilitated. They all understood one another, and readily responded to Ursula's poetry! At the start they settled on the open format suggested by Sandy, the youngest, without a power hassle. Ursula, not absorbed in herself, said that Sandy looked healthy when pregnant. Billie, of course, was quick to stop others from giving advice, but was herself the chief advice-giver of the day—not bad advice either, except for wanting Sandy to bring the baby. Elinor had sense enough to talk that down.

And they noticed they're all redheads! Suddenly she was singing, "Casey would waltz with a strawberry blonde!" and waltzing around the room in sheer relief and joy. Then, surprised at how hungry she was. she waltzed into the kitchen to enjoy dinner with Sarah.

Only in the evening did her thoughts become more realistic. Poor Elinor and Ralph! What will this threat do to them? And poor Steven! What a shock to his confidence in his relations with girls! And August may be suffering a lot of physical pain as well as emotional. He may be out of Ursula's life for good, but I predict she'll grievously miss him some day.

These developments are all sadly different from my hopes. It's great, though, that Sandy's going through only very normal ups and downs with her baby. And Billie heard from Mike and welcomed him home! That boy most likely has learned a big lesson, having for once met up with an authority big enough to control him!

And speaking of authority, in a one-on-one session I could have urged Billie to consider how she herself rejects it. But how can I do that safely in front of the others?

Maybe, when the strawberry blondes are all thoroughly acquainted, I'll be able to get them to focus on their real problems.

The process is promising.

32

What Does Billie Want?

As soon as the women were assembled for the second meeting of the group, Elinor blurted out, "Guess what? I have a job!"

"Lucky you," said Sandy. "What kind of job?"

"I'm secretary to the rector of our Episcopalian Church. I work in the office, less than a forty-hour week, but I'm brushing up on my skills and can get a good reference some day. I've always liked the rector, and his wife is very nice. What do you think?" She looked to Martha.

"This *is* news," Martha said, smiling but with some reserve. "What precipitated your decision at this time?"

"Well, Dr. Kaufman, we've discussed it but you didn't tell me to do it." She smiled broadly. "Billie told me, 'Get a job, for God's sake!' So I did."

Billie, pretending to be a bashful cowgirl, turned the toes of her boots inward, chopped her heels into the rug and drawled, "Aw, Ma'am, 'twarn't nuthin'. Ah meant ya to do it for your own sake, not God's." Ursula laughed.

Elinor continued happily. "I haven't had any money of my own since I got married, so it'll feel good to pay for my own therapy." Ursula clapped and Elinor became modest. "The church has a hard time filling the job, since it's only part-time and you can only get to it by car. I take my lunch."

Martha asked, "Does your ex-husband know you're working? As I recall, you were worried about his cutting off support."

"The rector says he knows a good lawyer for me if Howard stops paying either my monthly allowance or the mortgage. The divorce papers are for real, and the child support is so small that if we go to court, I'll probably get more, even if I keep on working. The rector says the lawyer knows the high cost of living where I live."

Ursula spoke with a depth of feeling which surprised Martha. "Elinor, you are taking charge of your own destiny. I salute you." Sandy clapped. Ursula continued, "I've been thinking about the divorced nineteen-year-old girl who said your son got her pregnant. How are things now?"

"No good news," Elinor replied dully.

"No plans for an abortion?" Billie asked.

"No plans."

"She shouldn't wait beyond the first trimester," Sandy said.

"Ralph and I talked about that but we can't force Helen. He says things like 'Live in hell with Helen,' but now that she's done something really awful, he blames *me* for not controlling Steven."

"That figures," said Billie. "Does he blame *his* mother for whatever he doesn't like about himself?"

"I don't know, but he blames his ex for the divorce."

Billie said, "You're a stand-in for his mother or wife when he blames you."

Elinor looked at Billie with acceptance. "That's how I feel, like a stand-in."

"Daughter Helen may have been a stand-in for her mother," Ursula said, "as Daddy's sex object, a playmate, while Mommy did the boring stuff—toilet training, punishments, and so on. It's lonely, being the mother of a teenage girl. I went through it twice. My husband joined in each of my girls' adolescent rebellions and hasn't stopped criticizing me since. At the same time, from their first dates onward, he got very ardent toward me. I think he pretended in bed that I was one of them."

"Teenage girls often drive their parents to divorce," Billie said. "A guidance counselor told me once the gals may not actually sleep with Daddy, but that it's amazing how many do. A girl may come to feel secretly that she has equal power with the mother."

Ursula made a little speech. "Men have strong primitive instincts. I've often wondered if Freud did the world a favor by bringing sex problems into the open, because they're probably more widespread now. To a lot of men, giving a name to a situation makes it legitimate. Like an Electra complex for a girl sleeping with Daddy."

"That's putting it well!" Billie said and looked at Ursula with respect.

Martha intervened. "There are Oedipus complexes, too, in which mothers claim their sons harmfully, and may actually sleep with them. So women are to blame, too. These human problems don't become legitimate because they're named." There was a silence. Martha sensed that her last remark had brought constraint into the room and waited.

Billie took the lead with, "Ursula, how are things going?"

"You be next, Billie," Ursula said. "I'd rather not."

"Well," said Billie, "I do have headline news. Remember, I said last week that I wouldn't know until I got home if Mike went to school that day? Well, he didn't. So Christopher and I drove out to Eastwick that same night. We stopped at the police station and persuaded a policeman to go with us to that Soul Only house. We got only as far as the front porch, but we could see kids sitting around inside, and sure enough, there was Mike, the big jailbird. When they saw us, they sort of melted away, but Mike came out and talked with the officer, who wasn't threatening. He asked Mike to help by riding with him to the police station to report some facts. We followed them and waited in front of the station a while until Mike came out. He wouldn't say much as we drove home. I hope he told the police something they could use to help those overworked kids in the diner.

"The next morning I woke him early, singing, 'The school bell is ringing!' and he started swearing and threatened to go out to Eastwick, but I told him to forget school, he needed sleep. So he slept. I called the school office and took the day off. He woke up about noon and over coffee told me that the reason he'd headed out to Soul Only was to get his 'big boom-box' but our arrival made him forget to get it. He was overjoyed when I told him to look in the pantry, where Christopher stored it. That ended the quiet, and the house began to rock! But I didn't mind. My boy is safe.

"I had to shout to tell him to shave and get dressed because our lawyer, Pat O'Neill, was due. I knew Pat because once after a PTA meeting a couple of years ago he and I started telling Irish jokes to one another, and later he drew up a simple will for me. I don't own much, but there's the car and the Steinway and my IRA savings account. He told Mike how I leave everything to him if he finishes college, but otherwise it goes to the nuns to educate other kids. Pat told him, 'You'll learn more at school than at Soul Only and earn a better living by using your brains than by waiting on tables.' He also talked about law school, and showed Mike his new red Jaguar. So guess who's doing homework and asking about college entrance exams? Our jailbird! He says he's going to write an article about runaway teens for the *Reader's Digest.*"

There was a silence. Martha sat very quietly, hoping nobody would notice that her eyes were filled with tears at Billie's good news.

"Maybe seeing the kids reminded him about restaurant work," Sandy said.

"Yeah," said Billie. "With all this going on, I'm making up my own materials again, because my boss scheduled new minicourses and we won't get any books for a week. It used to be worse. So I assigned everybody library projects. I'll be busy correcting them next week. In the meantime, Chris and Mike and I are painting the apartment." She broke off, scowling. "This is silly. We're going to bore each other to death if we drag in everything that happens. Talking for fifteen minutes on this sh—stuff doesn't make

374

sense. Why don't we discuss women's issues, like feminists do? They're at least programmed."

"What's their program?" Ursula asked.

"They have topics for weekly sharing of feelings, but don't try to be therapists like we do."

"I'm not trying to be a therapist," said Sandy.

"But aren't we all supposed to be? If we talk to one another all the time and never get the therapist's reaction, we must be therapists ourselves." Billie darted a bold glance at Martha.

Martha protested. "That's only one definition. A group can usefully test out the reactions of suitable peers, not just those of the professional therapist."

Elinor raised her hand, lost her nerve and put it down, then admitted to Martha, "I was expecting to continue working with you."

Ursula agreed. "I asked last week if you would be more active, but maybe you think it's best this way."

"The best use of the leader is determined by the circumstances," Martha said. "My method is to let group dynamics work unless someone is being destructive. And I haven't seen any sign of that here."

"I believe," insisted Billie, "that we should use this opportunity to raise our consciousness. Face the predicaments women are in and work toward equality. I like the idea that we can be our own leaders, but I think we need to discuss policies, like equal pay and abortion rights, or we'll just gossip."

Martha defended sticking to feelings. "Unless we explore our own emotions and their background we can't come to understand and can't change. We could avoid a lot of emotional trauma by rigorous self-knowledge."

"That leads to more soap opera stuff, not to feminism," Billie said. "We should *study* what's happening to women."

Hesitantly, Elinor asked, "Would we have time to talk about feminism and our feelings too? I need help right now."

"If we went around the circle twice," Ursula said, "we could discuss both."

"It depends on the topics," Sandy said. "What are they?"

"Well," said Billie, "the topics are still about personal stuff, like how you felt when you first realized you were female and has that downgraded you, and so on."

"It sounds like what I need," said Ursula.

"Me too," said Sandy.

Elinor, nodding, asked, "Which topics do they discuss first?"

"I don't know," said Billie, "but I'll ask my teacher friend. She's moved out of a therapy group with men and is into Consciousness Raising with women. She's sure to have a list of topics that I could bring in. Okay. I'm through with my turn."

"One thing more," said Ursula. "After being married for years to a teacher, I know your work is a big part of your life. I'd like to hear more about your classes."

"Well, I have four classes of about thirty kids each and right now everyone's either in Mixed Economies or Developing Nations."

"Sounds like college stuff to me," said Sandy.

"But I don't lecture, just get them to give daily reports on a lot of issues, mostly from current publications. And they write term papers."

"I'd like my kids to get courses like that," said Elinor. "What school are you in?"

"Middle Cove High."

"Oh," cried Elinor, "I can't believe it! My kids go to Middle Cove High—Steven and Susan Bates. Do you know them?"

"I have Steven now," said Billie with the matter-of-factness of an experienced teacher to a mother. "In Developing Nations, second period."

"For heaven's sake!" Elinor looked dazed.

Martha was taken aback that she hadn't made a connection before. "You all recall our rule, of course, that everything that's said here is confidential. It wouldn't be ethical for you, Elinor, to tell anyone about Billie's son, nor for you"—she turned to Billie—"to tell anyone about Elinor's son."

Billie frowned.

Elinor nodded, and said, "I'm very discreet. That's one reason I was a good Embassy secretary. I'll never breathe a word about Mike's being in jail, and I trust Billie not to talk about Helen's pregnancy."

There was a sudden heavy silence in the group. Finally Billie said, "Every high school has cases of pregnancy. Believe me, this isn't the only one I won't talk about." She reached over and shook Elinor's hand solemnly. "I'll relate to Steven only in connection with his classwork."

Unexpectedly, Ursula said, "I'll speak next." She directed her gaze at Martha. "Talking about how men are always blaming women made me want to throw things all around the room. But then I remembered that my husband has to stay in the nursing home and I'm safe at Blaine's. Still, my highest hope is to go home to my own house and find some young person to share expenses with me, maybe a college girl. Queens College is quite near my house. It might be interesting to have a college roommate—I never had one."

Sandy warned. "You may find college girls pretty immature, not very organized. I know—I was one not long ago."

"And don't they smoke a lot of pot?" Elinor asked.

"Please tell me, what's wrong with pot?" Ursula asked.

"It makes people irresponsible at times," said Sandy.

"Wasn't your daughter trying to find tenants for your house?" Elinor asked.

"I persuaded her to wait. Billie said last week that we'd think of something."

"We will," Billie asserted. "There are airports in Queens and you might rent a room to a flight attendant. They make good money, not like college girls. You might enjoy having someone who flies to exotic places. Some of my former students do that."

"Do you think I could find someone Japanese?"

"Sure!" said Billie, and then added, "Maybe."

Elinor was almost bouncing in her desire to help. "I could phone Japan Airlines and ask. That's one sort of thing I do on my job, get information to help people."

"Good," said Ursula. "Thank you." There was a pause. She was wishing that someone would ask her to share another poem, and had a new one with her. But no one asked and she said, "That should wind up my turn."

Eyes turned to Sandy who had been sitting tense, her face drawn. As the others looked at her, she placed her palms on her ribs and made her breasts flap up and down. "I don't have any milk," she said in anguish. "All week it's been low at this time of day."

"That happens," Elinor responded, feelingly. "When I was breast-feeding I had to rest in the afternoon or I wouldn't have enough milk later, just when the baby needed a full tummy for the night."

Sandy got to her feet. "I'm going to call home and tell Mom to give the baby the bottle. I did fix one, just in case. I swear to God, Jordy's never had a bottle."

Martha intervened. "Sandy, let's consider what's happening. Your mother has probably given him the bottle if it was needed. There's nothing habit-forming in an occasional bottle—it won't affect your milk. You'll be out of here in about fifteen minutes. Do you really want to interrupt our session just when it's your turn?"

Sandy stood irresolute. "I'm not trying to get out of speaking, just worried."

"That's understandable," said Martha. "But if you control your worry, you'll function better."

"Okay." Sandy sat down and made an effort. "Well, this week has been some better and some worse. I told Mom that I needed one of those baby carriers—I never know what they're called."

Billie spoke up. "They're called 'cradle boards' and were invented by the American Indians."

"Oh," said Sandy. "They didn't tell Mom that at Saks Fifth Avenue. Anyhow, she brought me one and I can get out of the house with Jordy for a change. But when I went to the post office I found out I'd been invited to be in a group show that was already over."

Elinor let out a motherly cluck of sympathy and received an annoyed glance from Billie who said firmly to Sandy, "There'll be other shows."

Sandy started to cry. "I don't know when. Nothing goes right any more. Sometimes I hate the baby."

Ursula patted her hand. "And so you should," she declared. "Horrid, selfish brat. Every baby is. Never does a thing to help."

Sandy's sniffles speeded up, became half laughter. "He *is* a brat sometimes." She blew her nose. "But I think what's wrong is David. He wants a new job but he's afraid his boss will find out he's looking, so he doesn't go out for interviews at lunchtime any more. He's been losing sleep too and it's hard on him."

"Can't you put some heart into him?" Billie asked.

"I try, but I'm too depressed myself. And I keep thinking how ambitious he felt when I was pregnant, but he couldn't job-hunt then because he couldn't say, 'My wife's having a baby.'" She began to weep again, then cried out, "Oh, now my milk has come in. I'm going home." Clasping her handbag, she pulled her coat off the hanger in the closet and kicked her way out the door.

The time was up and the others departed quickly. Martha sat at her desk and enjoyed a moment of quiet. She didn't feel like waltzing around the room this week.

Elinor's less infatuated with Ralph, getting to know him better through Helen's pregnancy. It has one good side—he's loyal to his daughter, who needs support. Steven probably had nothing to do with it. His mother's church job makes her seem less glamorous but shows

379

how warm-hearted she is, eager to serve. Ursula is more intellectual than I realized, knows a lot of Freudian theory. It's remarkable how focused she is on her own interests, like wanting a Japanese housemate, but sadly, she's still indifferent to the illness of poor August. Sandy is no longer a whirlwind blowing off about the hazards of marriage but just a young mother torn between domestic and artistic loyalties. She's the least concerned with the feelings of the others but that's youth. I picture her with her baby on her back and her portfolio in her hand doing the rounds of the galleries. I hope she gets life on her own terms, and can avoid hasty decisions, not be like my daughter-in-law who divorced Barry, seemingly without thinking. As for Billie, I'll have to study her more carefully, especially her motivations. What does she want most—to stand out as a bright, bossy leader or to become a harmonious person? I'm not sure but will try to look on her good side.

I'm glad they're all beginning to see their worlds and themselves more clearly.

I wonder if any of the changes in their lives are directly due to the group? Well, at least it may have speeded them up. Elinor got a job, not due to my advice but to Billie's bossiness. And Billie took Ursula's suggestion to move quickly to rescue Mike from a cult. Ursula's getting support in her hopes for a housemate. Sandy has taken the baby out of the house, an idea that came from Elinor, and went for her mail at the post office, because Billie ordered her to! Truthfully, in one-on-one sessions things might have taken longer. However, the most important change was that Billie's attitude toward Mike became loving, and I was working toward that long before the group started. Now the question that keeps bugging me is what does Billie expect to get from the group?

Sigmund Freud's most famous question was "What do women want?" Now we take this as a give-away of his male chauvinism. What do you think men would want, Sig, if half the people in the world had more rights than they? Of course, women sometimes destroy their own chances for power by not compromising. To the unempowered, power looks easy, but you have to keep negotiating and compromising to keep it. You have to know your goals and never stop working toward them.

The light on her desk signalled that someone was at the front door and she stood and looked out the window.

It's Sarah, letting me know that dinner's ready. I'm late like I was last week after the group. But it's annoying that she rings the doorbell. Does she feel like a patient, a supplicant who wants comfort? I work against time all day, and need to study my impressions while they're fresh, and come to dinner when I'm ready. She doesn't understand.

She buzzed the front door open and called, "Just coming!"

After turning off the office light, she stood a moment in the dark, realizing she was in a foul mood.

How can I claim the grace, even the simple energy, to preside over a healthy group when I myself feel antagonistic and lonely? The members of the group are at least members. They have me and one another to confide in, to level with.

Billie wanted to shift our whole purpose from therapy to consciousness-raising. I'll need all the skill I have to integrate her feminism into my therapeutic aims. While avoiding interfering!

Does a power struggle occur every time two human beings meet?

Good question.

33

Consciousness-Raising Is Free

When the group assembled for its third session, Sandy said, "I'm supposed to bring you a request. My mother wants to join our group. I told her about Elinor's getting a job and she thinks we might help her decide if she wants one."

Martha intervened, her voice shriller than she intended. "Sandy, we must remember our rule of confidentiality. It seems you broke it by telling your mother about Elinor's job."

"I don't see any harm in that," said Sandy.

"It's not a question of harm. It's respect for privacy."

"I forgot. I was happy for Elinor."

After a pause, Martha said, "I hope no one will break our confidentiality in the future." Heads nodded assent. "We can, of course, discuss the matter of Sandy's mother, since it came up."

Elinor began, "Well, knowing you, Sandy, I'm sure your mother is full of ideas. Of course, my getting a job was something Dr. Kaufman and I had been talking about. Would it work if your mother joined our group without the background of regular therapy the rest of us have had?"

Billie said, "Why not, Sandy? You and your Mom could wear matching outfits!" She laughed.

Martha said, "Let's not ridicule what may be a genuine need."

Ursula said, "I have a problem with our taking in a new member at this stage. I'm just getting to know this group."

Elinor said with quiet conviction, "It wouldn't be very nice of us to keep Dr. Kaufman from getting another fee. After all, we're not paying full price."

"I wouldn't decide for that reason," Martha interjected.

Sandy was looking worried and Elinor asked, "What do you think would be best, Sandy?"

"Mom's okay and she'd be good in a group, but I need her to keep the baby. I can't afford to pay for therapy and sitters too. Oh, why is everything so difficult now?"

"Bring the baby," said Billie.

"It wouldn't be appropriate to bring the baby, or to have a mother and daughter in the same group," Martha said. Billie shrugged.

Sandy's face screwed up with the onset of tears. "I love my mom, but Billie's right. I don't want to wear matching outfits. This is my group."

"There are other groups she could join," said Martha.

"She lives in Great Neck," Sandy said, stifling a sob.

Martha said, "There are therapy groups there. I'll look up a few names for her."

Billie said, "Let her call the Manhattan office of the National Organization for Women and ask for the NOW number in Great Neck. They'll tell her about their political action campaigns and how they get legal help for women who are harassed on the job. And they organize consciousness-raising groups, too."

Ursula asked, "Isn't Sandy's mother interested in a therapy group rather than a feminist one?"

"Yes, she is," said Sandy. "Dr. Kaufman, I'll phone you for the names."

Elinor spoke up, her voice brimming with good will. "I can report on the calls I made to look for a Japanese housemate for Ursula."

"Good," said Ursula.

Elinor warmed to her subject. "Well, two men at the Japanese airline office—two of them talked with me—surprised me with their big 'No.' They keep tight control of the girls, it seems."

"Not girls," interposed Billie. "*Young women.* The word *girls* means females who haven't gone through puberty and before puberty girls do not—repeat—*do not* work for airlines."

"We-e-ll," Elinor said doubtfully. "Anyhow, they have a company hotel in Anchorage, Alaska, where their *young women* stay. I asked if any other firms bring Japanese here, and finally got to a big news agency, but they hire only men."

"Are you surprised that Japanese men are chauvinists?" Billie asked.

"They're not with the program of the National Organization of Women," said Elinor.

"There you are, a feminist already!" said Billie.

Ursula spoke up. "Please, we should understand the Japanese culture. If someone who flew regularly to Japan stayed with me, my dream would be to go with her. That country has such wonderful treasures, not only art, but literature and culture. They may keep close tabs on their young women, but we have social problems here, like crime, that they don't have."

"I do have one lead," Elinor said. "The rector said there was a Japanese student at services last Sunday, with a church member who teaches comparative languages at Columbia University. The Japanese man—he's older than most students—is going to Poland to teach, leaving his adventurous younger sister in New York. She's working as a chemist in Queens, but can't afford to keep an apartment on her own and needs to find a place soon. Her name is Michiko."

"A common name in Japan," Ursula said.

Elinor went on, "She speaks English but you'll have to talk with her brother for a decision before he leaves." She held out a paper toward Ursula. "Here's his phone number. I wrote it large so you could read it."

Ursula, sitting very straight, slowly reached for the paper and sat holding it reverently.

Sandy turned to Billie. "Did you get the list of topics of feminism you were after, Billie?"

"Not yet. But I heard of a topic that my friend said went over well, 'Betrayed by Men.'"

"Ouch!" said Sandy, "that hits home. Why don't we talk about that today? Everybody knows about being betrayed by men. I'll go first, okay?" Heads nodded and Sandy said, "I don't mean betrayed by David, but my father left my mother, and my art professors never encouraged students to tackle big projects. I can't really leave David out of it, either. When we first became lovers he told me he didn't want to get married, and then later told his aunt we were getting married soon. He slept with a woman on his staff at a convention and explained that his boss had hinted that he could make me jealous so I'd marry him."

"Is that why you did?" asked Billie. "You were betrayed."

"Maybe. But mostly it made me realize how much he needs me, and I do love him. I love his honesty. He's so sweet I could eat him."

"That sounds sort of violent," said Elinor.

Sandy raised her voice. "No, I really love him. I love to hear him singing while he's shaving, and I love going to art galleries with him and discussing world affairs with him. I love everything I do for him, like cooking and taking his clothes to the cleaner. He's my David. And he does thoughtful things for me, and wants to earn money *for me*. We're perfect together. But I didn't want to be married, and I can't forget he betrayed me on that. Don't say it's because I don't want to be committed. I'm committed as a lover and mother for ever and ever, but I don't want to be called just a wife because of how people define the role."

"Define it? How?" Billie prompted.

"Hypocrisy," Sandy said, making the word hiss. "Like at family affairs, couples kissing when everyone knows they're fighting a lot, and wives afraid to express their own political views, and a husband talking as if he took time off to buy his wife a birthday present when she knows his secretary got it, and family pictures with everyone smiling— all a mockery."

"You're into my story now," said Ursula. "Add this to

385

your list—Golden Weddings that are celebrations of a long misery."

Sandy nodded and continued. "I also hate the role expectations, mostly because they creep up on me. Like before we were married, David cooked as much as I did. But now he doesn't. And when we have his aunt to dinner she eats like she's deciding whether or not to keep me. I'm their new investment."

Elinor broke in. "A lot of men cook now. My Ralph makes good Caesar salad."

"But does he actually prepare meals when you're busy or sick, and do it well and willingly? Does he take turns shopping for food and clean up afterward and make plans for the next meal even if nobody praised his salad? In the office, does he respect his secretary's work and do it cheerfully in a pinch, like she does his? There's not much democracy in men."

"Is there democracy in women?" Martha asked.

"Not always," said Sandy. "We need to work on that. All I'm sure of is I knew *beforehand* that getting married would give society the right to define me, and I wanted to define myself as an *artist* before I *got* defined as a *wife*, period. Nobody listened to that."

"I listened," said Martha.

"Did you?" Sandy said quietly. "I thought the bottle of champagne you gave us was part of the wedding hoopla. To celebrate that society won."

"It was to celebrate the birth of the baby," Martha said, softly. "That wonderful baby."

"But there are plenty of things a baby could use, right? I don't want to be ungrateful, but one bottle of Dom Perignon costs more than I can make in a week."

"What does Baby Jordy need now, Sandy?" Elinor asked. "I'd like to give you a gift for him."

"So would I," said Ursula.

"Doctor Kaufman," Elinor entreated, "could we have a little shower for Sandy next week? I could bring a cake."

"We need our full time for discussion, but you could each give Sandy a gift if that's your individual decision."

"Please," Sandy interjected, "we don't need anything. We hardly have space for the basics, which we have. The only thing we need is time for me to visit the galleries."

"I could babysit," said Elinor. "I come to town pretty often to meet Ralph for dinner, and I could come a few hours early some afternoon and stay with Jordy."

"Don't you have a job, Elinor?" Billie asked.

"Oops, I forgot." The group fell silent, in sympathy with Elinor.

"I'll speak," said Ursula. "Sandy, talk about betrayal—a long time ago I *lost* what you're taking for granted. You and David have interests in common and love each other, and you have long years ahead in good health and in your art. I've been betrayed so frequently for so long by my husband that I got even and shoved his copy machine downstairs. I didn't try to hurt him—didn't even know he was in the house. And his bones were already weak or it wouldn't have hurt him to pick it up. His betrayals boomeranged on him."

The room fell silent again.

"Did you say something about a Golden Wedding?" asked Elinor.

"I can't bear to think about it," Ursula replied. "It would be the ultimate betrayal. August is determined to live until it happens, no matter how sick he is, but no matter *what*, I'm going to insist on a divorce instead. I've had it with that man."

Elinor was shocked. "Is everyone here against marriage?"

"I'm not," Martha said.

"I'm not altogether against it," said Billie, "though mine didn't work out."

"I'm certainly not," said Elinor. "Even if it's risky."

"I've stood nearly fifty years of it," said Ursula, "and now August's accident is finally letting me out. He has cancer."

Neither Elinor's gasp nor Martha's sympathetic moan of pain reached Ursula, who went on, "So now I have emotional security."

"You didn't mention cancer before," Sandy said.

"No, it's a hush-hush word. But . . ." she turned to Martha, "Blaine told you, didn't she?"

"No," said Martha in a level tone. "I knew he had tests."

"He'll be staying in a hospice, so I'll never have to live with him again. Now he can't throw away my journals, or be rude to my poet friends, or shred and vacuum up my only copies of poems, or refuse to make copies for me. He had a plan for his life and we both followed it, and any plan I had he gave me bits of, as if I were a child being indulged. I had to scheme to get anything I wanted. He denied me my medicine. He betrayed me."

There was a silent moment of grief.

Ursula broke it by snapping her handbag closed on the paper with the phone number, and nodding in satisfaction.

"Let's hear from you next, Elinor. We can get out of here a little early if you can make it short," Billie said.

Martha winced at Billie's bossiness, but Elinor seemed to take it as a pep talk.

"Well, I'm not feeling betrayed totally and I'll be brief. My father, whom I loved, was kind in his way but wasn't home much, being absorbed in his pharmacy. He could have paid for college for me but wouldn't even consider it. All he did was work, and I guess it isn't surprising that I married Howard, a real workaholic with no time for kids. I was so lonely I got to the point of suicide, ten years ago, and came here to see Dr. Kaufman. She helped me a lot. But finally I got divorced last year. Howard makes a lot of money in the financial firm he owns, but he influenced the divorce lawyers and I'm not getting enough child support. He's betraying not only me but the kids, to the point of their health maybe. Trust Howard to know how to really hurt me. I got depressed at Christmas and am better now, but I still feel blue at times because with kids it's hard for me and Ralph to fall in love properly. Like right now my son needs me more than my lover does. End of story."

"Your turn, Billie," Sandy said.

But Billie dodged and asked, "Where's your fire and brimstone, Elinor? You should be outraged at the men you've put up with, your father and husband."

"Tell us about *your* fire and brimstone, Billie," said Martha.

"I've got it!" Billie shot back. "I never knew my father and you'd better believe that's a betrayal in itself. My Mom tried to cope sometimes but she was so mixed up she couldn't. After she died, my aunt sent me to be educated by nuns to be a teacher, and my political party gave me a philosophy. I tried to cope with marriage but my ex-husband Michael was even more alienated than I was, and took advantage of my having a job. And my son does the same. It's not only betrayal, it's exploitation. What more can I say?"

"I say 'Bravo!' to you for making something of yourself," said Ursula. The others clapped.

"What about men outside your family?" asked Sandy. "Any betrayals?"

"All the time," said Billie, cheerfully. "I don't see anyone else in this room who works with a bunch of men on a job and, believe me, *that's* betrayal. Like politics. The superintendent of schools in my district is the political choice of an elitist community. Luckily, my department chairman is not prejudiced against liberals and knew when he hired me that I'd written an article for a liberal magazine. As an administrator, he's constipated, but he has experimental ideas about curriculum which help our students get into good colleges. He started our mini-courses on real subjects. The betrayal came over the one on Mixed Economies, because after I turned in my draft of the course of study with discussion questions and tests and all, he gave it to Ed to teach. I guess his aim was to test it with a real conservative, but Ed liked it and started taking credit for all my work, spoke about it as *his* course."

"What did you do?" Sandy asked.

"Well, I'm sort of paranoid about being accused of being a socialist by people who have no idea there's useful socialism. My course of study is fair, and presents both sides about Sweden's mixed economy, England's Labor government, FDR's new deal and so on. I was afraid it might arouse questions, so before I even showed it to my boss, I sealed a copy in an envelope and mailed it to myself by registered mail. Last week in faculty meeting I made a show of opening it and revealing the date, and asked Ed to tell everybody that he didn't invent it. He's a charmer and covered himself by declaring in the department meeting that he enjoys teaching it so much he just naturally identifies himself with it! I then presented copies to everybody and asked for suggestions, and told them they can teach any of my new courses with my blessing. Now I get the credit along with the hard work. In fact, getting the credit is harder."

"This is good news," said Martha. "I hope we can hear more about your courses, but now since we've all shared our news, we should take a few minutes to decide on our topic for next week. I suggest something we touched on today, 'Are Women Democratic?'"

"Wouldn't it be more interesting to take turns rating each other on our respect for ourselves as women?" countered Billie. "Call it 'Mutual Evaluations.'"

"Uh, oh," Ursula said. "I'm sure to be shredded all to pieces on that one."

"Those topics are a lot alike," said Elinor, playing mediator. "We can be democratic in the way we evaluate each other."

Sandy, who already had her coat on, said, "I'll go for just plain mutual evaluations."

Martha sensed this remark settled the matter but

warned, "I hope each evaluator will respect other people's feelings."

The group left together and Billie stopped them on the sidewalk. "Look at that bombed-out sign!" she exclaimed.

Elinor said, "For a long time I've wanted to do it over."

"What does it say, Elinor?" Ursula asked.

"Psychotherapist. But it's missing some letters in the middle of the word."

"I'll fix it," Billie asserted. She took a black felt pen from her handbag and filled in the spaces with letters and dashes, so it said PSYCHO-the-RAPIST!

Sandy laughed. "Billie, that's very clever!"

Elinor, not sure of the implication, said, "I hope it won't scare off patients. I was going to do it in gold paint."

"Let her get it done," said Billie. "She's free, white and making good money."

Impressed by Billie's lack of sentimentality, Elinor said, "I enjoyed what you brought to our session, Billie."

"Me, too," said Ursula. "We're beginning to really talk."

"Yes," agreed Billie. "And there's a lot more to talk about. Does anyone want to go over to the Adam and Eve for a beer?"

"I do," said Elinor. "For more than beer. I'm starved by six o'clock, and tonight Ralph can't take me to dinner until nine."

"It's months since I had a beer," said Sandy, "because of nursing the baby."

There was a chorus. "One beer won't hurt!"

"Well, maybe," Sandy decided. "I'll phone Mom that I'll be home late and she and David can eat the dinner I cooked. She's probably giving Jordy a bottle like I do."

"I guess he knows all about being a baby now," said Elinor.

Sandy laughed. "Yes, he's a pro."

"I'm not sure I should go," Ursula said. "My daughter's group is booked for dinner, so she told me to eat at the

Greek Garden on the corner and they'd be there at nine. I told her I'd ask Elinor to walk me over there after the group."

"We're only going a couple of blocks from the Greek Garden," said Billie.

"Come with us, Ursula," said Elinor, "and I'll gladly walk you to the Greek Garden before nine."

"So come on," Billie said, leading the way.

When they were all settled at table with a large pizza and a big pitcher of beer, Elinor turned to Billie and asked, "How do you evaluate me, Billie?"

"Well, at first I saw you as a rich suburban divorcee, dating a stockbroker, all fluttery when you're talking to yourself, waiting for a man to define you."

Elinor was taken aback but answered with spirit. "I'm far from rich but I've always had to please a man, so I'm used to that. As for how I talk to myself, I have some strength there. I repeat beautiful litanies from the prayer book. They shape my thoughts. If you didn't grow up in the Episcopal Church you can't understand."

"I grew up a Catholic," Billie said, "so I do know litanies. But I avoid letting them shape my thoughts. My aim is to free myself from the crypto-bourgeois shackles of a faith that tells people even how to pray."

"What's crypto-bourgeois?" Sandy asked, but was ignored.

"I liked confessing," Billie said, "because it was my chance to talk about abstract concepts, something besides whether I had a clean uniform. That's why it hit me, the idea of taking a priest with me to rescue Mikey. I didn't do it, but I took Christopher and he's a forceful moral influence."

Ursula was lost in her own thoughts. "I'll bet you put me way down on the scale of liberated women."

"Not too far down," Billie assured her. "You know the problems of marriage, so you understand what Sandy wants. I rate you a generation younger than your age."

"Or two generations. I have a great-granddaughter."

Billie spoke slowly, her blue eyes wide open and serious. "What I don't comprehend—not just in you, but in anyone—is all that poetry. Mind you, when I was a kid I memorized poems, mostly religious, and once in my career I had to teach an English class. But as a social scientist I see the world going to hell for lack of socialism. Poetry seems an indulgence, all that personal suffering."

Ursula replied with equal conviction. "We won't get anywhere until people understand their emotions. I think liberation—human liberation, not only women's—will come from more attention to poetry, not less."

"I want to ask you, Sandy," said Elinor, "how do you see me?"

Sandy replied without hesitation. "I'd guess you're only about a half generation older than me, Elinor, but you seem old-fashioned. You seem to take having an affair frivolously, like a few dates for dinner, when what's really between men and women today is right down on the mat. Sex is a power struggle and you're Sleeping Beauty wrapped up in false femininity."

"You think my femininity is false?"

"Definitely," said Sandy. "The way you use makeup falsifies it."

"Don't you ever use makeup, Sandy?"

"Not really. Well, I did wear red polish on my toenails while I was in labor because I wanted to . . . well, show that the pain wasn't going to suppress me, the female."

"That's why I wear green eyeshadow," Elinor said.

Billie looked gravely at both of them. "Can't you be female without red and green paint?"

"That reminds me of a poem, 'The Emperor of Ice Cream,'" said Ursula, "which claims that our bodies feel like emperors with momentary pleasures like ice cream, but they melt away. Nothing stops death. Wallace Stevens wrote the poem, and it makes you think. Honesty and love are all that lasts. Poetry explains a lot." There was a pause.

She turned to Sandy, "What is your opinion of me? What about my husband's driving me crazy?"

"He was," Sandy said. "Like the baby is driving me crazy. I'm at a stage where I can't define myself."

"But you have time ahead to define yourself," said Ursula, "as I don't."

Elinor said, "Ursula, I like your independence, because I'm not a suburban clubwoman type, whatever Billie says. I probably spend more time alone, jogging and gardening, than any woman in my suburb."

"But your docility hides what you are," said Billie. "It's okay for Ursula to be a mystic at her age but you should be involved in the real world, protesting and changing it."

"I've thought of taking an art course," Elinor replied.

"What sort of art?" Sandy asked.

"Just art history. I'm not creative like you, Sandy."

Billie was shocked. "But art history's useless for earning a living!"

While this statement was hanging in the air, Sandy smoothed her hair with her hands like a little girl presenting herself at a party. "What do you think of me, Billie?"

Billie spoke matter-of-factly. "Come out of your swoon, Sandy."

"My what?"

"Your swoon. Your obsession with freedom and divorce."

"But I'm trying to avoid divorce!"

"Negative! What comes across is that you want a friendly divorce at the start of marriage. That won't work because you have to be fully in before you know if you want out."

Sandy was silent and Ursula defended her. "But, Billie, Sandy has come to grips with the problems of marriage early, and is trying to be true to herself."

"Marriage shouldn't be the whole solution for women," said Billie, "but it can be part of a solution right now for you, Sandy. You're in it and you put yourself in it, so it's something you have to accept. I think what you haven't accepted is your artistic commitment. You'll have to decide it and discipline yourself to work around it. I had to discipline myself to earn a living and work around that so I know it can be done. Your art and David and the baby can all be full commitments."

Ursula sweetened Billie's theme. "You're already doing it, Sandy—loving and taking care of your little family and keeping up with your creativity, hanging onto the idea of it, at least, while you're breast-feeding, which is temporary. So keep trying."

"I have no choice, now," Sandy said.

"You'll do it," Elinor said, and smiled warmly at Sandy, who relaxed and smiled back.

Noticing that Billie was putting on her jacket, Sandy said, "Hey, Billie, aren't you going to be evaluated?"

"Naw, I know you're going to say I'm bossy and butch, so forget it."

"Don't be afraid," said Elinor. "We love you as you are."

"Because I'm cute, right?"

Sandy grinned and then looked severe. "Billie, you can't evaluate yourself. You've got to take the heat like the rest of us. I, for one, think you have very good ideas."

"So do I," said Elinor. "I remember the first time I saw you, waiting for Dr. Martha to buzz you in. I thought you seemed hard, but I think now that you were impatient to get in to see her. Like you *needed* to see her. I figure your hardness covers up your shyness."

"I was jealous that she probably liked you better than me," said Billie. "But look, I want everybody's address and phone number." She passed around a paper, and when it came back to her remarked, "Everybody but Sandy lives on Long Island."

"Actually," said Sandy, "I grew up there, in Great Neck, where my Mom lives now."

Billie was looking at the list. "I can't read what you wrote, Ursula. Tell me the house number."

"It's three fourteen Maple Street, half a mile or so east of the New Hyde Park subway stop."

Billie, writing it down, said, "I pass very near there when I drive to that stop to go to Manhattan. I could pick you up on my way and take you to our group."

"That's nice of you, Billie," said Elinor.

Billie had her own idea. "Meeting in a restaurant worked fine today. We talked like grown-ups, not sick people in therapy. Where shall we meet next week?"

Ursula jumped in. "I'm really hopeful that I'll be able to move back to my own house—that's the address I gave you. Couldn't we meet there?"

Elinor reminded her, "Billie said she'd pick you up and bring you on the subway to Dr. Martha's."

"Sure," said Billie, without conviction. "And home the same way."

Elinor was relieved. "That's a better plan than meeting at Ursula's, because Dr. Kaufman couldn't get there very easily."

"Or are you suggesting we meet without her?" Sandy asked.

"I was thinking of that," Billie admitted, cheerfully. "There'd be no charge—consciousness-raising is free. And we don't need a leader. The subway to Ursula's would be just as easy for you, Sandy, as the ride to Kaufman's. One fare and one change of trains."

"And a short bus ride after that," Ursula said.

Sandy considered it and then said, "It would be a very long subway trip. Maybe I should drive to Ursula's from Mom's. I could leave the baby with her and borrow her car."

Elinor was alert. "You said, Billie, that you can bring Ursula to the office, and it's the most convenient for me. Your plan to meet somewhere else looks like a plot against our therapist."

There was a troubled silence before Billie said, "Okay. Back to the office."

"So what's our topic for next time, Billie?" Sandy asked.

"How about this one—'How Could Feminism Have Helped My Mother?'"

"Sounds great," said Sandy. "Now I'm going to dash to the bookstore to buy a book for David's birthday, maybe one about King Tut."

"Nice to have you aboard, Sandy," Billie said. "See you next week."

34

Blind Spots

The next Wednesday, Billie came bursting into the group a minute before the session was to start, carrying the lower board of the shingle. It still bore her revised lettering, PSYCHO-the-RAPIST. Two short chains dangled from it and she gave them a jolly shake as she extended the board toward Martha, saying, "On our way out last time we agreed this sign is a disgrace."

Elinor gasped.

Martha rose to her feet, and took a step toward Billie. The two women froze, confronting each other in silence.

Elinor said softly to Martha, "Billie's drawing the board to your attention. It needs new lettering. I could try to do it."

Without breaking her eyes from their lock with Billie's, Martha snapped, "Someone has done some lettering on it already."

"I didn't do what's on it now," said Elinor lamely.

Martha's silence made clear the impact of Billie's brashness. "My practice requires a professional shingle out front," she finally said. "Replace it, please." Her look was unwavering.

Billie, undaunted, made a mock bow and with exaggerated care laid the board on the floor at Martha's feet. Then she took off her jacket, rolled it up, and threw it down in the direction of the closet. When she turned to sit in her chair she came face to face with Martha, who stood blocking the chair with the board firmly in her two hands. She extended it toward Billie. "Hang this back, please," she said, in Thorny's voice.

Billie, like a tennis player who has lost a tough point, kept her movements deliberate and took her time fishing out pliers from her handbag. Then she accepted the sign and walked out the door. Her attitude was compliant but not submissive.

Martha walked into the inner office.

The three remaining women sat stunned. Then Elinor rallied. "It's cold out there. She'll need her jacket." She caught up the jacket from the floor and tap-tapped down the hall with it. It was refused, so she stood holding it while Billie struggled to rehang the sign, which was harder to put up than it had been to take down. It was finally in place. Billie was wiping rust from her hands as they came back to the waiting room. Martha had not returned. Ursula was saying to Sandy, "Seeking a guru is the admission of our need to accept life's contradictions."

"Tell me about it!" Billie said, and laughed. She and Elinor took their seats.

Martha came in, carrying a tray with tea in new mugs.

"Oh, tea!" Ursula exclaimed. Then she added, "We've been missing you, Dr. Kaufman."

Martha, busy passing tea to everyone, failed to ask what this remark meant, but smiled broadly in the hope that her loss of temper had not blighted cheerful exchanges.

"What pretty mugs!" Elinor said. "I like the delicate botanical flower designs."

Sandy opened the session. "There's someone who wants to visit our group, my old college roommate, Danielle. She lives on Long Island but comes into Manhattan often for her work as a decorator. She'd like to come with me next week."

"Why not?" Billie's voice was cheeky as ever, but her glance at Martha showed new respect.

"Could you tell us about Danielle?" Martha asked.

"She's a talented artist," said Sandy, "but her life isn't easy. She has two little girls to support."

"What did you tell her about us?" Elinor asked.

"Not a thing except what it costs and I like it."

Martha asked, "Would her visit be to explore the idea of joining this group? Subject to our approval?"

"I think so," Sandy said. "Is that all right?"

Heads nodded in agreement and Billie spoke up. "There's someone I want to bring, too, to liven up this lily-white sisterhood. She's a Black journalist, named Fern. She's about thirty-five and very intelligent."

"Uh, oh!" said Elinor, looking doubtful.

Billie raised her voice. "That is, if you honky suburban-ites can associate with someone from the real world."

"We can," Ursula said. "I'd like Michiko to join, too."

"Oh, has she moved in with you?" asked Elinor.

Martha intervened. "Let's wait to hear about Michiko until it's Ursula's turn."

Ursula couldn't wait. "Let me just say that Michiko works during the day so I'd like us to meet evenings at my house. She'll bake cookies."

Martha smiled affectionately at Ursula's enthusiasm, but murmured, "Please wait, Ursula—we were learning about Billie's friend, Fern."

Sandy said, "Billie, I'm no honky suburbanite, but if we're going into the real world thing, a Black journalist is okay."

"Aw, Fern'll fit in," Billie asserted. "She doesn't have an attitude, just believes in clean politics. She wears cornrows and long ear rings, and high-heeled boots. She's American."

Elinor genuinely felt better. "Okay," she said. "I could bring my neighbor, Adele, too."

Martha concluded, "Since there's no objection, all the people you've mentioned will be welcome to visit next week. We can meet in my living room upstairs, as it's larger than this room."

Elinor spoke up somewhat plaintively. "Before every-thing changes around here, I have some things to talk about."

"Sure, we agreed to that, not to just discuss topics," Sandy said. "What's up?"

"I'm not going to marry Ralph."

Martha winced at this news but remained silent.

Billie said, "Good!"

"We're changing to be just friends," Elinor said. "It's been coming for a while and it got definite with Helen's being pregnant."

"What did she do?" asked Sandy.

"She had an abortion last Friday. Ralph took her to a private clinic. He knew a good one because a woman got pregnant by him and he saw her through an abortion last fall."

"That recently?" demanded Billie. "The scum!"

"I wouldn't call him names. It happened that he got the woman pregnant on a one-night stand last summer, a month before he met me. He didn't plan to have an affair with her, he said, and I believe him. She's the mother of the kids Helen babysits. She called to get Helen to sit one night and he volunteered to substitute. Her name is Belinda, she's a divorcee, about forty, and a good sport. When she came home that night she made cocoa for him and he ended up spending the night. He didn't do it with a complete set of feelings, like he says he did with me, but partly out of gratitude to her for being friendly to Helen, who's given him a lot of grief. He also enjoys Belinda's three lively little boys. He was courting me but when he believed Helen's claims that Steven got her pregnant, I stopped spending nights with him. And he was torn because he was falling for Belinda."

Billie was irate. "I say he's scum."

"I'm not angry at him. Belinda had been desperate, didn't see how she could manage another kid, and was very grateful to him for arranging an abortion. Later she was the one who persuaded Helen to get one, and it was successful. Thank the Good Lord the doctor reported that Helen had been pregnant from before Thanksgiving so Steven couldn't have been the father. And now Belinda and Ralph are set to get married."

Martha gasped. "Ralph's marrying Belinda?"

Elinor nodded, matter-of-factly. "That's right."

"You didn't see this coming when I last saw you." Martha couldn't keep anger and grief out of her voice. "I don't understand these changes."

"Well, when my ex made me quit seeing you, I had to get through Christmas on my own. I made it, too—no depression—with the help of Ralph who took all of us, including Belinda and her boys, to the show at Radio City and to supper afterward. Later, Ralph and I had some frank talks and things came clear to me. First, his and my relationship had become eighty percent economics and twenty percent friendship. He provides for people he's fond of and wants me to profit by keeping Michele. Now that he knows about our good schools he's buying a house near us which will take care of her school eligibility. The three boys will go to one of our elementary schools. Ralph apologized for telling me to go to a singles group, and says it came from a guilty conscience. I told him I'd laughed it off. He says that's a good idea, and maybe if we kid Helen and Steven a bit, we can ease them into family friendship.

"Michele doesn't want to live in the same house with Helen. But she wants to see her father often and she can do that from our house. He also wants to raise Belinda's boys and plans to make grease monkeys out of them. They're going to keep both Cadillacs in shape! It's new to me, a man who cares so much about being a father, but that's Ralph. And my kids are too old for him to influence a lot. Well, Susan's young enough, and he's promised if she and Michele keep their good grades and earn Regents Scholarships, he'll send them both to college. As for Steven, he's always resisted what Ralph wanted to teach him about the Cadillacs. Anyhow, it's in the divorce agreement that his own father will send him to college.

"You know, I sometimes think Ralph fell for Belinda because of her boys. He's never had a son and I honestly don't want any more kids."

Martha found her voice. "Could you tell us more about your feelings? Were you hurt?"

"I was hurt that he was disappointed in Steven, but after all, Howard is also to blame for Steven's not wanting to fix cars. I fell out of love with Ralph over the Helen thing, but even before that, at Thanksgiving I knew I was more attracted to his money than to him. Actually, I like him better now. He says he's learning to love after a lonely marriage, and admires me because I work at the church. He expects me to understand he's always wanted to raise sons, and expects me and Belinda to be friends. She's a diet nut and he must have told her about my gourmet cooking, because she asked if we were drowning in cholesterol. I said we can't afford it, so she sent me a vegetarian recipe book which I really like."

"Do you think you can be friends with her?" asked Sandy.

"Maybe. She's happy-go-lucky. I liked her personally when we met on Christmas. When they move to Middle Cove I'll show her my favorite shops and we'll have lunch. She likes gardening, too. Ralph's going to continue giving Michele and Susan piano lessons and they've promised the three boys a puppet show. The other day the oldest called and asked when they could come to see it, and called me *Aunt Elinor!*"

Billie asked, "Is Helen jealous of Belinda and Ralph?"

"No, she's all for their getting married so she can live with them and go on babysitting with the boys. Ralph hopes she's learning a lot about homemaking and will get married again. His daughters have never been happy before. Their mother was wrong, somehow. And face it, the best thing of all is that I'll always have my house!"

There was a silence, during which everyone took a deep breath. Then Sandy said, "Wow!"

Martha, reassured that Elinor was weathering the storm, said, "You've told us quite a saga about Helen. I hadn't taken her for the babysitting type."

"Well, she is. She likes kids—didn't want to have an abortion, remember?"

"I'm sorry she had to have one," said Sandy.

"Hey, hey, Sandy," said Billie, "you haven't said a word during the saga of Helen."

"I've been wondering what's different about her and me being unmarried mothers," Sandy admitted.

"The difference is that in your case both the mother and the father wanted the baby," said Martha.

"Negative!" Billie declared. "The difference is that the father of Sandy's baby had a job. It's easy to want a baby if you can afford it."

Ursula said, "Thank God it's resolved."

"I used to think about the prayer, 'O Lord, let me never be confounded' in connection with Helen," Elinor said thoughtfully. "She was depressed after the abortion and didn't want to talk when I called her. It made me feel lucky I'm an adult and not a slave to sex."

"Michiko says abortions are common in Japan and keep the birthrate down, which everyone's glad about—but one of her friends was seriously depressed after one."

Elinor said, "Well, Helen's feeling better now. She called me this morning and asked how I roast chicken. Ralph told her I have a special recipe with lots of garlic. The plans we've made seem to suit everybody. I have every other Sunday alone with my kids because Michele goes into the City—you won't believe this—to clean Ralph's apartment, which he's going to keep and we can use after he leaves."

"Her cleaning for him may be a way for father and daughter to keep in touch," Martha said.

"Yes, he takes her to movies, and they talk."

"Where does all this leave you?" Sandy asked.

Elinor spoke with bravado. "I lose a husband, gain a daughter and laugh all the way to the bank."

Billie grumbled, "Elinor, you're too soft. You should sue him for palimony. He did expect to marry you."

"He did, but believe me, I'd rather get some education and make my own money than be the wife of a strong man, even a kind one."

"Are you sure you don't feel betrayed by him?" Sandy asked.

"Yes, I'm over him in that way."

Ursula spoke thoughtfully. "I think love affairs that turn into friendships are considered new, but there was George Sand, more than a century ago. She gave hospitality on her big estate to her lover, Chopin, while he was composing his greatest music. She still took care of him even when he was far gone with TB and she had another lover."

Martha asked, "How does Steven feel now?"

"He's like himself again," Elinor said, with a little chuckle. "Being taken for a Don Juan had a certain glamor to it! When I asked him how he felt about the whole thing he said it was *awesome*."

"He's so right!" said Sandy. "Kids say everything is 'awesome' but the word really fits having a baby!"

"He's doing okay in my course," Billie said.

"So am I," Elinor said. "I've done all the reading—it's too bad you can't require me to write a term paper."

"If you write it, I'll read it."

"I probably won't, but I want to tell you, Billie, I'm impressed with the research you did for this course. It should be used everywhere."

"Thank you. Research is easy, but to put it into good form for teaching, I'd need to record everything we do in class and that's too much work."

Martha saw an opportunity. "To whom would you send it, Billie, if you did prepare it? To textbook publishers?"

"Eventually. But first the curriculum people in Albany could do it as a pilot program in a few schools. They do a lot of new stuff that way."

"So do it," said Sandy. Billie looked thoughtful.

Elinor spoke up again, embarrassed. "Sorry to ask, but is it all right if I rattle on? I have a decision to make."

Martha nodded, and Ursula said, "Rattle, Elinor!"

"Well, Ralph has been wanting to give me a gift, something of value. Once he offered to pay my tuition for an art history course and I didn't take him up on it. This time he's insisting, and I'm signed up now for a course leading to an art appraiser's certificate. Billie said I couldn't make money from art history, but appraisers get paid. I've always been pretty good at telling real things from imitation—and will learn more. I'll take a string of classes next fall."

Martha felt a rush of jealousy over Elinor's taking Billie's advice again but comforted herself that good ideas came up in her group.

Sandy said, "That seems a neat career for you, Elinor."

Elinor warmed to her subject. "I'll have to be able to judge market values of collectibles, and give people advice about insurance and taxes. It's a lot but I'm going to love it."

Billie snorted. "I can't stand to collect stuff."

"I'll have to resist collecting for myself. Of course, in London I learned a lot about silver and china and furniture and can make them my specialties. They say if you scratch an Embassy wife you'll find a dealer in antiques."

Martha tested Elinor's sincerity. "You must have been somewhat depressed over not marrying Ralph."

"A little. But he'll always advise me about money matters. For a start, my friend Adele is hiring me to redecorate her house. And I'll still work at church."

Ursula said, "Ask me if you ever have to identify a Japanese print. I can use my magnifying lamp and spot a Hokusai or a Hiroshige."

"Thank you, Ursula. I will ask you."

Ursula took her turn. "I have something to celebrate. Last weekend Michiko and I moved into my house. Blaine drove me down, and we bought food for a month. We fixed up my husband's room for Michiko, and she loves it. She cooks good meals really fast, and gives a Japanese touch to everything. It's great how bits of sliced beef and spinach and soy sauce come out suki-yaki."

"I recall we heard she's a chemist," Martha said.

"Yes, trained in Japan. She uses August's chemistry books to learn the English terms."

"Are you alone all day?" Martha asked.

"Yes, but she leaves me lunch and gets home pretty early to cook, and during the day I often go walking and my neighbors have been stopping by. Blaine gave me a special attachment with large numbers for the phone so I call to chat with her and my grandchildren. I'm going to invite friends from my N.Y.U. class to poetry readings. My only worry is how to get here. Billie brought me today but I wish this group could meet at my house."

Elinor put in, "But Billie's willing to bring you, aren't you, Billie?"

"Sure," said Billie, without much conviction.

Martha looked at her watch. "Now if no one else has headline news, we can proceed to the topic we decided on, 'Mutual Evaluations.' I have some suggestions for that discussion."

"But we finished that topic," said Sandy. "We decided to discuss what feminism could have done for our mothers."

"My recollection is different," Martha replied.

"Dr. Kaufman," Ursula said respectfully, "your memory is of what happened here in the office. But afterward we went to a restaurant and held a session on our own."

Martha's posture went rigid. "Why didn't you tell me?"

Elinor drew a sharp breath. "You haven't been saying much."

"You don't tell us about your life," said Ursula.

"But I'm the leader," said Martha.

"I think feminism leaves more to the members than to a leader," Sandy said.

"That may be. But this group is not about feminism. It's therapy, a discipline for which the leader is trained."

Billie chopped the air with her hand. "Dr. Kaufman, you have convened us and done background therapy with us and I for one don't mind paying for this group. But you can't object if we continue talking after we leave here."

"I can strongly advise against it," said Martha. "As a psychiatrist I am responsible for the quality of the exchanges in this group and thus entitled—in fact, obligated—to know what's shared among you."

Elinor spoke up. "We didn't talk about *you*."

"I'm not implying that that you did. Although you obviously talked about my shingle."

"We did, but that was all," Sandy said. "We could have complained about a lot of blind spots."

"What do you mean by blind spots?" Martha demanded.

"Well, you made me mad when I was doing macramé, and you told me I couldn't do it in the office. Since I did it so I wouldn't smoke, when I stopped smoking I quit therapy."

"I don't allow handiwork here because your whole mind has to concentrate on getting a serious view of yourself and the person you want to be. When that's clear, you'll naturally do what's right for you."

"You never explained that," Sandy asserted. "I just wanted to quit smoking while I was pregnant."

"Good. I know quitting isn't easy."

"You never noticed that I was cleaning up my language," Billie said. Martha's face went stony at this dubious claim, but she remained silent.

"I noticed," said Elinor. "I'm glad you did, Billie. Or anyhow, sorta tried."

"Good," said Billie. "I'm a good kid. Now get this, Kaufman. We're talked out on mutual evaluations and plan to discuss how today's feminism could have helped our mothers."

Martha, summoning her reserves of self-control, refrained from shouting, "Billie, leave this group!" and managed to say, lightly, "Does anyone else need more hot water?" She stepped into her office, closed the door and struggled with her feelings.

I'm really angry at Billie, and she's pushing for another confrontation, having lost the battle of the shingle. I have the choice of swallowing my annoyance for now or challenging her. I could list the ways she's been snatching the leadership, but the catch is that some of her domination of the group has been helpful, in their view. And the irony is that right now while I'm out of the room they're discussing their mothers, the very topic I've been trying to get Billie to explore. I need to get back to the group and keep quiet while I think this through.

She poured water into her mug, and quietly returned to her chair. The discussion was proceeding.

Sandy said, "My mother got a B.A. in anthropology, which she never used in a job. I was her only child, so her energies weren't really challenged—and believe me she had energy!"

"So did my mother," said Ursula, "and it was needed. Cooking and washing clothes took work in those days. My mother could have taught school, but she honestly thought that if she worked for money, it would disgrace my father. If more women had worked outside the home back then, she would have."

Elinor said, "My mother might have disapproved of women's demanding equality, but I'll bet if there'd been more of it in her youth, it would have helped her. Her talents were social—she could have been in politics, but not many women were into that then. So she ended up concentrating on house work. My father's pharmacy supported us, and I believe if she'd had to earn money, she'd have developed herself."

Billie said only, "My mother was sick a lot and died when I was twelve."

Martha remained silent, conjuring up her own mother with fond but guilty thoughts about the barren landscape of her last years.

She was lonely, and I couldn't be with her daily because of struggling to become what she wanted me to be, a doctor. Sadly, ironically, she died while I was at the crisis of my efforts in med school, working too hard to be a reliable daughter. Still, we were never estranged, and to this day I think of us together as one person with many arms, an Indian goddess.

"It's five-thirty," Billie said,

"Yes," said Martha, "and to avoid any further confusion, I'm going to assign a topic for next time which is relevant, 'How Happy Are the Men in My Life?' We should include whether they follow their values and deepest feelings, and how we could help them."

There was silence. Then Sandy said to Martha, "We're not ready to consider men's feelings." Billie stood up abruptly, took her jacket and waited impatiently by the door.

Martha was firm. "What's happening to men is a central question."

"I've talked about Steven's feelings," Elinor said.

Martha ventured, "But how about Ralph's? Did you consider his feelings when you sent him away so he couldn't meet your son that Sunday morning? And did you ask him how he meant it that marrying you would be a financial help? From a man who values money, couldn't that have been a serious proposal? Haven't you said today that he does share if you let him?"

Elinor replied, "Yes, he does, but he's no longer the man in my life. And I'm really glad about that."

"I think about what the world looks like to men," Sandy said, "but women have been downgraded so long that now we come first."

"How true!" said Ursula. Her tone was placating but her sentiment was firm. "My husband never thought of my feelings."

Billie departed, banging the door shut.

"Billie's walked out," Elinor said.

Martha, a note of pleading in her voice, said, "Because it's our stopping time."

No one spoke. Billie had voted with her feet on the issue of men's feelings. Silently, they put on their coats and went out the door, Elinor murmuring, "Thanks for the tea."

They found Billie smoking on the sidewalk in front. Her greeting was that of a union organizer. "You know what's going to happen next week, don't you? We're going to stay home. I've had it with her picking our topics and stressing men's feelings."

"You mean a boycott?" asked Sandy.

"Yes. Let her have the whole meeting by herself next week. She can choose whatever topic she wants, so long as it's men."

"But if we don't come, don't we have to pay anyway?" Ursula asked.

"Not if we cancel two days in advance. That's what I'm going to do. How about you, Sandy?"

"Like I said, we have to think of women first."

Ursula nodded vigorous approval.

Elinor looked doubtful, then managed a little nod.

"You don't have to give an excuse," said Billie.

After they left, Martha sat a few moments at her desk, trying to calm her feelings. Recalling the shocking lettering on her shingle, she went to the window and saw the women still on the sidewalk, only now parting. Elinor, looking depressed, was walking away from Billie who gave her a jolly wave and victory sign.

Why does my shingle mean so much to them? Well, at least Billie got it back in place, hanging straight.

She went to the kitchen for a damp sponge and went out. The women were out of sight. Stretching her arm, she rubbed off Billie's lettering, and noticed the poor condition of Thorny's board. Back at her desk, she pulled out the phone book and jotted down the numbers of three signmakers.

At dinner she said, "The Wednesday Four will be bringing visitors next week. We'll have to meet in the living room."

"So get it fixed up, like you've been planning," Sarah said. "You could do it in a week. Make them comfortable."

Martha went into action. On Thursday evening she hastened to Bloomingdale's where she bought two sofas the color of linen and three matching easy chairs. She was promised a Tuesday delivery.

On Friday she decided to buy one large plant to place by the windows. It didn't turn out to be easy, even in a metropolis, to locate the perfect plant. Shopping by phone, she explained to several florists that she wanted a large plant with both asymmetry and balance, words learned from Ursula. She got one favorable response from a man with a teacherly voice who suggested looking for a *bonsai* tree, a favorite of the Japanese for its characteristic of seeming larger than it actually was. Cheerfully, he made clear that for a tree large enough to place by large windows she'd have to pay an amount in four figures. At her expression of amazement, he asked, "What would you pay for an oriental rug?"

Something in his voice made her trust him, and she knew what, sense or nonsense, she would decide.

This is my moonwalk.

"Could it be returned if I don't like it?"

"Of course. But because of its delicate handling, it'll be a hundred dollars each trip."

She shivered at this, but braced herself. Only in Manhattan, a city of crazy glorious gamblers, could such homage be paid to art. After a solemn pause she said, "I need it by next Wednesday—guests coming. Please find a beautiful big one and charge it to my credit card." She gave him the number, and he promised to find and send a beautiful *bonsai* tree no later than seven the next Tuesday evening.

On Sunday, she and Barry rolled shell-white paint on the living room walls. They left the old carpet down to catch paint spills and at the end cut it into pieces and trashed it. True to what Barry's friend Robin had discovered, the underlying floor was well-preserved hardwood. This lightened the large room and brought out its best features: the high ceiling, large front windows and simple, elegant fireplace. Martha placed Barry's white trophy of the runner on the mantel.

On Monday, a professional team cleaned and waxed the floor, Sarah supervising. That afternoon Martha received a phone call from Ursula, saying she couldn't come on Wednesday as she wouldn't have transportation. Martha felt sorry for her situation. Poor Ursula, she'd also miss seeing the *bonsai*.

To her anxious regret, the *bonsai* didn't arrive on Tuesday evening. Fortunately the sofas and chairs did, about eight o'clock. She fussed at the delivery men about the lateness of the hour and for a generous tip got them to put the new pieces in place and take the old ones out to the sidewalk. By Manhattan custom, people would help themselves and eventually she'd arrange to have any remainders taken away. Before the furniture men drove off she saw, to her surprise, the battered sofa being lifted into their truck, its ball and claw feet seeming to wave goodbye forever.

Upstairs she found Sarah looking comfortable on one of the new sofas, and sank down beside her, exhausted.

Sarah said, "I can't believe so much was done in so short a time. I guess all it takes is knowing what you want."

"And money," Martha added.

"The furniture looks good, and matches the drapes."

"Maybe I should get something for the walls, original art. For now, though, the bareness is soothing."

"But not the bareness of the floor," said Sarah.

Martha brought from her bedroom a long-treasured Turkish rug in earth tones and laid it in the center of the floor.

"They'll love this room," Sarah said. "It's perfect."

"Not until the *bonsai* arrives. As I hope to heaven it will." She went to bed worried about the astronomical gamble she had made with her credit card.

Before seven the next morning, Sarah, who had luckily gone downstairs early, came up to announce, "Your tree is here."

Martha dressed hurriedly and went down. Two young Hispanic men had deposited a big wooden crate on the stoop and stood waiting. Martha was interrupted by an early morning phone call, so Sarah gave the men a pep talk to get them to break open the box on the stoop and carry the tree up to the living room. After it was placed in front of the middle window they stood with her in awe of the strange living presence. The younger man seemed especially entranced with it, saying reverently, *"Muy eleqante."*

Sarah, unable to resist adding drama to the scene, made a bow in Japanese style and said, "Thank you for *Bonsai Eleqante.*" After showing them out the front door and making sure they removed the pieces of the box, she went upstairs again to examine the new arrival. She had expected it to be shaped like a Christmas tree! But it had a stockier look, with a long branch at one side bravely going up beyond several curved branches, and at the other side, a soft bunch of shorter branches. Its gnarled spine reminded her of an old patriarch.

When she went down again she wanted to ask Martha to come see it, curious to see what her reaction would be. But the office door was closed.

Martha's first caller was Billie, the second Sandy and the third Elinor, all saying they wouldn't be coming today. None gave a reason, although Sandy said her friend Danielle definitely wanted to visit the group next week.

What am I to think of this group action? That's what it must be. Ursula cancelled on Monday, explaining that she wouldn't have a ride. Dear Ursula had a simple reason and cancelled in time, and the others didn't. Right now, they're probably hoping I won't make them pay. It's a game, a power play, which is unfair.

She felt again her shock that the group had met without her. Recalling Billie's saying, "Get this, Kaufman!" she felt sure Billie was behind all the calls.

I should have asked her to leave the group. When I saw

them from my window, they all looked unhappy except Billie, who's excited by her own power. Why is she so angry at the world? She has tremendous energy from her need to dominate, only some of it is discharged in the classroom. And yet she is lovable most of the time! She even sounded like a kid, complaining that I didn't notice she's given up bathroom language—I'm waiting for the day! What I can't tolerate is her hostile spirit, so hard on group morale. Today, because of her, the others are being denied therapy. For which they may have to pay anyway.

What exactly went on last week?

She went over her notes.

I was right to correct Billie for taking down my shingle. We heard about Elinor's breakup with Ralph—too bad, but a sign of her new confidence. When I learned they'd held a session without me, I became forceful again. I was right to do so, but Billie's defiance had opened up complaints about my blind spots, starting with Sandy's claim that I made her smoke by not allowing handiwork. Then Elinor defended herself when I pointed out *her* blind spot in sending Ralph away on Sunday morning. I indicated that he might have been hurt, and used the opportunity to suggest they take men's feelings as a topic for discussion, but they refused. Sandy actually said, "We're not ready to consider men's feelings."

That's it. They didn't want me to assign a topic and didn't like the one I proposed. These fortunate suburban women are so absorbed in themselves that they can't think about their partners' feelings. Talk about blind spots! It makes me sad that we humans are blind so often, and so eager for conflict.

Now, after I've invited them here, they call in with late cancellations, chirping over the phone that they're not coming. Without any reasons! A lot of temper tantrums. They should be spanked, the whole bunch of stiff, wobbly Barbie dolls with no feelings.

All this, before I've even had a cup of coffee!

When she'd had it, with a brioche and apricot jam, she went upstairs to see the *bonsai*. Silhouetted against the window, it looked like an abstract sculpture.

It will take some getting used to.

Feeling suddenly weary, she pulled a chair over and sat near the tree, enjoying its nearness, a reminder of Vermont.

This beautiful room I've readied for them is serene like a place of worship. It's too good for them, with their boycott. So let them stay away. Maybe it's the best therapy for them, to probe and discover their own feelings. Still, I don't deserve a boycott.

What a strange morning this has been. Dear tree, I know you're old and wise. I promise to water you faithfully and get the right tree-barber to clip you, like the florist said I should. I don't want you to feel this is a strange place. Well, I'm in a strange place too, with my group, but I suppose time will settle things. Anyway, there's just a half hour before my first patient is due, and I have work to do in the office.

From the door, she took a backward glance at the *bonsai* and felt a thrill. "It's magnificent!" she said aloud.

Back at her desk, she sorted her old mail, mostly junk. The one item she opened contained an invitation to a one-day miniconference in a hospital near Gracie Mansion.

"Therapists! Come share professional theories and experiences," it offered. Scanning the list of workshop leaders, she found the name of her best friend, Dr. Lucille Woodward, and a handwritten note, "Come if you can. Lucy."

It's too bad I have to miss a lot of events, and Lucy's was no doubt worthwhile. When we were in training, she always got excited about ideas. I haven't seen her for months, since she and Dan had me to dinner at their place. And now I've missed her latest project. No, wait! It's today! I'll call her and check it out.

Lucy answered. "Oh, Maggie, how nice to hear from you! How are you?"

"Pretty well, just very busy."

"Are you coming to our miniconference today?"

"Yes. It sounds useful." Martha felt pleased to have decided so quickly. "But I can't get away until after noon."

"Too bad. My workshop's in the morning."

"Sorry to miss it. Is there any particular theory behind the conference?"

"A variety of theories. There's a new guy from California who claims he's cloistered serenely with Freud while the rest of us flounder in chaotic innovations! But this afternoon I'm going to a workshop at two o'clock offered by my old colleague, Tom Rappaport, who's awfully good. Why don't you come with me? We can meet at the registration desk at one forty-five."

"Sounds good. I'll be there."

35

A Career Opportunity

Sarah, after giving Martha lunch and seeing her off to Lucy's conference, took the opportunity to clean the office.

The regular cleaner hadn't come, and though cleaning wasn't Sarah's job, she'd rather do it than go off schedule. She vacuumed the floor, wiped finger marks off the white-painted woodwork and dusted all the furniture except Martha's desk. In the sunniness of the room with its new drapes the desk called out for attention, but it was off-limits to cleaners, and Martha herself kept the leather top waxed, as well as the leather-bound appointment book. This book held a separate fascination for Sarah because it had power over Martha's time, and the only time sure to be free for conversation was at dinner. She dusted the outside of the book, took one quick look inside to see the slots full of names and closed it with an unfriendly little thump of her thumb.

The telephone was dusty. Sarah believed a phone should be spotless like the one in her bedroom, which rang only when Barry called. Still she cleaned it frequently, and if it rang in her hands, she'd tell it, "Don't wet me while I'm changing your diaper." Today she thoroughly cleaned Martha's phone, relieved that it didn't have the nerve to ring.

She examined the tape recorder, also dusty. Martha had told her in Vermont that if you pushed two buttons at once, something might be erased.

I wish she'd show me how to work it, and let me hear what they say.

Like a child delicately running a finger around the icing at the edge of a cake plate without poking the cake, she cleaned around the buttons.

This button, "Record," is important. You don't need to go to therapy to learn about other people's troubles—people anywhere in town will tell you—but to record your troubles must be a treat. I'm not going to push it, just pretend.

Bent as her forefinger was from arthritis, she suspended it above the button and spoke to it. "This is Sarah. I'm still here at age seventy-two and getting homesick for Vienna, where life is like it should be, comfortable. I don't hold with women's liberation. I loved my husband and we each did our share. Most men try to be good. My son was good to me and left me a good daughter-in-law and a good grandson. I cook for them, so I'm still useful in this world. But I would like to schmooze with a few women once in a while because . . . well, I'm your friendly neighborhood bubbi."

She tossed her head, lifted her finger, then again held it over the button. "In this world it's not easy, but a woman can be a *mensch* too. Yes, a *mensch*." She raised her hand in mock feminist shock, and then said defensively, "Well, that happens to be the word. It means to be the best you can be." She stood straight. "So who's preaching? There's no magic button to *oisreden die hertz*. Even if I really pushed it."

She flipped her feather duster over the machine and started for the kitchen. She had unloaded her heart, now it was time to unload the dishwasher.

On the subway, Martha studied the day's workshop titles and mulled over one, "Rev Up That Slow Couch and Steer It into the Fast Lane." Lucy's workshop that morning had been called "Do You Get A or D—Analytic or Directive?" The two o'clock workshop Lucy had promised her was called "Repositioning," a word familiar to Martha because it came up frequently on her computer, reminding her of her teenage dancing classes.

At the registration desk, she wrote on her name tag:

"Martha Kaufman, M.D., Psychotherapist." She had just pinned it on her lapel when Lucy came up, looking professional in a Wedgewood blue suit, her soft brown curls as bouncy as ever. Beaming with pleasure, she greeted Martha and in feigned amazement pointed to her own name tag, "Lucille Woodward, M.D., Psychotherapist." "We've got the same bar code, so we're both smart!" she said.

"I may not be," said Martha, laughing. "I'm here to learn more about group therapy. I know you've done it for a while, and I'm giving it a try."

"I've done it since Bion was a baby! And soon I'm to lead a basic course for group therapy leaders—I want to tell you about it. But we'd better go in now to Rappaport's workshop. I hope you like him."

She led Martha into a nearby room where a dark-haired man, seemingly in his fifties, was about to address the group. Martha's first impression was that he had a pleasantly confident manner and personal warmth.

He began by saying, "Our concern in this workshop is how therapists may deal constructively with their own feelings when a patient leaves therapy. In training we were told to expect a day when a patient would claim to be ready to graduate, no longer feeling dependent. We learned that we'd quite possibly feel strongly that the patient wasn't ready to leave. Yes, we therapists are accused of wanting to prolong treatment but I think it's because we have standards to meet. You may recall that the great analyst, Kohut, named four qualities patients should demonstrate before concluding treatment: 'Empathy for self, creativity, humor, and wisdom.' Not perfection of character, please note."

There was a murmur of agreement from his audience, and he smiled. "Your reaction tells me you know your Kohut! Like Freud, he allowed a patient to graduate without having become perfect. I'm not a strict Freudian but it's part of our history to recall Freud's saying of one patient leaving therapy that she was 'no longer mentally ill, only capable of living in everyday neurotic misery.' My point is that the moment of leaving therapy should be more seriously considered.

"Of course, we all believe that goals like empathy for self, creativity, humor and wisdom should be built into the process from the beginning. But try as we may, there may come a surprise, notably when we work with groups. One day we may simply find an empty seat, or get a phone call, 'I'm quitting therapy.' We're indeed lucky if we also get the question, 'How much do I owe?'"

The audience laughed ruefully.

"We're left with a slump in our professional pride. And, even more hazardous, a slump in the morale of the remaining group members. They may blame themselves—or the therapist—for the departure. I find that for the health of the group, my feelings as leader must be mollified, to restore confidence."

How appropriate, Martha thought. I like this leader.

"So today we will imagine a suitable goodbye being exchanged between a therapist and a departing patient. All art requires practice, and in this role-play you can practice how to feel when a patient suddenly leaves you. In fact, even if the departure was planned in advance—and even if you yourself initiated it—a goodbye can cause you pain, which can be eased if you deal with it creatively, in a way to encourage the patient's return to you. Try for a suitable closure, maybe by mentioning some sign of growth which the patient has shown recently, even a small detail, like thanking someone for something. It must be true, not an exaggeration, something encouraging without being unduly so. It will show the patient that you've been observant, that you care.

"For this role-play, you'll work in twos and take turns playing the therapist and the patient. Draw on your real experiences, and invent a positive goodbye. I call this 'Repositioning.' Please choose a partner."

There was a hub-hub while participants chose partners.

When they were ready to work, Dr. Rappaport said, "There are extra chairs, so each couple should place one to be the 'hot seat' for the patient who is departing."

Martha and Lucy placed their empty chair against a wall so it directly faced them.

"I'll go first," said Lucy. "I'll be the therapist."

"Who is the patient you are facing?" Martha prompted.

"It's a real case, a man named Ross, a thirty-three-year-old jazz musician who suddenly dropped out with a hasty 'I'm broke!' after being in one of my groups for two years . . . Hello, Ross, I know you've come to see me about quitting therapy. I'd regret your quitting now, as you seem to be enjoying the group lately—coming on time, not walking out mad like you used to, and being interested in the others." Her voice became warmer. "Since you've come to terms with your relationship with your father, you've made efforts to change. In my view, it's early for you to graduate, but let's hope that with real effort you'll continue to make progress. If the going is rough, you may wish to return some time in the future and I'll be here."

Lucy then sat in the chair by the wall and, assuming the role of Ross, spoke to her old chair. "Hello, Dr. Woodward. This is Ross. I came to see you to get some things off my mind. Therapy costs too much and people are led to expect too much. The people in the group talk all around the point and you don't stop them. I'd rather walk out than listen. Well, I guess they don't like me walking out, and I wouldn't like them walking out. I'm learning to be friendlier to others and to myself, but money-wise, I can't come any more. I'm glad you expected me to improve, and I have gotten better. I'll keep trying, I promise. You're a caring person. I'll miss you,"

Lucy returned to her own seat, holding back tears. "I know his warm feelings really exist."

"You were great!" Martha exclaimed. "I guess this 'suitable closure' calls for 'Aha!' when the whole picture comes into focus, right?"

"I hope so," said Lucy. "What I need right now is to be quiet for a few minutes." She sat with her eyes closed.

Martha was moved by the sharing, which brought relief that it was all right for doctors to admit they cared deeply about patients. Her need for sharing had not been met in her old days at the clinic, where a sign, "Therapists don't blab" was posted on the wall of the staff room. Her fellow psychiatrists were close-mouthed and spoke of their patients passively in therapeutic terms. She had never revealed to them how devotedly she thought about her patients, nor how prayerfully she cherished real hopes for each one. Only Norman and Sarah knew. Today she could confide in a sympathetic professional.

Lucy soon opened her eyes, saying candidly, "I can't tell you how angry that patient was until he explored childhood causes of his anger and tried on new emotional patterns." She paused. "You see, I'm using your analytic methods!"

"Good!" said Martha.

"Then he suddenly quits therapy and leaves me with a hole in my heart. Two years' work just walked out. I feel like a potter must feel if somebody steals a bowl that isn't quite finished. The bowl is gone, as you expected, but so is your chance to see the design completed. It's a double hurt."

"Maybe it'll hurt less now that you recognize he's grateful."

"Yes, and he is, I know. I feel better knowing that."

"This is a good exercise," said Martha. "Is it original with Dr. Rappaport, do you think?"

"It may be. He's a wise person. He and his wife were friends with Dan and me before she died last year."

"I like his style."

"So, Maggie, you're on."

Martha sat in the "hot seat" and said, "I'll start out being my patient, Billie. She's a brainy teacher, always very frank, and sometimes condescending. She hasn't quit therapy but may be about to. You're going to hear some words that I don't normally use."

"Go, girl!" said Lucy.

"Okay... You, Kaufman, don't work hard enough. Shit, I work harder with a debater over facts than you do with a patient over feelings. You must be having a professional crisis, as I see you updating some of your methods. I never could count on my mother, and you often seemed to be flabby-minded and uncertain, like she was. Besides, you're sentimental, wanting me to love everybody. But when you made me put back your shingle, you did okay. I'm on a family track now with Mike and can thank you, so I'm quitting therapy with a good impression of you, even though I prefer a feminist group."

Martha explained, "Some letters of the word 'psychotherapist' were faint on my shingle and she took it down. Someone—and Ursula told me later it was Billie—lettered in the spaces so it looked like 'psycho the rapist.'"

Lucy laughed. "Shall I call you 'The Rapist'?"

"She's sharp, but I wasn't amused, the way she did it. I made her hang the shingle up again, and I sounded like Thorny. Do you remember Thorny's voice?"

"Who could forget?" They laughed.

Martha returned to her own chair and talked to the imaginary Billie. "You might before long reap the rewards of your long years of supporting your son. But you never say anything appreciative of him, just regard him as a chore. Your other relationships need fine-tuning also—in the group, you seem able to relate to people only if you're in charge or able to control them in some way. It was my aim to help you gain compassion, but you've dodged what therapy could do for you. After Mike's friends helped you find him, did you ever tell them you were grateful?"

Lucy intervened. "Maggie, try to stick to what you've seen in the office."

Martha paused, then plunged on. "Listen, Billie, in group therapy you've got a right to your own feelings, but

424

you can't treat the others like students you can dominate. A brilliant mind isn't enough—you need to develop some acceptance of others as well as of yourself."

"Bravo!" said Lucy, "But maybe you're a bit too critical of her to bring her back to therapy. Can you think of a way to praise her?"

Martha felt shaky. "Nothing recent. She once made a suggestion to help Ursula find a housemate. But it's hard to get her to remain inside the analytic situation. She's the sort who stays slightly outside the group, even when she expected to be their leader. But true leaders accept the hierarchies of power, the Establishment, which Billie doesn't recognize. I'm the Establishment now. Imagine that!"

Dr. Rappaport was calling for the end of the exercise. As they moved their chairs back to join the others, Lucy said, "I felt like saying 'Aha!' when you said she'd dodged what therapy could do for her."

"Thank you," Martha said. She felt lighter and glad she'd spoken frankly before her old friend.

Lucy didn't sit, but whispered, "Maggie, it's been fun. I have to make some phone calls at three but I must talk with you, and this room will be empty at three-thirty, so please stay here and I'll be back. Here's my flyer for you to look at."

She picked up her coat, then whispered, "In case I forget later, we're having a party on my birthday next month and I'm inviting you and Tom Rappaport." She tiptoed out.

Martha stayed through the final evaluation and when it was over, read about the six-week series Lucy was offering called Group Therapy Basics. It was to start in two weeks on Wednesday afternoons.

It would be good for me to take a course from Lucy, but of course I'm tied up Wednesday afternoons.

Or at least I *was*. Well, I could at least hear what Lucy's planning to do in her course, as there's a chance my wayward group might fall apart altogether. I won't tell her my problem, just be vague as to whether I can sign up.

Lucy soon came in, bubbling over with a question. "Maggie, did you look at my flyer? Would you please be co-leader? I'm still in the planning stage, but five people signed up this morning."

Martha almost gasped, not having guessed she'd be asked to join as co-leader, not a student. "I'd love to, but don't know yet if I'll be free."

"Can we talk about my plans, anyhow? I'd like your input."

"If you're starting two weeks from today, could you train me in time?"

"Hey," said Lucy, "therapists with your common sense and humor are hard to come by. You're creative, too. So let's plan."

They drew up a list of questions to send ahead to participants to learn their backgrounds, and Lucy took from her briefcase an outline of the course which Martha scanned with interest. The first topic, "Orientation for New Groups," included her own requirements: strict times for starting and stopping, democratic sharing of discussion time, no smoking, no handiwork, no talking to anyone outside about what anyone said. She praised Lucy for one rule she wished she'd made: no sharing among the group outside the office, going for coffee or telephoning.

Lucy grinned. "Some people might say this forbids free speech, but I justify the rule because everything said in the group is part of our understanding of one another, and absence of even one person or the leader distorts the process."

"That's a good rule," Martha said.

"Briefing on rules is never-ending. I often have to schedule an extra private session if I have someone who's always angry and aiming at subverting the group's purpose. I try to determine the type of anger that's present. There are so many kinds!"

"Like all the Eskimo words for snow!"

"Or like a poet's word for *love*! I'm getting good at quickly squelching a self-appointed *provocateur* who clearly threatens the survival of the group. But I don't call him or her a Drop-out or a Throw-out, but a Start-over. We have so many groups in Manhattan that some of us therapists have a network and can refer a difficult patient to a new group for a fresh start. It often works. Of course, whenever anyone leaves, there's the problem of replacement. There are usually people on a waiting list, but a newcomer is under a handicap and may need orientation. We arrange an invitation to visit a group session. Then, if the visitor wants to join and the group is agreeable, I brief the new person on some key items. If, for instance, the group already knows that one member has recently gone through the suicide of a family member, it's only right for the newcomer to know that."

"Does the group usually accept a new person?"

"Yes. I recall only once when it didn't work. I tried to introduce a man into a group of women. It happened he was terribly obese and a dominating talker, and they didn't want him."

Martha found this easy to believe.

"I do make it clear to a new member that polite masks have to come off. Feelings can and should be let loose and it's important to be prepared for angry outbursts which have to be examined. A new person can feel threatened."

"I've invented a little phrase," Martha said. "Feel, reveal, heal."

"That's good. I'm writing that down."

Impressed with Lucy's matter-of-factness, Martha was glad she hadn't told her how she'd agonized over problems which were apparently part of the process. But she knew she'd learned a lot on her own and offered to draw up a list of dos and don'ts. Lucy wanted it. Feeling she had to be frank about her own uncertainty, she said, "Lucy, I want to be your co-leader, but I honestly may not be free. I'll let you know."

"I hope and pray you're free. And thanks for helping today." She looked at her watch and rose suddenly. "I've got to go home and get dinner for Dan. I work a lot of evenings. You know, men get lonely too." She departed.

Martha sat thinking about what Lucy had said, so like what she herself had thought about Elinor's sending Ralph away on Sunday morning. Men get lonely too.

My Norman must have been lonely when he went twice a day to a bar, and I didn't realize it. My man with a bad heart had a wife with a hard heart. I thought I had good emotional patterns with men since childhood, as my father was so lovable. But maybe I kept my childish concept that a man is super-strong.

Here in this room something good is happening to me. I know it's not true that Norman drank kummel because he felt neglected by me. He loved our vacations of hiking and singing together in Vermont. We enjoyed raising Barry. We appreciated Sarah. We went to the theater, bathed together, and made love in deep tenderness. He knew and understood I couldn't be with him all the time, trying to establish my practice and earn enough to pay for his medical care beyond what insurance covered.

I've had about a year of grieving, and, most likely, have finished the hardest part. I can rest in the sure knowledge that Norman lived the life he chose. Always he chose to love me. I was happy loving him. Nothing could cure his heart, and his big spirit will always be with me. He was never bitter, always compassionate and always had a light touch. To show my appreciation of the wonderful person he was, I can keep my own life happily useful.

One thing I could do to steady myself is to have a quiet weekend alone in the cottage. I should go up there for a personal retreat. I can fly to Boston and rent a car—I'll phone in the morning and make a reservation on a plane for Saturday.

When she stepped out of the building, she felt uplifted. Here I am uptown, the evening is my own, and I have

428

something to celebrate, being back in touch with colleagues. I'm a connected person again.

She asked the taxi driver to take her to the Hilton. In the hotel, she went directly to the upscale grill, which she had missed the night of the omelettes with Berson, and ate a quiet dinner. Then she walked three blocks to Carnegie Hall and bought a ticket to the Rachmaninoff concert which was about to start.

During the music, she made decisions.

I will definitely send bills to Billie, Elinor and Sandy for their late cancellation today. Not to do so would be failing to teach them to face consequences. As for Billie, my unconscious was speaking when I role-played a farewell. It was wishful thinking but it made sense. She's not only dodging her own therapeutic tasks, she's interfering with the learning of others, seizing leadership she hasn't earned. It's right to ask her to leave.

Aha! That part was easy.

The music crashed, then soared, stiffening her resolve to deal with her regrets about Billie as she had dealt with other griefs in her life, as cool truth.

But her sorrow didn't dissolve under the buffeting of the music.

It'll be a painful struggle to let Billie go, after all my efforts with her. Her disruption of the group is a Pandora's box which I don't want to open.

The music became harmonious, problem-solving.

Today Tom Rappaport's exercise helped me pry open the lid of Pandora's box, and now it's up to me to deal with the hazardous contents. First, Billie is no monster, she's just a little girl in some ways, still feeling abandonment and rage at a mother who couldn't cherish three children properly, and who was ill. Billie transfers to me her anger over early neglects. She needs a velvet glove over a strong therapist's hand, and I was too lenient. Well, it was all right for me to let her show some affection for me, like teasing me and giving me a cactus. I praised her for buying a snow plow for Mikey. But I wasn't strong enough, didn't push her to learn about herself.

Definitely, if I dismiss her, it will be my failure as much as hers. Well, not to blame myself too much—I was succeeding, slowly, in getting her to acknowledge her affection for Mikey. She looked for him, he called her and came home to return to school as she wanted. They're learning to love one another.

It was the group that was too much for her. I overdid my efforts to be non-directive, and Billie, accustomed to leading, couldn't refrain from taking over. I should have stopped her the minute she tried, to protect the others. But since I've let her go too far, there may be nothing to do but let her go. Or lose them all.

The music didn't stop unwinding its conflicts. Majestically it pounded out its tremendous, unavoidable conclusion.

I started leading a group before I was ready. I thought knowing the patients as individuals beforehand would be enough preparation, but I should have observed some actual groups, or assisted in one first. People like Billie can show behavior patterns in a group that they don't show in solo treatment. The experts stress that all members have to share in the interactions of the group. It's a laboratory, a demonstration. I was right to intervene about the shingle and should have shared more of my commitments to the process. My real feelings. In a group, a confrontation with one may have repercussions on others, and the leader must bring out patients' gut interactions. Even violent ones can be expected and discussed down to their origins. There should be no stumbling over loss of privacy. The process truly is one of feel, reveal and heal.

In a taxi going home, she sat in silence.

I'm a sort of mentor for Billie. I don't call this countertransference, I call it professional responsibility. I also admire her for making her way in a tough world. Still, as long as she's in the group it can't function properly. She

430

makes it a power struggle, and as leader I have to see that peace prevails, without hurting her or the others.

Instead of asking her to leave, maybe I should finesse it and dissolve the whole group. They've all been getting better and I could give it to them full blast, convince them that they should all graduate!

That idea seemed promising until she was sitting at her desk that night.

How would a group graduation play out in terms of fairness to each woman? Well, Elinor seems serious about preparing for a job as an appraiser. My strong hunch is that there won't be any more suicide attempts, as she knows herself better now and wants to earn money herself, not be supported and dominated by a husband. She's lucky Ralph wants to finance her business course, but she'll need help in remaining steady through the new relationships he's throwing her into! Of course, these new friendships may benefit her kids. Even Steven may be helped.

No, Kohut wouldn't say Elinor is ready to graduate. Some day she will be. Then we can do it properly.

Sandy is past her emergency and learned when she was younger how to change course without collapsing under defeat. She keeps her show on the road and seems to be setting out as a promising starlet. Still, she'll need support through her struggles toward the big time as wife, mother and artist.

Ursula is like a beautiful sailing ship which is still afloat. Treatment can't cure her established quirks but can strengthen her strengths. Eventually she and August might have a simple Golden Wedding celebration in the hospice. He deserves that, having fathered and supported a family faithfully, even if he didn't have a poet's imagination. For herself, she'll probably be able to sail along with her Japanese housemate. If she shares her article with kindred souls and publishes a poem or two, there may not be a shipwreck.

431

Obviously, graduations would be premature at this time, and will probably be timed differently for each. The only threat is Billie's attempt to run things, which has to be dealt with, brought to what Rappaport calls a suitable closure.

Like throwing her out.

She went to bed and had a dream.

She was in the old office, before the remodeling. Norman took a bottle of champagne from the silver bucket and brought a glass toward where she was lying on the sofa face down, sobbing. "You don't know what I've done—I've let Billie ruin my group! After I've helped her and loved her all this time, now I hate her. She's started a boycott and they've all gone along."

Norman was quiet as he sat beside her. Always beside her. It was no ghost. In his own voice he said, "We try too hard for justice. Justice can be harsh. Try forgiveness. Forgive Billie. You've helped her to define herself. Draw a circle that takes her in. And forgive yourself. You were new to group therapy—why not learn more about it from Lucy?"

She looked at him, caught his dear smile, then brightened and quipped, "But what will the redheads do on Wednesdays? Will they all leave me and go with Billie?" He sat shaking his head.

She woke up early the next morning and lay in bed, her discard of Billie now challenged.

To learn to forgive is as hard as recovering from an addiction. I'll have to build up her strengths and see that she gets strong in herself, not in dominating others. It's odd how group therapy stirred action in all of them. And in me. There's a kind of energy in it that seems to speed things up. I'd like to learn to be good at it. In fact, I'd like to become a top-notch group therapist, as I might if I work with Lucy. That settles Wednesday afternoons. I work with Lucy.

But I won't graduate the Wednesday Four. They wanted

432

a break and they can have one! They're all well enough to withstand six weeks without me. After that I'll make them into a really working therapy group, with better techniques of analysis. I think they'll come. I'll sell them the idea. I'll try to make use of some of Billie's ideas, try a few consciousness-raising topics, and let her be a sort of co-leader once in a while. I can keep her on a string, maybe an elastic one. If she tries to use the break to organize the others into a consciousness-raising group, they'll get tired of her bossiness and come back to me. She couldn't steal my group even if she tried! I'll just have to suggest the right thing to keep her busy, and hope she'll come back when we resume. If she wants, she can get a consciousness-raising group together on Long Island. Ursula can invite women to her house and Billie can give them a lift-off into space, raising their consciousnesses to Venus and beyond!

She giggled.

Well, there I go, putting down consciousness-raising! Maybe she'll come back with us if I suggest that the experience of being in a real therapy group might help her run her kind of groups in the future. She may even decide one day to free her potential through therapy with someone wiser than I. Maybe Lucy. Or Tom Rappaport.

So we'll take a break and I'll work with Lucy and in six weeks meet my own Wednesday group again on a new basis. Also Lucy organizes new groups all the time and I'll lead a couple of evening ones in the place Lucy rents. What a good idea! I'll get one afternoon free and go to classes . . . in art history, foreign affairs, poetry. In Vermont this weekend, I'll sort out what I want to do.

As she went down the stairs to breakfast, Barry hurried past her on his way to work, saying, "Mom, I'm taking a long weekend off to go skiing."

She managed to call after him, "That's nice. Will the snow still be good?"

"Maybe not, but we'll clean the yard and have fires in the fireplace—maybe get out the old Scrabble game and find out how to spell 'commitment.' " The front door slammed behind him.

Well, I'm still Mom, the one who stays home. And it's great to see him so cheerful, more like himself. Bless him, he has a right to the slopes he climbed with Norman, and to the clouds and trees he shared with me. Not to mention romance that comes with starlight on the mountain! I was about to make a plane reservation, but I can have a weekend alone in the cottage any time. Or fly on a three-day special to a Caribbean island.

This weekend I'd rather stay home anyway. I'll sit by the fire and read my collection of the travel sections of the *Times*.

Wonder why Barry mentioned commitment?

To Sarah she said, "Would you like to go uptown on Saturday night and have dinner at the new fondue restaurant? I'll bet after you taste their fondue you can improve on it for us."

Sarah grinned. "Guess what? My appointment book says, 'Saturday night, fondue.' "

36

The Old Order Changeth

Back from the fondue restaurant, Martha sat relaxing in an easy chair in the living room. She raised her glass and said, "Here's to living in luxury!"

As her treat, Sarah had poured kummel, the weekly glass she called their Saturday Night Special. Her toast now was, "May this comfort improve our characters."

Martha nodded. "Like Ursula says, 'Simple elegance penetrates the soul.'" She patted the arm of her chair.

"What's your favorite improvement?" Sarah asked.

Martha spoke without hesitation. "The *bonsai*. It's the most necessary thing in here."

Sarah looked at it attentively. "It was a good idea of Barry's to put two track lights on it—it makes double shadows against the drapes."

"I never noticed before how the heat from the register makes the drapes ripple. *Elegante* seems to be waving in a breeze."

They gazed at it in silence until Sarah said, "It does have an astonishingly right shape!"

After Sarah went to bed, Martha sat alone.

I'm still vaguely sorry I moved Barry's trophies out. Norman would have wanted to keep them, but as the French saying goes, one must suffer to create beauty. Barry understands. He knows his childhood is significant to me and that I hope he'll have children who'll earn their own trophies. The Greek runner is enough in here.

Before going to bed she walked up to the third floor and looked into his room. As always, there were piles of books on the floor, now stacked neatly. There were no papers on the desk, only a few clothes in the closet.

Is Barry moving out?

A pang shot through her and she gritted her teeth, catching her breath.

It was bound to come. We've had a year of refreshing time under the same roof. I will miss him, yet I know we'll always be friends in a spirit of equality, beyond what either of us feels with anyone else.

Aloud, bravely, she said the lines of a Tennyson poem, learned years ago:

> "The old order changeth, yielding place to new,
> And God fulfills Himself in many ways
> Lest one good custom should corrupt the world."

At breakfast she asked Sarah, "Has Barry said anything to you about moving out?"

"No, but early Friday, I was on the stoop getting the paper and a young woman was helping him pack his car. They both waved to me."

"What did she look like?"

"Didn't see her face. Dark hair."

"He told me he was going to Vermont with someone. She may be the reason he's been gone so much lately."

"From the piles of stuff he brought down, he was taking all his clothes."

"And you didn't tell me?"

"Actually, he said as he went by, 'Don't tell Mom. Yet.' I thought he meant about the girl."

"Could be they were taking his clothes to her place before they drove north. He probably didn't want to explain that, figured I'd think he'd clutter the cottage. Could this be good news?"

"He will choose right," Sarah said piously. "He's being sure he's found the right woman before we meet her."

"I hope so. He was certainly in a good mood when we painted the living room, though he talked only about his work and that he likes my house improvements."

Sarah nodded and Martha turned to her. "Well, Sarah, some things are changing around here."

"Let's talk about it in a couple of months."

"What do you mean?"

"Well, if he moves out—and I'm guessing he will—there won't be much cooking."

"We'll eat out more often. And we'll go to matinees on Saturdays."

Sarah smiled as she stood up from the breakfast table and went to the sink. "I'm ready."

"In fact, we can see a show this coming Wednesday, as I'll be free. You can get tickets to whatever you think is good."

"Okay, I will. How come you're free?"

"I canceled the redheads for a week so they can cool off. Wednesday after next I'm going to meet them individually to talk over their personal agendas. Then we'll take a six-week break—because I have a new career opportunity. Lucy has asked me to be co-leader of a workshop that lasts six weeks. After that, the redheads will start meeting again, if my plans work out. I'll talk with them about it. They're coming here next Saturday evening."

"Oh, so they are coming?"

"Yes. Each of them is bringing a guest—this will be the session with visitors that started our fix-up frenzy in the living room."

"Oh, I'm glad they're going to see it!"

Martha laughed. "They'll never know the favor they did me, giving me a push to do it. Now my secret agenda is to serve them champagne to celebrate!"

"The room deserves a party!"

"Well, it's mainly a professional matter. We'll discuss some feminist issues, so their guests can join in. My four will give their evaluations of the group, and following that I'll be preparing them for when we meet again. I plan to intensify therapy with them, make it more rigorous, more like analysis. I figure that a little champagne could prepare them for getting down to work."

"I know they'll like the room."

"And my new shingle outside with the spotlight on it."

"Is everyone bringing a friend who might start therapy?"

"Not really. I think Sandy's friend, a young single mother, is probably the only serious prospect. Elinor's bringing a neighbor, Billie's bringing a friend who works for a Black newspaper, and Ursula's Japanese housemate is coming."

"It's nice for Ursula to have someone to go out with."

Each in her own thoughts, they sat silent, until Sarah said, shyly, "Martha, I want to tell you something. You know I can live on the investments my father left me—I don't need much—and I plan to go back to Vienna and live with my sister. She's getting old and so am I."

"Oh, Sarah, have you been thinking about that? How can I let you go?" She stood and walked over to Sarah at the sink.

"You'll be fine."

They hugged and both cried quietly.

Martha found her voice first, "I'll never forget how you stuck by me and Barry when we needed you."

"I needed to be needed and you helped me out."

"Well, if you really go, one of us will fly over to see you every year. Or I'll send you tickets to fly here for visits."

"Of course," said Sarah. She held out her arms like wings and bent from side to side, grinning. "Frequent fliers!"

"Let's not tell him you're going until the time is definite."

"If I leave first, I'll fly back for his wedding."

Teasing, Martha said, "For you I'll save the pleasure of thoroughly cleaning his room."

"*Ungelegt und ungepechget!* Well, today I'm making a real fondue and you'd better like it." She put on her apron and started shredding cheese.

That Sunday afternoon, while Sarah was writing letters as usual, Martha carried a stack of travel sections to the

438

living room, started a fire in the fireplace, and pulled an easy chair in front of it.

It makes more sense to sit here than to fly and rent a car and drive to the cottage. Now where shall I travel to?

Her first article was a full description of the pleasures and mind-stretching realities of Venice. She absorbed the details of the pictures, and remembered it all, the pigeons in St. Mark's square, the adventure of boarding a gondola and then the slow ride under bridges. Once again she succumbed to the bewildering, even appalling, thought of a city whose gardens were not dirt and flowers but water. And now, alas, decay. She closed her eyes in empathy with the Venetians in their endless efforts to preserve their great buildings.

I can grieve with them over the water damage, but Venice remains in my mind a perfect place, so powerful are my memories of being there with Norman. It was our honeymoon and I found some things about him surprising, like his easy familiarity with Italian money. But I found him to be no puzzle in bed, just my naturally masterful, lovable teddy bear with the power to make me happy. The power to be happy is stronger than anything that can bring us down. For me, Venice can never decay, it's immortalized in my heart.

Her next choice was an article about a world wonder she had never seen, the Great Wall of China. Its history was one of many challenges. The human costs of securing so massive a structure to hundreds of miles of uneven terrain. The vast number of horses and men needed to defend it! And today, the upkeep required. She scrutinized each picture.

I'll likely never see it but I feel as if I had, and I won't forget it.

What will happen here Saturday evening? How's Billie going to behave? What if she flares out at me or just sits being antagonistic all evening? Oh dear, how I'd like to hear just one sentence of approval or gratitude from that young woman! But it's my weakness, wanting it. Maybe I can think of a strategy for keeping her in the group. If I can, and also maintain the dignity of a gracious hostess, I'll deserve the reward of going to Lucy's party.

It will be fun at Lucy's, just being myself among friends. There's been so little of that in my life this year of work. Still, it hasn't been a bad year. Maybe, like Ursula I could write a poem. About missing Norman and disciplining myself to keep working. It must be satisfying to write poems. Maybe I should try it.

Aha! I joked to Lucy that I was joining the Establishment, and it's not a joke. Norman and Thorny always told me I could be a leader. Maybe someday I'll feel like telling them, "Dear dreamers, I have stayed the course." For now, I can say, "Thank you, dear Long Island Ladies, for letting me practice group therapy on you. Let's keep on until we get it right."

Life's going to be fun. Lucy says Tom Rappaport likes to dance and if he and I click tomorrow, she's promised we'll be a foursome at the Waldorf on New Year's Eve—I'll even wear my sparkling stockings! But only if we click. If we don't, I'll know. If Barry can take time to be sure, I can too.

She turned to her travel sections again and sat arranging around herself a nest of clippings about faraway places.

That evening, she tried writing a poem.

> I miss him, my sweet love,
> my conundrum, my teddy bear,
> my gondola.
> But death told me to disembark
> and live my transition through.
>
> I swore off love and its unknowns
> and engineered my way,
> defined a self for living out my time.
> I have a Chinese wall inside my mind,

and early learned to walk straight stretches,
keeping in line my teams of five horses abreast
and tens of soldiers side by side, on foot.

Walking alone I now am finding how
to wind through mountains,
curve around their bases, cling to the slopes
of valleys in far distances, exploring.
I walk this lonely wall because I am it,
a mystic above trees,
faithfully, wisely being who I am.
I stay aloft and find I somehow can
pass turret after turret,
not jump from the stony spine
nor abandon the righteous ramparts
but go the miles, singing to myself
of being free to merge into my uses.

37

Ten Feet Tall

For the session on Saturday evening, Martha wore a simple navy silk dress with a cut flattering to her figure. She pinned on a carved ivory brooch bequeathed to her by her grandmother, and wore her high-heeled sandals.

Ten minutes before her guests were due, she stood checking the lamp-lit living room. Champagne glasses were on a tray on the low table behind one of the sofas. A white linen napkin covered two bottles of Chandon cooling in the silver ice bucket. More bottles, previously chilled, were beside them. The easy chairs and sofas were arranged in an informal circle.

The statuesque *bonsai* tree looked green in front of its black shadow. Its wavery longest branch extended into a realm of hope, and the short branches on the other side lent stability and softness. She felt reverence for the tree's age, and murmured to it, "Dear *Elegante*, I'll never tell how much you cost, nor ever be so extravagant again. Please share with me your dignity and humor—I need them tonight."

She walked downstairs and soon greeted Billie and Fern. Billie quickly stepped inside and strode down the hall. Fern introduced herself and followed Billie. Ursula and Michiko were coming up behind them, Ursula taking time to look at the shingle. "It has a light on it," she said as she mounted the stairs of the stoop. "Dr. Kaufman, this is Michiko."

Michiko bowed politely.

"I'm glad you came and that Billie could give you a ride. Let's go to the office so you can leave your coats before we go upstairs to the living room."

Billie heard this, having already hung her coat and

Fern's, and marched ahead up the stairs. Fern waited with the others. When they entered the living room Billie was looking around like an inspector. To Martha she announced, "You have some nice things here."

"Thank you," Martha replied. "Please sit wherever you like. I'm going down to watch the front door." She hastened off.

As she descended she thought how predictable everything was. Michiko's bobbed hair was black like her skirt, in contrast to her simple white blouse. She hadn't said anything. Fern was tall and wore a tight red dress, long dangling earrings, and high-heeled boots.

I'm glad I'm wearing my high-heeled sandals.

Elinor arrived next, preceded by a fiftyish, bony-faced woman sporting a checked flannel shirt and low-heeled oxfords who introduced herself as Adele. Elinor lingered outside, exclaiming, "Dr. Martha, the sign looks wonderful! The lettering is just like I imagined it could be, and the light is really nice."

"Thank you," said Martha. Her voice almost failed her, she was so touched by Elinor's caring, and the nickname.

Adele said, "You're fortunate to have an authentic brownstone. I always forget how much good domestic architecture there is in Manhattan."

In the living room there was general chatter about the *bonsai*. From the moment of her arrival, Ursula had stood near it in meditation.

Adele moralized, "We all should plant a tree for the environment."

Elinor turned to Billie. "Does it count, inside the house?"

"I don't know why not," Billie replied. "It's good for the air, inside or out. Of course, we're supposed to plant new ones. This one's been around for a while."

"A very long while," said Martha.

"It's a lot like a famous one that's over two hundred years old," Ursula said reverently.

"Please sit wherever you like," Martha said. "I'll just watch the front door."

"I'll do it," said Fern.

Martha accepted this, having suddenly realized that it wouldn't be easy to lead a discussion from one of the low easy chairs. She brought a straight chair for herself from her bedroom.

Sandy soon trudged into the room, breathless.

Elinor said, "Sandy, please meet my neighbor, Adele. And this is Michiko, who came with Ursula."

"Hi," said Sandy. She dropped heavily onto a sofa. "I'm exhausted from driving."

"It's hard to go out in the evening when you're nursing," Elinor said.

"It's not only that," said Sandy. "I took the baby out to Mom's this afternoon, drove to Queens to get Danny's sitter, and then out to Sea Cliff for Danny. And later I have to do it all again."

"I'm glad you're strong, Sandy," said Martha. "Where is your friend?"

"She's downstairs, talking to the woman who opened the door."

"That's my friend, Fern," said Billie, who was fingering a cigarette but had not lit it.

Fern came in, explaining, "Sorry to be so long, but we got onto my favorite subject, art. I just love talking about art."

Danielle drifted in a moment later, smiling in a dreamy way. Her height and cool blond assurance seemed to belong to the room. Billie and Elinor, sizing up Sandy's choice of friend, exchanged a little approving glance.

"Everybody's here," Martha said, feeling at ease with these vibrant women in this now-beautiful room. "So, let's begin. Tonight we want our guests to join in a discussion along feminist lines. We'll tell our latest news and evaluate group therapy. We'll also talk about the future. For now, our discussion topic is one Billie once suggested,

'How Did You Feel When You First Realized You Were Female?'"

"That's fine," said Ursula. "But first I'd like to say I don't know if we're beginning something or ending something—but I'm glad to be here. I made two preparations for tonight. One is for a sort of game, giving a title to the evening to let Dr. Kaufman know we appreciate her opening her home to us. And the other is my new poem."

"Oh, read us your poem," Elinor urged.

"Not yet," Ursula said. "The game first. When I give a party, it gets a title, like a line from a song, or a quotation, or whatever comes to mind. It can add to the festivity."

"Could you give us an example?" asked Elinor.

"Well, you could start with the word 'Festivity.'"

"Oh, I like that word," said Elinor. "At church some young people had a party they called 'Festivity and Transformation.' The title made me think of all Dr. Martha has done for me. Only I'd put transformation first: 'Transformation and Festivity.'"

"Good," said Ursula. "Does anyone else have a title?"

Danielle spoke up. "When I saw this room, I thought of a song from an opera. 'I dreamt I dwelt in marble halls!'"

Ursula clapped. "That's nice."

Sandy said, "The shadows of the plant on the curtains remind me of an old song." She sang, "Just a song at twilight, when the lights are low, and the flickering shadows softly come and go."

Martha's face lit up and she said, shyly, "My mother used to sing that song."

"Anybody else?" asked Ursula. There was a silence, so she said, "My title is a line of poetry I used in my book on poetry therapy. You remember my book, don't you, Dr. Kaufman?"

Martha smiled and said, "Of course," touched by Ursula's pride in the book of poems she'd collected for the professor.

Ursula went on. "My title for tonight is by Rumi, a poet

445

who was an early follower of Mohammed and lived twelve hundred years ago. In one poem he compares himself to a bird and says he sometimes flies too high and gets lost. But then he says, 'Falling, I find wings.'"

"How does it apply to tonight?" Elinor asked.

"Well, when I get confused, I should realize the power I already have. Be like a bird and not crash but open my wings and start flying."

"Easier said than done," said Adele.

Sandy said thoughtfully, "It applies to all of us."

"And we have Dr. Martha to help us!" Elinor said, nodding enthusiastically.

Martha, also nodding, said, "I like your game, Ursula. The titles have been a sort of blessing for this room."

"Thank you!" said Ursula, and added, "Billie, do you have a title?"

"How about 'Habitat for Humanity'?"

Martha took this as a reproach for all the money she'd spent on the room. To make sure Billie didn't make a speech about "haves and have-nots," she said, "Now it's time for us to discuss Billie's topic about how you felt when you first realized you were female. Billie, would you be first?"

Billie flashed her an engaging smile, and said, "Okay. Probably until I was about six, I didn't even know I was a girl. My mother dressed me in my brother's hand-me-downs, which I was lucky to get and didn't object to. Later, I had to learn to wear dresses to school. So I found out I was a girl, and nobody cared if I played good baseball or not. Worse, in the group home I was expected to become a lady."

"But doesn't feminism make you proud of being female?" Danielle asked.

"It does, but it's pride you don't get early, when you need it. It comes later by your own effort," Billie said.

"What was your reference to a group home?" Martha asked.

"Oh, it was an old beat-up foster home in the City

where they put me after my mother died. They put my brother in a different one and he stupidly got himself killed on his bicycle. Then my aunt sent me to be educated by the nuns. I've told you about that." She closed her mouth as if no more was to be said.

Martha said, "Sandy, will you be next?"

"Okay. I knew I was a girl from the time I was two because Mom had me in pink hair ribbons and white ruffles. Before I had much hair, she used to fasten ribbons to my head with tape. And you should see the pictures they took of me running around with nothing on but a ribbon!"

Elinor said, "I bet you were cute."

"Well, my parents let me grow up without inhibitions, that's for sure. My mom decided I had a talent for drawing when she noticed my art work at the beach. I'd make abstract designs over big patches of wet sand by scraping the lines in with my heels. They looked good in the snapshots my grandfather took, and I liked making something big. Once, in grade school, I used a whole big blackboard for a design in colored chalk, and my teacher praised it. Then later I felt hampered by the small projects they gave us in art, so Mom enrolled me in a private art class. A couple of the boys in class felt the same way. It isn't being female that I mind, it's having to work too small.

"When I finished training at the Rhode Island School of Design, I came to Manhattan and ran into so much competition in the art world that I had to do macramé. I'm still doing it sometimes, but since I met David, who reminded me of my grandfather, I—"

Billie interrupted. "You said once that your professors betrayed you."

"They did, but not because I was female. They were good artists themselves, men and women professors in a prestigious school of design, so they could have fought for bigger art from us students, something really humongous. But that costs a lot. Now, in marriage I hold out for women's rights, but in art I hold out for all artists' rights. Mostly I don't think of myself as a woman, I'm an artist. Me. I hope you'll buy my stuff some day. It'll be signed *Sandra.*"

Michiko shyly raised her head and with a slight shoulder movement caught Sandy's eye. "Please excuse my English. What was the garment you didn't have, with hair ribbons?"

Sandy was puzzled. "I said I didn't have any clothes on."

Michiko persisted. "You said you grew up without—?"

"Inhibitions," said Martha. Adele laughed.

Ursula explained. "To have inhibitions is to be shy, have guilty feelings about being naked. In-hib-ishuns."

"No in-hib-ishuns in Japan. Our families bathe all together, naked."

"But don't they make more of a fuss over boys?" Ursula asked. "I know there's a big boys' festival every year."

Michiko smiled. "If girls work hard in school they get fuss too. I learned chemistry and worked for a big firm. I kept studying English and my brother helped me come to the U.S. and get a job in Long Island City."

Martha asked, "Can you recall when you first saw that girls' lives may be more restricted than boys'?"

Michiko obliged. "I was twelve when I got sore here—" she cupped her fingers and pointed them at her breasts as if circling them in baskets, "and had pains here every month." She rubbed her abdomen.

"But those cramps are only practice," said Sandy, equally unembarrassed, "to prepare you for real pains when you give birth. You forget all about the pain when you have a beautiful baby."

"I don't know about that," said Michiko. "I only had abortions."

There was a pause before Martha said, gently, "You have a lot of courage, Michiko, coming so far away on your own."

"My brother found Mrs. Friedrich." She made a slight bow to Ursula.

"How old are you, Michiko?" Sandy asked. Michiko giggled, her hand over her mouth.

Martha turned to Fern. "Will you speak next, Fern?"

"Okay," said Fern. "I knew from my mother and all her friends that being a Black female meant taking responsibility. It made me angry—still does—that women of my race, who earn the money and raise the kids and sing in the choir—pretend that men run everything."

"How old were you when you saw that?" Billie asked.

"About six, I think. My mother had a job and I did housework and my brother didn't have to help. But I wasn't a trouble-maker, so I got into a Catholic school, and he didn't. In the end I couldn't afford to finish college. But I knew how to write news stories and it wasn't too hard to get a job on the paper where I work. A Black woman like myself can't be concerned about equality—economic survival comes first. I pretend to know less than a man does rather than fight for women's rights. Like Billie, I'm for Socialism which benefits both men and women. Of course if I had kids, I'd be raising them on welfare by myself. Welfare doesn't let men live at home with a woman and kids."

"It's not only women like your mother," said Elinor. "A lot of women like me have to raise the kids and earn money. When I was little I played boys' games like Billie." Noting Billie's look of disbelief, she said emphatically, "I did, Billie, honestly. My dad wanted me to do sports, climb trees and build things, but he thought being smart was unladylike. So I'm still more athletic than smart."

"You never talk about athletics," Billie said. "Do you play tennis?"

"No, I can't afford it, but I jog every day. Hey, can you do this?" She stood, bent over, and pressed both open palms to the floor.

"Not my style," laughed Billie. "But I have great muscles in my arms." She stood up, pushed up her sleeves and bulged her muscles. "Sumo wrestler," she announced, swaggering as if challenging an opponent.

"Look!" cried Ursula, gleefully. She dropped to her

knees in front of her chair. "This is Simharsana. The lion pose in yoga." She made a fierce face, panting, and roared.

"I can't exercise at all now," wailed Sandy, remaining seated. "I'm just a milk cow."

"Bull!" said Billie.

Michiko helped Ursula back onto the sofa. There was an awkward pause until Martha said, "Will you continue, Elinor?"

Adele spoke. "Elinor, I met your father once. Do you remember? When you first moved next door."

"He was pretty old by then, I guess. He mellowed some before he died, and encouraged my Susan to read, more than he did me."

Billie was still standing. "Elinor, it bugs me, your comparing your life to Fern's mother's. You should learn the facts."

Elinor looked chagrined, and turned to Fern. "I apologize if I said something racist."

"You didn't," said Fern. "Some day you'll have to come with me to visit my mother. She'd love it." She raised her voice. "Billie, sit down."

Martha suppressed a smile, thinking to herself, Surprise!

But instead of sitting, Billie asked, "Is there a bathroom on this floor?"

"First door on the left," Martha said, keeping her voice normal.

Billie went out.

Adele was ready to speak. "I'm like you, Elinor," she said. "Growing up, I got the green light to be healthy but not brainy. So I used to read by a flashlight under the covers, mostly kids' books. Then later I read biographies, and now I read the *New York Times*. In their ads they claim that people who read it are interesting, but my old husband reads it and he's boring as hell." She laughed. "From cover to cover, and mattress to mattress, if you get my drift." Fern laughed, but Elinor was embarrassed by her friend.

Ursula spoke to Adele, "You have what I call intellectual

fire—a quality of doubting the male idea of the world. That's good. Women did that where I grew up out west. I was about nine when I first realized I was female. We kids were playing 'One Ol' Cat' in the street in Seattle, and I hit a home run, and had to run to my house to go to the bathroom. I was excited and sweaty, and stood up straight and thought, with a rush of happiness, 'I can do everything a boy can do, and also have babies.' My epiphany. More or less true—I had babies, but no career."

Billie came back in, and sat, again fingering a cigarette without lighting it.

"We've heard a wealth of stories, all well-told," said Martha. "I guess everyone has talked except you, Danielle."

Danielle spoke softly. "I had a nanny in England until I was four, but my parents came to the U.S. for my father's work. I stayed in college after they went home, and after graduation married an American. Who turned out to be Mr. Wrong. I'd always played with dolls, and invented a game about a boy doll fighting with a girl doll. I probably got the idea from my strong-willed mother who was dominated by my dad. She resisted by submitting, didn't develop her own talents but punished herself by martyrdom. So my dolls' games were power struggles. And, wouldn't you know, one of my twin girls is biddable and does what any lively kid does, and the other fights me all the time." Her voice faltered. "I need help, Dr. Kaufman. Sandy recommended you. I hope I can pay enough. My parents are in England and aren't rich—in fact they're feeling an economic pinch, but they'll help pay."

"We'll make an appointment before you leave tonight," said Martha. "Now, we've sketched in our first feeling about being female. It's time for the next act."

Billie pointed to Martha. "First tell us when you realized you were female."

But Martha had walked behind the sofa and dramatically whisked the napkin off the glasses and champagne. "Here's festivity!"

Elinor stood up and went over to look. "That's a hand-some ice bucket!"

Soon, two corks flew into the air, and Martha poured, while Fern and Elinor handed the glasses around.

"Here's my toast," Martha said. "To Festivity!" They drank.

"To Transformation!" said Elinor.

"To Redheads!" added Ursula.

Soon Martha asked, "If our guests don't mind, can the group members share what's happened since we last met? Who would like to start?"

"I'll start," Sandy said. "I'm glad Danielle came tonight because I think individual work with Dr. Martha will be helpful and they'll be a good combination. What's been happening to me has been the same, except the baby has stopped crying so much. I'm drawing every day. David didn't leave his job but spends fewer hours there, and is a consultant in another agency. With two jobs, he earns more! I stay home and keep house and play with the baby and am building up a portfolio of good drawings to sell."

"Bravo!" said Martha. "That's a good summary!"

"Yep," Sandy said, "I summarized!" She leaned back but sat upright again. "By the way, I really did want a nice wed-ding. I'm glad Mom arranged it. Everyone had a great time. As for marriage, I love David but don't know yet if I can love the role of wife. I'm just trying to be a partner." She smiled.

"We'll drink a toast to partnership!" Martha said, as she filled glasses.

"Sandy, you make me feel like crying," Elinor said. "We all have so much to thank Dr. Martha for. My evaluation is that it's been a great success."

"Thank you," said Martha. "Tell us more of what's been happening in your world, Elinor."

"Well, one thing—not a happening but a nice non-happening—is I've stopped wearing makeup at work and people seem to confide in me more. It's a funny feeling, because it's not like I'm a different person."

"You said you're going to take an art appraiser's course," said Billie.

"Oh, yes, and Ralph's going to pay for it and keep on paying me for Michele. Her news is that she's lost ten pounds. She and Susan do a lot of the cooking, mostly vegetables. My course doesn't begin until next fall, and in the meantime I'm working for the rector, who adjusts my schedule so I can go to auctions and bone up on collectibles." She turned to Billie. "I want to thank you for tipping me off to study something that leads to money. At least, I hope it will."

"It will," said Billie. "You've got a lot of class, and that counts in selling art."

"Will you tell us your news, Billie?" Martha asked.

Billie put the unlit cigarette in her mouth and took an off-hand tone. "I'm just grinding out my salary at school, and Mike's still in school and so's Christopher, we're *all* in school. And a lucky thing happened. You know your son's course that I teach, Elinor, that you did the homework for?"

"I didn't do any of his homework," said Elinor quickly.

"I know that. He contributed a lot in class from his own thinking. But the thing is, one of the kids took special trouble and taped our discussions, and photographed maps and what we had put on the chalkboard, stuff you have to catch as you go along. Of course I had test questions and bibliographies and kids' term papers, so I wrote a rough draft of a course of study. My chairman sent it to Albany and they like it. I'm promised a grant so I can work it up fully. Then it can be tested in another high school."

"That's wonderful!" Martha exclaimed. "We should drink to that? Shall I open more champagne?"

"No thanks," Billie said, "I'm driving home soon."

"It's really a great course!" Elinor exclaimed. "I understand what goes on in the world now."

"Billie," Martha said, her voice warm with approval,

"yours is truly front page news. Congratulations! And congratulations to you, Elinor, for selecting a career." Ursula clapped, followed by the others. Martha resumed. "Now, shall we hear from Ursula?"

Ursula said, "I'm feeling good, back in my own house. Michiko and I are doing fine—it's a whole new life for me. Thank God, my husband gets good care at the hospice, and I talk with him on the phone every day. He's trying to revise his chemistry course, and the hospice mails pages to me, and I walk to the library and make photocopies for him. Our library also has books on tape and I listen to them at home. Dr. Martha, I used to think I was going crazy, but you prescribed Doxepin and got me back into writing poetry. So I'm really better. I've enjoyed the group, too, and hope to keep coming on the subway with Billie. That's all I'll say now because I want to read my poem. After we talk about the future."

Martha said, "Yes, I look forward to hearing it. And I appreciate everybody's thanks. Working with all of you has meant a great deal to me, and I called you together tonight to talk seriously with you about our future work together. I'm sure you've all felt the energy of this group. And in that spirit, I ask you to concentrate on therapy, rather than feminism. No *ism* can take the place of true therapy, with its requirements that you each study yourselves and help one another do the same. We will discuss this further as we get into it.

"But I have something else to talk with you about, a plan that we take a break of six weeks. I've been asked to join another therapist in giving a course in basic group therapy. It's offered on Wednesday afternoons, and people have already registered.

"I'll have more wisdom to bring to our group when we get together again, and of course, there will be no charge to you during the break. I wouldn't suggest a break if I didn't recognize you've each reached a time in your life when you can integrate your progress. I say this not to promote overconfidence, but so you won't feel the break is coming at a bad time. I also believe you each have some real work to do when we resume work together.

"For example, three of you have children at home, and when parents are free from hang-ups, they can do a better job of raising children. And artists like Ursula and Sandy must shelter their creativity and find freedom in it. We can go deeper into matters like this in the group, fulfilling obligations to one another.

"My two questions for you boil down to this: Will you wait for me for six weeks, and come back to concentrate on the true tasks of therapy? And will you come individually once more next Wednesday so we can discuss your personal agenda? If you prefer another time to Wednesday, please call me. Otherwise, I'll expect to see you at your former time—at the lower group rate."

"I can't come at three because of my schedule at school," Billie said. "But I could bring Ursula here at four, then wait until five to see you. I always have something to do at N.Y.U."

"Five o'clock is Sandy's usual time," Martha said.

"I could come at three," Sandy said, "which actually suits me better."

"With those changes, then, we'll go ahead," Martha said, passing out some slips of paper. "Here's a note about the date for coming back to the group. Write it on your calendars."

Elinor, wiping tears from her eyes, said shakily, "This is like a reunion already. Dr. Martha, I want to do it."

"I want to continue in the group," Sandy said, "and a break is probably lucky for me, because David and I want to go on a honeymoon with Jordy."

Ursula nodded assent.

Billie averted her eyes and was silent.

Martha, watching her, said, "Billie, I believe you will be a success not only in creating courses, but in leading consciousness-raising groups some day. What you gain from seriously concentrating on therapy will be of real help to you. Of course, during the break, I expect you'll be busy working on your course of study. Do you have a deadline?"

Billie, looking thoughtful, nodded. "Yes. I'll be working like mad at it."

Martha, sensing a new solemnity in the group, said, "So we're agreed?"

Elinor and Sandy nodded, and Ursula said, "I do."

"That's what I'd hoped. So now let's hear Ursula's poem."

Ursula said, "First, I'd like to say something to Danielle. Okay, Danielle?"

"Carry on," said Danielle, a bit apprehensively.

Ursula smiled. "I'm sure you'd be very nice to know, but I think you should see Dr. Kaufman privately. The rest of us started that way, and I think that would be better for you than our group. Besides, our original four have a chance to really help each other because we know each other already." Danielle nodded. Ursula handed a paper to Elinor. "Please prompt me if I need it." She cleared her throat. " 'Beginning and Ending.' " She spoke hesitantly.

"The world of beginning
was books whispering riddles
and dreams of enchantment—"

She broke off suddenly and took the paper from Elinor. "Do you know what?" she said, in a definite tone. "This poem isn't really finished. I'll work on it and share it later."

"Okay, Ursula," said Sandy. "Maybe sometime I can make a drawing to go with a poem. But it's getting late and I have lot of driving to do. Dr. Martha, I want you to have this." She picked up a flat envelope from the floor and handed it to Martha. "It's my best print to date."

"Oh, thank you," said Martha sincerely. "I've been wanting to see some of your work."

Elinor exclaimed, "Please let us see it too."

Sandy helped Martha open it, saying, "The theme is dependable man, and a woman in all her moods."

The print was passed around. Ursula took it over by the *bonsai* to see it under the spotlight. Billie looked at it and declared, "This is good, Sandy. I'd like to take something you've done to show my partner, Christopher. He draws too, all the time."

Elinor said, "I'm no expert on prints yet, Sandra, but I find a pronounced evanescent rhythm in the flow of the dancers."

Billie was amused. "You've got the lingo, Elinor. But *evanescent* rhythm? You do know that means 'vanishing,' I hope?"

Adele laughed. Elinor nodded slightly, with a pasted-on smile.

When the print was back in Martha's hands, Sandy said, "Dr. Martha, after you've studied it, could you phone me your opinion?"

Martha said, "I will, but I can say right now, I like it very much."

"Call in the evening, when David's home." She started toward the stairs.

Danielle, following, said to Martha, "Don't forget my appointment."

Martha said, "Let's go down and put it into my book."

When they were out of earshot, Adele asked, "Is this doctor for real?"

Billie was unusually silent.

Fern volunteered, "She's like a woman preacher, who plays straight and is generous. Ten feet tall."

Ursula said, "Yes, Fern. If you can afford it, you really should make an appointment with her."

"She gave me a very reasonable rate when my son was small," said Billie. "And I've never thanked her." Then to her own surprise, she burst into tears.

Fern, astonished at tears from the imperturbable Billie, patted her on the back and said, "What's the matter?"

Ursula gave Billie a tissue. When her tears subsided, Billie said, with difficulty, "Without her, I could have lost Mikey."

Martha, alone in her office later, evaluated the evening.

I like my new nickname, "Dr. Martha." It's respectful, yet using my first name makes it personal. I noticed that others picked it up from Elinor. Billie was on her best behavior. She didn't get the membership vote to continue the boycott, but is finally getting some credit for her superior teaching. She deserves that. I hope she'll settle down to work on her course and stay in the group.

Ursula's writing poetry and talking on the phone to August every day. That'll help to make up to him the loss of her company. How ironic that she's making photocopies for him of his chemistry lessons—that's a switch! Poor guy, there isn't a lot of future for someone in a hospice. Elinor may have career fulfillment ahead, which she claims she needs more than a husband. Could be.

Nothing turned out as I expected, but that'll teach me to stop forecasting patients' lives. Each of the group had prior obligations whose strength I didn't understand. Well, at least I didn't stop them from going their own ways. And, I did predict my own desired direction.

When I decided to go to med school, with Norman's support, I vowed that I wouldn't have any more children. But I still had to grapple with my wish for a daughter. So it's okay to be fond of patients, so long as I listen and wait for them to work out goals for themselves and remember that I'm not in their lives. I can only give them challenges and guidelines. And a few rules.

She recalled how Elinor brought in bodily fitness by touching the floor, Billie became a Sumo wrestler and Ursula fell to her knees and roared like a lion!

We ain't got no in-hib-ishuns here in these marble halls!

She laughed heartily.

Going to bed, she looked to her own future.

Listen, honey, you're doing okay. Forget the part of your poem about marching soldiers and horses, all that feeling of being driven. You've got some new living room, not just in this house.

38

She Likes What I Like

The next morning, Martha happily put on a new outfit, a shirt and slacks in pale green.

They're the color of daffodil leaves, Elinor's color. Slacks are comfortable for a Sunday morning at home but I'll change into the matching silk skirt for Lucy's party.

On her way to the kitchen she stopped in her office and looked for Sandy's print.

Oh, here it is, right beside Billie's cactus under the fern in Sandy's hanging basket. I must have subconsciously put it there to start a collection of gifts from daughters! I think I've learned to see through my own impulses for counter-transference and keep them in check. Useful for me to know when I'm training therapists, especially in treatment of girls. Wanting to cherish a little girl is a natural human characteristic, and a healthy one. Feminism, I'm with you! So on Tuesdays when I'll be seeing Danielle, I'll refrain from playing grandmother to her twins. Well, I might a bit, within bounds.

When she got to the kitchen she told Sarah, "Sandy gave me one of her prints." She unwrapped it carefully.

Sarah studied it. "It's a big picture for its size."

"Yes, and I like it. It's a love story. In my opinion, it's really good."

Sarah, placing a waffle before Martha, regarded the print thoughtfully. "It reminds me of *Swan Lake* with the dancing girls. And the man is a prince."

They were joined by Barry, who came in from the back porch carrying the paint rollers he and Martha had recently used in the living room. He was borrowing them to paint a friend's apartment—Martha assumed that it was where he was staying nights, but didn't want to quiz him.

She was happy knowing he hadn't come only for the equipment but because he loved Sunday mornings at home and missed her and Sarah.

He glanced at the print, then stepped forward to examine it. "Who did this?"

"Sandy, my patient. The one who's your age. Her professional name is Sandra."

"The one who had the shotgun wedding," Sarah put in.

"I didn't know she was an artist. What are the dancing women all about?"

"It's a dependable man, and a woman in all her moods," Martha said. "I think that's what Sandy said. On the back it says 'Images of Woman.'"

"They're all doing something different. They'll never make the chorus line."

"I think it's all the same woman," Sarah said. "See the faces? She's dancing her moods, and he loves her. He's godlike, like a Michelangelo or a Rodin."

"I remember those guys from Europe," Barry said seriously. "This is a nice lithograph. World class, I'd say. See if you can get a print for me, and how much."

"My grandson: a patron of the arts," said Sarah, teasing but proud.

"Advertising has taught me something about printing," he said. "And I just landed a hot new account, so I can celebrate. This would look good in my friend's living room. The one we're painting. I like it and she likes what I like."

Martha, comforted by the word "she," reached over and patted his arm. "Then we're sure to like her. Or does that mean she's sure to like us?"

"Both ways," said Barry, sitting down in his usual spot.

Sarah, busy with her waffle iron, turned and faced him. "When will you bring her to see us?"

"I had thought about today, but we're painting."

"Any evening this week is fine," said Martha.

Sarah spoke up. "Bring her for dinner tomorrow. We'll eat in the dining room."

"Okay. Sounds good. I'll let you know tonight. Her name is Ruth."

"As in the Bible story, 'Whither thou goest, I will go?'" quipped Sarah. "Here's your waffle."

He looked up. "Thanks, Bubbi."

"Tell us about her."

"Wait till you meet her. I've told her a lot about both of you."

Martha stood up to remove the print from any chance of spilled syrup, and examined it again. "I'm going to hang this in the living room. And it'll be nice if you and Ruth have one like it. Sandra is serious about her work."

"She made a sale this morning," said Barry. "Be sure to order one for us. I want to surprise Ruth on her birthday." He became engrossed in the puzzle.

Martha leaned down and kissed him on the top of his head. "I love you," she said, "you awesome business man." He reached up and gave her arm a squeeze, his eyes still on the puzzle. Wrapping the print, she paused. "There's a date here in the corner. Last November. That's not long after she started seeing me."

"You inspired her," Sarah said.

"It would be nice to think so. But maybe she gave it to me now because it has to do with lovers' feelings, something we've been talking about."

Sarah pointed to a tray holding sparkling champagne glasses she had washed and dried. "I found nine wet glasses up there. So everybody came?"

"Yes, eight and me. And the room didn't feel crowded."

"Did anyone comment on your improvements?" Sarah asked.

"Well, of course none of them had seen the living room before. Elinor said the new shingle out front looked wonderful, just the way she'd imagined it. And Billie's comment on the room was, 'You have some nice things here.'"

"Only *some* nice things! I'd like to see her place. What did Ursula say?"

"She kept admiring the *bonsai* and said it was like a famous one that's two hundred years old."

"I guess you had an evaluation of more than group therapy!"

"I'm too modest to tell you all the nice things they said."

"I always thought Ursula would be grateful."

"She was. She named the evening 'Festivity and Transformation.'"

"Is anyone new coming to you?" Barry asked.

"Yes, an artist friend of Sandy's is coming next Tuesday."

"What's she like?" Sarah asked.

"Ethereal. In looks, anyhow. But practical, too. She's supporting twin girls."

Sarah clucked in sympathy. "She has her hands full. She's not joining the group?"

"No, but I'll allow her the group rate. If I lead one or two of Lucy's evening groups, I'll make all the money I need. In fact, I plan to take more time for my own enjoyment. Go to the theater, see art shows, give dinner parties."

"You have a life of your own now," said Sarah, stirring her glass of tea.

"We all have lives of our own," Martha said.

ABOUT THE AUTHOR

Betty Morris, née Betty Cole, grew up in Seattle and wrote poetry at a young age, like her character Ursula.

While a graduate student at Columbia University she lived, like Martha, in Greenwich Village.

She spent several years in London as an Embassy wife with two children, like Elinor.

She, like Billie, created curriculum and taught in a high school in New York.

Like Sandy, she has sought to remain devoted to both her family and her artistic ambition.

Her book of poetry, *Waiting for Climbers*, was published in 1992.

Falling, I Find Wings is her first novel.